Chop Suey

Barry Kalb

chop' suey' (chop'sōō'ē)

1. A Chinese-style dish consisting of small pieces of meat, chicken, etc., cooked together with bean sprouts, onions, mushrooms and other vegetables and seasoning. [1885-90, *Amer.;* < dial. China (Guangdong) *jaahp seui*].

2. Mixed bits.

For my brother, Steve

Prologue

2003: On the Hong Kong-China Border

The traders are trapped.

Late August. Ninety-six degrees hot. Ninety-eight percent humid. People packed so tightly you couldn't slide a chopstick between them.

The border crossing between Hong Kong and the Chinese city of Shenzhen used to be a breeze. Now it's hell any day of the week, almost any time of day: standing in line to get to the next line; trying not to twist an ankle on the wheeled suitcases and trolleys being dragged by the masses of people ahead; trying to maintain your dignity while giving the elbow to a little old Chinese lady who pushes in front. All the while enshrouded in the stifling heat and humidity of Southern China.

A knot of cross-border traders is trapped on the footbridge that connects the Chinese and Hong Kong sides of the border, trapped alongside backpackers, bargain shoppers, businesspeople – some of the scores of thousands who make this crossing daily. The lines ahead at the Hong Kong immigration counters are backed up, and the phalanx shuffling across the bridge from the China side has been halted until the lines thin out.

First-time travelers along this route accept the crush as another part of the China experience. To the professional traders who have made the trip hundreds of times, it's agony. When they first arrived from their homes in the West twenty, twenty-five years earlier, it was all fresh and exotic. China had just opened itself to the outside world, admitting foreigners like them for the first time in decades, and they felt a thrill every time they crossed

4

the border. They were bemused and beguiled by the Chinese people, dressed in their baggy revolutionary-era uniforms of blue or gray, staring in wonderment at any foreigner who crossed their path.

Now the thrill is gone. The traders roll their eyes and cast knowing glances at each other as another group of mainland tourists shoves its way forward, dressed in modern Western clothing, shouting into their mobile telephones as they head for the high-fashion shops and restaurants of Hong Kong and contributing to the back-up of foot traffic like this.

Why, they wonder, melting in the blast-furnace heat; why subject myself to this torture again and again?

So much for the romance of the East.

One of the veterans elbows her way to the rail at the outside of the bridge, which allows her a bit of wiggle room. It also means she receives the full effect of the open sewer, officially known as the Shenzhen River, that runs beneath the bridge and forms the Hong Kong-China border. In her mind's eye the stench of human waste below takes on visible form, rising like a hand from the black waters to claw at her sodden face. Pollutants spewing from the chain of factories that stretches from this border to the city of Guangzhou, belching from the vehicles increasing at a geometric rate on China's roads, envelope her in a fine mist.

But China's airborne excreta have no respect for borders. They hitch a ride on the jet stream and reach brown fingers as far as North America — reaching out to the world, like China itself, after centuries of slumber; affecting everything it touches. But here at the edge of the mainland, the pollution is especially fulsome. The air just across the border in Hong Kong is now thick with smog half the time. More than half the time. The crystalline vistas that used to be a feature of the harbor between Hong Kong Island and Kowloon are largely a thing of the past.

Most of the pollution is a consequence of the rapid modernization of the country to which Hong Kong, for most of its modern existence a British colony, now owes allegiance. Although, since Hong Kong businessmen own a large portion of the factories on the mainland side of the border, there's an argument to be made that Hong Kong is choking on its own shit.

The trader leans against the rail while she waits for the line to start moving again, inhaling the muck, feeling the perspiration trickle from her armpits and down her back, pasting her blouse to her skin. Fellow traders say the bridge will soon be enclosed and air-conditioned, but who knows if that's fact or just wishful thinking?

She tries to push the present away by envisioning the clean, cool, air-conditioned apartment that awaits her on the south side of Hong Kong Island. She leans out over the rail, in hopes of catching a passing breeze.

Something in the water below catches her eye instead.

She leans out as far as she can to get a better look.

She lets out the most godawful scream.

~

A body is face down in the water beneath the bridge, lapping gently against the Hong Kong side of the riverbank. Solid matter has gathered around the corpulent torso, and the white hair is stained dark by the sludge. Methane bubbles up about the ears.

Given the location and regional demographics, there are better than a billion chances that the floater is Chinese. But with a garment manufacturer's eye and two decades of experience in this part of the world to inform her, the woman knows different.

Dark pinstriped suit. Double-vented jacket, pinched much too tightly at the body's midsection. Wool and cashmere blend from the look of it.

She doesn't need to see the face to know the dead man isn't Chinese.

She tells herself: only a Brit would dress like that in this kind of weather.

One

If a plane crashes smack on the border between two countries, where do you bury the survivors?

All right, it's an old joke. Survivors aren't buried. But if somebody *dies*...

The Hong Kong Police argued: the body was found on our side of the river, and the victim looks like one of ours. The death is ours to investigate.

Maybe so, the Shenzhen Police replied, but the entire Hong Kong side of the river is tightly patrolled, off limits to civilians. It's highly unlikely anyone could have sneaked a body through the closed and guarded Hong Kong border zone, not to mention hoisting the considerable bulk of this particular body over the high security fence topped with razor wire, in order to reach the river's edge — and why would anyone bother, when there are hundreds of miles of easily accessible coastline, plus a couple of hundred square miles of wilderness park, in which to dispose of a body in Hong Kong proper?

It was far more likely that the death had occurred somewhere inside the city of Shenzhen, and the body then floated downstream to the border crossing. That, the Chinese cops said, would put the death within *our* jurisdiction.

Not that they were arguing the point too forcefully. If they had really wanted to take control of the case, the Chinese could have settled the matter with a word. Hong Kong was again a part of China. Britain had handed the colony back to Beijing six years earlier, in 1997. These days, the folks on the mainland had but to make their wishes known and – as the old imperial edicts from

Beijing were wont to phrase it – the Hong Kong government trembled and obeyed.

But investigating a crime like this required time and effort, and that wasn't what the Chinese police did. They carried out political directives from their superiors in the local government and the Communist Party. They aided local officials in corrupt enterprises and shaking down the masses. They arrested people at random, under a system called *shourang*, and then made them buy their way out of custody. They did whatever they could to avoid what much of the modern world would consider normal police work.

The Shenzhen cops did the calculations: there wasn't any money to be had in this one that they could see, only a lot of hard work. Too much trouble. And the murder victim – for the bullet hole in the back of the head strongly suggested that murder it had been – was a foreigner. *Much* too much trouble.

Shenzhen was already gaining a reputation as a lawless pit, what with stories of muggings and beatings making regular appearances in the Hong Kong newspapers, and the publicity was threatening to scare off the thousands of visitors who came across the border from Hong Kong each day to shop for bargains and transact business. The Shenzhen authorities needed a murdered tourist like they needed rubber chopsticks. Better to go with the fiction that this particular crime had occurred in Hong Kong.

"*Suibian!*" they told their Hong Kong counterparts.

Help yourselves.

~

A group of Hong Kong police officers was gathered around the body, which now lay desludged, disinfected and deodorized on a metal slab in the coroner's office in the town of Sha Tin. A puffy European face topped by a shock of white hair protruded from one end of a white sheet, a pair of naked feet from the other. In between, the sheet rose expansively into the frigid mortuary air over a well-nurtured belly.

No identification had been found on the body. The suit did contain the label of a Hong Kong tailor shop, but as best the police could determine after a quick enquiry, the tailor had emigrated shortly before Hong Kong's change of sovereignty and the shop was closed for good. It would take days if not weeks to locate the tailor in America or Canada or Australia—whichever refuge he'd chosen in order to escape the approaching embrace of his motherland. If he could be located at all. Even then there was no assurance he'd be able to identify his former customer on the basis of a jacket and a pair of pants.

One of the cops was shouting at his mobile phone, calling in a photographer to take a shot of the dead man's face. The others were discussing the situation in high-decibel Cantonese as Brian Ross, deputy chief commissioner of police, entered the room.

Ross luxuriated for a moment in the air-conditioned coolness, tugging at the damp spots of his shirt to detach them from his body. The humidity was at one of its seasonal heights. Step outdoors at times like this and the dampness slapped you in the face like a hot, dripping towel. At certain times of the year Hong Kong is so damp that mold grows on walls, on the clothing in closets, on anything that doesn't move. The Peak, the mountain rising above the western tip of Hong Kong Island from which the territory's wealthy and powerful have traditionally surveyed their world, is permanently shrouded in moist cloud and mist during the spring months. One morning a friend who lived there called Ross to say his bedroom wall had sprouted mushrooms.

Hong Kong got by with air-conditioning, the great enabler of the tropics. Many Chinese had come to depend on air-conditioning even more than the expatriates. On a cold day, it wasn't unusual for the interiors of some local taxis to be set at temperatures that could shrivel genitals. On a day like this one...

Ross waited for the air-con to stem the flow of perspiration. He wiped his face with a handkerchief. He leaned over the body. *Oh, dear,* he said to himself. The features were bloated and indistinct from their submersion in the river, but it took just a single glance for him to recognize the victim. Ross had joined the Royal Hong Kong Police in 1979, fresh out of his native Scotland, and was one of the few British cops still on active duty since the 1997 handover. He was familiar with most of the prominent personalities in the former British colony, including those in the still-sizable British contingent. The lump of flab on the table, alas, was an old friend.

"There's no need for the photographer," he said aloud, still staring at the face. "It's Rupert Rackley. The political affairs columnist for the Hong Kong *Star*. Poor bastard."

"Are you sure?" the medical examiner asked.

"I'm sure," Ross said. "Rupe and I put away many a pint together over the years. He was a decent old guy, even if nobody paid much attention to the rantings and ravings in his column. How did it happen?"

The examiner turned the dead man's head and pointed to the bullet hole just behind the right ear. "No exit wound, so I'm assuming the killer used a small-caliber pistol. No other wounds that I can see. No signs of a struggle." He recounted the Chinese theory, with which he and Ross's colleagues now reluctantly agreed, that the death had probably occurred somewhere on the Chinese side of the border.

"So he was dead before he went into the water?"

"I'll know once I examine the lungs, but I can't see any other scenario. Why would he get into the water with all his clothes on if he were still alive? Why would anyone under *any* circumstances" – the examiner grimaced as if he'd bitten into a fresh Sichuan peppercorn – "get into the Shenzhen River?"

Ross grunted agreement. The notion that any Westerner would voluntarily enter that cesspool was far-fetched in the extreme. There was hardly a body of water in all of China that wasn't fouled beyond salvage with human and industrial waste. The Shenzhen River was worse than some, better than others, but definitely no place for a cooling dip. "Did you find anything at all that might help us?" Ross asked.

The examiner shook his head. "Whoever did this was quite thorough. There was no wallet, no watch, no passport, no business cards, no phone, no keys, no nothing. The killer took the trouble to make the body as anonymous as possible before dumping it in the river, which in my inexpert opinion suggests a professional hit. If this was some common mugging, maybe one of your out-of-work laborers from the northern provinces who are crawling all over the South, you would have expected the perpetrator to grab the victim's wallet and watch and run as fast as he could. Would you not?"

Ross would. He knew the average mainland citizen could occasionally obtain a gun by buying one off a soldier, but most violence in China was committed with knives or meat cleavers or homemade bombs – China was the undisputed world leader in the settling of common disputes by means of explosive. And shootings on Ross's side of the border were virtually unheard of. Hong Kong had one of the most restrictive gun-control regimes in the world. This one did look professional, and it did look Chinese.

"So, we're faced with a quadruple mystery here," Ross said.

"Quadruple?" said the examiner.

"Aye," said Ross, and he ticked them off:

"Who killed poor Rupe?

"And why – what could he have done to warrant a professional hit?

"And precisely where was he killed?

"And most intriguing of all, assuming our mainland colleagues are right: why was he in China to begin with?"

"He could be there for all kinds of reason," said Winston Wai. Wai was Ross's right hand, and he had already taken copious notes by the time his boss arrived. "Business, sight-seeing, buy a fake Gucci wallet, have a massage, order new curtains. You know how busy two-way traffic at the border is these days," he said. "Chinese, *gwei-lo*, makes no difference. Everybody goes."

"Not this *gwei-lo*," Ross said. "Rupert hated China. I mean, he loathed the place with all his being. I remember him telling me more than once that the only way they'd ever get him across the border was over his dead body."

13

"Wah!" said Wai. "And look at him now."

~

People live, people die, the world turns. The passing of an individual is normally of no great moment in the cosmic order. But Rupert Rackley's death resonated beyond this semi-rural corner of Hong Kong. It resonated to all of China – and that being the case, even farther. Known during most of its recent existence for Stone Age poverty and harsh communist rule, the country had suddenly exploded onto the international stage as a major economic and political power. It had not quite ascended to the status of superpower, but already, if China developed heartburn, the rest of the world belched in discomfort.

And now, six years after the handover, China was still struggling to digest Hong Kong, the city Rupert had left behind: close to seven million people, living in forests of high-rise metropolis sprouting from four hundred and twenty-five square miles of hilly land and rocky island, the whole extending like an afterthought from China's Guangdong Province and into the South China Sea. Ninety-five percent of the inhabitants were Chinese, but its barristers still appeared in court wearing the powdered wigs of the British Empire. Its masses ate Pizza Hut pizzas and McDonald's hamburgers along with their dumplings and steamed fish. Its elites dressed in Armani and Chanel (or very good knock-offs they bought for a song across the border).

Yet despite the foreign overlay, Hong Kong's daily life was guided to a remarkable extent by ancient Chinese tradition and superstition. Ancestors were venerated and their graves tended to. The stars, the gods, the spirits of the mountains and sea, the auspiciousness of certain words and numbers, could dictate actions and set large sums of money in motion. Westerners might poke fun at the Chinese insistence on molding their lives to the dictates of intangible forces, but the Chinese ignored the guffaws and flowed on like a river, carrying their ancient ways with them, absorbing whatever worked from cultures they encountered along the way.

During a century and a half of British rule – and this accounted to a large extent for Beijing's dyspepsia – the Hong Kong Chinese had absorbed a lot. In the deal that saw the colony revert to Chinese sovereignty, Beijing's rulers promised to preserve Hong Kong's western-style legal system and personal freedoms – both alien to the communist state – for fifty years: "One country, two systems," they called the new arrangement. That left the rulers in Beijing with a dilemma: how to pound this liberal, semi-westernized peg into the slant-eyed hole of the modernizing but still totalitarian Chinese state.

Which was part of a greater challenge: how to take the entire sprawling entity, the *Zhonghua Renmin Gongheguo,* the People's Republic of China, and integrate it into the modern world, where it might soon challenge the economic and military might of the United States, without relinquishing the Communist Party's monopoly on political power. "How," as Rupert had put it in one of his many columns vilifying China's leaders, "to become a modern nation while continuing to deny more than a billion people the civic and political rights that, however imperfectly some nations apply them, are becoming the world-wide norm."

He had a point. The Chinese people were delighted that the ideological insanity of the Maoist years was gone. They were

15

delighted with the steadily rising standard of living that economic reform had brought. But they were angry about the corruption and pollution that had accompanied that reform. Protests against abuse of power by Communist cadres were breaking out by the thousands all over the country each year. When it realized that material goods were no longer enough to ensure social harmony, the Party had turned to the old stand-by, nationalism:

Redress the humiliations inflicted by foreign powers in the 19th and 20th centuries! Reunite Taiwan with the motherland!

The masses had bought into the call to patriotism, but the anger was growing nonetheless. How long the lid could be kept on, nobody could say. Truth be told, no one was sure the lid could be kept on at all.

Enough to occupy any government, one would think. It seemed unlikely that the leaders in Beijing would notice, let alone care about, the death of an old, fat scold like Rupert Rackley, whose voice had reached only a small number of people on the periphery of the nation.

And yet it appeared that they did.

~

As he contemplated Rupert's remains, the Communist Party's concerns were the farthest thing from Brian Ross's thoughts. He was happy to let those in the distant capital grapple with transcendent issues while he and his men saw to law and order in their small corner of the nation. "If there's nothing else, then, I'm off," he said to Wai. "Call me as soon as the autopsy is finished."

"Actually," Wai said, "there is one thing." He fished in his pocket for his notebook. "A call come from one of the security people in the mainland just before you arrive. This fellow wants to know is there any new information on our DOA."

"On our what?" Ross said.

"DOA. '*Dead on Arrival*,'" Wai said with a self-satisfied grin. "That's how they call the dead body on *NYPD Blue*. I watch every week. Last week—"

Ross harrumphed. "We're becoming far too Americanized around here. I'm not surprised about the phone call though. It looks like the Public Security Bureau in Shenzhen is going to end up involved in this investigation whether we like it or not."

"This not Public Security," Wai said. "This fellow says he is State Security."

"*State* Security? Are you sure?" Public Security was China's cops. State Security handled protection of state secrets, espionage, counter-intelligence and the like; it didn't normally get involved in common crimes like this one. It certainly was not in the habit of making person-to-person calls to Hong Kong police officers.

But Winston Wai was not in the habit of making mistakes. For all his comic English, he was a deadly serious cop, a veteran of the Homicide Squad, and before that the Triad Bureau, which dealt with Hong Kong's violent organized gangs. "I asked him repeat it, just to be sure," he told Ross. "*Guojia Anquan Bu* – State Security. Here, look, I write his phone number."

Ross looked. A mainland Chinese name, a phone number with a Beijing area code. Why in the world would someone in Beijing – State Security, no less – be interested in the death of Rupert Rackley? Did the man who called even know who the victim was?

And if he did know...*how* did he know? The Hong Kong cops themselves didn't know until Ross had identified the body a few minutes earlier.

Ross began to feel queasy, the way he did after eating sea slugs, or stinky bean curd, or one of the many other curiosities the Southern Chinese considered delicacies. He loved Hong Kong. After a quarter of a century it was more his home than Scotland had been. But too much Chinese at any one time didn't agree with him.

He copied the name and number into a notebook. "We'll also have to get in touch with that bloody American journalist, Sturges," he said as he scribbled. "He was Rupert's best friend. Maybe he can shed some light on the situation. Although..." Ross shook his head and turned away with a look of distaste on his face. Sometimes the people one had to deal with during a murder investigation turned one's stomach as much as the murderer himself.

He sighed and gave the flaccid lump under the sheet a gentle pat before heading once again for the cauldron outside. "Well, well, Rupe old boy," he said under his breath. "It looks like your flailing away at China attracted more attention than any of us here realized. I just hope we don't have to depend on Chinese security to find out what the bloody hell you were doing over there in the first place."

Two

If Rupert Rackley's death was a mystery, his life had taken unexpected turns from the start. It became inextricably entwined with China long before he left England for Hong Kong in 1963.

His working-class background denied him the opportunity to attend college, but as a boy he fell in love with all things Chinese, and by the time he first set foot in the British colony he had fashioned himself through diligent self-education into something of a China scholar. He arrived with an academician's knowledge of Chinese history. He could discourse knowledgeably on the subtle intricacies of Chinese culture. Above all, he knew the country's art. He was enraptured by it: the wispy landscapes, the incredible detail and grace of the carvings, the bold statues and bronzes, the delicate porcelains. They spoke to his soul, and he spoke back with his admiration and devotion.

He also spoke a bit of the language. He was a self-made man and proud of it (even if he later had to acknowledge some rather glaring flaws in the end product.)

In 1963 he was young, lean and ambitious, and soon after his arrival he landed a job as a reporter for the Reuters news agency. It was a dream assignment for a young foreign correspondent: based in Hong Kong, covering the whole of East Asia including the then-fourteen-year-old People's Republic. The mysteries of the Orient to savor. Revolutions and wars on all sides to write about. Gorgeous, accommodating Asian women for the taking. (Or men, if one was so inclined.)

Rupert's expertise and passion showed in his reports from the field, and three years after his arrival, having added practical experience to his résumé and now approaching fluency in Mandarin, he was hired away by the *Daily Telegraph* to be their man in East Asia, specializing in coverage of China. Life didn't get much better.

Unfortunately, as so often happens, life was soon to get considerably worse.

~

There was talk in Hong Kong that Rupert was working for MI6, Britain's overseas intelligence service, but foreign journalists could only occasionally obtain a visa for the mainland in the late '60s, and he had little in the way of first-hand knowledge of China to pass on. Even if Rupert had been providing information to the secret service, it's unlikely he could have told them much they didn't already know: China was a mess.

Like a lot of successful revolutionaries, Mao Tse-tung had proved a disaster as a governor. Instead of improving lives, he bombarded his masses with brutal political campaigns and utopian schemes. Executions of landlords and "rich peasants." Purges of "rightists" in the Communist Party. A particular bit of insanity in the late 1950s called the Great Leap Forward, which created a nationwide Great Famine that led to upwards of forty million deaths – that's a four followed by seven zeroes – and almost destroyed the country.

After that the Party's leaders decided it was time to put the Great Helmsman out to pasture while they struggled to piece things back together. But Mao was determined to hold on to power. In 1966, he launched the Great Proletarian Cultural Revolution, ostensibly to re-ignite revolutionary fervor among the masses, but in truth to get rid of his enemies in the Party before they got rid of him and his lethal fantasies.

While Rupert and other observers watched aghast, normal life in China screeched to a halt. Chaos ensued. People went at each other hammer and sickle, denouncing fellow citizens as "capitalist roaders" and "poisonous weeds," torturing and killing on a mass scale, all claiming to uphold the banner of Mao Tse-tung Thought.

Worst of all from Rupert's perspective, armies of fanatical young Maoists known as Red Guards rampaged through the country destroying huge elements of China's cultural heritage – paintings, sculpture, porcelains, books, temples, historic buildings and monuments – because only brand-new Mao Tse-tung Thought was valid, so anything "old" was by definition bad.

This, keep in mind, in a culture that stretched back beyond the country's three thousand five hundred years of recorded history and into the mists of unrecorded time. Five thousand years of continuity, with all its attendant writings, art and architecture. There was a massive amount of "old" around to destroy.

Nobody but Mao had the power to halt the chaos. The more rational members of the Communist leadership at least tried to shelter the few foreigners in the country from the madness in the streets, but every now and then some unlucky outsider fell prey. In the winter of 1968, Rupert's turn came.

He had managed to get a visa by latching onto a tour group from the Organization for Irish-Chinese Cooperation. British security personnel in Hong Kong warned him against going to China at this dangerous time, even as an ostensible tourist, but Rupert replied that it was his duty to report on the atrocities taking place there – which for him more than anything meant the insane destruction of historic buildings and priceless art. Once on the ground in Shanghai, he was en route to an interview with an expert on Chinese antiquities when he ran into a patrol sent out by some crazed political faction or another. When they spotted a vile foreign devil walking unguarded through the streets, their day was made. They dragged him off.

China's ties with the outside world were already coming unraveled by the spectacle of a nation gone mad. Chinese diplomats in foreign capitals periodically ran riot to demonstrate their revolutionary zeal to the leadership back home. A band of Red Guards attacked the British embassy in Beijing in 1967 and beat the occupants. The Party did not need the added burden of some foreign visitor being bludgeoned to death by a band of lunatic teenagers.

It took a unit of the People's Liberation Army, accompanied by a high-ranking Communist Party official and a representative of the Foreign Ministry, to pry Rupert loose. The soldiers broke into the abandoned school where he was being held, shot three of his captors on the spot and beat the rest senseless. After a frantic search of the building they found Rupert lying naked on a frigid cement floor, blabbering incoherently, his gangly body purple with cold and bruises. He'd undergone several days of "struggle sessions," in which his captors would surround him and demand that he admit to transgressions he hadn't committed. They forced him to stand for hours in the "airplane" position, wrists tied together behind his back, arms pulled straight out and forced high into the air while his head was pushed downward. They beat him repeatedly when he couldn't understand what they were saying (they were shouting in Shanghai dialect while he spoke only

Mandarin and a bit of Cantonese) and failed to satisfy them with confessions.

After his rescue he spent a week in a Beijing hospital before the doctors declared him well enough to be transferred to Hong Kong. He needed a couple more weeks in the hospital there before he could begin the road back to a normal existence.

His injuries weren't life threatening, but the outrage he had suffered could not be erased. Like many a person who has had a love affair go bad, Rupert saw his infatuation with China mutate into abject hatred. As he resumed work he made a vow: he would never return to the mainland while the Communists were still in charge. From his perch in Hong Kong he would take every opportunity to expose the commies, and the Chinese people in general, for the barbarous madmen that they were. An epidemic could wipe out all seven hundred million of the bloody beggars, and Rupert would cross the border only to piss on their graves.

For the next thirty-five years he made good on his vow. He limited his dealings with the Chinese to those who were locally born or had fled the PRC. They would hate as much as he what China had become under the Communists.

Once, in 1988, twelve years after Mao had died, Rupert allowed himself to be cajoled into signing up for a press junket to Guangzhou – Canton, as most of the world knew it. Mao's co-conspirators in the Cultural Revolution were long since dead or behind bars. One of Mao's archrivals, Deng Xiaoping, had taken charge, and a semblance of sanity had returned. The press trip was to be a benign affair to commemorate the tenth anniversary of Deng's *kaifang*, his post-Mao "Reform and Opening up:" a speech or two by local officials, a visit to a few factories and historical sites, several days of extravagant eating and drinking, and what have you.

It was still too much for Rupert. As soon as he laid eyes on the PLA troops at the border he began to hyperventilate. His friends thought he was having a heart attack. He was escorted back to Hong Kong while the rest of the contingent carried on. As far as Brian Ross or anyone else who knew him was aware, Rupert never came any closer to China after that than the Royal Hong Kong Jockey Club golf course in Fanling, several miles short of the border. And yet...

The Chinese theory of Rupert's murder was impossible to ignore. The killing could only have taken place on that side of the border. Ergo, Brian Ross's fourth mystery: why had Rupert broken his long-standing vow and returned to China after all those years?

To which Ross now had to add a fifth, equally vexing question: why in God's name was Chinese State Security so interested in the death?

Someone had left a note on his desk with that same Beijing telephone number: State Security had called for a second time.

Three

Ross and Wai had budgeted fifteen minutes for the border crossing, but even with their police credentials to grease the way it had taken half an hour from the time the Kowloon-Canton Railway dropped them at the Lo Wu train station on the Hong Kong side of the border. That only got them across the border bridge to the street on the China side, where a sign informed them they were in Luo Hu. Same location, different Chinese dialect. In any language, they were running late.

Ross had taken that phone call from State Security and immediately passed it up the line to his superiors. Dealing with the central Chinese authorities was something he rarely had to do and invariably disliked. He turned now to people he could at least identify with, his fellow cops across the border, the Public Security Bureau. The PSB was the *Gong An Bu* – the "*gong an*" to the Hong Kong cops. Unfortunately, the Shenzhen *gong an* seemed far less interested than State Security in pursuing the Rackley murder. Ross had had to send repeated requests for a consultation before they grudgingly told him to come along.

He had visited Shenzhen only a few times before this, and never with any enthusiasm. There was first of all the traffic they would have to navigate, which had metastasized on the roads along with the country's economic explosion. Most vehicles were guided by first-time drivers who lacked the experience to respect the dangers of the road. They ran red lights, they rode the shoulders in the wrong direction, they turned in front of oncoming traffic. "Sweet Jesus!" Ross shrieked as a massive truck outside his window changed lanes without warning, threatening to crush them and their tiny taxi like kumquats.

More than the traffic, though, Ross was unnerved by the frenetic pace of China's development. The Communist Party had set the wheels in motion only twenty-five years earlier, and now it was all threatening to speed out of control, like the machines in some apocalyptic fiction that turn on the men who create them.

Before Deng Xiaoping began to lift China into the modern era, Shenzhen had been a sleepy agricultural and fishing village, the gateway to an alien world. Beyond the immigration building, uncountable hordes wallowed in poverty and ignorance. A faded sign behind the immigration counters bore the Chinese characters *chu* and *kou*. "Go-out mouth." Exit. It might easily have said, Here Be Dragons.

The transformation to the 21st century madness Ross and Wai now encountered began when Deng selected Shenzhen to lead China's way to modernization. The goal was prosperity for all. "To be rich is glorious!" Deng told his countrymen.

Hardly a revolutionary war cry in most places. But for decades the Chinese masses had been indoctrinated with the evils of wealth. Now they took Deng at his word and began grabbing everything they could get their hands on, with the same enthusiasm they'd shown just a few years earlier for clubbing each other to death in the name of ideological rectitude. Marxism vanished like the air from a punctured balloon. Corruption, already endemic, expanded to fill the void, and members of the Communist Party led the charge. From time to time Beijing shot a couple of errant cadres to set an example, but the media continued to record staggering new heights of thievery.

And yet, as the high-rise buildings stretching as far as Ross and Wai could see attested, Deng's goal was being met. The country was modernizing at an unheard of pace.

It was a hugely uneven sort of modernity: a ladleful of Chinese tradition, a generous portion of American robber-baron-style capitalism, with a clenched fistful of Leninist control orchestrating it all from behind the scenes. This New China was a chop suey of mixed bits, neither fish nor fowl, neither communist nor democratic. It teetered on the edge of chaos, it heaved and bellowed, it grew and changed shape in front of one's eyes like an alien life form. But grow it did. Not even China's harshest critics – not even Rupert Rackley in his prime – could deny that.

As Ross and Wai made their wary way to police headquarters, New China in all its raw exuberance spread its arms to greet them.

~

A Public Security Bureau officer was pacing the lobby of the municipal building, checking his watch nervously. As soon as Ross and Wai appeared they were rushed upstairs and into the office of Bai Yongchao, a vice director-general of the Shenzhen Municipal PSB. Ross smoothed his rumpled uniform and wiped his sweat-soaked hair as they entered.

Vice Director-General Bai was broad and stolid, with a lopsided grin splitting his jowly Northern Chinese face. His uniform had a faint *Student Prince* air, far more ornate than the understated uniforms of his Hong Kong visitors. A second man wearing the same uniform with a bit less braid stood at Bai's side.

"I'm terribly sorry we're late," Ross said after introductions were made and business cards exchanged. "Getting through the border took longer than we expected."

Ross was speaking English, although like most ex-pat Hong Kong police officers he spoke fluent Cantonese, the dialect of Hong Kong and Guangdong Province. Wai translated the English into Cantonese for their hosts' benefit. Bai's Guangdong-born assistant translated for his boss from Cantonese to Mandarin, or *Putonghua*, China's national language and the native dialect of Beijing and the Northeast.

A secretary scurried in with a tray of tea and cups. "Please," Bai said in Putonghua, "have some tea. You must be tired after your journey." His accent confirmed what his looks suggested: his Mandarin was replete with the exaggerated R's of the Northeast.

The aide translated Bai's offer into Cantonese. For the sake of form, Wai translated it into English for Ross. "This is going to be slow going," Ross said in an English aside to Wai.

Bai and his aide also exchanged a few words. The vice director-general looked up and said, in English: "Maybe we can speed things up, Mr. Ross. My English is not good, but I can speak a bit."

"Your English sounds excellent," Ross said with a relieved smile. "I would guess that you're from somewhere in the Northeast, Mr. Bai? Liaoning province, perhaps?"

"Heilongjiang province," Bai replied. "Harbin City." Ha*rrrrr*bin.

"Not here long enough to have learned Cantonese, I expect," Ross said.

Bai made a face. "I do not think I will ever learn it. Very difficult language, Cantonese," he said, and then to Wai: "No offense, detective, but I just cannot get my mouth around it."

Wai gave a wan smiled. He knew most northerners had difficulty with Cantonese. It was spoken with seven or eight intrinsic tones (depending on who was counting) compared with Mandarin's four. It was an older dialect than Mandarin, and like their cuisine, like everything of a cultural nature, the Cantonese considered it superior to any other in China.

Bai's status, however, meant he did not have to bother with Cantonese sensibilities. He turned from Wai and asked: "How can I help you gentlemen?"

"We would like to propose," Ross said, "that our two forces cooperate on the murder of the English journalist who was found on the border here a few days ago."

"Ah, yes. I've been reading about that in the Hong Kong newspapers," Bai said, reverting to Putonghua and addressing his subordinate instead of Ross. The Chinese have an aversion to delivering bad news. Bai had switched languages so as not to have to inform Ross directly that the Shenzhen cops wanted absolutely nothing to do with the investigation into Rupert's murder. "Your people were quite adamant that the incident took place on your side," he said.

"Actually," Ross said after the comment had made its way through the language relay, "we've now concluded that the victim must have been killed on *this* side. As your people originally suggested."

"I believe that was only mentioned by our people as a preliminary hypothesis, before we had time to look into the facts," Bai said.

"We have also looked into the facts, quite thoroughly," said Ross, "and they lead us to conclude that our original theory of the case was wrong."

"And what are these facts that support this revised theory?" Bai asked, raising his head. His body language made it clear that he was unhappy with the direction the meeting was taking. He had returned to English to speed the conversation to a conclusion.

"Our people have determined that the victim took the direct train from Hong Kong to Changping Station, outside Dongguan City, the day before his body was found," Ross said. "We have no record of his returning to Hong Kong through any of our immigration points. So the inescapable conclusion is that he died somewhere on this side."

"Aha," Bai said after a moment. "Dongguan." The principle city between Shenzhen and Guangzhou. "And of course you have considered the possibility that the murder took place in Dongguan City itself?"

"We have asked your colleagues in Dongguan for any information they can give us, naturally, but since the body was found here in Shenzhen..."

"Yes," Bai said. He paced the room, hands clasped behind his back. "Well, we will look into this. But you realize that we are seriously short of staff." He raised his arms to the city erupting outside his office window. "Shenzhen has grown so quickly. And the killer has had days to disappear and cover his tracks. We will try to do our best, but I'm afraid I cannot hold out much hope."

"Any help you can give us will be appreciated," Ross said. "Mr. Rackley was a rather well-known figure in Hong Kong and a lot of people there would like to see the case solved." He signaled to Wai, who produced a stuffed manila envelope. "We brought along what information we've been able to obtain so far, including photographs and descriptions of the bullet we took from the body. Perhaps this might help your detectives in their inquiries."

Wai held the envelope out to Bai. Bai gave it a look one might give an offer of the Ebola virus. The aide stepped in and took the envelope from Wai's hand.

"Detective Wai here is leading the investigation on our side," Ross said. "I trust your people will contact him with any information you might turn up."

"Yes, yes, of course."

"By the way," Wai said, "had you talked to the State Security about this?"

"State Security?" Bai bristled at the suggestion. "This is not their concern. Why do you ask?"

"We have got a couple calls from them since the murder. They want to know what's going on."

The look of pain told them Bai had been taken by surprise. "Well," he said, "I am sure they have communicated with someone on my staff. My assistants handle such, uh, routine communications for me. As I say, I am extremely busy..."

The interview ended with ritual pleasantries all around. Ross chose his parting words carefully. Many an innocent *"Let me know if I can help you in any way"* to officials on the mainland had been followed by a request for an expensive watch, a Mercedes sedan, an American university education for an official's child.

"What do you think?" Ross asked once they were back in a taxi.

"I think we not gonna get nothing out of the *gong an*," Wai said.

"I agree. Mr. Bai was very obviously not interested in helping us. Even if they do learn anything, and that's hardly a given, they're unlikely pass it on to us, especially if it reflects badly on the local authorities in any way."

Wai chuckled. "Boss, how long you been in Hong Kong now?" he asked.

"Going on twenty-four years. Why?"

"Still you can't read Chinese people, that's why. That guy, it's not just a case he's not interested. It's a case his superiors don't tell him what's going on. He suppose to be the boss, and still they wouldn't keep him in the loop. You can see he's very embarrass when you mention State Security. He lose much face."

"Yes," Ross said. "That one obviously took him by surprise."

"If mainland people don't talk to each other," Wai said, "I don't think any way they gonna talk to us."

"No novelty there," said Ross. "The only time they talk to us anyway nowadays is to tell us what to do." His mobile phone rang as he was speaking. He held it to his ear and Wai could hear a voice leaking out the edges, delivering some long-winded message. Aside from telling the caller that he was in Shenzhen, Ross's only contribution to the conversation was an occasional grunt or a *yessir*. When the voice disappeared, Ross flipped the phone shut and shook his head.

"Anything important?" Wai asked.

"I'm afraid so," Ross said. "That was the chief."

"Chief of police?"

"Himself. He just received a call from the Chief Secretary's office. They'd just received a call from the Hong Kong and Macau Affairs Office."

"Why our chief calls to tell you that?" Wai asked.

"It's about our case," Ross said. "The affairs office wanted to let us know they are very interested in the Rackley case and wish to be kept informed. The chief says the CE's office wants to be kept informed, too."

"Chief Executive. Chief of Police. Chief Secretary. *Wah!* So many chiefs. I thought you said Mainland China don't even like Rupert. So how come all the *dai lobans* suddenly so interested in who killed him?"

Ross shrugged. All the big bosses, indeed. He'd thought that by passing that message from State Security up through channels, he'd be free of political interference. Yet here were the *dai lobans,* out in force and clamoring to be kept informed. "You're Chinese, they're Chinese: what do you think?" he asked.

"Don't ask me," Wai said. "Hong Kong Chinese, I know how we think. And Hong Kong Chinese government don't go to toilet now unless Mainland government says go. But how Mainland Chinese think? Shit, I got no more idea than you *gwei-los* do."

They were interrupted again by the ring of Ross's phone. He said a few words into it and slid it back into his pocket. "Well, there's a surprise," he said.

"Let me guess," Wai said. "Chief of Communist Party?"

"Almost as strange," Ross said. "That was Bill Sturges. The editor-in-chief over at the *Mail*? He wants to get together for a wee chat about the case."

"Why strange?" said Wai. "You already say you planning to talk to this guy anyway."

"I am, but I never would have expected *him* to be the one to call *me*." Ross disliked dealing with journalists almost as much as he disliked dealing with mainland officials. He acknowledged the value of a free press in principle, and occasionally he encountered a sympathetic soul among the press corps – he'd been friendly with Rupert, had he not? – but like many cops he viewed most of Rupert's colleagues as unwelcome meddlers. An obstacle to solving crime and keeping society safe. And the most unwelcome of all, from Ross's point of view, was Bill Sturges.

"He and I have a bit of unpleasant personal history," he said. "Truth be told, I'd rather not have to deal with the bugger at all. But, as I said, he was Rackley's closest friend, so one of us has to talk to him. And don't forget Rackley's widow. Have you arranged for her to come in for a conversation yet?"

"Tomorrow we talk to her," Wai said. "Today she burying her husband."

Four

Bill Sturges was running the facts of Rupert's death through his mind when his phone rang. He took his eyes off the road long enough to glance at the screen. "What the hell?" he said. Olivia Chen, Rupert's widow, was calling. He'd just seen her at the cemetery minutes earlier, stopping to take her hand and voice his condolences as he joined the throng filing from Rupert's graveside. Outwardly, she'd seemed as cool as an icicle radish. Yet he sensed that beneath the dignified bearing, she was overwhelmed by events, and Sturges wasn't sure his presence had even registered. He'd mumbled what he thought was a perfunctory *"If there's anything I can do"* – and here she was ten minutes later, apparently taking him up on the offer. Asking him to escort her to the reading of Rupert's will the next day.

"Of course I'll join you Olivia," he said. "But pardon me for asking: why me?"

There were always questions when Olivia was involved. Along with the new mysteries Rupert's murder had thrown up, an old had been reverberating at the back of everyone's mind: Why had a highly successful, meltingly sensual woman like Olivia Chen married a dissolute old fart like Rupert, who was almost twenty years her senior? It certainly wasn't his looks, which were plain at best. It wasn't money: he'd been comfortably well off, but nothing more. The match had been a matter of gossip and speculation in Hong Kong since long before someone put a bullet into Rupert's brain.

People looked in vain for the answer in Olivia's past. She straddled three worlds, that much was common knowledge. Born in China. Not quite ten when she and her widowed father sneaked across the border into British Hong Kong in 1968, fleeing the Cultural Revolution like so many others. Her early education was a combination of those first two worlds: the modern curriculum of Hong Kong's British schools by day, tutored instruction in the Chinese classics and traditions in the evenings. Then, at the age of fourteen, she was sent to continue her education in the United States.

There, she excelled. *Magna cum laude* at the University of Michigan. Top of her class at Harvard Law. She became a citizen. In the mid-'80s she joined a leading Wall Street law firm, and in several years of effort she worked her way up to junior partner. Then she made a sideways move into investment banking, and in 1993 the bank sent her to open a branch in Hong Kong.

Olivia's family was originally from the city of Suzhou, and by popular belief the most beautiful women of China hail from Suzhou. Olivia was true to the stereotype. Her lustrous black hair framed skin like fine shell porcelain. She had long and shapely legs, modest but firm breasts, and the elegant and finely etched features that the Southern Chinese lack. She carried herself with the air of an aristocrat. Upon her return to Hong Kong at the age of thirty-five, three-quarters of the colony's rich and eligible bachelors, not to mention a goodly portion of the married men, went weak in the knees.

Olivia did nothing to discourage the attention. She dressed like a twenty-two-year-old secretary prowling the singles bars: Versace mini-skirts, low-cut tops exposing vistas of cleavage, stiletto heels. La Perla underwear, according to several men who dated her before she married Rupert. To hear those same several men talk, the image that her style of dress broadcast was no false advertising: more than one fellow claimed she had worn him out with her sexual voraciousness. She was the kind of woman men fantasize about when they're having sex with their wives. Among those who knew her intimately, she had earned a nickname: "The Man-eater."

She'd moderated her wardrobe in the last couple of years as she passed forty, but not by much. Good genes and regular workouts in the gym kept her looking almost as young and luscious as when she arrived.

Rupert may or may not have known what brand of underwear his wife wore – he was English, after all – but if he did, he never said. He never said much about her at all, as if he enjoyed the speculation that surrounded the match and liked to encourage it by ignoring it. None of the men who drank with him regularly at the Hong Kong Club or the Cricket Club or the Foreign Correspondents' Club or the Football Club or the Yacht Club – none of them could figure the marriage out, especially given his antipathy toward the Chinese. If someone was sufficiently lacking in tact to bring the subject up in his presence — typically around eight p.m. after a long lunch at one or another of the clubs — he would smile Buddha-like into his glass and say, in his deep, sonorous voice: "Some chaps just know how to please a woman."

But nobody bought that for a nanosecond. Rupert Rackley was no stud and never had been. Like many an expatriate man in Asia he did cut a sexual swath as he traveled the region in his younger days, but his was a highly particularized swath. For Rupert – and this only compounded the mystery of his marriage – liked his women young. Far younger than Olivia was at the time they were married. He wasn't a pedophile in the strict sense of the word, he didn't go in for pre-pubescent children, he wasn't interested in boys of any age, but during his early days in Asia, while other men were having their fill of fully-grown women, Rupert roamed the brothels and back alleys in search of teenage girls.

He didn't trumpet his preferences, but neither could he hide them from the men he traveled with as they followed the stories of the day around Asia. Some found it mildly amusing. Some found it repulsive. Most simply didn't discuss sexual matters with him. They didn't often discuss Rupert's proclivities with people outside their circle, either, although there was one story that occasionally made the rounds late in the evening at some Hong Kong soirée or other when the company was convivial and the storyteller was well oiled.

One night in Taipei, it seems, Rupert was sitting at the bar of the hotel where he and several other journalists were staying. He was unusually subdued. He stared at his whisky, occasionally emitting a plaintive sigh.

"You're uncharacteristically pensive this evening, Rupe," one of the hacks said. "What's on your twisted mind?"

Rupert shook his head without speaking.

"Come on, old man, out with it: what's up?"

He let out another long sigh. "This girl I saw today," he said. "She was...I can't describe her. She was magnificent."

At that there were hoots and catcalls from around the bar. "Yeah, yeah, we know," one of the men said. "She was magnificently *young*, right, Rupe?"

"This one was special," Rupert said with quiet insistence.

"They're all special to you, Rupe, as long as they're barely old enough to bleed."

"Probably didn't have a hair on her snatch, you filthy old bugger."

"You don't understand," Rupert said.

"What's not to understand?" another said. "You like to stick it to sixteen-year-olds."

"Ah," Rupert replied, "but *this* sixteen-year-old..."

The others were becoming impatient. "Come on you miserable pervert, spit it out."

"This one..." He paused, and those around the bar thought they'd lost him. Then his eyes shone with an inner brightness. "This one had the body of a *thirteen*-year-old."

But those days were long past. By the time of the marriage Rupert was in no shape to have sex with anyone. He was already extremely large, grossly out of shape. A serious heart attack a year after the wedding left him weakened, and yet he continued to drink heavily despite it all. He was no longer interested in sex as far as anyone knew, and couldn't have done much about it if he had been.

Nor was he unusually well endowed. Had his Jade Stem (as the Chinese erotic classics had it) been notably large, and depending on which woman one asked, and given the whispered stories about Olivia's proclivities...

But men had stood shoulder to shoulder with Rupert at urinals throughout East Asia and they all knew: he was perfectly average in that department.

Some chaps did indeed know how to please a woman, but it was highly unlikely that Rupert Rackley was among them.

Certainly not by the time he went for a final, fatal swim in the Shenzhen River. Certainly not sufficiently to win the heart of a piece of ass like Olivia Chen.

In Hong Kong, beautiful young Chinese woman are born to marry impossibly wealthy Chinese men. Once married they typically spend their time shopping, lunching with the ladies, taking yoga classes. Having their colons irrigated or whatever the current health fad might be. Taking a brief time out to have an average of 0.9 children.

A superficial glance might have suggested that Olivia was headed in the expected direction. She was courted fervently by one of the territory's richest playboy-socialites, Jackson Liu, the son of a famously wealthy property developer. Liu was in his early forties at the time, twice divorced, first from the daughter of another leading Hong Kong Chinese family, then from an Italian woman he had met in Modena while buying his first Ferrari. He was sophisticated, good-looking, intelligent enough. He had what Hong Kong assumed was everything a girl like Olivia could want: cars, a multi-million-dollar yacht, a house on the Peak, a duplex in New York, shares in a winery in Tuscany, money coming out of every pore. Three years after her arrival, having broken half a dozen Chinese and Western hearts, Olivia began to be seen in public with Liu.

It was obvious to anyone who really knew her, however, that Olivia would never be content with the empty life of a Hong Kong *tai-tai*. She liked to party, true; she pampered herself unabashedly; she had a third-degree black belt in shopping. But she was serious about a career, serious about making her own mark. It was stamped on her face. It showed in her walk.

The insularity of most Hong Kong Chinese contrasts glaringly with the sophistication and worldly outlook of the city. Despite a century and a half of foreign influence, despite the frenetic activity visible any time of night or day, those who have never left the cocoon of the Chinese family tend to display a remarkable absence of curiosity about the world around them. Ask a question about current affairs and they'll offer only a blank stare. Ask the location of a shop three doors away and they'll shake their heads in ignorance. Follow them down the street: it's like following a sleepwalker. They'll wander absently left and right, right and left, with little awareness of anything except whatever lies directly ahead.

Chinese who were born or have lived in the West have a different aspect. An awareness of the wider world is apparent in their eyes. They carry themselves with assertiveness. It was awareness and assertiveness that showed on Olivia Chen's face.

One cannot escape one's origins, however. Her western veneer, like that of Hong Kong itself, went only so deep. If someone asked, she would describe herself as the same traditional, respectful Chinese daughter that her father had raised. "The things you grow up with never leave you completely," she was often heard to say.

Perhaps, but those who knew her from childhood insisted that she was a very different person from the teenage girl who had left Hong Kong, and not just in years. Given her Western demeanor, then, Hong Kong was not totally surprised when Olivia dumped Jackson Liu a year after they started dating. American women did things like that.

Hong Kong was positively blown away, on the other hand, when seven months later, she and Rupert Rackley ran off and got married.

Nobody was more flabbergasted than Jackson Liu himself. The break-up was not only a terrible disappointment, it was a devastating loss of face. And face to the Chinese is almost everything. Give a Chinese man the choice of losing a million bucks or losing face and he'll be torn with indecision.

When Liu finally began venturing out after the initial disgrace wore off, he took what little revenge he could. He would describe in great detail their escapades in bed, Olivia's prowess – we're talking clinical detail here – in the performance of oral sex.

It was obvious to those who knew him, though, how massively Liu had been wounded. When he walked into the member's bar at the Hong Kong Club several days after the news of Rupert's death, one of the old boys clapped him on the shoulder with boozy familiarity and said: "I say, Jackson, no love lost between you and old Rupert, what? I wouldn't be surprised if you'd run him under with your Testa Rossa."

~

If anyone should have known about the marriage of Rupert Rackley and Olivia Chen, it was Bill Sturges. He had known Rupert since he, Sturges, was a child. Rackley was Uncle Rupe, a tall, dignified-looking man who used to drop by the house when Bill was young to spend time with Bill's father, George.

George Sturges had arrived in Asia from America in 1954 as a newspaper photographer. He married the granddaughter of a former British governor of Hong Kong, a member of one of the colony's elite British families, and their son was born in 1960. Like many a journalist roaming Asia during the middle third of the 20th century, George Sturges had become an amateur collector of Asian art, and Rupert, the acknowledged expert among them, became George's mentor.

George was killed in Vietnam during the communists' Tet Offensive of early 1968, and Rupert took eight-year-old Bill under his wing. He always made it a point to bring the boy some small gift from his travels – a piece of jade, a Buddha's head, an intricately painted snuff bottle – and then instruct him on the item's significance. Rupert's trips to the mainland and his fondness for the Chinese people came to an end after the trauma he suffered there in 1968, but his love for Chinese art and traditional culture was undiminished. If he now deplored what China had become, he could still revel in what it had been.

He drilled young Bill on the language: the written characters, which were more or less identical no matter which dialect of Chinese was being used; the vast spoken differences between the Cantonese that Sturges had learned from the household servants as he grew up and the Mandarin used on much of the mainland. "To know a people you have to know their language, lad," Rupert told him. "You will never understand the Chinese without understanding how their language is put together. Although..."

At this his words would trail off, and he would disappear into his own thoughts. Could anyone, seeing how China had evolved under Mao, really understand the Chinese? Could the Chinese understand themselves?

But to Rupert knowledge was sacrosanct, even knowledge of evil. He continued to pass on his own, and along with it his philosophy of unwavering intellectual rigor. "Things are rarely as they seem, lad," he would tell the boy. "Always look for the underlying truth. Learn not only what happened but also how and why it happened. That's been the secret of my success as a journalist. Only when you know the root causes of a situation can you truly claim to understand it."

Over the years he distilled this dictum into a simple two-word Chinese slogan. The Chinese language is malleable. Individual words have many shades of meaning, depending on the context and the emphasis placed on them. Rupert's pride and joy aside from his art was a 1982 Morgan roadster, the famous British sports car, whose name in Chinese is rendered with the characters "摩根", and pronounced "*Mo-gun.*" The characters had been chosen because they sounded like "Morgan," but Chinese characters do not merely represent sounds: each also has a meaning. Rupert realized one day that the two characters could be read to represent his personal motto: *Determine the root cause.*

It tickled him that his car was a rolling admonition to seek the truth. "*Mo gun,*" he would warn when someone jumped to a careless conclusion in his presence. It was his version of the clever puns and plays on words of which the Chinese were so fond.

Few people got the joke, and Rupert's sexual shenanigans had earned him no small number of detractors, but young Bill worshipped the man. He was well into his teens before he learned of Rupert's skewed sexual leanings, but growing up in Asia he had seen and heard far stranger things. Sturges's mother had her misgivings about her son spending so much time with a man of Rupert's reputation, but George had valued Rupert's friendship and Rupert was always discreet around the boy. She saw how her fatherless son reveled in the attention and soaked up Rupert's teachings like a sponge. She allowed the relationship to continue.

Bill received his initial education in the British schools of Hong Kong. Then, with a bow to his American side, he studied at Yale, but like many Hong Kong kids he was eventually drawn back home. He returned as a correspondent for *Newsweek* in 1995, two years before the British handed China the last of their great colonies. In 1999, he was forced to make a choice: *Newsweek* was planning to move him to the Middle East. The *South China Mail*, the territory's leading English-language newspaper, offered him the job of political editor.

He opted for Hong Kong. Two years after that he was promoted to managing editor, and shortly before Rupert's death he moved up to editor-in-chief. His decision to stay had been guided primarily by personal considerations, but the *Mail* job paid well, it conferred a reasonable amount of prestige, and it was an excellent vantage point from which to observe the city's transition from British colony to that strange new entity known as the Hong Kong Special Administrative Region of the People's Republic of China. The SAR.

By the time of Sturges's return to Hong Kong, Rupert was already fat and out of shape, but his enthusiasm for life was undiminished. The two resumed their friendship as if it had never been interrupted. As the millennium approached, Sturges assumed he knew Rupert as well as anyone in town, and better than most. He knew among other things that Rupert had occasional dealings with Olivia's father, another renowned collector of Chinese art. Yet he had no idea that Rupe was seeing

45

Olivia socially, let alone that they'd developed any kind of relationship.

The two men might have been close as father and son, but Rupert had said not a word to Sturges about the impending marriage.

Once the shock wore off, Sturges expected he would get to know Olivia in the normal course of events. Wrong again. On the rare occasions they did cross paths she seemed happy enough to see him. She'd give him a little hug and a kiss on the cheek, they'd exchange a bit of small talk. But that was pretty much that.

He'd been confused, therefore, when she called a year earlier, just after his own marriage had disintegrated, to inquire about his wellbeing. "My poor Bill," she began, and launched into a stream-of-consciousness dialogue of sympathy and affection. As if they'd been close all along. "If you need anything...friends have to stick together...come for dinner...help you get past this painful moment..."

She began e-mailing: chitchat about Rupert, bits of local gossip, passing on the odd joke. When Sturges was invited to the Rackley house she was now there to share the evening. Once or twice as he was leaving she appeared to hold a hug a bit longer than was normal between friends.

Sturges was a healthy man, and he couldn't avoid occasional fantasies of getting into Olivia's pants. He'd heard the rumors about her sexual appetites; he'd held her in his arms for however briefly and felt her allure first hand. Still, he never seriously considered trying to take it beyond the fantasy stage, even after his divorce left him free to play around. He respected old Rupe too much for that.

He convinced himself anyway that she had no sexual interest in him. Not that he was uninteresting. He was comfortable with what he saw in the mirror. Slim and fit at forty-three. Full head of wavy black hair. Always ready with a knowledgeable comment or a good joke. Dark eyes fixed in a journalist's skeptical squint, set above high cheekbones. For reasons unknown to him, women placed great store in cheekbones; Sturges often caught women giving him and his cheekbones the eye. The divorce had been a massive blow to his ego and the recovery was slow in coming, but he was confident he'd have no trouble hooking up with other women once he got past the pain.

When he did, though...no, not with Olivia. The two were something beyond friendly, yes, but not even close friends, let alone potential lovers. Despite their long acquaintance, at the time of Rupert's death Sturges barely knew Mrs. Rupert at all.

~

The reason Olivia wanted Sturges at the reading of the will was quickly forthcoming, at any rate, and like just about everything else since the murder, it entailed a surprise.

"I think here's something in the will for you," she explained over the phone. "Rupert told me he planned to leave you something when he was gone. Didn't he ever mention it?"

"Never," Sturges said. "Not a hint."

"Ah," she said. "Well, the old bastard was full of surprises, wasn't he?"

Five

The things you grow up with never leave you completely, Olivia Chen liked to say. It was a lesson she had learned from her father, who knew more than most how the actions and circumstances of youth can return to haunt the most exemplary of lives. In turn observers, participants and victims, Olivia's family was 20th century China writ small, flung to and fro by the tides of history until its path ultimately intersected with that of Rupert Rackley.

Olivia's grandfather, Chang Daorang, was born to a wealthy landholding family in Suzhou in 1899. The Sino-Japanese War had ended four years earlier with Japan victorious, and Japan's war booty included the Chinese island of Taiwan – one more humiliation foisted on China by foreigners after a century of humiliations. Daorang's father was a modern-minded man who despised the decrepitude of China's ruling Qing Dynasty. He saw how the West, by contrast, was flexible in its thinking, innovative, and strong. He decided: Western ideas were needed if China was to confront the coming century from anything but a position of inferiority.

He turned Daorang's education over to American Protestant missionaries, who steeped the boy in Western thinking and gave him the biblical name Jacob. On October 10, 1911, Jacob Chang Daorang's class was discussing America's Declaration of Independence when they heard shouting in the street. They ran out to learn that a revolt had taken place in the city of Wuhan, in Hubei province, and the rebel leaders had taken the opportunity to declare the province's independence from the Qing Emperor.

Other provinces followed suit in seceding from the empire, and the next year, as Jacob prepared to leave for college in America, the six-year-old emperor in Beijing abdicated; the revolt had officially became a revolution.

This particular revolution, however, had occurred with scant popular participation, little central leadership to bind the parts together, and not the slightest idea of where it was going next. "China" was now a republic in name, but the nation Jacob sailed way from had disintegrated into a checkerboard of independent fiefdoms and political factions.

When he returned to China in 1916, Jacob followed the expected path. He joined the family business in Suzhou. He married and started a family. His father was a famous collector of antiques, and Jacob, too, became a collector of no small expertise. Life was good, and he might have been content with his lot. But during his time in America he had come to embrace notions of nationhood and freedom; while building his own future, he had taken on board his father's dream of building his divided nation into a strong and free China.

Jacob studied the available options, and decided he could be most effective as a member of Chiang Kai-shek's Nationalist government. In 1929 he accepted a position with the finance ministry, and moved his family up the Yangtze River to the capital in Nanjing. "Chiang Kai-shek will cure China's weakness," Jacob assured his father as they sailed away.

If only Chiang Kai-shek himself had been so clear of purpose. Instead of concentrating on building a strong nation, he became fixated on destroying the young Communist Party. He chased the Party across the country and back, eventually to Yanan, a remote district in Shaanxi province just south of the Great Wall. While Chiang's attention was elsewhere, Japan had begun a slow, insidious invasion, snatching pieces of the country from under his nose. Jacob Chang was among those who stood by Chiang, but many Chinese began looking for someone who would forget about the pesky Communists and lead the Chinese nation instead against the Japanese.

The Communists themselves answered the popular yearning. They called for an anti-Japanese front. They spoke at the same time of an end to the exploitation of China's peasants and workers – the vast majority of the population – whose lives had traditionally been an abysmal hell. This vision, so dramatic a break with Chinese tradition, appealed not only to the poor, but also to students and intellectuals who dreamt of a modern nation, and who began making their way to Yanan to join the fight. Among them was Jacob Chang's son – Olivia Chen's future father – Peter.

Peter was educated by American missionaries like his father before him. The boy studied western literature, history, mathematics and the sciences. He spoke English as well as he spoke the various Chinese dialects around him: Mandarin and its Nanjing variant, plus his mother's native Cantonese.

He was twelve when the Japanese first took territory on the mainland, and he watched with burgeoning political consciousness as they annexed more and more. By the time the Communists had established their stronghold in Yanan, in 1936, Peter was seventeen, and old enough to question the Chiang government's policies. Jacob, however, had seen that the boy also studied the Chinese classics: Confucius, Mencius and other ancient texts.

When his father forbade discussion of politics, Peter, the good Confucian son, retreated.

But if he was master of his own house, Jacob could not control the world outside his door.

In 1937, Japan shifted from piecemeal annexation to all-out invasion. As Japanese troops approached Nanjing early that December, Chiang's government fled. Those it left behind were treated by the invaders to a six-week orgy of rape and murder.

In simple numbers, the Nanjing Massacre ranks somewhere in the middle of humankind's scale of atrocities: between a hundred fifty thousand and three hundred thousand killed; twenty thousand or so women raped.

Still, credit where credit is due: for pure sustained barbarity, Japan's actions in Nanjing were world class. Any Chinese who crossed the path of a Japanese soldier risked instant death. The soldiers raped almost any female they found, and after the rape was finished the women were subjected to humiliating tortures: their breasts sliced off, their abdomens cut open.

Those caught in the maelstrom, like Peter Chang, could be forgiven for thinking that here, the most profound depths of human depravity had been laid bare.

~

The assault on Nanjing began December 9th. On the 12th the Chinese defenders began retreating through the walls and across the Yangtze River, leaving behind a city swollen with civilians and wounded soldiers. Jacob Chang had seen what was coming and began to prepare his family for evacuation, but by the time he had everyone ready it was too late to run. He gave money to the household staff and told them to save themselves. He locked his doors and hid each family member separately, parceled out the food and water he had collected for the flight from the city, and prayed they would survive the coming onslaught.

The Japanese entered the city on the 13th. They opened fire on the unarmed populace, and the killing continued throughout the day. The next morning tanks rolled into the city to join in the slaughter. On the 17th a Japanese general on horseback led a victory parade into the city, but the invaders' blood lust was not yet satisfied. Thousands more were drowned, sprayed with kerosene and set afire, thrown into pits and buried alive.

The Changs cowered in their holes for three days, listening to the rattle of machine gun fire in the streets and the screams of the dying. On the fourth day there was a massive crash downstairs, and then the sound of soldiers' boots running across wooden floorboards. The family members were located one by one and pulled into the open. Only Peter escaped detection behind a false wall in the cellar.

He could hear little from his refuge. There was shouting shortly after the soldiers arrived. Once, he stuck his head into the open and heard what he thought was a woman's cry somewhere above.

When his food and water were gone he climbed gingerly out of his hole, listening in the dark cellar for any hint that the soldiers were still there. Hearing none, he crept up the stairs. He stuck his head into the hallway and listened again. There was no sign of any living human being.

There were splatters of blood in the living room. He opened the door to the study and his eye fell on a jumble on the floor. His mind could not immediately identify what it was seeing, but bit by bit the picture came into focus: two bodies, a haphazard pile of limbs and torsos surrounded by pools of their own blood. Two round objects lay not far from the bodies, and Peter resisted for a moment before acknowledging that they were the heads of his father and grandfather, severed by some samurai's sword.

His soul shriveled. Images of the two men's last moments flooded his thoughts. He imagined the edge of the sharp blade slicing into the flesh on the back of his own neck. When his head cleared, he set off to explore the rest of the house, telling himself, be brave. But the horror only intensified.

His mother's body lay on the dining room table, wearing only a blouse that had been yanked up to her armpits. Her abdomen was split open from breastbone to vagina. Her head was tilted to the side, and the horror she had experienced before the end was frozen into her dead eye.

Peter felt ill and ran to the kitchen for water, where a similar scene greeted him. His grandmother's naked, withered body was spread-eagled on one of the counters. Her legs had been forced open, and a bayonet jutted at an angle from her vagina.

He climbed the steps to the bedrooms. The body of his younger sister, Rebecca, lay naked in her bed. The little girl's throat had been cut and her thin thighs were smeared with blood.

Rachel's body was seated in an armchair. Her torso had been tied to the back of the chair with loops of rope that pinned her arms to her sides but left her small breasts exposed. Her legs had been tied high over the chair's arms, throwing her naked thighs open to view, and her vagina was torn and bloody, as if some animal had ripped it apart. Later, Peter understood that Rachel had been trussed that way to make her an easy target for repeated rape. All the women in the family had been violated.

There was nothing to be done for the victims. Peter covered the bodies to give them as much dignity as possible. He went through the house and collected family photographs: at least he would take something of them with him. Then he gathered what food and water he could find. It was mid-winter and overcast, and he was able to sneak through the darkened streets at night without being spotted by a Japanese patrol.

As he made his way from the city, the course that would propel him through the next phase of his life formed in his mind. He told himself: the Nationalists had not saved China as his father said they would. They had certainly not saved the Chang family. Nor had the family's Western education, nor had its adopted god, Jesus Christ.

The family's fate had hinged on race. Jacob had tried to mold the family into little yellow versions of Westerners, but nature would not be denied: the Japanese had singled out every Chinese they could get their hands on, educated or illiterate, Buddhist or Christian, rich or poor. They had attacked a race they considered inferior – and did their effortless victory not suggest that they were right?

Peter concurred with his father and grandfather that the only way for the Chinese to stand up as a nation was to overcome the weakness that had been inbred during centuries of self-isolation. But he added a caveat: China should borrow only selectively from the outside. The Chinese should not attempt to *become* outsiders, as his father had done. They had to make themselves strong as Chinese. Peter would embrace what was good of Chinese culture, and abandon whatever had made his country weak. He began by jettisoning his western name.

He made his way across the Yangtze and headed northwest, through Anhui and Henan provinces, toward the city of Xian. Once there he would turn due north, to Yanan. He'd heard that the Communist Party had its base there. He'd heard that the Party was led by a man named Mao Tse-tung, a patriot who dared to challenge both Chinese tradition and the Japanese invaders.

Chiang Kai-Shek had fled, but Mao, according to the rumors, had stood and fought. Chang Dongfeng would find this man Mao and his Communists, and under their guidance, he would learn the way to a strong China.

Six

Bill Sturges contemplated the day's news. Beijing was in one of its recurrent snits over Taiwan, threatening the use of military force unless Taipei agreed to a peaceful reunification. There were earthquakes and typhoons, Muslim insurgencies in South Asia, nuclear weapons in North Korea.

But the story of the moment in Hong Kong was Rupert Rackley.

Hong Kong was one of the safest big cities in the world. Guns were tightly restricted, murders by any means were rare. Granted, it appeared that this murder had taken place across the border, and Shenzhen was becoming known for its flagrant crime. Even so, the cold-blooded gunshot murder of a well-known personality like Rupert so close to home... *Aiyeeah!* Nobody in Hong Kong could remember a case like it. Who among the seething masses on either side of the border might have ordered the hit?

Rupert had pissed off no end of people with his writing, castigating politicians and businessmen, bureaucrats and celebrities, men and women, Asians and Westerners, locals and mainlanders, with egalitarian scorn. Everyone had his favorite suspect.

Someone Chinese was at the top of everyone's list, for that's where Rupert had aimed his sharpest barbs. He had rather shamelessly named his column *"The Last Word:"* it gave him the advantage of having the last word in any debate, and he'd exploited that advantage ruthlessly to attack the Chinese leadership. Yet even he realized his writing did nothing to change minds in Beijing. On the contrary, the China of the Communist

Party was becoming fabulously successful even though the Party completely ignored his criticisms and advice.

Back in the 1980s, when China was just beginning to claw its way out of the dark ages of Maoist rule, its economy still primitive and its masses mired in poverty and ignorance, Rupert had posed a facetious question: Come 1997, will China really take over Hong Kong, or...ho-ho!...will *Hong Kong* take over *China*?

Those were the days of what Hong Kong derisively called the "two-billion-armpit syndrome," a reference to a mythical Western deodorant manufacturer peering wistfully across the then-closed Hong Kong-China border and sighing: A billion people; *two* billion armpits!!

Foreign merchants in fact had dreamt of selling to China's masses for hundreds of years – but what would those impossibly impoverished millions have been able to buy? Even if they had money to spend, what would they *desire*? Deodorant was probably not at the top of their wish list. Might foreign manufacturers sell them...potholders? Potato peelers? Underwear? Did the Chinese under Communist rule even wear underwear? No one on the outside could say for sure. Rupert's little joke seemed apt.

Yet neither he nor anyone else could ignore the inescapable reality of 1997.

The British forced the Qing Emperor to cede Hong Kong Island in 1842, and in 1850 they grabbed the Kowloon Peninsula, the small spit of land across the harbor. Both cessions were made in perpetuity. The little colony prospered, and in 1898, the British more than quadrupled its size by leasing a swath of the mainland surrounding Kowloon. The land was dubbed the New Territories. The lease would run for ninety-nine years, until 1997.

As the expiry date approached, Britain suggested renewing the lease, but the Party said no way – and while we're at it, we're not just taking back the New Territories in 1997, thank you, we're taking back the whole thing. Perpetuity doesn't last forever, you know. Regaining Hong Kong was fundamental to the Party's goal of making the country whole and erasing the humiliations she had suffered at foreign hands. Britain had no choice but to agree.

At the time of the handover, China had already begun its march toward modernization. By the time of Rupert's murder, the dawn of the 21st century, the country might still have had one foot planted in the 19th, but even Rupert could not deny that it was the fastest-growing economy on the planet. Governments and corporations were tripping over each other to take up where the deodorant maker had quit in frustration. Jokes like Rupert's were heard no longer.

Still, he had continued to lambaste China's leaders for their suppression of political rights. He excoriated provincial and municipal officials for their untrammeled brutality and corruption. "China has come full circle," he wrote in one Chinese National Day column. "The Communist revolution was ostensibly fought to free the country's masses from the greed, the corruption, the exploitation and the almost indescribable inhumanity of the ruling classes. Now that ideology is dead in China, corruption and grasping once again rule the day. The common people are again subjected to unspeakable greed, exploitation and barbarous treatment – but now the exploiters are all members of the Communist Party."

Another of his favorite targets was Hong Kong's tycoons, who embraced the motherland with enthusiasm. They parroted the official Beijing line on everything from politics to pork dumplings, and received favorable treatment for their mainland investments in return. They joined in calls for a clampdown on the "irresponsible" free expression of ideas, such as the suggestion that Hong Kong should move rapidly toward full democracy – a suggestion whose most vociferous proponents included Rupert.

The Hong Kong newspapers, while careful not to accuse any individual of the murder, focused with glee on the many enemies Rupert had made over the years. It was no problem to name several dozen of his fellow Hongkongers who would be delighted to see the back of him.

"I didn't kill him," a leading businessman who had been a frequent target of Rupert's vitriol was quoted as saying, "but I'd be happy to pay for the bullet."

I'd be happy to pay for the bullet. The standard method of judicial execution in the People's Republic was a gunshot to the back of the head, and then the government sent a bill for the bullet to the family of the deceased.

I'd be happy to pay for the bullet. The allusion was lost on no one.

Had some offended Hong Kong bigwig graduated from allusion to action? Had Rupert gone too far in lambasting some official across the border for stealing from the public purse with both hands — and might one of those have ordered him whacked?

The Hong Kong police had no idea. They had little evidence and no solid suspects. As they scanned the long list of possibilities, they could only ask themselves: who would *not* have wanted to murder Rupert Rackley?

~

Sturges was determined to see the mystery solved. He had fond memories of his real father, George, but for most of Bill's young life George was gone, off in some Third World hellhole covering war or revolution or famine, and then one day he was gone forever, and Rupert had taken his place. Sturges's mother was now five years dead, he had no siblings, and his wife was gone, too. Rupert might have been a flawed human being, but he'd been the only family Sturges had left.

Sturges had immediately taken personal charge of the *Mail's* coverage of the story, vowing to make some sense of the tragedy, only to learn that Brian Ross was in charge of the police investigation. Sturges had clashed with people he'd written about before, but those disagreements were always fleeting. The animosity between him and Ross had taken a personal turn that would be difficult to overcome – yet here they were, thrown together not only by their respective responsibilities, but also by the desire to figure out who had killed their mutual friend.

Sturges had been taken aback by how readily Ross had accepted his invitation to lunch. "Actually, I was going to call you myself," Ross told him. "We might be able to do each other some good."

Right, Sturges thought: like you did me some good before. But he breathed deeply and kept any dark thoughts to himself. He did that a lot these days.

He had grown up Anglo-American in British Hong Kong and could call up proper British reserve whenever it seemed appropriate, but his years at college in the States had allowed his

American side to win over. His default persona became pure Yank: direct, wisecracking, profane, irreverent.

The divorce had changed him. Where he'd previously accentuated the positive, he now gravitated automatically to the worst-case scenario. He would sense rage building inside him for no good reason and be helpless to stop it. He was still always ready with a pertinent observation or learned commentary, but his quips had become darker and his rejoinders more bitter.

His staff came to recognize the signs of an impending explosion, and would scatter to avoid his scathing tongue. His friends endured his outbursts for a time, but finally they told him: this is most unattractive, old boy. We like you, we feel for you, but we don't want to have to relive your pain every time we meet. Deal with it, or find some new friends.

Most days now, he was dealing with it. It required studied effort – but look how civil he'd been on the phone to Ross. More than civil: he'd been positively engaging.

Good for me, he told himself with a mental pat on the back.

Attaboy, Bill.

Seven

Sturges and Olivia met for the reading of the will at New Alexandra House, one of the prestige addresses in Hong Kong's Central District. She was dressed appropriately in black. A black Versace dress revealing a considerable portion of leg. Black pumps and black broad-brimmed hat by Ferragamo. Black Fendi bag. Her well-defined features were partly obscured by black-rimmed Giorgio Armani sunglasses. The chiseled contours of her breasts were framed by the top edge of a black lace bra. Northern Chinese women tend to have decent-sized knockers, nothing huge, but with her small back and tiny waist and the assistance of an uplift bra, Olivia bulged this day like Dolly Parton.

Since the collapse of his marriage, Sturges had run the emotional gamut, now chasing like a rutting teenager after any skirt that walked by, now doubting his own manhood and walling himself off from the world with work. He was several weeks into a cycle of celibacy when Rupert's murder occurred. The death had struck like a hammer, reminding Sturges how short life was. The sight of Rupert's widow now reminded him that there were things worth living for.

His ambivalence toward women flowed from the circumstances of the break-up: his wife had cheated on him, and then she had walked out. He despised her, even though he had to admit that he was partly to blame for the situation. He never should have brought her to Hong Kong in the first place. To a professional expatriate like Sturges, waking up in a strange country where you know not a soul and speak not a word of the local language was as natural as breathing. It hadn't occurred to him that his wife might not share his love of travel and adventure. Not every spouse is eager to drop a carefully constructed life and be dragged by a partner to some alien land. Sarah Sturges, American born and bred, never made the adjustment.

Their first foreign posting was Paris, and who could not like Paris? But French food was too heavy for Sarah on a regular basis. French wine was different from what she knew at home. There were endless strikes. She spoke no French, and the French anyway can be a difficult people to like; she confided that she wouldn't have wanted to converse with most of them even if she could have.

Sturges was delighted several years later when *Newsweek* said it was moving them to Hong Kong, and Sarah tried to be enthusiastic. He had always spoken with great affection about the place he was born and raised, about the exotic East.

At least this time the westerners all spoke English, but it grated on her that the British spoke English...well...they spoke it differently from Americans. They even spelled it differently. *Cheque* instead of check. *Programme* instead of program. *Aluminium*, with an extra "i," instead of aluminum.

The truth was, she had arrived secretly fearing the place, and her fears had been realized. She hated the overcrowding, the noise, the traffic, the climate. She couldn't get used to driving on the left side of the road.

She didn't like the food, most of it. Sweet & sour pork and chicken chow mein pretty much exhausted her Chinese repertoire, but here there were not only new dishes, there were entire regional cuisines she'd never heard of: Shanghainese, Yunnanese, Taiwanese, Chiu Chow.

Others in her position delighted in the plethora of choices the city offered, but it only made Sarah dizzy. She could enjoy boat trips that ended on Lamma Island with huge seafood feasts, but she shrieked in horror the first time prawns and fish arrived with heads and tails attached. She preferred her fish and seafood cleaned, decapitated and looking as little like fish and seafood as possible by the time they appeared on her plate. The way they were served back in America.

Like many ex-pats raised on a Westernized version of Chinese cuisine, she would whisper to like-minded friends: it doesn't taste like *real* Chinese food.

Then there were the Chinese themselves. If Sarah had disliked the French, she despised the Chinese. "They fart and burp in public, they pick their noses, they spit, they push their way into elevators and subway cars without waiting for people to get out first," she said. "And they're so goddamned *loud*." To top it all off *Newsweek* had her husband on the road half the time, leaving her to suffer in solitude.

The expatriate life tends to be a hard-drinking life under the most benign of circumstances, especially in a place like Hong Kong, where British culture prevails. But Sarah was soon drinking far more than someone who was merely fitting in. Sturges could sense trouble brewing. When *Newsweek* decided to move them to Beirut, Sturges told himself: she would never make it in the Middle East. The offer from the *Mail* came along at the same time and he took it. It would keep him at home.

Then he began to hear whispers about Sarah and other men.

He'd seen marriages unravel before. It was usually the husband, off for extended periods on business and faced with an array of seductive women, who did the screwing around. And nowhere was the array greater than in Asia; nowhere were the pickings easier. Sturges knew all that even as a teenager.

He knew that the women in the region's girlie bars and massage parlors wore big buttons with numbers on them to made it simple for the customers to make their selections:

I think... Number 31 tonight. No, no, wait: let's make it Number 107.

He'd sat with Rupert at the bar of the Foreign Correspondents Club and listened as journalists and bankers and businessmen and diplomats passed around the latest hot numbers like men elsewhere passed around tips on stocks or the horses.

The next time you're in Bangkok, forget about your interview with the prime minister, cancel your meeting with your most important client, but do not, I repeat do not, under any circumstances, fail to experience Number 169 at the Darling massage parlor. I swear this woman could suck a tennis ball through a garden hose.

Now it appeared that his wife was the one exciting other men's imaginations. He went from disbelief to shock, and ultimately to humiliation. A phone call from the police:

"My name is Brian Ross, Mr. Sturges," the caller began. "We spoke once before."

"I'm quite aware of who you are, Mr. Ross," Sturges said. As Hong Kong's change of sovereignty was approaching in 1997,

Sturges had written an article recounting the colony's history, including the corruption that had once been endemic in the colonial police department. Ross, who joined the force as the corruption was finally being rooted out in the late '70s, had been mentioned in the article as one of the few high-ranking ex-pats still on duty. It was an innocent statement, but Ross felt the story implicated him by association in the crimes of his predecessors.

Ross's friends told him he had misread the story, and Sturges tried to tell him the same thing when Ross called in a blind fury. Ross was having none of it. "Bloody hacks!" he shouted into the phone. "You don't care who you hurt as long as you sell your bloody newspapers. I promise you, Sturges," he said with an ominous growl, "you'll pay for this one way or another."

Now Ross was calling again. "What did I do to piss you off this time?" Sturges asked.

"It's about what your wife has done, actually."

"My wife?" Sturges said. "What about her? Is she all right?"

"She's well enough. She's enjoying our hospitality for the moment."

"What the hell does that mean? Has she been arrested?"

"Not formally," Ross said. Twisting the knife in slowly, exacting his revenge.

Sturges fought to keep his voice calm. "What happened?"

"We received a call early this afternoon from one of the love hotels in Kowloon Tong," Ross said. "You know, those short-time places that are used for..."

"I know what a love hotel is, thank you. And?"

"And...the manager reported that a female guest was horribly drunk. Shouting and throwing things about. The manager wanted our lads to come take her away."

Sturges's heart sank. "Is she okay?" he said.

"She's sleeping it off," Ross said. "Her dress was torn a wee bit in the scuffle."

"What scuffle? Your men attacked my wife?"

"Quite the other way around. She attacked one of them, with a desk lamp. Gave him a nasty lump on the head. It took both men to subdue her."

"Two men to subdue one small woman? Don't you fucking cops teach your men to deal with people without roughing them up?"

"If you'd teach your wife to behave, Sturges, we wouldn't be having this conversation."

"Look, Ross," Sturges said, "my wife has a drinking problem. I'm sorry about that, but it's not easy to 'teach' people how to control problems with alcohol. You being Scottish should understand that."

Ross ignored the implied commentary on Scottish drinking habits. "When I refer to behavior it's not just your wife's drinking I'm talking about," he said.

"Meaning?"

"Meaning," Ross replied, his voice now cold, "that the problem is not with us 'fucking cops,' as you so eloquently put it. It's your wife fucking other men that's the problem here. What do you think she was doing in that hotel in the first place?"

Sturges knew full well what Sarah or anyone else would be doing in that hotel. Hearing it in so official a manner was like being kicked in the stomach. "I...I didn't realize," was all he could say.

"Did you not? Well you'd best get your house in order, laddie," Ross said. "The manager says your wife has been there two or three times before today. And not always with the same man."

Sturges had no reply to that. "You're enjoying this, aren't you?" he said.

"I have no idea what you mean," Ross said. Sturges could almost see him smiling as he said it. "I'm just a police officer doing his duty."

"What you are, Ross," Sturges said, "is a shit. Reveling in another man's misfortune, all because of some imagined insult years ago. The colonial government might have eliminated corruption in the police department but it sure as hell didn't eliminate bloody-mindedness."

Now Sarah was gone. So was Rupert, and as Sturges and Olivia arrived at the entrance to New Alexandra House, he found himself eyeing Rupert's widow with lust in his heart. He leaned over and gave her a peck on the cheek. He felt the urge to lower his face further, to bury it between those satin globes and taste their contours with his tongue.

With an effort he turned his eyes instead to the elevator, and they rode side by side to the law offices of Lee, Li, Lai, Lo, Lam, Leung & Gillespie.

~

The Morgan.

That's what Rupert had left to Sturges. The *Mog*, as the British called the car; *Mo-gun* to Rupert and the Chinese. Rupert and Sturges had shared a passion for cars and motor racing. They loved to debate the relative driving skills of Stirling Moss and Jim Clark, Ayrton Senna and Michael Schumacher. Sometimes on a Sunday they'd work all day on the Morgan, polishing its chrome and touching up nicks in its paint. In the evening they'd sit together in Rupert's living room, pints of British bitter in hand, watching the Formula One races on satellite TV while Qing Dynasty patriarchs stared from the antique paintings that papered the walls. The Morgan creaked and groaned, it was sprung so stiffly it would rattle your back teeth, but Sturges had always loved that car. Now it was his.

Grissom Lam, Rupert's attorney, handed Sturges a bulky manila envelope. "The car title and what-not," the lawyer said. "There's a note from Mr. Rackley in there for you as well." Sturges was surprised and touched. As he clasped the envelope, thinking beneficent thoughts about his late friend, Lam began reading the rest of the will, and the real surprise of the day emerged.

It turned out that Rupert was rich after all. Not just well off: really rich. He had somehow accumulated nine properties in Hong Kong, including his and Olivia's house on the south side of Hong Kong Island, all in prime locations, all with mortgages now fully paid. The value of Hong Kong real estate had only recently started to creep back upwards from the depths of a five-year recession and the SARS outbreak earlier in the year, but given their locations, Sturges calculated that Rupert's holdings were still worth an average of at least thirty million Hong Kong dollars apiece. The eight that were rented out would be bringing in a half million or more a month in income.

Sturges did his sums: nine times thirty million, divided by seven-point-eight – the Hong Kong properties were worth in the neighborhood of thirty-four million U.S. dollars, plus that rental income. And there were two flats in the best sections of London, also fully paid, plus another ten million Hong Kong in stocks, bonds and cash. All told, Rupert had easily been worth almost forty million large. And that didn't include his art collection, which had yet to be valued since his death.

Rupert had no other living relatives. The standard phrase, *except as otherwise specified*, was included in the will, but the only thing otherwise specified had been the Morgan. The rest was Olivia's. As the details of Rupert's net worth came spilling forth, she and Sturges could only look at each other in stunned silence.

"None of this is official until the will goes through probate," Lam told them. "But I don't anticipate any problems or challenges. You're a wealthy woman, Mrs. Rackley."

~

"Did you know about any of this?" Sturges asked once they'd left the law offices.

"It's a complete surprise to me," she said. "Rupert and I never discussed money. He had his financial affairs and I had mine, and that included our respective incomes. You seem as surprised as I am."

"I'm gobsmacked," Sturges said. "I mean, Rupe always seemed like he had enough cash to enjoy life, I never saw him take a second look at the size of a dinner bill, but even so..." He cast his thoughts back to Rupert's lifestyle. "His only extravagance, if you can call it that, was his full-time driver, Mr. Wong, but he was still being chauffeured around in that old diesel Mercedes. I'm absolutely floored."

"Like I said…"

"Rupe was full of surprises. I know," he said.

Surprised she might be, but Olivia did not seem as impressed by her newfound millions as one might have expected. Partners in investment banks, Sturges told himself, must make even more money than he thought.

They rode the elevator down in silence. In the lobby she pulled out a mobile phone and said a few words in Cantonese. Then they waited, watching the heat waves percolate up from the sidewalk outside the lobby's glass doors, until the car rolled up to the curb. Old Mr. Wong ran splayfooted to open the rear door, flashing an ingratiating smile of stained and crooked teeth beneath a squashed dumpling of a nose.

"Hallo Mistuh Stooges," Wong said, in as close an approximation of Sturges's name as he could manage. Sturges noticed that he was wearing new chauffeur's livery, with a proper driver's cap: Rupert had never bothered with that kind of formality.

"Call and let me know when you want to come around and pick up the Morgan," Olivia said.

"Olivia, wait," he replied. "We haven't had a moment to really talk since this all happened. You do know I meant everything I said at the cemetery about Rupert. He really was a close friend."

"He felt the same about you," she said. She reached up and her fingertips traced the sharp angles of his face. "You're a good man, Bill. That's something I haven't been able to say about most of the men I've known."

It was an odd remark coming a day after her husband's funeral. Before he could pursue the thought she stretched on her toes and gave him a soft, lingering kiss, which landed so close to his mouth he couldn't tell if she had aimed for his lips or not. This was the widow of his life-long friend, whose body hadn't yet settled into the ground, yet Sturges watched her mouth form the words *thank you* and, God forgive him, he couldn't help but picture what Jackson Liu said she liked to do with that mouth. The skin of her bare arm, which he held to steady her, was like silk. Her perfume filled his nostrils. His eyes wandered again to her Partonesque parts, which heaved and fell beneath their skimpy covering just inches below his face.

"I've been wondering when you were going to take a look," she said.

His head jerked up in surprise. Then he realized she was pointing at the manila envelope, which was still clutched in his hand. He stared as if seeing it for the first time. "Later," he said. Inspecting the contents would mean taking his attention away from her, and he realized he was enjoying himself too much.

He watched her climb into the car and arrange herself in the back seat, and as she did so he caught a flash of minimalist black lace panties framed by milky thighs. Olivia followed his eyes, and he thought that she would blush or make some dismissive comment out of embarrassment. Instead, she looked directly at him from beneath the broad brim of her hat. "It's not polite to stare, Mister Sturges," she said.

The casual tone took him by surprise. His mind was assaulted by the thought that she had exposed herself to him on purpose. He was unable to form a coherent thought. "I...I wasn't really..."

She giggled, a sound like wind chimes on a warm evening. "You really must get out more, Bill," she said. "I'll have to show you around some time. Call me."

She slid her sunglasses onto her nose and pulled the door closed, and the car drove off. The spell was broken and the world came rushing back, but a frisson of excitement remained at the back of his mind, that premonition of intrigue and pleasure that comes when an enticing possibility suddenly seems within reach.

Call me, she had said.

Call and let me know when you want to fetch the car?

Or just...call me?

~

He turned with a sigh in the opposite direction and walked among the soaring office towers of the Central district. Left on Pedder Street and up toward Queen's Road, blending into the swirl of commerce and humanity that made Hong Kong hum. Shanghai Tang was advertising the last markdowns of the summer sales. The Louis Vuitton shop in The Landmark shopping center was undergoing renovation. The Marks & Spencer window told of new autumn arrivals.

Chinese and Indians, Europeans and Americans, Japanese and Filipinos, stood in line at the Hong Kong and Shanghai Bank's automated teller machines while the hordes flowed around them. An ancient Cantonese woman threaded her way through the choking traffic in the middle of the road, bent almost double as she pushed a trolley loaded with flattened cardboard boxes and bulging garbage bags, while Shanghainese princesses with impeccable faces and bodies stood on the sidewalks with shopping bags from Gucci and Hermès and waited for their chauffeurs to collect them.

The sea of heads bobbing in Sturges's line of vision was an artist's palette of black, brown, red, purple, blonde—occasionally orange where a hair stylist had miscalculated the amount of dye needed to lighten jet-black Asian hair. The heads eddied and flowed, skirting obstructions, yammering into mobile phones, darting in and out of buildings like ants carrying nourishment for the life of the city.

Sturges moved effortlessly through the crush, an Anglo-American comfortably at home in this improbable Sino-Western mélange. Kipling was right, East and West were unalterably different, but this was as artful a blend of the two as the world had yet achieved. Much of Hong Kong was gleaming skyscrapers and ultra-efficient transportation systems. The people thronging the streets carried the latest in cell phones, personal digital assistants and mobile music players. There were no longer any of the clichés of a Hollywood director's vision to be seen, no rickshaws being pulled through the streets by men in straw hats and black pajamas, no Chinese junks in full sail tacking through the harbor, no women dressed in *cheongsams*. The average Hongkonger dressed, if not always as fashionably as the Italians or the French, at least indistinguishably from the average Brit or American.

And yet Hong Kong's soul was Chinese through and through. Now that the Chinese were in charge, the former colony's genetic signature was that much more discernible beneath its Eurasian features.

Who were the Chinese, these people so surrounded by myth? Those that Sturges knew on both sides of the border didn't fit the

Western stereotypes any more than Hong Kong itself did. They had no inside channel to the world's truths. They didn't observe the comings and goings of the world with Buddha-like serenity. They didn't dispense Eastern wisdom and ancient Chinese sayings in slow, trenchant phrases. Classical Chinese culture might be infinitely subtle, but the bulk of the Chinese people were anything but: they pushed, they shoved, they clawed and grabbed, they hocked and spat, huge numbers of them were crude and uneducated and ignorant of the world around them, and even the educated ones often jabbered superstitious nonsense. They all scrambled to get by, some through hard work, some by stealing whatever wasn't tied down.

Sturges had always resisted the tendency of wide-eyed Western visitors and impressionable writers to see Eastern thought as somehow superior, just as he refused to join his fellow expatriates in viewing Asians as irredeemably illogical and incompetent. Different cultures saw the world differently and dealt with it in different ways. None had a patent on perception or wisdom. All groped their way toward equilibrium and a modicum of enlightenment. Each had its own way of getting from here to there, and the Chinese had fashioned their style over the course of millennia.

There were just so many of them! Sturges elbowed his way through the lunchtime throng at the corner of Pedder Street and Queen's Road, which flowed as thick as migrating lemmings. More than one visiting westerner, suddenly finding himself engulfed by this flood of human bodies, had had to brace himself against a wall until his heart rate could return to normal. It was worse on the other side of the border: now well over a billion people and still growing despite government-ordered limits on childbearing.

Sturges made his way to D'Aguilar Street, where the broad streets and sidewalks of Central gave way to the steep hills, narrow lanes and weathered low-rise buildings of an older Hong Kong. He hopped and skipped his way through the scrum of people and buses, taxis and private cars, delivery trucks and vans.

As he walked he replayed the events of recent days. Olivia's forwardness had flustered him so much he'd forgotten to ask if she had any idea why Rupert had gone to China. The most logical assumption was that Rupe had been on the hunt for some information for his newspaper column, most likely something that was would reflect unfavorably on the Chinese government. But given Rupert's hatred of the place...

Murders tend to underline truths and reveal secrets. Investigate a man's death, learn about his life. What new revelations would Rupert's murder force into the open? Did Olivia have more surprises in store – and was there a chance they would include Bill Sturges? As he made his way uphill toward the bars and restaurants of the Lan Kwai Fong district, the feel of her skin was still igniting fires on his fingertips. The smell of her perfume lingered in his nose. The swell of her breasts...

That reminded him of the package from Rupert, and he opened it as he walked. There were ignition keys dangling from a Morgan key ring, along with the owner's manual. There was an envelope with his name on it, as the lawyer had said, but instead of a note inside, there was a small, carved ivory box of the type that typically slid open to show a couple in erotic embrace, a common Chinese motif. It seemed a strange thing to leave a friend.

He tried to slide the two pieces apart, but they were stuck. He could hear something rattling inside: perhaps the interior carving had broken off and that had caused the box to jam. He put the envelope under one arm, grasped the two ends of the box tightly between his fingers and yanked hard. They resisted for a moment, then surrendered. As the sections came apart, another small key chain with three keys on it popped out and landed with a clink on the brick roadway.

Sturges picked them up and searched through the envelope: nothing to indicate what the keys were for, only a cardboard tag attached to the ring with a twist of wire, and written on the tag, in Rupert's distinctive calligraphy, the two Chinese characters for a familiar injunction:

摩根

Learn the root cause.

Eight

For the lunch with Brian Ross, Sturges chose the American Club's downtown facility, which sat high atop the harbor-side complex of towers that housed the Hong Kong Stock Exchange. The American informality of the place, he calculated, just might put an old colonial like Ross off his stride.

Now Ross stood in the entryway of the club's forty-eighth-floor bar, staring at portraits of U.S. presidents going back to Calvin Coolidge and waiting for some living soul to make eye contact with him. He was every bit the British officer, tall, upright, with a long face and a prominent nose. He was dressed in one of the smartly tailored safari suits preferred by expat officers.

Sturges studied him from afar, working up his resolve. He took a breath and walked forward with his hand out. "Commissioner Ross," he said with forced calm, "this is uncomfortable for both of us. I'm sorry for that misunderstanding about that magazine article. But our differences pale beside what happened to poor old Rupert. I'm hoping we can forget the past and have a civil conversation about him."

"Let's hope we can, yes," Ross said, returning a stiff handshake. He too was struggling for civility, but he had checked out of work early this day to give the meeting as much chance for success as possible. "I'm, ah, sorry I had to make that call about Mrs. Sturges."

"Ex-Mrs. Sturges."

"Yes," said Ross. "Well, one might have expected that under the circumstances." His accent was pure Highland Scots. Syllables rumbled around in his mouth like cricket balls in a cement mixer.

"What can I get you to drink?" Sturges asked.

"A whisky and soda would be lovely, thanks."

"Ah, you've come to the right place," Sturges said, happy to find common ground. "This club might be run by Americans but we members have soaked up enough British culture to appreciate good Scotch whisky. We have quite a decent selection of single malts on hand."

Ross eyed the row of bottles at the back of the bar. "Not bad for a bunch of Yanks," he said. "But I'm afraid you have a wee bit more culture to soak up. You see, no self-respecting Scot would sully his single malt with soda or ice. As my dear father likes to say, the only two substances that should be added to single malt are highland spring water at ambient temperature, or more of the selfsame whisky. Besides," he said, "malt is a cold-weather drink, and it's still bloody hot. A wee dram of whatever blended whisky the bartender is pouring with plenty of ice and soda will do me just fine."

"You'll have to pardon my ignorance," Sturges said. "I'm only half British, you see."

"Half-*British*, did ya say? That half wouldn't be Scottish by any chance?" There was latent empathy in Ross's voice, but the look on Sturges's face dashed any hopes. "Welsh?" Sturges shook his head. Ross made a final, hopeful, stab. "Irish?"

"English," Sturges said, and braced himself.

"Ach," Ross said, "an Anglo-Yank. You're doubly cursed. Still, I might take pity on you some day and teach you about whisky." He raised his glass and looked Sturges in the eye. "Cheers," he said. "I gather you're getting on with your life, at any rate." He flashed a hesitant smile and the tension eased a touch. "I see your photo in the society pages with some rather smashing looking women."

Sturges shrugged the comment off. "In my position I'm obliged to attend a lot of society receptions, and you know how it is: the photographers grab a few people, line them up and snap a photo. The people in the picture haven't necessarily arrived with each other. They often don't even know each other."

"I'll wager they sometimes leave with each other, though," Ross said.

"Sometimes, yes," Sturges said, and he allowed himself a small smile.

They followed the headwaiter to a table in the main dining room, set alongside tall windows that looked across the harbor to Kowloon. The water far below was a beehive of ferries and barges, sampans and passenger ships, one of the few bits of old Hong Kong that had survived the relentless Chinese quest for newness. The elegant old buildings of the colonial era, with their stone facades and graceful arches, now existed only in faded photographs. The fact that any historic buildings remained at all was thanks in large part to a few Westerners who thought age and architectural charm might actually have some value, and had convinced some of the locals to agitate for preservation.

"It seems just yesterday that nothing over there was more than six or seven stories high," Ross said, gesturing across the harbor to Kowloon. Since Kai Tak Airport on the Kowloon harbor front had been closed in favor of a new facility on one of the outlying islands, the height restriction beneath the old glide path had been lifted, and skyscrapers and construction cranes soared above the low rooftops like trees sprouting from the underbrush.

"It seems just yesterday that you could actually see over there from over here," Sturges said, squinting through the gray mist that shimmered outside the windows. The government referred to it as "haze," but that was to avoid admitting how much it had allowed the air quality to deteriorate. "I remember standing on Kowloon side and looking across at the high-rises of Central framed against the Peak, and it was so clear and vibrant it didn't look real. Can you imagine what it's going to be like when another few hundred million across the border own motor vehicles?"

"Frightening," Ross agreed. "Unless it all goes up in flames first, of course. We get reports almost every day of a new anti-corruption riot in the provinces. I'm not one to cry doom, but I do wonder how they're going to hold the country together. Their officials are out for nothing but to please their superiors and line their own pockets, and even when they make real progress it's quickly overwhelmed by sheer weight of numbers. There are just too bloody many people, and that's the bottom line."

"And we have to breathe in the muck all those people spew out," Sturges said. "I like bumping into old Hongkongers who knew this place when it was still Never-Never Land and the air was still clean."

"Old-timers like Olivia Chen?"

So: the small talk was over. "Olivia?" Sturges said.

"I'm wondering," Ross said, "if your meeting her in Central yesterday was one of those coincidental get-togethers you were just talking about."

"Are you having Olivia followed" Sturges asked.

"We're off the record here, are we not, Mr. Sturges?"

"As you wish."

"Right, then: 'followed' is overstating it, but I'm sure you realize we always take a hard look at the spouse in the case of a murder. You also know that the Rackleys were not particularly close. That and the fact that she stood to inherit a sizable fortune on Rupert's death gave her a plausible motive to kill him. To be truthful, Mrs. Rackley is the perfect suspect in this case."

Stated so bluntly, the notion made perfect sense...and yet her surprise at the extent of Rupert's wealth had seemed genuine. "I was at the reading of the will yesterday — which is the reason I was with Olivia," he said, "and I can tell you, she seemed as blown away as I was when we learned of Rupert's assets. She said he'd never told her about any of it, and I believe her."

"Perhaps," Ross said. "May I ask why you were invited to the reading? I know you were quite close to the victim, which is why I wanted to talk to you, but as far as I've been able to gather you were not close to Mrs. Rackley."

Ross had done his homework: the size of Rupert's estate, Sturges's relationship with the couple. He told Ross about the car.

"A Morgan! Wonderful car," Ross said. "A throw-back to the day when sports cars were something special. Do they still make them with that wooden upper frame?"

"They do. I haven't picked mine up from Olivia's house yet, but Rupert and I used to work on it together. I know every nut and bolt and wooden strut on the thing."

"Do you have any idea how he came by all that money, though?" Ross said. "I always thought a print journalist's salary was no better than that of a copper."

"I have absolutely no idea. It's like I told Olivia: except for the fact that he never hesitated to pick up a dinner check or buy a round, there was never a sign that he was anything more than comfortably well off."

"I have to ask: when did you last see Rupert?"

"I guess it was at his house, about ten days before he was killed," Sturges said. "Or ten days before the body was found, at any rate. Do you know exactly when he died?"

"The heat and the submersion in water complicated things, but the medical examiner's best guess is that death occurred about twenty-four hours before he was found. Can you tell me what the two of you talked about on that last occasion?"

"Nothing out of the ordinary," Sturges said. "Chinese politics. Chinese art. Cars. He asked about my love life, how I was getting on after the divorce."

"Did he give any indication that he was thinking about going to China, or why?"

Sturges shook his head. "I assume he went for some journalistic purpose. But even then...I was as shocked by his being there, given his history, as I was by his wealth. You do know about his run-in with the Red Guards during the Cultural Revolution?"

"Aye," Ross said. "I also knew Rupert personally, although not as well as you did. He never made any secret of his dislike for China, or the reason why."

"And I take it from what you're saying that there's no question he was killed inside China."

"That was easy enough to pin down. He picked up a visa at China Resources here on August 22nd. He passed through Hong Kong immigration at Hung Hom train station the morning of the 27th, to catch the early train to Dongguan. Our counterparts on the other side aren't telling us much, but they do confirm that he passed through China immigration in Dongguan about an hour and a quarter later. Immigration here have double-checked all of our several crossing points. Rupert never came back through – not while he was alive, anyway."

"It's strange that he was even able into get to China," Sturges said. "I mean, we journalists don't just line up at the China visa office along with tourists and businesspeople. We have to go through the Foreign Ministry press office here when we apply for a visa. Given the things Rupe had written about China, they must have thought long and hard before they agreed to issue his visa."

"Our mainland colleagues don't make us privy to such matters," Ross said dryly.

"According to what you just told me, the death would have occurred several hours after he arrived in Dongguan on the 27th. So how did the body end up in Shenzhen on the 28th?"

"He could have been killed in Dongguan and the body transported for some unknown reason," Ross said. "But the more plausible scenario is that he did whatever he had to do in Dongguan, took the train back to Shenzhen, and was shot when he got there. It's a short distance between the two cities, and plenty of people take the train and then walk across the border to Hong Kong. I don't have to tell you what crime is like in Shenzhen itself: your newspaper carries enough stories about it. It's mainly been muggings and purse snatchings so far, but we've been waiting for the casual murder of some tourist from Hong Kong, and this may well be it."

"Is it all right if I put that much in a story? What's known of his travels, I mean."

"Just that – and as long as it doesn't come from anything more specific than a 'police source,'" Ross said. "The public would expect us to have learnt that much."

Sturges pulled out a notebook and made a few notes. "You mentioned your suspicion of Olivia. Surely she's not the only one you're looking at?"

Ross laughed. "I wish she were," he said. "We have more potential suspects than we can shake a cricket bat at. There is a thought I've had, it's pure conjecture at this point: do you think there's any possibility that antiques might have been involved? Rupert was quite the collector, as you know."

"You mean did he go to China to buy an antique? I would seriously doubt it, even though he was an aficionado of Chinese art for fifty years and had what was reputed to be one of the best collections in Hong Kong."

"Perhaps even better than you know," Ross said. "We took a bunch of Rupert's effects to the police station for examination the other day — with Mrs. Rackley's blessing. We found a valuation that was done a year ago for insurance purposes. His collection was valued at more than a hundred and fifty million Hong Kong."

"My god," Sturges said. Another twenty million U.S. on top of all his other wealth. Olivia's net worth was rising by the day. "I never realized it was that valuable."

Ross studied him with a skeptical eye. "Didn't the quality of the collection ever suggest to you that he might be worth a lot more than he let on?"

"I never gave it any thought. The art was always there as I was growing up, just part of the scenery. I do know that he didn't pay anything remotely like the figure you mentioned. Many of his best pieces were bought thirty or forty years ago, when you could get them in China or here at a small fraction of today's value. And you think antiques somehow figured in his death?"

"As I say, it's only conjecture, but the antiquities business is a somewhat questionable one. There's smuggling involved, and when you put money and illegal activity together, you tend to attract some unsavory characters."

"You're referring to 'grave goods,'" Sturges said. Chinese peasants were paid by black-marketers and smugglers to break into the thousands of years of burial tombs that peppered the Chinese countryside and search them for antiquities. It was illegal under Chinese law and occasionally a grave robber would be arrested and executed, but more often, the tomb raids were carried out with the connivance of local officials. Most of the items recovered were smuggled into Hong Kong, where they ended up in local collections or were sold to collectors abroad.

"Aye," Ross said. "Rupert usually bought through reputable shops here. But we're told he also dealt directly with the people the shops buy from – meaning, by definition, smugglers. He might have got into a dispute over payment for some item or other and a bullet in the head was his reward. It wouldn't be the first time someone from our side ended up being punished because someone from the other side lost money on a business deal, would it? Although murder would be taking it to a new level."

"That still doesn't explain why he'd do any of this on the Chinese side. He vowed he'd never go back," Sturges said. "Anyway, I guess we now have to add a few pissed-off smugglers to the list of potential suspects. How about Hongkongers? Rupe made a lot of enemies here."

The policeman waggled a hand in the air. "We are looking at one or two."

"Any names you'd care to share?"

Ross hesitated. "I'm being more open with you than I normally would with a journalist," he said. "I'm convinced this was something more than an ordinary homicide, but the fact that it occurred over the border makes it extremely difficult for us to look into. Given our personal histories with Rupert, I'm thinking that you and I together might bring more to the investigation than either of us could bring separately. I'm willing to share information as long as I think that doing so will help solve the murder. But I need your absolute assurance that anything I tell you will be off the record unless I specifically say otherwise. And of course I will expect some quid pro quo from you."

"You have my assurance about anything you give me," Sturges said. "As for quid pro quo, we journalists are not in the habit of giving information to the police. But if it helps find Rupert's killer, and it doesn't hinder me from doing my job of telling my readers what happened, then I suppose we can reach some accommodation. You understand that my reporters will continue to follow any independent leads, just as they would under any other circumstances, and we won't necessarily consult you on those before we publish?"

"Understood," Ross said. "So, you were asking about potential suspects: I believe you know Ricco Tang."

"Ricco Tang!" Sturges glanced around to see if he had blurted the name out too loudly. Nobody else in the dining room seemed to have noticed, and he turned back to Ross. "You can't think Ricco had anything to do with this," he said in a lowered voice.

"He was never one of Rupert's editorial targets. He and Rupert were good friends, in fact. He's also another of the most prominent art collectors in the city – is that why you mentioned antiques earlier?"

"I'm told they had a falling out not long before Rupert's death," Ross said. "A rather serious one, the way I understand it. I was rather hoping that you might be able to tell me something about that."

"Sorry," Sturges said. "I don't know anything about it. What makes you think I might?"

Ross thought a moment before answering. "I believe," he began slowly, "that you're friendly with Mrs. Tang."

"Ricco and Claudia are social friends of mine, Ross," he said. "If you're implying there's anything more to my relationship with her..."

"I don't mean to keep intruding on your personal life," Ross said, "but yes, I'm enquiring officially. We talked about those society page photographs. I've seen pictures of you and Mrs. Tang together there on a number of occasions. She's a striking woman, and a good deal younger than her husband. The possibility did occur to me that she might be seeing...someone else."

Could Ross have picked a more sensitive topic than marital infidelity? The anger Sturges had been keeping at bay welled up inside him. His cheeks flushed and his breathing became heavy. "I hope you're not suggesting that I'm anything more than friends with Claudia Tang, or that our friendship has anything to do with Rupert's murder," he managed to say.

Ross flinched at the vehemence of the response. "I'm simply trying to determine relationships, to see if they might have some bearing on circumstances," he said, doling the words out carefully. "Sometimes one has to take a circuitous route to the truth. It would be nice to come across someone wearing a sign that said, 'I killed Rupert,' but we're rarely so lucky."

"I *told* you," Sturges said, and he realized he was almost shouting again. He lowered his voice and continued: "I told you, the photographers like to group people into the same shot, especially if the people happen to be well known on the social scene."

"Which you and Mrs. Tang are."

Sturges's fist slammed the tabletop, rattling the silver. "Which a lot of people are, Ross! You seem to have an unfortunate propensity to jump to misguided conclusions."

"And that's all your relationship with Mr. Tang is? Purely social?"

"You and I talked about my former wife," Sturges said, enunciating each syllable slowly. "That episode might suggest I don't have a high opinion of men who play around with other men's wives. I don't do that myself, with Claudia Tang or anyone else."

Ross weighed the words while Sturges fumed. "Fair enough," he finally said. He was not here to hold Sturges's hand, but he did want his help. "I apologize. You realize I have to explore every possibility in a situation like this. As a journalist you'll be familiar with the necessity of asking uncomfortable questions at times."

Sturges closed his eyes and breathed deeply, willing himself calm. "Sure, sure," he said. "Sorry. The divorce and everything surrounding it...I'm still a bit touchy."

A bloody sight more than just a bit, Ross thought. But he had no desire to reignite the animosity. He waited for Sturges to compose himself.

Sturges forced a smile to his lips. "You were talking about Ricco and Rupert."

"Aye," Ross said with relief. "I need to know what that argument was about."

"I gather — I don't mean this as a criticism, but you don't seem to know much of anything about the case."

"There is one thing I know."

"What's that?"

"I need your promise that this information will never be attributed to me or anyone else in the department," Ross said. "You might come across it on your own, but it never came from the cops. Agreed?"

"Agreed."

"The mainland is interested in the case. Quite interested."

"Nothing particularly surprising in that," Sturges said. "You've conceded that the murder took place on the other side. Public Security in Shenzhen has to take an interest."

"I'm not talking about Public Security," Ross said. "In fact, they've made it clear they want nothing to do with the case." He told Sturges about his encounter with the Shenzhen police. "No, it's the Communist Party that's interested in Rupert's death," he said.

"Would that be 'the Party' as in some local cadres just across the border, or are we talking about the serious folks up in Beijing?"

"The latter. State Security. They've made inquiries about the case directly to my office. For some reason or another, this murder has excited interest far above the level of the local authorities."

"More than one inquiry?"

"More than one. The Chief Executive's office is also asking, and since they do little on their own initiative, I'm assuming they're asking at the direction of the Party."

"Do you have any idea why they're so interested?"

"If I knew the answer to that question," Ross said, "I might be able to tell you who shot Rupert."

Sturges pondered the possibilities. For State Security to get involved, Rupert would have to have been onto something that could challenge the Party politically, or at least cause it serious embarrassment. Sturges had no doubt that the Party would resort to murder if it felt seriously threatened, but what could Rupe have stumbled across that would cause such fear? "He never hesitated to attack the Communists, did he?" he said to Ross. "Maybe State Security wants to find the killer so they can give him a medal."

Ross chuckled. "That's not so far-fetched. But communists are not big on whimsy, Mr. Sturges. I have to I assume they have some more substantial interest in the matter. I've had our staff monitoring the Shenzhen newspapers for any clues, but the journalists there haven't exactly been breaking the story wide open."

"I don't have to tell you that mainland journalists are extremely limited in what they're allowed to print, especially if the topic is sensitive," said Sturges, "but some of them know quite a lot about their local scene, and sometimes their way of getting that news out to the public is to pass it on to foreign journalists like me. I'll see if our people can scare anything up."

"I'll take any information I can get, from any source," Ross said.

"Ah, that reminds me." Sturges reached into his pocket and brought out the keys from Rupert's ivory box. "Rupert left me a packet of materials along with the car. Most of the contents had to do with the Morgan, but these keys were in there, too. Three keys from the murder victim, and I have no idea what they open."

Ross took the keys and studied the piece of cardboard attached to them. "Any idea what this Chinese means? I speak the language but I don't read it."

"Well, like most Chinese words, the individual characters can have many subtle differences in meaning, but the two words together were a personal motto of Rupert's, one he used to drum into my head when I was a kid. Basically, he meant it as "learn the underlying truth" – or as he liked to put it, "learn the root cause." He was always pushing me to look beyond the obvious when I was confronted with a problem."

"So what are you suggesting?" Ross asked. "Rupert knew someone was out to kill him and he left this note behind to encourage you to find the truth about the murder if it actually happened?

Sturges shook his head. "I checked with the lawyer, and he says Rupert gave him the packet of materials more than two years ago, at the same time he put me into his will. Even if Rupe did learn that someone was out to kill him, it's unlikely he would have learned it that long before the fact – and it's even more unlikely that all he'd do about it was leave me a cryptic message that I might not even be able to decipher. He had his eccentricities, but this would have been too weird even for him. My guess is that this writing was just a final reminder of the message he'd given me so many times before."

Ross studied the keys individually. The first, which had the cardboard tag attached, was small and unexceptional. It could have fit a door, a padlock, almost anything. The second was a complex affair with a square cross section instead of the normal flat blade, protruding from a thick black plastic handle. Like the keys that come with expensive European cars, with a microchip inside designed to combat theft. Or perhaps to open a secret door.

"This one," Ross said, holding up the third key and examining the markings on it, "looks like it could go to a safe deposit box."

"That's what I thought. And there are an awful lot of safe deposit boxes in this town. If anyone has a chance of finding which box the key fits, it would be you cops."

"The chances of a connection between these keys and the murder seems rather remote," the policeman said. "But at this point, I won't turn anything away." He turned the cardboard over. "There's something written on the reverse side, too," he said. "Do you know these two characters?"

"*Rongren*," Sturges said. "It basically means 'patience.'"

"Was that another of Rupert's sayings?"

No. I have no idea what he might have been trying to tell me with that."

"Maybe he's saying be patient and you'll learn the root cause?"

Sturges rolled his eyes. "One trait Rupert picked up from the Chinese was inscrutability. He liked to talk in riddles. I'm not sure even *he* knew what he was talking about some of the time."

"It's all fascinating, but if you don't think the messages or the keys have anything to do with the murder, why give them to me?" Ross said. "I'm a bit confused here."

"I said I don't think the messages are relevant. The keys themselves could be. You have no leads. I have some keys Rupert obviously considered important, but I have no way of knowing what they're for. You're right, the notion that they're connected to the murder is a stretch," Sturges said, "but who knows? They just might open the door to some of the answers we're looking for.

Nine

It took Olivia Chen's future father the entire winter of 1937-38 to travel from the killing grounds of Nanjing to the caves of Yanan. When he arrived, Chang Dongfeng's only thought was to fight the Japanese. "Give me a rifle," he begged the Red commanders. "I will shoot them down like the animals they are. If there are no rifles, give me a spear. If there are no spears, I will kill them with a rock."

The officers were impressed with his enthusiasm, but the Red Army was primarily an army of peasants, men and women who had never seen an electric light or a flush toilet, who had the most rudimentary of education at best. People of Chang's learning were in short supply. He would eventually see combat like everyone else, but for now the leadership had better uses for him.

The Party's exodus to Yanan had involved a six-thousand-mile trek that lasted more than a year, and became known in Party lore as the Long March. Tens of thousands of people started the march in 1934 carrying tons of excess baggage: artillery pieces, printing presses, boxes of archival material, items that would be counted as normal had this been the orderly removal of a government. In this case, the removal was anything but normal. This was a flight, a retreat from Chiang Kai-Shek's forces, which attacked the column incessantly as it snaked up and down mountains, across glaciers, through bogs that swallowed men and equipment whole.

The communist leadership realized not far into the trek that the load had to be lightened. Political tracts, position papers and other non-essential documents were tossed over cliffs and into rivers along with heavy equipment.

Chang Dongfeng, who could read and write, was assigned to a unit in Yanan in charge of reassembling and maintaining the Party's archives. He sorted and filed documents that had survived, and during long sessions with individual cadres and Party leaders, some of whom were barely literate themselves, he helped reconstruct what had been tossed away. As he became known and accepted he found himself taking notes in his elegant and sophisticated hand while the leaders planned the military campaigns and debated the political doctrines that would be used to conquer and rule all of China. Despite his youth, he found himself privy to some of the seminal discussions and declarations of Mao Tse-tung, Chou En-lai and other Communist leaders.

His situation was still precarious. According to Party doctrine, the sins of the father were also the sins of the son, and the son's son: once a member of a bourgeois family such as Chang's, always a member of a bourgeois family. This family had been landlords, a capital offense in the People's Republic: the elimination of landlords and so-called rich peasants had been essential doctrine since the Party's earliest days. And Chang's father, Jacob, had compounded the sin by siding with Chiang Kai-shek. Had Jacob Chang and his family survived the Japanese rampage in Nanjing, it was unlikely they would have survived the Communist revolution twelve years later.

Yet Chang Dongfeng, Jacob's son, had proved himself with his devotion. He eventually proved himself under fire as well, first against the Japanese, and after they had been defeated, against the Nationalists in the fight for China itself.

With his impeccable personal credentials he was eventually given the honor of joining the Party. Quite a few like him, whose family backgrounds would normally have branded them enemies of the revolution, were given positions of responsibility after the victory against the Nationalists in 1949 and the establishment of the People's Republic.

Such people could only rise so far in the Party's ranks, but Chang had not joined the revolution for personal glory or power. He was happy to contribute to the creation of an independent and egalitarian nation. The leadership felt confident – as confident as anyone could ever be in the paranoid world that communism and Mao Tse-tung had created – that Chang Dongfeng could be trusted with the most sensitive documents of the Party and the state.

Some of what he saw from his elevated vantage point unnerved him. First in Yanan, and more frequently after the Party had ensconced itself in Beijing, he saw high-ranking officials grabbing privilege and the scarce amount of high-quality goods for themselves and their families. But he made allowances: the Party was still learning how to rule as a national government from the capital city. It would take time. Mao had often said there would always be opportunists and deviationists to deal with. If individual cadres were corrupt, Chang was confident that the Party's goals remained pure.

Once the new government was in place he was attached to the General Office, whose job was to help the Party and its leaders function on a day-to-day basis. The General Office provided everything from bodyguards to food and clothing for the officials, it handled monetary matters, it appointed confidential secretaries, it guarded Party secrets and communications. The General Office's subdivisions included the Bureau of Archives, and it was there that Chang Dongfeng was assigned.

One day in 1950, when the People's Republic was barely a year old, he received a note that would alter the course of his life once again.

~

He was ordered to report the office of the minister of culture. A post-script at the bottom of the note instructed him to bring a suitcase with clothing for several days. There was no indication where he might be going or when, but everyone knew that in the New China, one did not ask questions.

The furnishings in the minister's office were plain, little more than Chang himself enjoyed. What captured his attention were the pieces of art that brightened the otherwise drab room. There was a silk carpet of a fine weave on the floor, and a Ming Dynasty scroll painting on a wall. The greatest prize of all sat on the desk, two pieces of exquisite, light-green Song Dynasty celadon – the late Jacob Chang's special passion. The beauty of the porcelain almost took Chang's breath away, and he moved in for a better look.

"They are lovely pieces, are they not, Comrade Dongfeng?" the minister asked.

Chang realized he'd been staring, and he snapped to attention. "They are superb, comrade minister," he said. "I have not seen pieces of this quality for many years."

"I understand that such items were not unknown to your family," the minister said. Chang fumbled for an answer. He had spent too much time in the company of China's highest leaders in Yanan to be flustered by the presence of a government superior, but discussing his personal background was always a delicate matter. For even though Dongfeng had embraced the Communist cause wholeheartedly and acknowledged his family's sins, he secretly revered his father's memory. It was learned Confucian behavior, but it was more than that. Jacob had been an honest man. He had treated the common people humanely and with solicitude. He had refused to indulge in the corruption that engulfed so many of his colleagues, and he had made powerful enemies in the Nationalist government by condemning the practice openly.

Nevertheless, the son had to walk a careful line in the presence of other cadres. He mouthed the ritual condemnation of his father's politics and family history whenever protocol dictated. "My father, although a bourgeois reactionary, was very interested in preserving our nation's culture," he told the minister with head bowed. "He encouraged the study and preservation of Chinese art."

"And you became something of an expert yourself?" the minister asked.

"I was able to acquire a certain amount of knowledge," Chang said.

"Good. Come along, then. And bring your bag."

The minister led the way to a courtyard, where a car was waiting. No sooner had the door closed than the car pulled out and began a dash across a city almost devoid of motorized traffic. Within minutes, the capital's ramshackle airfield came into view, and the driver turned the car toward a barrier warning of mortal danger to anyone attempting to enter without authorization. At the sight of the ministerial flags flapping on the front fenders, two Red Army soldiers raised the barrier and snapped to attention as the car sped through.

An Ilyushin-12 was warming up when they arrived, and the plane began taxiing for takeoff as soon as they were on board. It was Chang's first ride on an airplane, and for him, as the plains and lakes of Hebei began rolling past far below their wing, the flight was a combination of exhilaration and white-knuckle terror. Almost before he could sort out which emotion was the stronger, the plane crossed a mighty river. Not long after that, he saw that they were descending toward one of China's many walled cities, and then another airstrip stretched out beneath them. The plane landed with a bounce and a squeal of the tires and rolled to a stop next to the terminal building, and Chang's heart missed a beat.

The words *Bei Jing*, where the flight had begun, mean "Northern Capital." A large sign on the terminal roof outside the plane's window now bore the two Chinese characters for this new city's name, "Southern Capital." For Chang Dongfeng, though, the voyage represented far more than the distance between two old imperial cities. He was back in *Nan Jing*, the place he had grown up – the scene of his family's slaughter – for the first time since he'd sneaked out through the Japanese lines thirteen years earlier.

~

There was no time for emotion. A car flying the Communist Party flag was waiting with engine running. Chang followed the minister into the car and again they sped through nearly empty streets. The driver picked the way through a decrepit district of crumbled buildings, a part of town destroyed by the advancing Japanese Army those many years earlier and still not rebuilt, and stopped in front of a wall devoid of any markings. At a signal from the driver a gate was opened to reveal a large courtyard surrounding a warehouse. The car rolled into the courtyard and the gate closed behind it.

The building's lights came flickering on as the minister entered with Chang on his heels. They were in a cavernous room, high-ceilinged and stretching into the distance, and as far as Chang could see in the dim light, crates of wood or iron had been stacked four or five high on the concrete floor. He estimated that there were several hundred crates in the room, maybe more: it was difficult to see how far the room stretched. Although the neighborhood they had passed through was rubble and filth and the exterior walls of the warehouse were covered in grime, the interior of the building was pristine.

Chang walked forward, hesitantly at first, then with more confidence when the minister did nothing to stop him, until his face was only inches from one of the crates. He read the writing stamped onto the side, but the characters there told him nothing. "What are these, comrade minister?" he asked. "All I see are rows of numbers."

"What you see," said the minister, "is what remains of the national treasures of China. All this and more was once in the Palace Museum in Beijing. The bandit Chiang Kai-shek shipped several thousand crates like these to Taiwan in late 1948 and early 1949 before fleeing himself. This," the man said, patting one crate but signifying them all, "is what he did not have time to steal."

"The Palace Museum," Chang repeated in an awed whisper. The Forbidden City, the sprawling home in central Beijing of China's emperors. It had been renamed the Palace Museum after the last Qing emperor, Puyi, was expelled in 1924. The palace had housed many of China's most precious art treasures, a collection begun a thousand years earlier by the Song emperors. Once Puyi and his entourage were gone, the complex and its contents were opened to the public as a museum.

"In 1933, as the Japanese invaders approached Beijing, Chiang Kai-shek packed the treasures into many thousands of crates and shipped them out of the city," the minister told Chang. "The crates went first to Shanghai, and then to the Nationalist capital here in Nanjing. When the Japanese aggressors began their full-scale invasion in 1937 and an attack on Nanjing became inevitable, most of the treasures were packed up once again."

The minister continued: the treasures passed the war years hidden in remote locations scattered around Sichuan and Guizhou provinces. At the end of the war the crates were consolidated in Chongqing, Chiang's wartime capital, and in 1947 they were finally returned to Nanjing.

But civil war between the Communists and the Nationalists followed immediately on the heels of world war, and by late 1948 the Red Army was gaining the upper hand. Chiang, seeing the writing on the wall, began shipping selected crates to Taiwan for "temporary" safekeeping, amid the same level of secrecy that had accompanied the collection's earlier movements. Chiang and his government followed the next year.

Chang Dongfeng was horrified at the thought of the delicate treasures being shuttled to and fro around the country, always just one step ahead of war and destruction. "There must have been considerable damage, comrade minister," he said.

"One would think so. But we have opened several of these crates, and so far almost everything inside is in perfect shape," the minister said.

"That is good news, then," Chang said. "And at least the Nationalist bandits were not able to take everything. I'm sure Chairman Mao and the Communist Party will soon announce plans to recover the stolen items and return them to their rightful place."

"That is for more senior minds than ours to deal with. In the meantime, comrade, it is our job to prepare these items that we have here for display in a new People's Palace Museum. With your expertise in archiving, combined with your knowledge of art, I feel you will be the perfect person to lead the team that will carry out the preparation," the minister said. "You will have the assistance of the country's leading experts in art and antiquities. Are you willing?"

"The Party commands and I obey, comrade minister," Chang said with a slight bow. "It will be my honor to serve the people in this way." Even as the words left his mouth, he knew he was volunteering for a monumental task. The minister had mentioned thousands of crates; that suggested there would be tens, even hundreds of thousands of items to catalogue. "If you will arrange for me to obtain the list of the contents, I will start immediately."

"There is no list," the minister said. "That is to say, we do have an inventory prepared in 1925 of almost one and a quarter million separate items, but it was done rather carelessly. The list does not include a number of items the reactionary Puyi stole in the years before he was kicked out of the Forbidden City. In addition, tens of thousands of items were added to the collection between 1924 and 1933. And we are not sure which pieces the Chiang bandits stole and which they left behind. Although we are told," he added darkly, "that they took many of the most important pieces.

"Your job and that of the people working under you will be to prepare a completely new and authoritative inventory," the minister said. "While you are finishing that task, a renovation and modernization of the Forbidden City will be carried out to prepare a proper home for the collection."

Chang ran a hand over the crate nearest him. "A million and a quarter items you say, comrade minister?"

The minister grunted acknowledgment. "Your work is cut out for you comrade Dongfeng," he said.

Ten

Ricco Tang, Rupert Rackley's fellow art collector, was a member of one of Hong Kong's prominent Shanghainese families. Although the vast majority of Hongkongers were Cantonese, with origins just across the border in Guangdong Province, an inordinate percentage of the territory's wealthiest and most influential traced their ancestry farther north to the Chinese financial center of Shanghai and surrounding cities in Zhejiang and Jiangsu provinces.

Many had been industrialists before fleeing the communist victory of 1949. Many had succeeded in rebuilding their fortunes after their arrival in the colony. In Hong Kong they considered themselves an elite, and they quietly disparaged the Cantonese, whom they viewed as peasants and small businessmen. The Cantonese looked down on the Shanghainese, along with Beijingers and most other northerners. People from Beijing didn't like either the Cantonese or the Shanghainese. Everyone disparaged the Sichuanese. It was one of the immutable realities of China: national unity might have been an overriding preoccupation, but nobody had much time for anyone from anywhere else in the country.

Still, Cantonese, Shanghainese: all were Chinese. Several thousand years of history is hard to erase from the collective psyche. Chinese raised in the West might grow up with an ambivalence toward their ancestral homeland – many a Western-born Chinese had come to Hong Kong in search of his or her roots, only to be appalled at the outward boorishness of the local people and the filth of the country itself. Native-born Chinese like Tang and his wife, on the other hand, might become thoroughly British (or American, or Canadian) in tastes and speech, but China tugged incessantly at their souls. They were happy to contribute to the motherland in one way or another.

Tang's contribution was a quiet campaign to bring home items of China's art that had made their way into foreign hands over the centuries. Bringing the art "home" often meant only to private collections in Hong Kong or on the mainland: Tang's collection was renowned throughout Asia. But he also donated pieces to mainland museums. Repatriating a national treasure was a way of satisfying nationalistic stirrings, and it didn't hurt an individual's standing with the officials who granted approval for mainland business ventures. If Chinese personal life revolved largely around the family, establishing connections – *guanxi* – with influential outsiders was the way to succeed in business. Ricco Tang's *guanxi* were excellent.

Tang's avocation also had another consequence. Through art, he had become close with Rupert Rackley. Bill Sturges knew the two men had been good friends. He was surprised to hear that they'd had a falling out.

"I was just discussing that with that police chap, Ross," Tang said when Sturges called.

"And what did you tell him?" Sturges asked.

"The same thing I'll tell you. Rupert and I did have a brief difference of opinion a couple of months back about a Tang Dynasty *sancai* horse. A misunderstanding that was quickly resolved. No big deal."

"What specifically was the argument about?"

"I bought the horse from Evelyn Chin, a very reputable dealer here. Rupert thought he had reserved the piece, and he accused Evelyn and me of unethical behavior. Evelyn said there was never any deal between the two of them, just a casual expression of interest from Rupert that he never pursued, and when I came along and made her a firm offer she sold the piece to me. After Rupert calmed down he conceded that she was right. Ask her yourself: she'll confirm everything I've said."

"I'm sure she will. But it sounds like an odd thing for Rupert to do, flying off the handle like that with a close friend like you. What do you think set him off? Was it an especially good piece?"

"Rupert and I never bothered with anything but especially good pieces, Bill. His taste was impeccable, and I like to think mine is, too. This one happened to be an excellent example of the genre, but there's nothing unusual about it that would get him so excited. Yet when he called me he was ranting like a crazy bloke. Called me all sorts of names. I know he could get pretty nasty in his writing, but I'd never seen him that way in person."

"But you say the two of you made up?"

"Well, he never actually called to make personal amends before, you know, the thing happened. It's a shame: as you say, we were close for many years. I'd go to his house if he bought a new piece, he'd come to mine. I don't know how many times we got drunk together."

In fact, Sturges noticed that Tang was slurring his plummy British-accented words right now. One of the habits Tang had picked up while becoming, as the saying went, more British than the British, was serious drinking. Since like many Asians he didn't metabolize alcohol well, he often sported a bright red face as a result.

"I'ss painful to think old Rupe might have gone to his grave hating me," he said.

"First you say it was a minor argument, now you say he might have hated you. Which was it, Ricco?"

"Right, 'hated' is an overstatement. The point is he told Evelyn that he was no longer angry with me, but he never had a chance to say it to me directly. It would have been nice to have heard it from his mouth before he died, tha'ss all I'm saying."

"Have you asked Olivia if Rupert ever talked about the argument?"

Tang's reply contained a hint of annoyance. "I hardly know Olivia," he said. "Not that I'd mind. I mean, you know, she's quite – but anyway, she was never around when I went to their house. And we move in different social circles. I couldn't exactly call her after the murder and say, 'Sorry your husband got whacked, old girl, but on the remote chance that you happened to see him any time before he died, did he mention anything about me?'"

"I know what you mean," Sturges said. "I knew Rupert from the time I was a kid, yet I probably don't know Olivia much better than you do. Do you know who she sees or where she goes outside work?"

"Ah," Tang said, "I've heard rumors..."

"Yeah, yeah, everybody's heard those rumors about Olivia. But it's all third- and fourth-hand gossip. What about Claudia: does she ever see Olivia?"

"She's bumped into her while shopping or at the hairdresser, but that's it as far as I know. Like I said, different circles. Claudia and I never discuss Olivia. Why so interested?" Tang asked. "Are you thinking of getting to know her better now that you're both single?"

"Come on, Ricco, that's a bit crude. I was her husband's close friend and he's just been murdered. And I'm sure she has things besides dating on her mind."

"Oh, bollocks!" Tang said. "Everyone knows it was a loveless marriage. Now Rupert's gone, Olivia is still sexy as hell, she's free to let loose like before. If I were you I'd hop into the queue right away, old boy, before too many chaps get there ahead of you."

"Yeah, I'll give it some thought," Sturges said. In fact, he'd been thinking of it ever since that morning at the lawyer's office. There was no longer any ethical barrier holding them back at this point. It could have been Sturges's male imagination working overtime, but he was almost sure Olivia was throwing signals his way the other day. Visions of her breasts and thighs kept popping into his mind. And that kiss she gave him...

Better to change the subject. "I'd like to talk to Evelyn Chin," he said. "Do you have her phone number handy?"

"Gonna check up on me after all, eh?"

"You know us journalists," Sturges said. "We suspect the worst in everybody. But what I really want is to ask her about Rupert. Maybe she knows something that can help explain what he was doing in China."

"Maybe he was raiding a tomb."

"Brian Ross raised that possibility – that Rupert's presence in China had to do with antiques, I mean. But, damn, it doesn't seem likely, does it? There was all the art he could want right here in Hong Kong. His adventuring days were long past. He certainly didn't need to go to rummaging around the Chinese countryside to add to his collection. And he was in no shape to do so."

"Anything was possible with Rupert."

"Are you saying this out of knowledge, Ricco, or is this just speculation?"

"You mean do I know for sure that he crossed the border on the trail of some piece of art? No," Tang said. "But we all know how much he loved his art and hated the bloody commies. Stealing their treasures would be one way of getting back at them."

"Theoretically, sure," Sturges said, "but he'd been getting back at them pretty regularly with his writing for thirty-five years. I can't see him suddenly hopping across the border after all this time just to give one more twist to the knife by stealing some piece of art. Unless you know something specific?"

Tang took longer than expected to reply. "There is *something,*" he said. "I mean, I don't know if it means anything. But I got the distinct impression from Rupert in the last few weeks – until he stopped talking to me – that he had something important in the works."

"What gave you this impression?"

"It was his general behavior. He seemed on edge the last couple of times I saw him, but in a positive way, as if he was anticipating something good. Like a kid just before Christmas. And about a month before he died, he said to me, 'I might have some big news soon.'"

"And...?"

"Tha'ss it."

"That's it? 'I might have some big news'?"

"Afraid so."

"Christ, Ricco, Rupert was in the news business. 'Big news' to him could have been anything."

"I told you it wasn't anything solid," Tang said. "But he said this in the context of a conversation we were having about art. We always talked about art when we got together. When he said 'big news,' there was no doubt in my mind that it had something to do with art and antiquities."

"Didn't you ask him what he was referring to?"

"I did, but he changed the subject, and I let it drop. I figured that if it really was about art he'd tell me eventually, like he always did. But then...anyway, try Evelyn Chin. She knew him well. She might be able to give you something more concrete."

Tang hesitated a moment, and then said: "I hope you're not gonna disappoint me, Bill."

"Disappoint you how? By asking Chin about your argument with Rupe?"

"No, no, I told you, you're welcome to ask her about that."

"What, then?"

"Olivia, man!" Tang said. "I hope you're going to call *her*. Jesus, half the guys in town would like to get into her knickers. You know her as well as anyone does, you're young, you're unattached: you're in a perfect position to score. I hope you won't let the side down. The boy'ss and I are sort of betting on you, in fact."

"You've been discussing me and Olivia with your friends?"

"The subject has come up. The subject of Olivia has come up a lot since the murder, to be honest, and, you know, some of the guys have been speculating..."

"Like I said, Ricco, I'll think about it."

"Well if you do—" Tang stopped in mid-sentence.

Sturges waited, but there was only silence. "Ricco, are you still there?" he asked.

He heard muffled voices on the other end of the line, and then Tang was back. "Sure, great to talk to you, Bill," he said. "Let me know if anything interesting turns up."

"Are you okay?" Sturges asked.

"Right. I'll call you and we'll have lunch." Then Tang's voice dropped to a whisper: "Claudia just came in. Gotta go."

Sturges had to laugh. "She doesn't let you talk on the phone?"

"It's not that," Tang whispered. "It's the subject matter. She knows I was friendly with Olivia's old man – he and I had a common interest in art. But she really hates it when I talk about Olivia."

"Wait a minute, Ricco," Sturges said, "you just got finished telling me you and Claudia *never* talk about Olivia. Now you're saying...Ricco? Hello?

But the line was dead.

Eleven

Brian Ross called three days after the lunch at the American Club. His voice was guarded. "I have good news and bad news," he said.

"What's the good news?" Sturges asked.

"Those keys that Rupert left you: we found out what one of them opens. It's a safe deposit box, just as we thought."

"Fantastic!" Sturges said. "Which bank?"

"The Consolidated Bank of Singapore. Rupert had a box at their branch in Tsuen Wan."

"He couldn't have found a much more out-of-that-way location than that, could he?" Tsuen Wan was an old manufacturing town at the edge of Kowloon. Most manufacturing had long since been moved across the border to take advantage of cheaper labor and laxer environmental rules, and Tsuen Wan was now mainly a place of warehouses and relatively inexpensive housing. There was something about the name of the bank that rang a bell in Sturges's mind as they spoke...

"So when do we open the box?" he asked.

"Ah, that brings us to the bad news."

"And that is?"

"Do you no' read your own newspaper, man?"

A copy of that morning's paper was lying on Sturges's desk. He picked it up, and there on the front page was the reason the bank's name had sounded familiar:

Bank Accidentally Destroys Full Safe Deposit Boxes

"You've got to be kidding," Sturges said.

The bank, one of the most prestigious in Asia, was in the process of renovating its Tsuen Wan branch. The management had engaged a leading contractor to oversee the renovation project, part of which included removing fifty small customer boxes in the vault and replacing them with larger boxes. The overseer had hired a leading manufacturer and installer of safe deposit boxes to make the switch. None of those leading companies had bothered to send supervisors to the construction site, and the prestigious bank's staff was too busy with its daily routine to pay any attention. The demolition crew had removed five stacks of ten boxes each as directed...but they were the wrong five stacks.

By the time the mistake was discovered all fifty boxes, full of only the customers knew what, had been sent to a scrap yard, where they'd been compressed into a cube of crushed metal the size of a hatbox.

"Rupert's box was one of the fifty?" Sturges asked.

"I'm afraid so," Ross said. "He'd had the box there since 1993."

"All these fucking 'leading' companies, and none of them had the fucking good sense to put someone with a fucking brain in charge of the fucking operation?"

"So your own newspaper says – in somewhat less scabrous language. We've verified the facts for ourselves, of course."

"Fifty boxes out of" – Sturges glanced at the story again – "a total of three hundred seventy-five. All those to choose from, including the empty ones that were supposed to be removed, and these dolts happen to mistakenly select the row containing a box that might hold the answer to a murder mystery. What are the chances of that?"

As suspicious as the destruction seemed, the story quoted a bank official as saying the change of boxes had been planned months before Rupert's death. And Rupert had kept his ownership of the box secret. The possibility that someone had targeted it because it was his was remote. The two men agreed that it had to be an accident.

"We've questioned everyone involved," Ross said. "It looks like it was just lack of attention, stupidity, and plain bad luck from our point of view."

"I can guess the answer to this one, but was anything still intact inside the boxes? What's left of them, that is?"

"They'd already melted the cube of metal down for scrap," Ross said. There's nothing left inside but ashes and bits of melted gold."

"So, one key down, two to go, and we're no closer to solving the mystery," Sturges said. "At least I have an interesting second-day story on the destroyed boxes."

"Hold on," said Ross. "I'm not sure whether it would help or hinder the investigation for people to know Rupert's box was included in this. Or that he even had a box. No, I don't think I want this published at the moment."

"But it was my key!" Sturges said. "Rupert left it to me, which can only mean he wanted me to open the box, so there must have been something for me inside."

"And you and I have an agreement," Ross reminded him. "We cops are the ones who found out which box the key fit and in which bank, remember, and that's covered by our agreement. You had no idea what the key opened, and you still have no idea what might have been inside. If you want to write a story saying he left you a mystery key, be my guest, but I'm not giving you permission to take it beyond that. I'm holding you to your word here, Sturges. I need to know I can trust you, or we call off our cooperation right now."

"Okay, okay," Sturges muttered. The thought of his needing police permission to write a story was infuriating. But a deal was a deal. And Ross was right: they didn't have the slightest idea if the contents of the safe deposit box had anything to do with the murder. Anything Sturges wrote would be speculative in the extreme. "So where does this leave the investigation?" he asked.

"The same place it was the last time we spoke," Ross said. "Which is to say, nowhere."

"There are still the other two keys."

"Aye – if we can find out what they open. And if *they* have anything to do with the case. Have your people had any luck? I keep opening my newspaper in the morning hoping I'm going to read something that breaks the thing open."

"One of my reporters checked with his contacts among the Shenzhen news media. They said they'd been ordered by local Party headquarters not to go near the story of Rupert's death. One reporter who did what he thought was some routine digging was hauled in by the cops and held for two days while they grilled him to see if he had learned anything."

"And had he?"

"Nothing. And that's what's interesting," Sturges said. "Our mainland colleagues can usually give us some useful information, as long as we protect their identities, but an editor there I've known for years told my man he had rarely seen such a total blackout on information. Whoever's responsible for Rupert's death has done a masterful job of covering the trail."

"What do you plan next?" Ross asked.

'I have an appointment tomorrow with one of the art dealers Rupert used to frequent," Sturges said. "I'll see if she has anything interesting to say. What about you: nothing new from the mainland cops?"

"Nary a word. No surprise there: based on what little we know, our suspicion is that the order for this killing came from high up. The *gong an* are certainly not going to start sharing information like that with the likes of us."

"You think some Party official ordered the hit?"

"It would hardly be the first time a Chinese official was involved in something dirty, would it? If Rupert had learned something that would seriously embarrass the Chinese leadership, I don't doubt that he'd do almost anything to write it – even cross into China to get the facts. And I wouldn't put it past one of those organized thugs who pass for officials up there to put a bullet in his brain to keep him from revealing it. The Communist Party is that paranoid about losing control."

"The sonsofbitches keep passing new laws, just like a normal country, but they ignore them whenever it suits their purposes," Sturges said in agreement. "I'm sure there are individuals in the leadership who care about the country and its development. But at the institutional level, the Party's primary concern is still the preservation of the Party."

"Rupert had it right about the buggers, didn't he?" Ross said. "All the talk in the West about China these days is of GDP and cheap exports and trade imbalances, as if it *is* a normal country. But we who live here know it's still one of the most corrupt, lawless societies on earth."

Twelve

"I appreciate your talking to me," Sturges told Evelyn Chin. He'd arrived at closing time at Chin's antique shop on Hollywood Road, a stretch of old Hong Kong just a short walk uphill from the gleaming towers of Central.

High-rise office towers now punctuated the skyline here, too, but for the most part Hollywood Road was still a narrow, curving lane of low-rise buildings housing art and antique shops. The Man Mo Temple, with its peaked, green-tiled roof, occupied the halfway point on the road. Local Chinese used to come to the temple to ask the gods to settle disputes when British law had failed them. Residents and tourists still prowled the surrounding shops to buy porcelains, jade, ivory and bone statuettes, and antiques that might or might not be genuine. Serious collectors like Rupert sought out the dealers like Chin, who could be trusted to stock the real thing.

Even if the items were genuine, however, an inescapable fact was that the vast majority came from illegally raided tombs, and had been spirited out of the mainland by smugglers. Hong Kong was a center of the antiques trade, and Evelyn Chin was among the most prominent dealers. She dressed with the understated elegance typical of a woman of her age and class, but Sturges knew that the string of apple-green jade beads around her neck could have paid for a house in most countries. There was one anomaly in her wardrobe, a pair of ungainly hiking shoes, but Sturges ignored them out of tact. If Chin's wardrobe was problematic, her English was flawless, Oxbridge pronunciation with hints of a Cantonese accent peeking through, indicative of an upper-class Chinese who had studied in one of Hong Kong's church-affiliated schools during the middle third of the last century.

"I'll tell you what I can," she said, and led the way through the shop past treasures whose beauty would be evident to anyone, but whose names and provenance only an aficionado would recognize: bright green *Qingbai* and white *Yingqing* ware from the Song Dynasty, a *Long Chuan* funerary vase also from the Song, a rare amber-glazed bowl from the Liao. "Rupert and I were friends. He bought from me of course, but oftentimes he'd just stop by to talk about antiquities," she said, gesturing at the beauty around her.

"This is a business but it's also my passion, as it was Rupert's," Chin said. "He and I could spend hours discussing a single piece. Any time I got a new shipment in, he was one of the first people I called. He had an excellent eye – and he was as good as they come in spotting the fakes. As the science of identifying and dating antiquities progresses, the forgers are working hard to keep up. In fact, they're usually a step or two ahead of us."

"I know what you mean," Sturges said. "Experts tell me fake fashion items coming out of China are now almost impossible to tell from the real thing. Even the fake certificates of authenticity that come with them look genuine."

Chin turned to a shelf and picked up a small ceramic statue of a pot-bellied woman. "You might be aware that this piece is referred to as a 'fat lady,'" she said. "It's typical of the Tang Dynasty, the 7th to 10th centuries A.D. The genre has always been popular with collectors. This particular piece has been tested by a very reliable dating procedure called thermo-luminescence, or TL, and it definitely dates to the Tang. And this is a particularly fine example of the type. It could be worth quite a lot."

"But it's not?"

"It's a fake," she said. "It was re-carved last year from another Tang statue called a '*lokapala*,' which is a kind of tomb guardian. The clay itself was fired during the Tang, so the statue passes the TL test. And the pigments used to paint this re-carved piece were ground by hand in a mortar, like it was done back in the Tang era, instead of by machine as it's done today. Something like this can fool even an expert."

"Then how do you know this one isn't real?" Sturges asked.

"Because I bought it from a factory in Guangzhou that's doing nothing but this kind of re-carving."

"I assume Rupert also helped you assess genuine pieces," Sturges said.

"He did. Just because a piece is old doesn't mean it's valuable. Rupert was one of the best at separating the good from the bad and the great from the merely good."

"And we all know that most pieces coming out of China, good and bad, are from tombs that have been illegally plundered."

Chin sidestepped the remark. "Once a piece is in Hong Kong," she said, "it's perfectly legal to buy and sell it. How it got here is irrelevant."

"I realize that," Sturges said. "I'm only asking because I wonder if this might be why Rupert had gone to China."

"To raid a tomb, you mean?" She put a hand over her mouth to stifle a laugh.

"You find the idea funny?"

"Quite. Those digs are extremely labor-intensive, dirty, and often physically dangerous. Rupert with his fancy suits and his huge tummy and his bad heart would have been totally out of place slithering down a rope into some pitch black, water-logged tomb. My Lord, he used to be out of breath after climbing the one flight of stairs to my office here!"

"So you don't think his presence in China had anything to do with antiques?"

"Certainly not if he had to dig them up himself. Why? Did someone tell you differently?"

"Ricco Tang told me yesterday that Rupert was all excited about something just before he died. He told Ricco he was expecting 'big news.' I've seen Rupert when he was about to score an important piece, and he behaved very much the way Ricco described him. So it occurred to both of us that maybe it was some special piece of art that drew him across the border. Given your relationship with Rupert, I thought he might have said something about it to you."

"That's all Ricco told you? 'Big news?'"

"I'm afraid that's all Ricco knows."

He waited for her to dismiss the notion out of hand, but instead, after a moment's thought, she said: "I don't know if this will be any more helpful, but the last time I saw Rupert he was hopping around with a smile on his face like a kid entering a candy store, just as Ricco said. He made references to 'a big discovery.' He said something like, 'I'm going to knock all their socks off.' Like Ricco I assumed this big discovery was some fantastic piece of art, but he never came right out and said it, or whose socks were going to be knocked off."

"When was this?"

"A week or so before his death."

"And he said nothing else?"

"I'm afraid not. But wait: do you know Fritz Giesler?"

Sturges shook his head.

"Fritz is another expert on Chinese antiquities. He does a bit of buying and selling, but he leans primarily toward the scientific side of the business, if you will, helping to identify and authenticate pieces. He consults for museums, big auction houses, and wealthy individuals. He also consults for Chinese government agencies on officially sanctioned digs. He's one of the few people I know who was Rupert's equal when it came to assessing art.

"I was speaking to Fritz shortly after that last time Rupert stopped by here," she said. "He told me Rupert had been peppering him with all sorts of questions about looted goods, how they were dug up, and how they were smuggled into Hong Kong."

"Which suggests that Rupe might have been contemplating a tomb raid after all."

"I still find that extremely unlikely," she said, "But Fritz and I agreed that Rupert might have been thinking of bringing in something that was already out of the ground."

Sturges digested the information. There was still no specific utterance of Rupert's to confirm that he'd gone to China to score a big piece, but three people who knew him well had apparently all received signals from him that might point in that direction. "I'd like to talk to Mr. Giesler about this," said Sturges.

"He travels a lot," she said. She leafed through a box of business cards. "Here's his card." As Sturges copied the information, Chin said: "I hope you'll be discreet in what you write, Mr. Sturges. I don't want to harm Rupert's reputation by raising the possibility that he was doing something illegal. I don't want to give the Chinese an excuse to disparage him, even if he is dead."

"Rupert gave the Chinese all the reason they ever needed to dislike him while he was alive," Sturges said, handing Giesler's card back.

"I suppose you're right," she said. She'd begun checking her watch and fidgeting in her chair as they spoke. "Is there anything else? I'm sorry, but I have to leave for another appointment soon."

Sturges hesitated for a moment, while curiosity got the best of him. "Well, since you ask...this might be rude of me, but" – he pointed at her feet – "your shoes. They're so out of place. I couldn't help wondering."

She glanced down, and laughed. "They do look terrible, don't they?" she said.

"Then why...?"

"Don't you know? Today is Mid-Autumn Festival. As soon as we're finished here I'm going to meet some friends to climb the Peak and watch the new moon."

The moon festival, of course. "It's tradition," Chin said. "And you know how we Chinese are when it comes to tradition."

Sturges knew. Anyone who knew the Chinese knew. Through thirty-five hundred years of recorded history and for uncounted centuries before that, warlords and kingdoms and dynasties had appeared and vanished from the Chinese scene like heartbeats on a hospital monitor. Floods, famines and predators had wiped out whole regions at a time. Through millennia of ups and downs, through disasters and atrocities that would destroy most civilizations, Chinese culture had endured, sustained by tradition.

Climb a mountain like Evelyn Chin at Mid-Autumn Festival. The celebration dates back more than three thousand years to the first historical dynasty, the Shang.

Arrange your surroundings in harmony with the forces of nature – the *feng* and the *shui*, the wind and the water. If bad luck haunts a home or a business, call the *feng shui* master to trick the *qi* into more propitious channels with a plant, a scroll, a mirror.

Don't get start a business, don't move a household, don't marry, without selecting an auspicious date. The number eight is considered lucky because the word for "eight" sounds like the word for "wealth." Get married on a date with an eight in it. Buy an apartment in a building with an eight in the address. Avoid the number four: it sounds like the word for "death." Even the most modern and sophisticated Chinese Sturges knew subscribed to such beliefs and superstitions.

Worship your ancestors. China's only truly native religion predated Confucius, and endured to the present day. After a funeral, set up a home altar with a portrait of the deceased. Make offerings at the altar for forty-nine days while the deceased undergoes judgment. Afterward, light incense at the altar and offer food and prostrations. Every April on the *Ching Ming* holiday, trek to the cemetery to tidy up the ancestors' gravesites.

Live in the modern world, adapt to its ways, but never forget what it is to be Chinese. Outsiders dealing with the Chinese or living among them may ignore such customs and traditions, may even mock them (as many do), but all should be aware: these beliefs, this reaching back to ancient beginnings, holds powerful sway over the thoughts and actions of those around you.

Even so capricious an act as murder...even that can be guided by tradition.

~

Sturges walked along Hollywood Road toward Central, replaying his final exchange with Evelyn Chin.

She confirmed Tang's story about the disputed horse: that Rupert had thought he'd reserved the piece, and had calmed down after she explained the situation. "The thing is," she told Sturges, "I suspect there was more to it. I'm hesitant to bring it up – but you were his close friend. I'm telling you this personally, though, not as a reporter."

Sturges nodded, and she continued: "I think he blew up because he was already angry with Ricco. After he apologized for accusing me, I said to him, 'I guess you're going to call Ricco and apologize to him, too.' But this sour look came over his face, the kind of look he usually had when he discussed the Chinese government. He said: 'In his case, it's not just the horse, you know. The horse was just the last straw.'"

"Do you have any idea what he meant by that?"

"All I can tell you is some gossip I heard. I have absolutely no idea if it's true."

"And that would be...?"

"I heard," she said, "that there might have been something going on between Ricco and Olivia Chen. Olivia is Rupert's wife."

"Yes," Sturges said, "I'm quite aware of who Olivia Chen is."

He'd been putting off seeing Olivia, uneasy about how he might act once they were alone. But enough procrastination: it was time to pick up the Morgan.

Thirteen

Sturges felt like a high school boy calling a girl for a first date. Butterflies in the stomach. Fear of rejection. Fear of looking like a fool.

This is silly, he told himself. Olivia and I aren't kids. We've known each other for years. I'm only calling to make an appointment to pick up the Morgan. What's to be nervous about?

He was nervous. He'd tried to get her out of his mind, and couldn't. Her beauty, her body, Ricco Tang's remarks about her – they'd all come back to him repeatedly over the last few days. The suspicion that she'd been flirting with him outside the lawyer's office had grown into conviction.

When he did call and she was pleasant on the phone, when she said, sure, mid-day Sunday's fine...he wasn't sure what he felt. He hadn't asked her for a date, he'd only asked if he could come by to get the car. She'd told him even before he called to come by to get the car. Why should he feel anything at all?

And yet he did. Relief?

Yes, but more than relief.

Elation? That, too.

And he was nervous.

This is not me, he told himself. He'd never been easily intimidated. He was at ease in the company of presidents and prime ministers, sports stars and movie queens. He scoffed at authority, bristled at any attempt by anyone to tell him how to act. "I've forgotten the Alamo, the Maine *and* Pearl Harbor," he would tell people, in a voice that allowed for no challenge.

So why was his stomach doing double axels at the prospect of meeting Olivia?

He climbed out of the taxi and the first thing that caught his eye was the new black Mercedes sedan parked in the driveway. Rupert's old car hadn't lasted long.

The door to the house opened and Olivia appeared, dressed with studied casualness: a tight, low-cut tank top that accentuated the shape and firmness of her breasts, bare midriff that revealed a lightly muscled stomach, and low-rider slacks of a soft knit that clung to every curve. She looked closer to thirty than forty. Her face was soft and smooth, with none of the hard lines Asian women often develop as they age. Her hair was pinned up seemingly as an afterthought, but he suspected that there was nothing unplanned about Olivia.

"You look fantastic. As always," he said.

"I got impatient waiting for you, so I was trolling the Internet for cybersex," she said, batting her eyelashes. "I had to look my best for the guys on line."

There was that easy banter about sex again, so different from the way she had acted around him when Rupert was alive. He supposed that anyone released by death from the confinements of even a happy marriage might let loose for a while. The little allowances and compromises that one makes for a spouse are no longer necessary. A person can be more spontaneous, even reckless. Maybe this accounted for her behavior.

Or not. He wasn't sure how to characterize Rupert's and Olivia's marriage, but "happy" certainly didn't leap to mind. He did know that the Olivia he'd been seeing since the murder was the

Olivia he'd heard about from people who knew her away from Rupert's company: forceful, risqué, overtly sexual.

The twinkle in her eye now suggested she was just teasing him, but he suspected he was blushing anyway. Definitely nervous. He had a hundred questions he wanted to ask, about the marriage, about Evelyn Chin's suggestion that Olivia had been having an affair with Ricco, about a lot of things. But he held his tongue for the moment and planted a kiss on both her cheeks.

She pulled her head back and looked him in the eye for a moment and he braced for another sexual innuendo, but all she said was: "I would have pulled the Morgan out for you, but I couldn't find the keys."

No problem." He dangled the set in the air. "Rupe left them for me."

"Well, then, your baby's waiting for you over there," and she pointed to a carport at the side of the house.

Sturges walked to the car and rolled the fitted canvas cover back, unveiling his new possession one section at a time. He traced the graceful, dark green curve of the fender the way a man might run his hand over the curves of a woman's body. He climbed into the front seat and caressed the polished walnut dashboard. He slipped on a pair of black driving gloves he'd bought for the occasion, molding the perforated leather to the spaces between his fingers. A twist of the key and the engine rasped into life. He turned to see Olivia studying him.

"How do I look?" he asked.

"Like a schoolboy with his first set of wheels," she said.

"Are you sure it's okay if I take it now? According to your lawyer, Rupert's will won't be official for another couple of months."

"Take it," she said. "I'm sure you'll be careful. It's still insured anyway. And if you wreck it, it's your problem, not mine."

"Well, then, want to go for a ride?"

"Maybe later. Let's celebrate your new possession first. Can you stay for lunch?"

"Hah!" he said. "I own this baby one minute and already the good-looking chicks are coming on to me."

"You guys and your cars," she said. "Come on in, Ayrton, I'll make drinks." She walked to the house with what looked like a purposeful shake of the hips, bidding him to follow. "You can lose the gloves. You're going to need full use of your hands."

This time he was sure he blushed.

~

The house had changed. Olivia had rearranged some of Rupert's antiques, removed others altogether. The large Tang Dynasty stone Buddha that had guarded the entrance for as long as Sturges could remember was now in a less conspicuous spot. The bronzes and porcelains that once seemed to fill every level surface and the scrolls that had covered most of the wall space had been thinned out.

Rupert's calligraphy table, at which he used to sit evenings when he was reasonably sober to practice his brushwork, had disappeared from the ground-floor sun room, and comfortable new furniture and a large flat-screen television had taken its place.

To a first-time visitor the house would still have reeked of Asia and China, but to Sturges the changes were jarring.

"You've been redecorating," he said when Olivia returned with a Bloody Mary in each hand.

"The place feels lighter, don't you think?" she said. "I have some other changes in mind. No disrespect to Rupert's memory, but now that I'm alone I'm going to make the place my own."

"Still, it's funny," he said. "Here was Rupert, the Westerner who hated China, yet he surrounded himself with its art, while you, the Chinese, want less of it."

"It was just too much. I appreciate the art – I got that from my father, who was no mean collector himself. But Rupert had every square inch filled with some piece or other. It was like living in a museum. I was always afraid that if I turned around too quickly I'd break something valuable. I want to create a bit of living space for myself."

"But you also have several new pieces here," he said, examining an exquisite carving of purple-and-green jade. "At least I've never seen them before."

"I brought a few items over from my father's apartment after he died. Pieces that I grew up with and that mean something special to me. God knows where I'm going to put all the rest. I haven't even had time to think about it with all that's been going on."

"Speaking of which," he said, "have you heard anything new?"

"About the investigation? Nothing. What about you?"

"Very little," he said. He decided not to recount his conversation with Ross. It had been nothing but speculation. "I did talk to Ricco Tang. Do you know anything about him and Rupert having an argument just a little while ago?"

She shook her head. "What about?"

"I'm told it was about an antique that they both thought they'd reserved from one of the major art dealers in town," he said. "Ricco said it was no big deal, a momentary fit of pique on Rupert's part. I just thought he might have mentioned it to you."

"Ricco? No," she said, "I haven't seen Ricco or spoken to him for several weeks."

"I didn't mean Ricco," he said. "I meant, did Rupert say anything about it to you?"

"This is the first I've heard of an argument between the two of them," she said.

He looked in vain for a sign that she was hiding something. "It was probably nothing, as Ricco said. So, what have you done with the stuff you moved?"

"Rupert's art? For now, I've put it in his study. I'll probably sell some of the pieces. Keep the really best ones of course, but in many cases he has five, six, even ten of the same thing. I can do with far less."

"I probably don't have to tell you, but get some expert advice if you do sell anything. Some pieces may look like clutter, but they could still be worth a hell of a lot of money."

"Oh, I learned enough from my father to know that a lot of this is extremely valuable," she said.

"A lot of it?" he repeated. "You mean you don't know?"

"Know what?"

He told her what Ross had said about the valuation of Rupert's collection.

"A hundred and fifty *million*?" She surveyed the paintings and statues with new respect, then struck a pose and cocked her head. "I don't really need the money, though, do I?" she said. "I mean, I'm already one rich little chickie, aren't I?"

"That you are," he said. There was still no sign that she was anything but bemused by her newfound wealth. "I'd love to know why Rupe hid his money all those years. What difference would it have made if people had known he was rich?"

"I've been asking myself the same question ever since the lawyer's office," she said. "I don't know, maybe he thought if I knew how much money he had I'd have wanted us to live differently. But this is a great house: I wouldn't trade it for one of those fancy high-rise apartment blocks in Mid-Levels or Repulse Bay. We've always had the best of food and wine. I have all the clothes and jewelry I need and plenty of money of my own to buy more. And my father's estate was substantial, not even including *his* art collection – I can't wait now to find out how much that's worth. If I'd wanted to live differently while Rupert was alive I wouldn't have needed his money to do it. I guess it would have been nice if he'd shared more of his secrets with me, but believe me, it wouldn't have changed our lifestyle at all."

So why had Rupert kept the secret, from Olivia and everybody else? It could have been his distrust of the Chinese – but he had married her, after all. Sturges's mind was running through all the mysteries the murder had thrown up when her voice pulled him back to the present. "Pardon?" he said.

"I said, I can just imagine what the men are saying about me."

"Which men?"

"In the clubs, on the golf courses: I'll bet I'm the subject of a lot of talk these days. Sophisticated broad, still fairly young, reasonably good-looking – she puffed her chest out, inviting him to admire – "suddenly unattached, and now worth a fortune to boot. I must be providing nighttime fantasies for dozens of guys."

"Listen, my dear, the men in this town have been fantasizing about you for years. Your money is just the icing on an extremely attractive cake."

"Is that so? And what about you, Bill Sturges? Do you fantasize about me?"

He felt the heat rush to his face again. "Come on, Olivia, this is awkward," he said.

"Why? Because of Rupert?"

"Yeah, partly because of that." His eyes roamed over her body. "Mostly because of that."

"Rupert's gone, Bill. You didn't kill him. I didn't kill him. We can mourn his death, but neither of us has to feel guilty about it."

"It's not a question of guilt, it's just that he was my friend, and you were his wife, and I've never given any thought to, you know..."

"Oh, come on yourself!" she said with a laugh. "I saw you looking up my skirt outside the lawyer's office the other day Mr. Sturges. Maybe you kept things kosher while Rupert was alive – but are you trying to tell me you're not the slightest bit interested now? Jeez, keep a girl's hopes alive, Bill, even if you don't mean it."

"I never know when you're serious and when you're teasing. But I meant what I said outside about good-looking chicks: you're gorgeous and you know it. A man would have to be dead two weeks not to be interested in you."

"Hah! So you've been mad for me all along. The real Bill Sturges reveals himself at last."

He hadn't expected the conversation to take this turn, and he was tempted to follow it to its logical conclusion, but he forced himself to change the subject.

"The police have determined for sure that Rupert was in China when he was killed," he said. "I meant to ask you the other day: do you have any idea what he might have been doing there?"

"I've been wondering when you'd get around to that." She hesitated for a moment. "Okay. Let me show you something." She turned to walk toward the stairs, but stopped and turned back. "That is, if you don't mind entering a lady's bedroom."

"You're not going to try to get me into bed, are you, Olivia?"

"There's an interesting thought," she said, starting again for the staircase.

They climbed the stairs, she in front, his eyes level with her perfectly proportioned behind and her well-muscled thighs. The line of a thong was visible beneath the thin fabric of her slacks, separating her buttocks and accentuating their roundness. The expanse of bare skin around her middle reminded him of the satin feel of her arm the other day, and he felt a tingling in his fingertips.

"Keep those hands where I can see them," she said over her shoulder. She laughed and led the way into the master bedroom. Sturges had only had an occasional glance through the open door when Rupert brought him up to the study on previous occasions, but he could see that the room was now totally redecorated. It was no longer a marital bedchamber, it was a woman's boudoir, soft, frilly, all whites and pastels and bright sunshine, redolent of perfumes and powders and a strong smell of incense. The four-poster bed was covered with a white net canopy, and the duvet was all but invisible beneath throw pillows covered in Thai silk. No Asian statue stood on the white-carpeted floor, no Chinese painting graced the walls. Instead, there were soft paintings of flowers, and some feminine bric-a-brac on the make-up table.

The only anomaly was a small, red, wooden shrine holding joss sticks in a jar of sand, sitting on a low wooden table in a corner of the room. The joss sticks were smoldering, which accounted for the scent of incense. Two framed photographs sat on the table next to the shrine, one of Rupert and the other of Olivia's father.

"That looks rather out of place in here," he said.

"Respect for one's ancestors," Olivia said. "It's only six weeks since my father died." She stared at the two photos for a moment. "I didn't think I'd be putting Rupert's photo here before I even took my father's down."

"This doesn't exactly fit with the image of a hard-nosed international banker," he said.

"The things you grow up with never leave you completely, do they?" she said. "It might be difficult for anyone who knows me now to accept, but I was brought up as a very traditional Chinese daughter. Respect for one's elders, reverence for one's ancestors. You can't turn learned behavior off just because you've gone to live amid another culture. Here, this is what I want to show you."

She had converted a walk-in closet into a work area, with phone, fax, a desktop computer and a printer. "This was Rupert's computer," she said as she took a seat. "I often used it here at home before he died. On the morning of August 24th – that's three days before he left for China, according to the police – I came to check my email and things. I started to type in a website address and one of those drop-down menus appeared at the top showing the sites he'd logged onto recently."

She showed him the list. Judging by their names, the sites all dealt with sex.

"Have you ever surfed sex on the web?" Olivia asked. "I took a little ride after I discovered what Rupert had been looking at. It was amazing. You go to one site, it has links to other sites. You click on those, and they take you to something brand new. I don't know much about computers but I do know how the Internet works, and I thought I knew just about everything when it came to sex, but some of the stuff I came across...I'm telling you Billy boy, there's a whole new world waiting out there."

"Did you make a habit of spying on your husband's Internet activity?" he asked.

"No," she said, "and that's not what I intended this time. But when I saw what he'd been browsing, I couldn't resist taking a peek."

She clicked on one of the addresses and a Chinese-language site appeared. She clicked again and a gallery of photographs filled the screen. They were only small thumbnail photos, but it was easy to see that they were all of young Asian women.

Sturges took the mouse and enlarged the first picture. The girl looked Chinese. She was seated with her face and torso toward the camera, and she was nude from the waist up, showing the breasts of a teenage girl. Hardly more than bumps. Just the type Rupert reportedly liked in his younger days. "Jesus," Sturges said. He clicked on several more photos and they all had the same format. When he looked more closely he saw that the photos had captions in Chinese giving the girls' names and ages.

"This was one of the websites you came across in your research?"

"No, this was one that Rupert had bookmarked himself."

"I don't suppose you know why he was looking at these photos."

"I can only guess. But when I found all this, I began looking through the rest of the computer to see what else might be there." She went to the computer's *pictures* folder and clicked again, and the same gallery of photos appeared on the screen. "He obviously downloaded these off that website. I'm afraid to guess why he did it."

Afraid with good reason. The potential ramifications were not something one would normally discuss with a man's widow, but it was clear they were both thinking the same thing.

"But it doesn't make sense, does it?" Sturges said. "Here's a man who, let's be honest, who was not really capable of sex...I mean...in recent years..."

When she said nothing, he took a breath and resumed: "Or, well, so he sort of indicated to me a couple of times. Anyway, my point is, back when he *was* interested..." He stopped again, wondering if he was digging himself into a hole he wouldn't be able to climb out of. "I'm uncomfortable bringing this up, Olivia, but I have to assume you know about Rupert's somewhat odd tastes. Don't you? Before you and he got together, I mean?"

"I heard some things about Rupert when I was growing up, yes."

"Well I heard a *lot* of things as I grew up," Sturges said. "The point being, as far as I know, Rupert never used to be interested in, shall we say, 'mature' women."

"By 'mature' you mean a girl older than fifteen or sixteen."

"Then you do know about that." No need to tiptoe around the subject any longer. "Yes, the girls in these photos were more his type – back then." He turned back to the computer. "And judging by the faces, I'd say these are all Chinese girls," he said. "Not only that: look at the faces closely. At least two-thirds of them are northern faces. That suggests that the pictures came from the mainland."

"Then this could be a clue to what he was doing in China – couldn't it?" she said.

"You mean Rupert might have snuck across the border to spend time with teenage girls? It's no secret that young girls are still bought and sold on the mainland the way they have been for centuries. I'm sure there's more than one online service today offering underage girls. But why would the old bastard, after all these years...?" He had to stop himself again. "Have you told the police about the photos?"

"God, no! I'd be mortified if anyone else saw them. You can imagine what it would be like if this ever became public knowledge. Even if there's some innocent explanation, there would be talk. Most of the people who knew Rupert in his younger days are dead or have moved away, but I'm sure there are still a few around who knew of his old habits. I don't want to hand them fresh justification for tittering behind my back, and I certainly wouldn't want to let the entire city in on such a secret."

She was speaking more frankly than he'd ever heard before. Maybe she was finally ready to open up completely. "I just can't see it," he said. "I mean, here was a man who, for reasons that frankly nobody can understand, found himself married to one of the most gorgeous, enticing women in all of Hong Kong. The thought that *your* husband would have to surf the Internet for sex..."

She turned her head to avoid his gaze. "A lot of people would like to understand our marriage, wouldn't they?" she said.

"That's putting it mildly. Look, tell me if I'm overstepping any bounds here, but I'm only repeating what people have been saying for years. Your marriage was a huge mystery to everyone." He waited, but she said nothing. He'd handed her the ball and she'd refused to run with it. "If I've offended you I'll drop the subject," he said. "Tell me to take my Morgan and go."

"There are a lot of busybodies in this town," she said. "I'm not including you in that description, by the way."

Another non-answer. "Okay," he said, "I'm going to ask you straight out Olivia: why did you and Rupert get married? Nobody could ever figure it out. *I* could never figure it out, and I think I knew him better than anyone. You admit you 'heard things' about him when you were young, so you had an idea of what you were getting into. Please, explain the mystery."

She stood and moved toward him until their bodies were almost touching. "I like you, Bill," she said, running the backs of her fingers across his cheek. "I've always liked you."

"I like you, too, Olivia. But that's not—"

"We're not talking about drinking buddies here. The topic of the moment is sexual attraction."

He tried to appear in control, without much success. "Go on," he croaked.

"Let me ask you a question. Suppose I offered you a choice: I'll tell you about Rupert and me, or I'll let you take me to bed. Which would you choose?"

He reached out a hand, and when she didn't stop him he ran his fingertips over the bare skin of her belly, and again the sensation was electric. "Are you giving me that choice?" he asked.

"It's just a hypothetical," she said. "I'm still a grieving widow; sex wouldn't be appropriate at this moment, don't you agree?"

"The only thing I'll agree to right now is that I'm totally confused," he said. "That taking-you-to-bed thing: that was really just hypothetical?"

"A what-if, yeah."

"Then my answer will wait until the offer is serious," he said. "But I'd still like *my* question answered...about you and Rupert."

She grabbed both his hands. "Later, I promise. Just give me some time: I'm still trying to digest everything that's happened." The limits of candor had been reached for the moment. She planted a kiss on his lips, and this time there was no question about where she had aimed it. "Let's have lunch."

He sighed and let her lead him to the stairs. "At least answer my original question before we eat," he said. "Can you think of any other reason why Rupert would have gone to China? When you first learned of his death, and before you discovered the photos of the young girls, I mean: did any possibility occur to you?"

"My assumption was that it was some newspaper thing."

"Yeah, that's the obvious assumption. But a couple of people I've spoken to in the last few days said Rupert had been hinting just before he died that he was about to score some major piece of art on the China side. Did anything he said to you over the last few months suggest, even in retrospect, that that's what he'd been planning?"

"He didn't say anything to me about that," she said. "Antiques were his great passion, of course, so it would make sense."

She turned, and now there was urgency in her voice. "He and I obviously didn't have the most normal of marriages, and we didn't share secrets," she said. "But I don't want to see him humiliated, Bill. Or myself. I'd love to learn that some antique was the only thing he'd gone to China for."

~

So, Sturges thought as he left the house: there were now three theories about what Rupert was doing in China. The original thought, that he had gone in search of a story. Two, that he had crossed the border to buy antiques. And now, three, that he'd gone for shabby sex.

Given Rupert's age and his physical condition, one of the first two seemed far more likely. Sturges definitely preferred those two. He'd hate to have to report that his old friend had been shot while diddling a teenage girl. But those photos on the computer were hard to ignore: the old boy had downloaded them for some reason.

He still didn't know the secret of the Rackley marriage, but he knew more than he had known two hours earlier. Olivia admitted that she knew of Rupert's predilection for teenage girls before she married him. According to men like Jackson Liu, she was very fond of sex herself. She had to realize, in other words, that her prospective husband was probably not going to be scratching that itch of hers...and still she married him. Why? Okay, there's more to life and marriage than sex – but where was the attraction in this case? What did the two possibly have in common?

Very little on the surface. And indeed, the gossip had always been that Olivia was fooling around while Rupert was still alive. Evelyn Chin heard that same gossip just before the murder. When Sturges had pressed her, Chin revealed that a friend of hers had seen Olivia talking to Ricco Tang in the lobby of a hotel in Macau a few weeks earlier. That by itself didn't prove anything, the two could have run into each other while visiting one of the new Las Vegas-style casinos. But where murder is involved, the most mundane of acts becomes suspicious. Olivia's and Ricco's own words only added to the suspicion.

When Sturges had spoken to Ricco a few days earlier, Ricco was at pains to say he hardly knew Olivia, yet his parting comment on the phone was that his wife "really hates it when I talk about Olivia Chen." That suggested that he spoke about Olivia a lot – and if he spoke *about* her a lot, wasn't it possible that he also spoke *to* her a lot? Olivia just said she hadn't spoken to Ricco Tang "for several weeks." She said it in a way that suggested that she spoke to him with some regularity.

Maybe Olivia had been sleeping with Ricco or some other married men while Rupert was still alive. If so, might the wife of one of Olivia's lovers, wounded by her husband's infidelity, have taken revenge on Olivia...by killing Rupert?

That made no sense. If the fact that your husband is boffing another woman drives you to violence, you kill the boffee, not the boffee's spouse. It was true that insane jealousy did not always make for logical thinking, but this would have been...

Nonsense, in all probability. The ravings of his fevered mind. The closeness of Olivia, her sexual innuendoes – she had said it right out, after all: *The topic of the moment is sexual attraction*; *What if I let you take me to bed*? Sex wouldn't be appropriate *at this moment*. Maybe it was just sophisticated banter on her part, but he'd heard the words, and it was a hard thought to put back into the bottle. The whole thing was fogging his brain.

As he rattled and jolted his way home in the Morgan, enjoying the looks of appreciation the car received from people he passed, another thought occurred to him. The captions on those photos on Rupert's computer: the writing was in the simplified characters that the communists had devised in the 1950s. That didn't prove Rupert had gone to the mainland to meet one of the girls, but it was powerful evidence that the photos had originated on that side. Simplified characters were hardly used anywhere but in the P.R.C., which added to the complexities of the Chinese language.

As if the Chinese language needed any more complexity than it already had.

Fourteen

As a news story, Rupert's murder was fading. With little in the way of solid new facts to report and with speculation having run its course, the media were starting to turn their attention elsewhere.

Sturges refused to give up. He left a message for Ross, hoping for some new development, and began skimming the on-line edition of the newspaper while he waited for the call to be returned.

Another major milestone in the Chinese economic miracle: the economy had expanded almost eleven percent in the previous quarter. At this rate it would soon catch the U.S. as the world's largest economy.

Another major riot in the Chinese countryside: thousands of villagers in Hunan province poisoned by an illegal chemical factory set up by local Party leaders. Would the country hold together until the leadership could bring it fully into the modern world?

Another new law passed. Bit by bit, the government was enacting modern legislation on legal reform, civil rights, environmental protection, building toward a nation of laws.

Another person thrown into prison on bogus charges for having questioned government policy. Modern legislation was all well and good as long as it didn't conflict with the interests of the Party. China remained a nation of men, not laws.

Another...mistake in the newspaper. "Dammit!" he growled. "How many times do I have to tell them?"

He walked to the door and scanned the heads in the newsroom. "Quinn!" he shouted. The head of Colin Quinn, one of the paper's young reporters, swiveled in the direction of the voice. Sturges waved him into the office.

"So, Colin," Sturges said, "how's it going?" The young Briton had arrived in Hong Kong only three months earlier, to help keep up the native-English-speaker quotient among the predominately Chinese staff.

"Getting it sorted out," Quinn said with more confidence than his voice betrayed. "It's a bit of a blur. Especially the names. I'm still trying to figure out the difference between Tsim Sha Tsui and Tai Kok Tsui," he said, grievously mispronouncing both.

"That's actually why I called you in," Sturges said. "I was just reading your story about Hong Kong opening a trade office in Nanjing."

A look of unease flashed across Quinn's face. "Did I get something wrong?" he asked.

"Yeah, you did." Sturges pointed to Quinn's story on the computer screen. "You wrote...here it is: you wrote, '...*Nanjing, whose name was changed from Nanking...*'"

Quinn's face was blank. "And?"

"Well, see, the name wasn't changed. It's only the romanized spelling of the name that was changed."

"The romanized spelling?" Quinn repeated.

"The spelling of a Chinese word using the Roman alphabet."

"Why would anyone change the spelling?"

"Do you know anything about the Chinese language?" Sturges asked.

"God no!" Quinn said, this time with unalloyed fear. "Don't tell me I'm expected to learn that, too."

"Relax," Sturges said. "A lot of Westerners have lived here twenty or thirty years without ever learning much more Chinese than their home address. But you're going to be using a lot of names in your stories, and for that you do need to understand some basic facts about the language." *As if I don't have enough to worry about*, he thought.

"I'll keep this as simple as possible," he told Quinn. "I assume you know first of all that Chinese doesn't use an alphabet like the Western languages do to spell out words. For the most part, each individual character represents a whole word. There are also a lot of compound words. The characters *dian* and *hua*, for example, individually mean 'electric' and 'speech.' Put them together, *dianhua*, and you have the Chinese word for 'telephone.' Are you with me so far?"

Quinn nodded.

"Next, every Chinese word has an integral tone – rising, falling, high, low, dipping. If you don't include the tone as you say the word, if your voice doesn't rise or fall as you utter the sound, you literally haven't said anything; to a Chinese person, if the tone is not included, it simply is not a word. The Mandarin dialect has four tones. Cantonese has seven or eight – there's a debate among linguists about the exact number. If you utter the right sound but the wrong tone, you've said something completely different from what you meant to say. The word *bai* with a falling tone" – Sturges's voice fell as he spoke, like the sound of an airplane in a steep dive – "means something completely different from *bai* with a rising tone.

"And third," he said, "the way a given character is pronounced changes depending on the speaker's dialect."

147

"Like Mandarin and Cantonese," Quinn said, happy to contribute something meaningful to the conversation.

"Those are two of the dialects, yes. There are seven or eight major dialects, plus hundreds of sub-dialects. Which means there are all sorts of ways that a given character might be pronounced, and that includes the characters for names. Mr. *Wong* of Hong Kong would be known as Mr. *Wang* or Mr. *Huang* in Beijing. Mr. *Xiang* of Beijing would be called Mr. *Heung* here."

Quinn made a face somewhere between skepticism and horror. "It's not a very efficient way to communicate, is it?" he said. "Why don't they switch to an alphabet?

"They do sometimes," Sturges said. "That is, Chinese words can be written using our Roman alphabet. That's what I meant about romanizing a word. But there's more than one system, so the same word can be romanized different ways."

"Does any of this have anything to do with Nanjing?" Quinn asked. He looked like he was close to tears.

"I'm getting to that," Sturges said. "The standard romanization system used outside China until about twenty-five years ago was the Wade-Giles system. Unfortunately, Wade-Giles frequently gives an inaccurate idea of how the Chinese word is actually pronounced, because it's a hodge-podge of Mandarin and Cantonese sounds. Like the city you wrote about: 'Nan-king,' which used to be the standard romanization of the city's name, is a combination of Mandarin and Cantonese sounds. Chinese speakers wouldn't actually say 'Nan-king.' The Cantonese pronounce the characters '*Nam*-king.' It's 'Nan-*jing*' to a Mandarin speaker. Nanjingers themselves pronounce it either 'Nan-jing' or '*Lan*-jing.'"

"My God," Quinn said.

"Frightening, isn't it?" Sturges was about to continue when his phone rang, and Ross's phone number came scrolling across the phone's face. Finally. "Excuse me," he said, "this might be important." Then, into the phone: "It's about time you called."

"I've had a pisser of a day," Ross said.

"I can't wait to hear all about it," Sturges said. "I have someone with me right now, but let me call you back in a—"

"I won't be able to tell you anything," Ross said. He sounded weary.

"I was actually being facetious," Sturges said. "You haven't had anything new to tell me for more than a week now."

"Well I'm being bloody serious," Ross said. "I'm off the case."

"You're what? It's your case. How the hell can they take you off it?"

"Not just me. All of us. The Hong Kong Police are off the case." Before Sturges could speak, Ross said, "Look, I can't talk right now either. Are you free later? Maybe dinner?"

"Absolutely," Sturges said. "Where and when?"

"How about the Yacht Club?" Ross asked. "It's my turn to treat."

"Seven p.m.?"

"Make it 7:30. I should be finished with my work then – assuming I still have a job by the end of the day."

"It's that serious?"

"I might have said some intemperate things when my superiors gave me the word."

Ross hung up and Sturges stood staring at the phone. "Is everything all right?" It was Quinn's voice. Sturges had forgotten the reporter was in the room.

"I'm not sure," Sturges said. "Sorry, what were we talking about?"

"You were saying that Wade-Giles is no longer the standard transliteration system."

"Right. Well, the communists came up with a somewhat better system, which they call *Pinyin*, and that's been creeping into international usage since the 1970s."

Sturges picked up a notebook and wrote several names. "Going from Wade-Giles to pinyin, '*Mao Tse-tung*' becomes '*Mao Zedong.*' '*Chou En-lai*' becomes '*Zhou Enlai*' and '*Teng Hsiao-p'ing*' becomes '*Deng Xiaoping.*' They're exactly the same names, they're renditions of exactly the same characters, and they're pronounced exactly the same. They're just romanized differently.

"It's the same with your story today: "Nan-*king*" was the accepted transliteration outside China for many decades; "Nan-*jing*" is the modern pinyin transliteration. You were wrong to write that the *name* Nanking was changed to Nanjing. Nothing has changed except the romanized spelling. Is it clear now?"

"I guess," Quinn said. He scratched his head, trying to digest everything he'd just heard. "So the only way to be sure is to learn the characters?" he said.

"Theoretically yes, but even that presents problems. When the Communists conquered China the population was essentially illiterate. To speed up instruction in reading and writing they removed some of the strokes in about a thousand characters to – in theory – make them easier to learn. They also invented some brand new ones, and the changes are known as 'simplified' characters."

"Did it work?"

"China is now estimated to have ninety percent literacy," Sturges said, "but whether changing those relatively few characters made any difference is a matter of debate. Meanwhile, a lot of mainlanders can't read much of what's published outside China, which is all in classic characters, and most outsiders can't read the simplified characters."

"Crikey," Quinn said. "Where does that leave a poor foreign devil like me?"

"It leaves you in difficulty," Sturges said. But Quinn's difficulties, he thought, were nothing compared to those of a foreign devil named Brian Ross. "At least you now know the difference between the names Nanking and Nanjing," he said. "Which is to say, there isn't any.

"And now if you'll excuse me," he said, showing Quinn to the door, "I have a very important dinner date to keep."

Fifteen

The Royal Hong Kong Yacht Club. The venue Bill Sturges and Brian Ross had chosen to address the harsh realities of the present. A sublime evocation of South China's romantic past.

The club was founded in the early years of the colony. For expatriates born there, like Bill Sturges, and those who came to live there, like Brian Ross, colonial Hong Kong had been a real-world Neverland, a name to excite the imagination of all who dreamt of faraway places, an island of exotic tranquility in a sea of intrigue and turmoil. Such people commonly lived on generous expat packages. Most had live-in housekeepers to cook and clean and take care of the children. Many owned sailing yachts or converted fishing junks, which they used for weekend outings to the surrounding islands. They ate lavishly, drank hard, and played hard. "Borrowed Place, Borrowed Time" was how they described it, in the days before anyone gave much thought to when the borrowing would have to be repaid.

For the Chinese, colonial Hong Kong was less a place of romance than of practicality. From the start, the enclave was an orderly refuge in which to do business and raise a family; in the decades between 1949 and 1976, it was a safe haven from the madness of Maoist China.

Still, anything "royal" smacked of the colonial master, and resentment had always lingered not far below the surface. To the Chinese, the Rosses and Sturgeses were *gwei-lo*, "ghost people" or "devil people," barbarians from outside the embrace of all-superior Chinese culture.

The *gwei-los* knew they had a very good thing going, and a bit of quiet opprobrium from the natives was not going to ruin that. They happily applied the pejorative term to themselves, with the kind of ironic self-mockery the Chinese could never understand. Sitting on the deck of their boats after a swim and a lavish lunch, watching the sun set over the South China Sea while their Chinese boat boys served them gin-and-tonics, the foreigners would turn to one another with a smile that was instantly recognizable to anyone living the life. "*Ahhh,*" they would sigh. "Another shitty day in paradise."

As Sturges now strode to meet Ross on the Yacht Club's outdoor deck, bracketed on both sides of the harbor by skyscrapers that lit the nighttime sky, with the waves of passing ships lapping softly against the sea wall, a vision of that past came rushing back, and in his mind's eye he could picture Hong Kong as it had been in the day.

But that day, he knew, was irrevocably gone. The *gwei-los* had come to terms with their new reality – which meant among other things that an investigation into the murder in Hong Kong of a British subject could be shut down with a simple word from faraway Beijing.

~

Ross was feeling anything but romantic when Sturges found him, seated at an isolated table on the deck, half illuminated by the lights blazing inside the clubhouse.

"Why?" was the first word out of Sturges's mouth as he took a seat.

"He's not here," Ross said. "I thought we *gwei-los* should talk alone."

"I wasn't asking about Winston. I meant *why* was the investigation shut down?"

"The obvious. Everyone knows Rupert was killed in China. We've exhausted every lead we could come up with on this side of the border, which is precious little, as you know. The Chinese have made it clear they're not going to invite us over to their side again to continue the investigation. In the view of my superiors – officially speaking – there is nothing further that the Hong Kong Police can contribute to the matter. We are to remain vigilant for new information, of course, but in the meantime, we are ordered to stand down. '*A drain on manpower that could be better utilized elsewhere*' is how it will be put in the official announcement tomorrow morning."

"And unofficially?"

"People in power across the border simply don't want us to pursue the case, as you and I guessed early on. Full stop."

"So the investigation is now completely in the hands of the Shenzhen Police?"

"Officially, yes."

"Who can be expected to do..."

"Fuck-all. I haven't heard a word from them since I paid them that visit just after the murder happened. I didn't expect much, but I thought they'd at least pretend they were making some effort."

"I know you're pissed off, but do you think your superiors might have a point? To be frank, you and your men haven't exactly been breaking the case wide open."

"Are you asking me that question on the record?"

"Would you answer me if I were?"

"Absolutely not. I value what's left of my job. Although – bloody hell: I'm fifty-five in a year. I could retire now with almost a full pension. I might just do it, and God damn them all."

"Let's hope we can find out what happened to Rupe before you do," Sturges said. "Off the record, then: how do you feel about being pulled off the case like this?"

"It's a bloody fucking disgrace," Ross said. "Rupert was one of ours." A burst of laughter came from the clubhouse, where a party was in noisy progress. "One of *theirs*," Ross said, gesturing toward the source of the noise. "He was a cantankerous old fart, and a perverted one on top of that, he'd pissed off everybody and his *amah* on both sides of the border, and for all we know he was up to something illegal or underhanded just before he died. But he was a Hongkonger, and he stood up for our rights while our politicians and big businessmen were happily stripping them away on behalf of the central government. We owe it to him to try to find out who killed him."

"I assume you made that argument to your superiors?"

Ross grunted.

"Do you know who gave the order for the case to be dropped?" Sturges asked.

"The higher-ups in the department know I've been talking to you up to now," Ross said. "If they read any of this in the *Mail* I'll be deader than old Rupert."

"Nothing will appear, I promise," said Sturges. He realized as he said it that the two men had found the common ground they had sought from the start. He'd even begun to suspect that he liked Ross as a person. "This conversation," he assured Ross, "is strictly off the record."

Ross finished his whisky and motioned to one of the aged Chinese waiters. "I'm drinking eighteen-year-old Macallan," he said to Sturges. "Does that come up to your American standards?"

"So you're finally showing me through the single malts," Sturges said. "It's about time. Yes, I think I can suffer with eighteen-year-old Macallan."

"You know," Ross said, looking him in the eye, "for a journalist, you're not too terribly bad a bloke. I'd almost go so far as to say you were a decent human being. Two more of these, please," he told the waiter. When the old man had shuffled out of hearing range, Ross turned back to Sturges and said: "The order to drop the case came directly from the mainland."

"You know that for a fact?"

Ross nodded.

"Who exactly?"

"That I don't know, but an order like this only comes from high up."

"Were you at least told why they chose now to make this decision? I was serious when I said you weren't getting anywhere with the investigation. With no new revelations coming out, the media here have been losing interest in the story. The Chinese could have waited another week or two and the thing would have died a natural death."

"Again, I can only guess. At first, it was too hot a story: there was nothing Beijing could do to stop the Hong Kong media from swarming all over it. They couldn't even have tried to squelch it without raising a firestorm about freedom of the press here. But now, as you say, the story has cooled down, and they probably figure the public is getting tired of it. I'm guessing the powers-that-be think that whatever information is still dribbling out has been originating with us coppers, and this is their way of plugging any residual leaks once and for all."

"Which only reinforces our suspicion that there's something about the case that they're desperate to keep secret."

"I'm convinced of it even if I have absolutely nothing to prove it," said Ross. "At least," he said, "we'll now have those bastards off our backs."

"Which particular bastards would that be?"

"You have to pay attention, Sturges. I told you we keep getting calls from important people. Somebody from State Security started calling immediately after Rupert was killed. Then they started calling the chief of police to pass messages to me. I've never spoken to any of them personally, but we keep getting requests for information. I assume whoever it is will now leave us alone."

"And if you do come across some new information?"

"We're to pass it on to Shenzhen PSB and return to our own duties."

The waiter returned with their drinks. Sturges stared into his for a long moment after the waiter left. "Something's on your mind," Ross said.

"I'm having a debate with myself," Sturges replied. "You see, I actually do have a bit of new information. It's speculative to a large degree and it's partially contradictory, like just about everything we've uncovered so far. But I feel like I might be closing in on why Rupe went to China."

"So what's the debate about?"

"I'm debating whether to share the information with you. I'm wondering, given this new state of affairs, if you'd really have to pass what I tell you on to the PSB. I wouldn't want that to happen before I published anything."

"You have a point," Ross said. "If I were you I wouldn't tell me jackshit." He snorted as the phrase left his lips. "I'm beginning to sound like a bloody Yank," he said.

"Even if you can't follow up officially, though," Sturges said, "you could still ask the odd question on an informal basis, couldn't you? That badge gives you access and powers of persuasion that we civilians don't have. I'm thinking that with what I might learn, and what you have the ability to pry out of people..."

"You're suggesting we continue to work the case together. Unofficially."

"That's what we've been doing all along, isn't it?"

"Aye, but there's risk in it now for both of us. If I'm caught violating these new orders I could end up with my arse in a sling. Officially. And you'd best be careful, laddie: it's clear some pretty powerful people don't want this story told – whatever this story is."

Sturges waved off the suggestion. China controlled its own journalists with an iron hand, and it occasionally made life difficult for Hong Kong Chinese reporters when they ventured to the mainland. But foreign correspondents like Sturges were rarely interfered with, and never physically harmed. "Anyway, remember, this is more than business for you and me. Rupert was a friend of ours. You said it yourself: we owe it to the old boy. If you were discreet, nobody else in the department would have to know if you turned over a rock or two for a quick look. I might be able to point out some likely rocks."

Ross pursed his lips and nodded his head. "I want the answers as much as you do. Even if we can't bring the killer to justice, I'd like to know how it happened. And we're just a couple of mates trying to satisfy our curiosity, right?" He lifted his glass. "So...Bill: to Rupert Rackley. Damn the Communists, whom he hated with so much passion. And damn the sniveling cowards here in Hong Kong who so willingly do their bidding."

"To Rupert...Brian," Sturges said, matching the salute.

They drained their glasses, and Ross again signaled for the waiter. "Tell me then, laddie," he said as they waited. "What's this new information of yours?"

Sturges proceeded to recount what he had pieced together so far: indications that Rupert had gone to China in search of some piece of art; an undefined relationship between Ricco and Olivia. He did not mention Olivia's suspicion that Rupert had gone to renew his old obsession with young girls. If that turned out to be the case, Sturges would eventually have to tell Ross about it, and he'd have to write about it, too, but he wasn't about to besmirch his old friend's reputation unless he was sure of his facts.

"Right," Ross said when Sturges finished. "As you said, all very speculative. But at least it gives us several leads to follow. Perhaps we can make some sense of this after all."

Sixteen

On returning from his visit to Nanjing in 1950, Chang Dongfeng resumed his position as an archivist in the General Office. Few people in China had ever heard of the General Office or knew what it did, and fewer still would have any way of knowing who worked there — in a society where even the weather report was considered a state secret, Party functions carried the highest security classification. A position that almost nobody knew about, in a department whose existence was top secret, was the perfect cover for his new assignment, the cataloguing of the Palace Museum treasures.

The task was overwhelming in size and complexity. Identifying the provenance of hundreds of thousands of items, many of which were thousands of years old, took an enormous amount of time. In some cases, to be sure, identification was provided. Paintings bore the calligraphy and chop of the artist. Porcelains and snuff bottles were often imprinted with the seal of the emperor in power at the time the piece was produced. During some reigns, certain colors were reserved for imperial use, and certain ancient glazes had never been recreated, and these also provided reliable identification marks. In other cases, though, if identification had ever existed, it had been lost during the centuries of storage in the Forbidden City or the years of transporting and hiding the treasures from the Japanese and Communist armies.

Despite the obstacles, Chang was ordered to confirm identification and authenticity whenever possible. Millennia before anyone had conceived of digital video disks or Louis

Vuitton handbags, the Chinese had perfected the art of making expert forgeries.

Experts in different eras, different types of art and individual artists were called in to help. Long discussions ensued. Chang's team examined and debated under the impatient eye of Party officials, and the stress at times was extreme. But with it all there were moments of exhilaration, when some new piece of surpassing delicacy was freed from its wrappings for the first time in decades and the staff would gather round to admire its beauty. All in all, after several productive years, Chang could tell himself that the project was going well.

He could not say as much for the People's Republic of China.

The euphoria of the revolution had lasted hardly longer than it took for the Party to ensconce itself in Beijing. Fear quickly took its place. The Party controlled every aspect of an individual's being. People hunkered down in response, trying to make themselves as invisible as possible. The traditional Chinese reluctance to take responsibility under any circumstances was exacerbated by fear of being denounced if a project went sour; the safest course was to do only what was expressly ordered. People waited for the Party newspaper, *Renmin Ribao*, the People's Daily, to come out each morning, and parroted the political line of the day. Whether or not it made sense was irrelevant. Like hundreds of millions of their fellow citizens, Chang and his colleagues went about their assigned tasks, asking no questions, volunteering nothing.

Still, Chang had access through his position and his contacts to more information than his inferior rank would theoretically allow. From discussions with colleagues and documents passing through his hands in his archivist position, he could see how comrades in powerful positions were taking the best of everything for themselves even as they mouthed slogans about equality. He could see how production figures sent to Beijing from the provinces were being falsified to meet official quotas and make regional leaders look good.

He was distressed by the hypocrisy. He told himself: Chairman Mao would rectify the problems and punish the guilty...if only he knew what was going on. But to speak out in this climate would be to commit suicide. Like everyone else, he watched silently while the rot to set in.

~

In 1957, the possibility of reform appeared.

Mao launched the "Double Hundreds" campaign, urging people to speak their minds. "Let a hundred flowers bloom," Mao said, encouraging candor and criticism of the Party and its policies. "Let a hundred schools of thought contend."

Slowly at first, and then with increasing confidence, individuals began to vent their frustrations. They spoke them aloud at party meetings, or wrote them on *dazibao*, big-character posters, which they stuck up on walls for others to read. Some writers were circumspect. Others openly questioned policy.

Amazingly, nobody was being punished. But Chang Dongfeng, with a caution born of experience, kept his counsel. Still, as the criticisms continued for week after week, ever more open and ever more bold, he wondered: might this be the chance to expose the abuses he knew about? Might he publish what he knew to help the Chairman?

Chang was particularly distressed at the state of agriculture. Large gains in grain production were being reported routinely in the documents flowing into the General Office, but the Communist system discouraged telling a superior anything the superior did not want to hear. If the five-year plan called for a hundred tons to be produced, a hundred tons – or more – were reported, even if the real figure was only half that much. Eliminating obvious exaggerations in the reports and extrapolating from the rest, Chang realized that the food situation in the country was actually deteriorating. His research showed that grain harvests under communism were smaller than during the years of Japanese occupation.

To possess such information was dangerous. Even more dangerous was his discovery of the main reason for the decline: Mao's policy of forcing the peasants into collectives.

When collectivization was formally introduced the previous year, peasants began slaughtering their animals instead of turning them over to the collectives, because selling the meat brought far more than the collectives paid for a live animal. That left a shortage of animals to pull the plows. Women began to hitch themselves to yokes to turn the fields. China's age-old system of agriculture had been disrupted, and famine started to appear in the countryside. Mao's policy, Chang realized, was a failure.

No one who recognized the burgeoning disaster had been brave enough to question the Chairman's wisdom. So after weeks of agonizing, Chang decided that he must be the one to sound the warning. He drafted a *dazibao* providing specific examples of falsification and corruption. He wrote with more circumspection than many of his colleagues had shown since the openness campaign began, but when he read what he had written, the truth was there for all to see: China's peasants were being exploited and abused as they had been over thousands of years of history. A revolution ostensibly waged to eliminate such abuse had changed nothing.

Chang didn't sign his poster. He hung it late at night when there was no one around to see. Even in this air of openness, it was foolhardy to let others know what one thought.

~

The backlash to the Double Hundreds campaign was sudden and merciless. It mattered not whether Mao had been surprised by the torrent of abuse the campaign had unleashed, or whether he had set out from the start to trap his detractors. Anyone who had dared to publish criticisms was accused of "right deviationism."

As usual, the Chairman did not define his terms, so "rightism" became whatever an accuser wanted to make of it. In the end, a rightist was anyone who had the misfortune to be accused, whether or not the person was guilty of anything at all. Like production figures, offenders were created to fill quotas. Personal scores were settled. Nobody was safe. Those careless enough leave a denunciation meeting to use the toilet returned to find that they'd become "toilet rightists," denounced for made-up crimes while they were out of the room and unable to defend themselves.

Millions were accused. Hundreds of thousands of those were persecuted for their ostensible crimes, torn from the lives they knew and shipped off to the countryside to do brutal manual labor and "learn from the masses" how to be good communists.

Chang realized as soon as the backlash began that he should have heeded his initial caution. His family background already made him an easy mark: in this paranoid atmosphere he was at risk of being accused no matter what. By speaking out, he had as much as invited disaster.

He learned he'd been fingered when Wang Sheyu, his immediate superior in the General Office and one of the most egregious of toadying falsifiers, arrived in the cataloguing office with three subordinates in tow. "Your anti-Party crimes have been discovered, comrade Dongfeng," Wang said.

"I have done nothing wrong," Chang protested.

"Really?" the man said. "You thought you could disguise your deviationist tendencies by failing to sign your *dazibao*, did you?" The confidence in his voice indicated that the verdict had already been decided. "But we all know your calligraphy, comrade. It is so distinctive." His face darkened. "It is so...bourgeois. Your class origins betray you."

"I have renounced my background. Chairman Mao personally absolved me of any guilt while we were in Yanan. My record of service to the Party is spotless."

"You have renounced your background?" Wang said. "Then what is this?" He reached into his shirt and pulled out a photograph. It was the picture of Jacob Chang, Dongfeng's father, that Dongfeng had taken from the Nanjing house before his escape from the Japanese in 1937.

Chang turned red with rage. His voice shook so violently he could hardly speak. "You have invaded my home and stolen my property," he said.

"You seem to have forgotten, comrade," the superior said, "that all property is the property of the people. And the fact that you keep a photograph of this class enemy" – he waved the photo of Chang's father in the air – "proves that your denunciations of your family have been lies. It is no surprise, however: once a bourgeois, always a bourgeois."

"Ask the minister of culture," Chang said. "He knows I have been loyal to the Party. Any criticism I made was only meant to inform the Chairman and strengthen the Party."

Wang laughed out loud this time. "The minister of culture has been exposed as one of the chief right-deviationists in the Party," he said. "He has been stripped of his position and his Party membership. He is probably on his way right now to some commune in Gansu, where he will have his rightist soul re-educated by the masses."

Chang swallowed hard as the full import of the man's words sank in. Argument was futile. Rightism was any act that brought Mao's policies into question, and Chang had exposed the lies at the core of the Chairman's pet program. He rose and looked his accuser squarely in the eye. "I have only told the truth," he said. "The peasants are being robbed. People are starving. I have spoken out so that Chairman Mao could learn about lies and corruption and cure the country's weakness."

The words had hardly left his mouth before he realized they were identical to his father's assurances of twenty years earlier, that Chiang Kai-shek would solve China's problems. Then, China's problems went beyond the failure of any particular policy. Ambition and greed had been more important to Chiang and the Nationalists than whether the people had enough to eat. As Chang

Dongfeng faced his accusers now, the realization struck him that the same was true of Mao and the Communists.

For eighteen years, Chang had labored for China. He'd renounced his family and vilified his father, whom he secretly revered, in the name of the revolution. Once he became part of the power structure, he had watched silently as frauds were perpetrated on the people. He'd consoled himself with the conviction that the aim was a better and more just China, that the end justified the means.

As he now prepared to be transported to a new home somewhere in the remote countryside, the full weight of reality came crashing down. It had all been a lie. The Communists were no better than those who had come before them. Mao Tse-tung was a fraud. China was once again under the thumb of an oppressor and he, Chang Dongfeng, had helped to make it possible.

He refused to despair. He was tough: the Party had at least given him that much. He'd lived for years in a cave. He'd gone for months at a time with barely enough to eat. He'd been wounded in battle. He and his family would endure whatever awaited now. He would keep his head down and his mouth shut, and they would survive.

He and his newly pregnant wife packed the few belongings they would be allowed to take with them. They and their two young sons shouldered their meager packs, and waited for soldiers to take them away.

Seventeen

Ricco Tang's mobile phone rang. He snatched it off his desk and glanced at the incoming number. "Bill!" he shouted into the phone. "So tell me: have you gotten into Olivia's pants yet?"

"Where are you right now, Ricco?" Sturges asked.

"I'm in my office. What's up?"

"Can you talk freely?"

"Sure," Tang said. "I have no secrets."

"Really? Because I called to ask whether *you* have been getting into Olivia's pants?"

"What!" Tang yelped. "What kind of a question is that?"

"I'm a journalist, Ricco. We ask all kinds of unusual questions."

Tang leapt up and peeked into the hallway to make sure no one was eavesdropping. He slammed his office door shut, holding the phone close to his ear all the while. "But what would make you ask *that particular* question?" he said in a lowered voice.

"There's gossip about the two of you going around, that's what. I ask questions about Rupert and antiques, I get comments about you and his wife. Call me crazy, but I figure where there's smoke, there's fire."

"There's no fire!" Tang insisted. "There's not even any smoke!" He composed himself. "Have you had lunch yet? We can discuss this over lunch."

"I thought you'd never ask. What did you have in mind?

"How about Sichuan?"

"Sichuan sounds good. Where do you suggest?"

"Let's go to Man Jiang Hong. My driver will take us. Where are you now?"

"I'm walking along Wyndham Street, making my way down to Central."

"Wait in front of the Hong Kong Club. I'll drive by and pick you up in twenty minutes." Tang lowered his voice again. "And I haven't slept with Olivia. And for God's sake, please don't even *suggest* that in front of anyone else."

"I won't," Sturges said, "as long as you convince me it's not true. What kind of car do you have?"

"Dark blue Lexus. Brand new."

"You should see the Morgan that Rupert left me in his will. Almost twenty-five years old, but she looks like she just came off the assembly line."

"Look for my license plate," Tang said, ignoring the change of subject. "HK8898."

"Wow! That must have cost you a bundle, Ricco." The government regularly auctioned off license plates that were lucky or prestigious, and wealthy people like Tang paid small fortunes for them. This one, with the "HK" prefix and the plethora of lucky eights, was both. "I'm guessing, what: eight, ten million?"

"You don't want to know how much it cost," Tang said.

"Whatever it was I'm sure it was a ridiculous amount. Don't tell me you of all people believe that nonsense about lucky numbers?"

Tang hesitated, and when he spoke, his voice contained more resignation than conviction. "You don't want to muck about with fate," he said. "Besides, Claudia insisted. Her *feng shui* man told her it would be bad luck if I didn't buy the plate."

"You're kidding. You let some peddler of superstition dictate how you spend your money?"

"Would I lie to you?"

"I honestly don't know, Ricco," Sturges said, aiming himself down Ice House Street and toward the Hong Kong Club. "That's what I'm hoping to find out."

~

They ate *shui zhu rou pian*, boiled slices of pork swimming in a brown broth redolent of chilis. They had *la zi ji*, a blanket of bright red chilis with miniscule bits of fried chicken lurking amongst the peppers. As a sop to Sturges's acclimated but nevertheless western tastes, Tang ordered *gong pao ji ding*, kung pao chicken, with peanuts and spring onion and chilis, one of the few authentic Sichuan dishes to make its way intact to western palates. He also ordered *mao xue wang*, "bubbling blood," rectangles of coagulated duck's blood, pieces of duck's liver and pig's intestine, some pig's throat thrown in for added flavor, all served in a bubbling cauldron of fluorescent red oil laced with chilis and Sichuan peppercorns. The kind of seriously authentic Sichuan dish that somehow never made the hit parade in Los Angeles or London.

Tang plucked bits of innards out of the satanic broth and popped them into his mouth with a look of satisfaction, while Sturges wondered anew at the Chinese delight in eating anything that once moved. He looked around to make sure nobody could hear them. The nearest person was a lone man who had seated himself three tables away, and he was absorbed in a Chinese-language newspaper as he ate. "So you swear you haven't slept with Olivia?" Sturges asked.

"Never!" Tang said, wiping a dribble of chili oil from his chin and taking a slug from his second large bottle of Tsingtao beer. His already red face grew redder. "I swear. Shit, Bill, if Claudia ever caught me messing around she'd take a cleaver and chop my gonads into little pieces. Her *feng shui* master would probably help her."

"And they'd probably stir-fry the pieces with chilis and bean paste," Sturges said. "I've got to say, Ricco, I grew up here, I'm used to Chinese food that is nothing remotely like what people in the West are familiar with, but there are still things you Chinese eat that totally mystify me. Like abalone, which is like chewing a rubber eraser. Like shark's fin, which has no taste at all." He gestured at the *mao shue wang*. "Like this shit."

"It's our secret weapon," Tang said, stirring the chilis of the *La Zi Ji* with his chopsticks and extracting a tiny morsel of chicken on the bone. "This stuff gives us super-strong sperm. How do you think the Chinese population got so big?"

"You were spotted in Macau not long ago in the presence of Mrs. Rackley, Ricco. Are you sure you weren't swapping a little super sperm with her there?"

Tang laid his chopsticks across the edge of his plate. "How did you find out about out our meeting in Macau?"

"I told you: I ask questions, I get answers. Somebody saw the two of you there. Everybody from Hong Kong is going over to see those new super casinos: what did you think, you'd have privacy there? And if you and Olivia weren't exchanging bodily fluids, what were you doing there together? Neither of you is a gambler as far as I know."

"That's just it: we met in the lobby of one of the hotels – a public place. If we'd been having an affair, don't you think we would have been more discreet? Olivia wanted to discuss Rupert, that's all."

"Which means you and Olivia were closer than you let on when we spoke on the phone a week or two ago. Why didn't you tell me about all this before?"

"I didn't tell you for exactly this reason," Tang said. "I was afraid you'd jump to the wrong conclusions."

"Why did she want to discuss Rupert with you?"

"It had to do with antiques, of course." Tang paused a moment, drank some tea, pondered his next words: "Olivia told me that Rupert was going to China to pick up a very important piece. An illegal piece. And he was planning to carry it back himself. She said she knew it was dangerous for him to get involved in smuggling, and she thought that given our relationship, I might be able to talk him out of it."

Sturges slapped the table in anger. The man sitting nearby started at the noise and looked up briefly from his newspaper, then returned to his lunch. "Dammit, Ricco!" Sturges said. "I've spent days trying to pin down the fact that Rupert had gone to collect some piece of art, and here you knew the truth all along. You could have told me instead of giving me some bullshit about 'good news.'"

"I'm sorry," Tang said, staring into his *Mao Xue Wang*. "Olivia swore me to secrecy." Sturges looked away. "Bill?"

"Oh, eat your fucking boiled blood," Sturges said. "I'm thinking."

"I said I'm sorry," Tang mumbled.

Sturges didn't hear the apology. He was too busy trying to digest this latest bit of information. He should have been delighted at Tang's revelation. But Ricco said the information had come from Olivia: Olivia had told Ricco that Rupert was preparing to go to China for a piece of antique art.

How did that square with what she had told Sturges a couple of days earlier, that she feared Rupert was going for a piece of teenage ass?

Rupert could have been after both. But Olivia had specifically told Sturges that Rupert hadn't said anything to her about antiques. Why had she told Ricco one thing and Sturges exactly the opposite? She was lying to one of them, that was the only conclusion he could reach. And if she'd lied about something as important as the reason for Rupert's trip, what else had she lied about? Could he trust anything she said?

"So," he said to Tang, "she told you Rupe was going to cross the border to bring back a special piece of art, and she was worried that he might get into trouble doing it. Did she say where she got this information? Did she say Rupert had told her?"

"She didn't say it in so many words," Tang said, "but the way she phrased it, it could only have come from Rupert."

"Okay, then what: did you talk to Rupert like she asked?

"I tried to. I invited him to my office. I told him smuggling artifacts was a dangerous business and if he really wanted whatever he was after he should let some professional bring it into Hong Kong for him. But he became furious that Olivia had told me he was planning the trip. He accused me of having an illicit relationship with her. I told him he was wrong, but he told me to mind my own business and warned me to stay away from her. He – he said some pretty nasty things. And then, a couple of days later, we had that disagreement about Evelyn Chin's horse. That was the last time we spoke."

"And that's why he said the argument about the horse was 'the last straw?' "

"Evelyn told you about that, eh?" Tang hung his head. "Like I said, it would have been nice to get it straightened out between us before he died. We knew each other for years. We ate together, we drank together – bloody hell, we were friends."

"But he did at least confirm to you that he was going to pick up a piece of art?"

"Well, not in so many words, no," Tang said. "It's more a case of he didn't deny it. He just got angry when I brought it up, and then he stormed out. When we argued about the horse a short time later the subject of his trip to China never came up."

"Jesus Christ on a cross," Sturges said. "You're a fucking fount of non-information, Ricco. *'Olivia seemed to imply this.' 'Rupert didn't deny that.'* Did it ever occur to you ask any straight questions?"

"I told you, I was hoping Rupert would tell me all about the plan when he came to my office," Tang protested. "He never did. Did you ask Evelyn if she had any more information?"

"I did, and she didn't," Sturges said. "She suggested I talk to a guy named Giesler, but he's out of town and not due back for a week or two. Do you know him?"

"Of course I know him. I know everybody in town who's involved in antiques. You know I'm crazy about antiques, Bill. The thought that Rupert was after some monumental score really got my blood flowing. But he was just so furious that Olivia had told me about it. I mean, you don't want a friend to go to his grave angry at you, do you? If you have an argument with someone there's always the chance you can make amends. But if the person dies first...it's like the anger is set in stone forever."

Tang was looking for sympathy, but Sturges wasn't giving. "Ask Claudia's *feng shui* man to hang a mirror on you to deflect the anger," he said.

"You're mocking me, Bill. It's not your style."

"Rupert isn't the only one who was angry, Ricco. I'm angry too. I'd like to find out why my friend was killed, and if possible, who killed him. It seems a lot of people are trying to prevent me from doing that. I'd appreciate it if you weren't one of them."

~

They left the restaurant and Sturges refused Tang's offer of a ride. "I need some time by myself," he said.

"Check with Olivia," Tang shouted out the window as his car pulled away. "She'll back up what I told you. She made me promise not to tell anyone about Rupert's plans. I was just keeping my word. I'm the good guy here!"

"Yeah, I'm sure you are," Sturges said to Tang's multi-million-dollar license plate as it disappeared into the maelstrom of mid-afternoon traffic.

He watched it go, and an odd feeling of unease, almost dread, began to roil his insides. His stomach felt queasy. His head was pounding. Maybe the knowledge that Olivia had lied to him had set off another one of his uncontrolled rages. Or could it be something he ate in the restaurant? It wouldn't be the first time.

But no. He looked up, and there was the answer. Despite the early hour, the sky was darkening and the city was bathed in an unnatural half-light. Dragonflies were circling aimlessly. The humidity, which had abated in the past week, had returned with a vengeance, and now hung in the leaden air like a hot, damp cloth.

He punched a few buttons on his mobile phone to call up the weather: sure enough, a typhoon that had been heading north toward Taiwan for the past couple of days had veered westward, and was now near enough Hong Kong to cause typhoon signal number one to be issued. Signal number three, indicating that the typhoon had in moved in close, was expected to go up at any time. The Hong Kong Observatory did not expect a direct hit, but the proximity meant the storm's rain band would come near enough to drench the city for several days running.

The low air pressure that accompanied a storm like this was what was making him feel nauseous and unsettled. He always suffered when a typhoon was in the neighborhood. But the main cause of his distress at this moment was the information he'd just received from Ricco Tang – that Olivia was lying about Rupert's last days. What was she up to? He started assembling the pieces in his mind when a high-pitched voice behind him said:

"Mr. Sturges? Might I have a few moments of your time?"

The owner of the voice was a short, intense-looking Chinese man. He appeared to be in his mid-forties. He had a thin, sour face that peered up at Sturges through black-rimmed glasses. He looked vaguely familiar, and after a moment, Sturges realized: this was the man with the newspaper who'd been sitting near him and Tang in the restaurant.

"My name is Wu," the man said, holding out a name card.

Sturges checked both sides of the card as the man watched. The only thing that appeared was a name, Wu Zhemin, written in Roman letters on one side, Chinese characters on the other. No phone number or e-mail address was listed. No company or organization, which in this part of the world usually indicated someone who was unemployed, or whose profession was too sensitive to be advertised. "What can I do for you, Mr. Wu?" Sturges asked.

"I wonder if we could go somewhere private to talk," Wu said. He had the air of a person who was used to having his requests granted.

Sturges was a man of well-developed instincts, and his instincts told him to stay away. The non-Cantonese name, the simplified characters on the card, Wu's features and Mandarin accent, all identified him as a mainlander. It was possible Wu had come across Sturges by chance in the restaurant and recognized him, but Sturges's was not a well-known face. Certainly not a face that would be known to a total stranger. That suggested the man knew who he was in advance, and perhaps had even followed him into the restaurant.

The weather had already poisoned Sturges's mood. Having a mysterious stranger from the mainland stalking him was not designed to bring sunshine to a dark afternoon. "Sorry, but I'm really quite busy," he said. He started to walk away, but Wu was not easily put off.

"I need only a few minutes," he said.

"Why don't you call me at my office to make an appointment?" Sturges reached for one of his own cards and held it out. Instead of taking, it, Wu said:

"I am here, shall I say, on behalf of certain high-ranking people across the border, Mr. Sturges. I have a matter of some importance to discuss."

"High-ranking people: in Beijing?" Sturges asked. Wu closed his eyes and uttered a low-pitched "Hmm," which Sturges took to be a yes. As Sturges debated whether or not to believe the man, Wu raised an arm, and a car with official PRC license plates rolled to a stop at the same spot where Ricco Tang's Lexus had stood moments earlier. A silver SUV with local plates and blacked-out windows pulled up behind it. The two cars sat there, engines idling, while Sturges considered the situation.

Wu was wearing a well-tailored suit cut from good fabric, his hair was neatly cut and combed, his nails were clean and manicured. This was not the kind of crude and inexperienced bumpkin that Beijing often sent abroad. Perhaps he really did have a message from on high. "All right, Mr. Wu," Sturges said, "you have my attention."

"I would prefer we talk some place more private than a busy street corner," Wu said, and he held the car door open for Sturges. "Please. This won't take long."

"Step into your government car? Just like that? You must realize how this looks," Sturges said. "Where were you thinking of taking me?"

"We will go wherever you like, Mr. Sturges. I'm not kidnapping you. I only want to talk."

"Anywhere I want to go?"

"Anywhere."

Sturges glanced around. Broad daylight. Streets thronged with people. This was not the mainland: they were in Hong Kong, where the rule of law still applied. People like Wu couldn't just show up and spirit him away to some secret spot for interrogation and torture, even if they did represent "high-ranking people." He could tell Wu to go to hell and be done with it. He *should* tell him to go to hell.

But I'm a journalist, he told himself. It appears that there's something new to be learned here. That's the beauty of this profession, learning something new every day. That's what I do.

He stepped into the car and Wu slid in beside him. Sturges gave the driver an address and the car eased away from the curb. He looked back: the silver SUV was right behind them.

Eighteen

The government driver dropped Sturges and Wu Zhemin without drama at the newspaper's offices, as Sturges had directed. Wu seated himself across Sturges's desk and got to the point with un-Chinese directness. "I have come to enquire about the investigation into the Rackley murder," he said.

"The place to enquire about that would be police headquarters," Sturges said.

"We are in touch with the Hong Kong Police, of course," Wu said, "and I have to say, they do not seem to know very much. It is just as well that they decided to hand the whole case over to our Public Security Bureau."

Of course they don't know much, Sturges thought: the people you're speaking on behalf of have thrown every possible obstacle in their way. "It's Public Security headquarters that I was referring to," he said. "The murder took place in Shenzhen. Since you represent high-ranking people in Beijing, I'm sure Shenzhen Public Security will be delighted to fill you in on how their investigation is going. A lot of people here would be interested in that information too, by the way. Shenzhen PSB has told the Hong Kong police nothing."

A thin facsimile of a smile flashed across Wu's face and Sturges braced for an evasion of some kind, but Wu simply ignored the remark. "My superiors are concerned that Southern China might be acquiring a reputation as a dangerous place, and a high-profile murder like Mr. Rackley's, which has been reported around the world, reinforces such an image, isn't it?" he said.

"So many foreign tourists enter the mainland through Shenzhen, Mr. Sturges. We want the world to know that China is a safe place to visit. The world pays attention to what Hong Kong's newspapers say, especially English-language newspapers such as yours. That being the case..." He let the thought hang in the air for a moment. "That being the case, we are naturally interested in knowing how Hong Kong journalists like you view the situation surrounding Mr. Rackley's unfortunate death."

Naturally. Except that Beijing didn't normally send State Security, which Sturges assumed Wu to be, to discuss tourism with newspaper editors. It was far more likely that the authorities in Beijing were afraid the Hong Kong cops or the news media might be close to learning who committed the murder, and perhaps even why. If Ross and Sturges were right, the who and the why were something Wu's high-level people already knew, and they didn't want that knowledge shared with the rest of the world.

Outside his window he could see massive black rain clouds rolling across the harbor from the Kowloon side. The typhoon was nearby and darkness was spreading across the sky like a stain, mirroring the darkening atmosphere inside Sturges's office. Beijing was used to mainland newspaper editors jumping at its command. Sturges assumed Wu's approach was an attempt to find out what he knew and then, in typical ham-fisted PRC style, to try to intimidate him into killing any story that wasn't to Beijing's liking. He had no intention of obliging.

One of the books Rupert had insisted that Sturges read as a boy was Sun Tzu's "*The Art of War*" – a guide, Rupe always said, to preparing for the battles of life. It was claimed that modern-day Asian businessmen and politicians still lived by Sun Tzu's principles. Sturges guessed that was another of those myths about China that had percolated to the West and was repeated unthinkingly, like the myth that the Great Wall could be seen from space. All he could remember about the book these many years later was the basic philosophy and a few of its stilted injunctions.

Avoid battle whenever possible. Well, it didn't appear that the little man peering across his desk was going to give him that option.

Know your enemy if you can't avoid battle. No problem there: Sturges knew well enough how the Chinese authorities operated, and he'd run into Wu's counterparts in other parts of the world as well.

He recalled something about being *"extremely subtle, even to the point of formlessness,"* whatever that meant. *"Those who face the unprepared with preparation are victorious."* The kind of hokey-sounding philosophy that made its way into Chinese fortune cookies in the West.

Hokey or not, Sturges knew he wasn't going to out-Chinese a Chinese when it came to ancient Chinese philosophy, especially one who was probably trained in modern intelligence and interrogation techniques. He did recall that most of the book's advice was just common sense: plan your strategy carefully, don't extend yourself beyond your resources, avoid frontal assaults whenever possible, use the element of surprise whenever possible, and so on. You didn't have to be a Chinese sage to figure out things like that.

"You were reading a Hong Kong newspaper in the restaurant," he said to Wu. "That should tell you pretty much how the local media view the situation. We journalists aren't complicated people. We learn something, we publish it in the paper."

"I have studied the foreign media," Wu said. "I believe that not everything that is learned will show up in print immediately. Good journalists wait until they have full facts in hand before they write anything, isn't it? You might know certain things but not yet be ready to publish them." He brushed a fleck of dust off his trouser leg, evidently pleased with his analysis. "That is the type of thing my superiors would like to know," he said. "What has not yet been published about the murder that might appear in the Hong Kong newspapers in the near future? I thought that as a friend of China, you might be kind enough to give me some guidance – off the record, so to say. Just so we can be prepared for any problems or bad publicity that might arise."

"If the Hong Kong newspapers are holding anything back," Sturges said, "it's because they're worried about the reaction from Beijing. Your superiors only have themselves to blame if they're not getting the full story."

"Under our handover agreement with the British, Hong Kong has retained its free press, isn't it?"

Sturges hesitated before answering. "Do you want a candid answer, Mr. Wu," he asked, "or do you want me to tell you what you'd like to hear?"

"Candor would be most appreciated," Wu said.

"Very well. In theory and in law, yes, the press here is still free to print what it wants. But ever since the handover, the desirability of being 'patriotic' has been drummed into the heads of Hong Kong's media owners, especially the Chinese-language media, by people like you who speak on behalf of high-ranking people on the mainland. Everyone in our business knows that being 'patriotic' means keeping unfavorable news and criticism of the mainland to a minimum."

"Mr. Rackley certainly never refrained from criticizing China," Wu said.

"Yes, but his column had become such an institution that his editors didn't dare try to muzzle him. Those editors knew he'd cry bloody murder if they tried it, and his complaints would have found a lot of sympathy here."

Wu looked ready to rebut the suggestion, but Sturges decided, fuck Sun Tzu: it was time for that full frontal attack. "But let me ask *you* a question: if Beijing really wants to see the case solved, why did it order the Hong Kong Police to drop the investigation? My readers would be very interested in knowing the answer to that question."

"That was purely a local decision, Mr. Sturges, based on local manpower needs, as the police themselves announced this morning. You know that under the 'one country, two systems' framework, the Hong Kong authorities have complete autonomy in matters like this. Mainland China does not interfere."

This was typical PRC: stick to the official script, mouth the official slogans, and you can't be accused of saying anything wrong. What did Sun Tzu say about letting the enemy know you were on to him? Sturges couldn't remember if that was a good idea or a mistake. But what the hell, once more into the breach:

"With all due respect, Mr. Wu," he said, "I and just about everybody else in Hong Kong knows the Hong Kong authorities follow Beijing's lead today on any sensitive matter, whether Beijing's orders are explicit or not. There has been every indication from the start that Beijing considers this case to be extremely sensitive, and your presence here today confirms that. I happen to know that the Hong Kong Police were quite eager to follow the case through to its conclusion. There's no way they would have dropped the investigation on their own initiative, because of manpower needs or anything else. So..."

He paused. *Occam's Razor: the simplest solution is usually the best.*

"...so experience, backed by common sense, tells me the order to drop the case came from your side of the border." *There's a little Western philosophy for you, Wu baby.* "I'm sure my colleagues at the other newspapers here would tell you exactly the same thing."

Wu parried the thrust effortlessly. "I will turn your question around," he said. "What reason would we have for calling the police off the case when we want to see it solved? That would not be logical, isn't it?"

He was fishing, hoping this challenge to logic would lure Sturges into blurting out his true theory of the murder. *Sun Tzu: Good warriors cause the enemy to come to them.*

But Sturges refrained from mouthing the obvious next step in his line of reasoning: *We assume Beijing closed the investigation down because Beijing has something to hide.* He didn't need an ancient Chinese philosopher to tell him to stay away from that one.

"All I can tell you," he said, "is that we'll be writing at length in tomorrow morning's paper about how the Shenzhen police have contributed absolutely nothing to the investigation while the Hong Kong police have been called off the case. We'll be quoting some knowledgeable people here as saying that someone in Beijing ordered the investigation closed and the Hong Kong police had no choice but to obey. It would add to the public's understanding if you'd explain why your superiors gave that order."

Wu's features reassembled themselves into a frown, and for a brief moment Sturges thought he saw a look of indecision flash across the man's face. "I'm sure the people I represent would want you not to print such baseless speculation," he said, his high-pitched voice taking on whatever menace it was capable of.

Finally, the veiled threat. Sturges had been wondering when it would come. "I expect you are right," he said. "I'm sure they would prefer that. Fortunately, as you pointed out, we have retained our right to a free press here, so we are not obliged to take the preferences of any government into account.

"However, we're also committed to fairness in our reporting. So if you wish, I'll be happy to quote you, by name in fact" – he pulled Wu's card out of his pocket and glanced at it once again – "as expressing your unhappiness with any suggestion that the mainland was involved in the decision." He looked up. Smiled. Waited.

Wu's frown returned and his skin flushed a bright pink. "Our entire conversation here is off the record," he said. "I assumed that was clear. I do not wish to be quoted on anything."

"Oh?" Sturges replied. "It seems your study of the foreign media didn't go far enough. The rule is, if you want something you say to be off the record you have to make that clear before the conversation gets started. Otherwise everything you say is printable." The color of Wu's face shaded toward the purple.

"However," Sturges continued, holding up a hand of conciliation, "I don't want to take unfair advantage." *Sun Tzu: A surrounded army must be given a way out.* "I'll agree to keep your comments off the record if that's what you want."

Wu's face lightened slightly.

"We'll just write..." Sturges pretended to consider alternative formulations, "...we'll write that 'a Chinese source close to high-ranking people on the mainland refused to deny that Beijing had ordered the Hong Kong Police off the Rackley investigation.' How does that sound?"

Now he could see Wu struggling with the complexities of English grammar. Verb tenses, which don't exist in Chinese, cause the Chinese particular difficulty. "A source *refused to deny* that Beijing *had ordered...*" Wu couldn't be entirely sure, but he didn't think what Sturges had just suggested sounded very good at all.

He uncrossed his legs and rose, willing himself to remain calm. It appeared he had misjudged this foreigner – an error, according to Sun Tzu: *If you know others and you know yourself, you will not be imperiled in a hundred battles; if you do not know others but know yourself, you win one and lose one.* Wu had to admit to himself that he had lost this one.

It was hard enough, he thought, dealing with the Hong Kong Chinese. They were all Chinese, the Hongkongers and the mainlanders, were they not? All sons of Han, all with the same thousands of years of history and civilization behind them. They should all think alike when it came to the welfare of the motherland, no?

No. Wu, like many Chinese from both sides of the border, had learned since 1997 that they did not think alike. The Hong Kong Chinese had soaked up too many foreign ways during their century and a half of intimacy with the British — including being able to think exactly how they wanted to think — while mainland thinking had been stultified by decades of repression and censorship.

And what were the Hong Kong Chinese to begin with, Wu thought, but a bunch of motherfucking Cantonese? Crude, unsophisticated, petty shopkeepers who cared for nothing but money. Not fit to sit at the same table with their cultured northern compatriots. He hated the people, hated the city with its miserable heat and humidity, its monsoons and its typhoons.

How much more difficult, then, for Wu to have to deal with this *yang guizi,* this foreign devil, with his alien notions of "individuality" and "free expression"? What could an outsider like this possibly know of loyalty to the motherland? What would he care? The owner of Sturges's newspaper was Chinese. Hong Kong Chinese, yes, but still Chinese. *He* would understand: Wu would make sure of that. Enough of wasting his time with outsiders.

"I appreciate your time, Mr. Sturges," he said with the slightest of nod of his head. "As I said, I would be very unhappy to find that any mention of myself or this meeting made its way into your news stories."

Sturges had no intention of quoting Wu, but he refused to give him the satisfaction of an affirmative reply. "I'm sorry I don't have any guidance to give you," he said. "Except to say, keep reading the local newspapers. The moment we learn anything, we'll make sure you and everybody else knows about it." There was more bravado in this comment than he truly felt, and that frightened him. Was the unease coursing through his body at this moment still just a physiological reaction to meteorological disruptions? Or had the encounter with Wu unnerved him?

As he opened the door to show Wu out, the first sheets of typhoon rain slammed into the office window with a roar, like a blast from a fire hose. "Thar she blows," he said. "I hope you came prepared, Mr. Wu."

"You needn't concern yourself, Mr. Sturges," Wu said, flipping open his phone as he made for the elevators. "I am always prepared for any eventuality."

The elevator doors closed. The man was gone, but the feeling of unease he had brought with him remained in the room like a physical presence. Sturges forced himself to turn his thoughts elsewhere, to the puzzle he'd been grappling with before Wu Zhemin had bullied his way onto the scene: who was Olivia Chen, really, and how did she slot into the mystery that was her husband's murder?

Nineteen

Chang Lili was a fighter from the moment she arrived on the scene. She was born in the squalor of a mud hut in a Chinese countryside village in August 1958, howling and squawking at an unjust world as she squirted out of her mother's womb and into the hands of a peasant midwife. The timing was propitious, however. For the first year of her life there was food aplenty in the village – more food at one point than most Chinese had eaten in their lives – and the abundance helped toughen her little body against the horrors that would soon accompany the famine-that-wasn't.

Lili's father, Chang Dongfeng, had arrived at the Hong Xing agricultural collective with his wife and two sons eight months earlier. Chang's banishment to this fetid grouping of villages in the Taishan district of Guangdong Province was his punishment for having questioned Chairman Mao's agricultural policies. "So, this is the man who knows more about agriculture than the Chairman," an Interior Ministry functionary said mockingly as he signed the Changs' travel papers. "We will send the comrade to a place where he can put all this agricultural expertise to work for the people."

The utter barrenness of the village was a shock after the comfort the family had known in Beijing. Yanan, the revolutionary base where Chang had spent almost 10 years, had also been primitive, but in Yanan there was plenty to stimulate the mind: the excitement of the revolution, debates over ideology, military battles against the Japanese and the Nationalists. There was even music and dancing for the privileged few. Here in the Changs' new home in the Pearl River Delta there was only mud and dung, the heat and enervating humidity of the southern coast, and mind-numbing, soul-stultifying toil from sunrise to sunset.

The peasants were a sullen and nasty lot who resented the soft city-dwellers they'd been forced to accept in their midst. The local Party cadres, themselves ignorant peasants for the most part, took delight in humiliating the right-deviationist and his family. They assigned them the filthiest of tasks. They taunted them in their crude *Toisan* dialect, a rural version of Cantonese. At least Chang arrived speaking decent enough Cantonese to communicate – it was his mother's native dialect. He even understood a bit of Toisan: when she moved from Guangdong to marry Dongfeng's father, Madame Chang had brought along a family nanny who was originally from Taishan herself, and the girl used to sing to Dongfeng in her native dialect when he was a small child.

Despite the hardships, Chang did not complain. He had arrived determined to be humble and cooperative no matter what awaited them. He knew that keeping his mouth shut would be their only chance of resuming even a semblance of their former lives. As the family unpacked its belongings and surveyed the mean hut that would be its new home, he told his wife and sons: "Be strong. We will survive."

For Chang had learned a lesson: never question the Party, never question the Chairman, no matter how unjust, no matter how insane their directives. The same lesson had been learned by the hundreds of thousands who believed Mao when he said he wanted candid criticism of the Party. It had been learned by the millions who watched as those foolish enough to take him at his word were fed into the Maoist meat grinder.

Go along with the Chairman and his ideas no matter what, that was now the guiding principle for six hundred million-plus Chinese. And the Chairman had some real dillies up his tunic.

~

Village life in China was hell for everyone. It improved marginally for the Chang family one day shortly before Lili's birth, as Dongfeng was hauling buckets of human waste from the village latrines to the fields.

For days a woman had been staring at him whenever he passed her hut. He wondered who she was, but he knew that asking one of the locals would only invite scorn and ridicule.

There was another political exile in the village, a man named Sun Ming. Sun was originally from the Northeast, and Putonghua was the only dialect he spoke; he was grateful for any chance to talk to Chang, a fellow Putonghua speaker. The two had to be discreet: having been found guilty of ideological crimes and speaking a dialect none of the villagers could understand, they could easily be accused of hatching some new rightist plot. Sun, however, had arrived several months before Chang and knew the lay of the land. The next time they crossed paths, Chang grabbed the opportunity to pull him aside and ask about the woman.

"She is Zhang Jieliu," the man said. "The wife of Huang Yanchi."

Huang was the collective's leader. The fact that his wife was watching Chang could only mean trouble. After that Chang took a roundabout route to avoid her whenever possible. If forced to pass her hut, he kept his head down and refused to look her in the eye.

On this day, she stepped in front of him as he passed by and blocked the narrow walkway. "Why do you walk with your head down?" she asked. Her voice was firm, but not hostile.

"The load is heavy, comrade," he answered. "And the sun is bright. I walk this way to shield my eyes."

"You are Chang Dongfeng," she said.

"That is right."

"Do you know who I am?" She was speaking accented but proper Cantonese.

He raised his eyes for an instant, then lowered them again. "You are the wife of comrade Yanchi, the esteemed leader of this village," he said.

She said nothing for a time, and her silence fed his unease. Then: "You are originally from Nanjing?"

She and her husband would have learned this from his official dossier. But if she already knew, why ask?

"Your father was Chang Daorang, an economist for the Nationalist government?"

Worse yet. Discussion with a village official of his family's bourgeois past could only presage bad news. His mind whirled, searching for an answer, afraid that whatever he said would be the wrong thing.

"*Hai-ah*," he mumbled in Cantonese, confirming his father's identity but adding nothing more. Yet two things struck him even as the words left his mouth. First, the woman had not asked the last question in Cantonese, but in the Mandarin spoken in Nanjing. Chang had used that dialect for most of his young life; the meaning of the woman's question had registered on his brain before he gave any thought to the actual words.

Second, she had omitted the usual pejorative adjectives – *"Nationalist bandits," "bourgeois"* – that invariably accompanied mention of the elder Chang's name or Chiang Kai-shek's government. A verbal error like this was not something one committed lightly in China's super-heated political atmosphere. Anyone could inform on anyone else for the slightest perceived violation of ideological correctness.

Before he could speak, the woman asked: "Don't you recognize me, comrade Dongfeng?"

With that he raised his eyes again. She took off her Mao cap and let her short hair fall free to give him a better look. She did seem familiar, he thought...but he wasn't sure...could it be...?

A huge smile creased her face. "I am Cheung Je-luk!" she exclaimed.

Cheung Je-luk? His nanny from his days in Nanjing! *Cheung* was the Cantonese equivalent of her family name, *Zhang*. *Je-luk*, the Cantonese equivalent of *Jie Liu*, meant Daughter Number Six. She was from a typically large peasant family, two sons and seven daughters. Her parents couldn't be bothered to remember so many names, and daughters were anyway more a burden than a blessing in China, so the parents had simply given the girls numbers: Daughter One, Daughter Two and so on. She and Dongfeng often had a good laugh about her name when he was a child.

"Wah!" he shouted in surprise. Alarmed at his outburst, he lowered his head again, but Je-luk put a finger under his chin and raised it gently. She grasped the pole holding his two slop buckets and lifted it off his shoulders. "This is no work for Chang Daorang's son," she whispered in his ear.

She led him to the collective's office. Many times since their marriage, in the privacy of their hut, she had told her husband stories of Jacob Chang, how he had treated the common people well, how he fought the corruption of the Nationalist government; how he had saved her life and those of the other household servants by giving them money and sending them off to safety just before the Japanese reached Nanjing.

Jacob had been guilty of class crimes, yes, but she had known him well: he was a good man at heart. Dongfeng, the son, was also a good person – and highly educated, she pointed out. He had given the Party two decades of excellent service: his dossier confirmed that. Dongfeng was accused of political infractions, but the couple was experienced enough to read between the lines of any official document, and they suspected the charges against him had been manufactured as in so many other cases.

Now, she said, composing her words carefully, he had been sent to the village to serve the people. Huang had been complaining bitterly about the difficulties of running this new-style agricultural collective, which grouped more than a thousand families from several dozen villages under one administrative umbrella. The collectives were Mao's personal project: it was Huang's duty, she said, to show respect for the Chairman by making the project a success. "Could not Comrade Dongfeng's intelligence and experience help you with the administration, husband?" she asked. "It would be for the good of all."

Huang Yanchi was a gruff, middle-aged peasant who'd had only minimal formal education, but he hadn't risen to a leadership position by being stupid. He immediately grasped the wisdom of his wife's words. Chang Dongfeng's days as the village honey bucket man were over. He would work in the administrative office, helping Huang to serve the Chairman.

~

There had been localized famines in 1956, largely due to Mao's collectivization policy, but famine was nothing new to China and this one did not cause great concern at the time. In 1958 the weather was good, and despite widespread discontent with collectivization there was a bumper harvest. Hong Xing's granaries were bursting at the seams, and the animals were strong and plentiful. That summer, Mao announced that China would embark on a *da yue jin*, a Great Leap Forward into the modern industrial age. The basis of this rapid advance was to be huge increases in the production of grain and steel.

Simultaneously, he reorganized the countryside. The collectives that had already vexed Hong Xing's leadership now became "people's communes." Private enterprise of any kind was banned in the communes; people could not even cook for themselves; all were forced to eat in communal kitchens. This was to be the ultimate communization of the peasantry, transforming rural society and the nation's agriculture in one masterstroke under Mao's brilliant leadership.

The large harvest that autumn seemed to validate his wisdom. Local officials bombarded Beijing with reports of record food production, and for once the reports were largely true. Party leaders in turn declared that a period of unprecedented abundance was at hand. People were encouraged to eat as much as they could, because from now on, under the Chairman's guidance, there would always be a surplus. "To eat meat," the people of Hong Xing were told at the end of the year, "is a revolutionary act."

Never question the Party. Never question the Chairman. Animals were slaughtered, and people gorged themselves like never before. Everyone from nursing babies to doddering oldsters grew plump and strong.

The reckless consumption left severely depleted food reserves. This, of course, would only become a problem ...if the Party was wrong...and permanent abundance was *not* just around the corner. But the Party could not be wrong.

As it turned out, the feasting was a final hopeful moment before all of China descended into one of the darkest episodes of the twentieth century.

It would require a great leap, indeed, to vault a country to the top rank of that century of horrors.

~

Mao based his leap in agriculture on pseudo-scientific gibberish he had borrowed from Stalin. He ordered agricultural experiments that proved disastrous. Grain production plummeted.

The second leg of the great leap magnified the damage. Mao had been shown a small furnace and was told that peasants were making made high-quality steel in it. It was more nonsense, but Mao was impressed. "Why are foreigners so stupid as to build huge steel mills," he asked aloud, "when our people can make so much steel in little furnaces like these?"

Never question the Chairman. Hundreds of thousands of "backyard furnaces" sprang up all around the country. Where there was no iron ore to feed them, the peasants were ordered to hand over any metal they had to be melted down: kitchen implements, bicycles, the tools they used to till the fields – even the hinges from their doors. The furnaces produced only useless lumps of metal. *Niushi geda,* "cattle droppings," the people called them. But quietly. Never question the Chairman.

With so many peasants diverted to making "steel," those crops that managed to survive Mao's revolutionary science rotted in the fields for lack of anyone to harvest them. The harvest failed in 1959. Yet Mao had declared that food output would continue to increase, so local officials continued reporting impossibly huge gains. Grain taxes were based on reported production, so the more food a commune claimed to produce, the more the Party confiscated. Soon there was little left for the villagers to eat. Cadres visiting Hong Xing began to whisper stories of serious hunger in the surrounding countryside.

Two years earlier, while still in Beijing, Chang Dongfeng had tried to warn that the false reporting was dangerous. Now it was literally killing people.

~

Hong Xing Commune fared well until late 1959 thanks to Chang's organizational skills. He had limited the number of people assigned to steel making and to ill-conceived irrigation projects, to ensure that there were enough people to work the fields. He'd persuaded Huang and the other officials not to sacrifice the commune's agricultural tools to the backyard furnaces.

"Chairman Mao has called on the people to increase grain production," he told them. "He cannot want us to destroy our ability to do so by melting our plows and scythes. Ours is a fertile area and our strength is food production, so let us place our emphasis there. Where the soil is poor people can turn their energies to steel, and in this way, both of the Chairman's targets will be met."

The commune's leaders already had an inkling of the disaster occurring around them. Visiting cadres now brought news of whole villages going hungry, of wasted bodies littering the fields and on the roads. The leaders followed Chang's advice, and the commune made it safely through most of 1959.

Yet common sense could not stave off the inevitable. Hong Xing had been forced like the others to adopt Mao's disastrous theories for the 1958-59 planting season. The 1959 harvest was far smaller than 1958's, but the commune's leadership was forced to report huge increases anyway. Based on this ostensible abundance, tax collectors took away much of what was left.

Outside, state granaries were full. Outside, district Party officials and their families had enough to eat. Everyone else was eating whatever they could get their hands on – dogs, rodents, birds, snakes, insects – until they'd stripped the countryside bare. If Hong Xing was hungry, China was starving to death.

Yet there could be no starvation, because there was no famine. There could be no famine: record harvests had been reported. To suggest otherwise was to suggest the unthinkable, that Mao's ideas were failures.

Never question the Chairman.

By 1960 all of China was starving. But even those who knew the true extent of the disaster had to play the game.

Soon, the tax collectors began coming back empty-handed. Impossible, their superiors said. Since there was no famine, there had to be more food; the peasants must be hiding it. "Anti-hiding" campaigns were launched to show Beijing that local officials were not soft on hoarders.

In February of 1960, a contingent of cadres and soldiers arrived in Hong Xing to search for hidden food. The soldiers went from hut to hut, poking holes in the walls and floors with their bayonets to look for stashes of grain or meat. Every now and then a cry came from inside a hut, and a soldier would emerge with a meager bag of rice held high in triumph. The owners would fall on their knees and beg for mercy, but they were hauled off to labor camps to die more quickly.

As the famine-that-wasn't deepened, Party officials became desperate to find more hidden grain. Cadres devised novel tortures to wrest "the truth" from the peasants. People were forced to stand naked in freezing weather. People's hair was set on fire. When one group shaved their heads to prevent this, their ears were cut off instead.

The situation worsened and the abuse escalated. One day in mid-1960 soldiers arrived again at Hong Xing Commune, and after a fruitless search, five women were grabbed at random and accused of hiding grain. They were stripped naked before a crowd and tied, spread-eagled, to stakes pounded into the ground. A Party cadre went down the line and shoved rice stalks into their exposed vaginas. "You claim your rice is dying in the fields?" he said to the assembled villagers. "Then plant it here," he said, jamming a finger in after one of the stalks. "There is plenty of moisture here to make the rice grow." He laughed, and the head of the military contingent joined in the laughter. Chang Dongfeng groaned.

"Turn your head," Huang Yanchi whispered in a voice trembling with horror. "Ignore this. We can do nothing to help the women until the soldiers leave."

"I cannot ignore it," Chang said. "I have seen this kind of thing before. The memory still haunts me."

"You have seen such a horrible thing as this?" Huang asked. "Where?"

"In Nanjing. When the Japanese came in 1937, this is the way they treated our women." Chang let out a sigh as the horror continued to unfold. "We called the Japanese monsters for doing such things to our people," he said. "Now look: we do it to ourselves."

~

Some people wasted away. Other swelled up as their tissues disintegrated from lack of nutrition. By now, anything that crawled or flew had long since been eaten. People turned to cornhusks, tree bark, even mud, to fill their stomachs. They foraged in the fields and forests for edible grasses from which they could make "grass soup" – although since private property had been outlawed, cooking utensils that hadn't been melted down for steel had been confiscated. Individuals could not even cook grass to eat. In the winter of 1960, people began eating each other.

Cannibalism is not unusual in times of famine, but the eating of human flesh has been a recurrent theme throughout Chinese history. Victorious military chieftains had often feasted on the livers of their dead enemies. The practice of *gegu,* "cutting the thigh," was an accepted act of filial piety: if normal medical means failed to cure a dying parent, a child might slice a piece of flesh from his or her thigh and cook it into a soup for the parent to take as medicine. When a famine did strike, children were the most likely to end up in the cooking pot. If people couldn't bring themselves to eat their own young, they sometimes swapped them for a neighbor's children.

"*Yi zi er shi.*" There were words that did not carry the moral authority of pronouncements by Confucius or Lao Tzu. These were words that never made their way into some American diner's fortune cookie. These were words, nevertheless, that comprised a venerable Chinese saying:

"*Yi zi er shi:*" "Exchange children, obtain food."

In Hong Xing Commune, there were only whispers of cannibalism at first. Miss Ng died but the Ng family performed no funeral rituals. Mr. Wong was last seen on a Tuesday, and on Thursday, people passing Mrs. Wong's hut insisted they smelled meat being cooked.

Then old Mrs. Leung was caught red-handed boiling the leg bones of a sister who had died several days earlier. The sister's butchered haunch was found in a secret compartment in the hut, hung like a ham to dry. The commune officials called for punishment – but how to punish a person who is starving to death?

When the Changs' first child was born in Beijing they named him Mingfu, "Bright Happiness." He was to be their great joy. In fact, the boy had brought his parents only anguish during his six years. He was sickly from the start, constantly in and out of a doctor's care. When food in Hong Xing started running short, he was one of the first to suffer. The entire Chang family was showing signs of gross malnutrition, but it was clear to anyone who saw Mingfu that he was already in extremis.

Mrs. Chang was frantic. She left the boy's bedside only go to the communal dining hall and bring their two pitiable portions of food back to the hut. She fed him half of hers while she herself starved, hoping to build his strength. Mr. Chang could only stand and watch, helpless, as his son faded before his eyes.

One evening as the boy lay near death, the head of a neighboring family approached. Chang Dongfeng did not recognize the man at first. His skin hung loosely from his bones. His teeth rattled in his gums. His hair was falling out. "Comrade Li," Chang finally said. "You are still alive."

"How is your son?" the man rasped.

"Very bad," Chang replied, absently rubbing his shrunken stomach in hunger. "I fear he will leave us at any time."

"I have a proposition," Li said. He leaned his mouth next to Chang's ear and spoke in a low voice. "My daughter is also near death. I propose that as soon as your son dies, we exchange the bodies, your son for my daughter. Then we will both have food."

Chang was horrified, but even in his horror he could not dismiss the suggestion out of hand. His other two children were also showing signs of serious malnutrition. Chang and his wife were almost down to skin and bones. He had to find them food. "But wait," he said, hardly believing he was pursuing the discussion. "We can't know when your daughter will die. It could be days, or even weeks, after my son. We couldn't just hide the boy's body and wait for your daughter to pass."

"*Mou mantai*," the neighbor replied. "No problem. As soon as your son goes, I will end my daughter's life. It is no matter: she is only a girl." His eyes glowed at the thought of food, and a line of spittle ran out of the corner of his mouth as he spoke.

Chang Dongfeng cursed all the gods in heaven and all the spirits of the earth for leading him to even consider such an obscenity. He cursed those whose false denunciations had sent him and his family to this hell. Most of all, he cursed Mao Tse-tung. "No!" he cried with what little energy he could muster. "Leave my house and never come back!" He would have struck the man if he'd had the strength, but all he could do was give him a weak shove to send him on his way. The man tottered off, muttering to himself.

Three days later, Mingfu expired. Mrs. Chang was hysterical. Chang had spared her the story of the neighbor's approach, but she knew what was happening around them. "They are eating dead bodies. Don't let them eat my boy," she begged her husband. "You must not let them eat him."

"I will not," Chang said. "I promise."

That night, he wrapped the boy's body in a cloth and dragged it to a nearby forest. He dug as deep a grave as his weakened condition allowed. He spread leaves and twigs over the freshly dug earth and left only a small marker to indicate the grave's location. His son's body would not be dug up for someone's dinner.

"Did you bury my boy?" his wife asked when he dragged himself back to their hut the next morning. "Is my Mingfu safe?"

"He is safe," he assured her. "Nobody will find him." As he spoke, the younger son, Xilian, whimpered with hunger from a corner of the room. But who will keep my other children safe when they die, Chang Dongfeng asked himself. Who will bury them deep when I am also gone and can no longer protect them from the starving mob?

~

Spring came, but the villagers were too weak to plant new crops, and most of the seed had been eaten anyway. The thin gruel of grasses and husks that the dining hall cooked up was barely enough to keep a person alive. Xilian had reached the end stages of starvation, and little Lili was not far behind. Chang and his wife were walking skeletons. "We must find meat," the mother said through her tears. But there was no meat, and Xilian died.

Mrs. Chang was inconsolable. If she could have found a knife she would have taken her own life, but all their knives had gone to the backyard furnaces except one, and her husband had hidden that. All she could do was blubber like a madwoman, delirious from starvation and grief. The only rational thought that came from her mouth was another plea to her husband: "Bury him deep. Don't let them eat my boy."

Chang walked outside to be alone with his pain. Was his entire family to be destroyed like this, by the megalomania of Mao Tse-tung, just as his parents and sisters had been destroyed by the barbarity of the Japanese? He was cursing Mao when another ghost shuffled up to him, and Chang recognized his fellow right-deviationist, Sun Ming. "So, you are still with us," Chang said. Sun nodded weakly. "And your family?"

"All gone but one," Sun said with a shake of the head. "The second of my three children died this morning. My wife passed weeks ago. Just one son and I are left."

"I have also lost two sons," Chang said. "The younger one died just minutes ago. My wife is inside with him now, mad with grief. Our baby daughter is still alive, but how much longer any of us will last I cannot say. Not long, I fear."

The two men stared at each other through sunken eyes. A silent thought passed between them. Sun said: "We must...We must dispose of both boys' bodies."

Chang nodded. He straightened his frail frame and said: "We are both weak. Two will be better than one. We can help each other with the bodies."

"Let us prepare then," said Sun. "I will meet you at the edge of the village, on the path to the mountain. Bring a knife if you have one – in case we come across food."

~

This time Chang did not return for two days. When he reached the hut, the baby was crying with hunger, and his wife was unconscious on the floor.

He pulled her with difficulty onto the bed. She opened her eyes, but there was little comprehension behind them. "You will not believe our good fortune," he said softly. "Mr. Sun and I went to the forest looking for food after we buried the boys, and we came across a small deer. Its leg was caught in a hole and it could not run away. We found rocks and smashed its head. Then we cooked the meat in the forest so nobody else could see. Look!" He unwrapped the cloth he was carrying, and there were several blackened slabs of stringy meat inside. "Mr. Sun and I ate in the forest, and we smoked the rest of the meat," he said. "This is for you and the baby."

He lowered her head gently, and made sure the door to the hut was closed. Then he uncovered a compartment he had dug into the floor and took out a pot of baked clay. He filled the pot with water, then sliced a piece of the meat into thin slivers and dropped them into the pot. While the broth simmered, he set fire to some leaves he had gathered in the forest, and the acrid smoke masked the aroma of cooking meat. If the neighbors got a whiff of real food they might tear the hut apart with their bare hands to get at it.

Chang had read about starvation in Beijing while studying the 1956 famine. He learned that giving a starving person too much food is as bad as giving none at all. The weakened body cannot handle it. He accordingly began to feed the broth slowly to his wife and daughter. The woman could barely open her mouth to take the food in, but after several spoonfuls she began to stir. He left her and turned to feed the baby in the same way. The little girl slurped the broth greedily, and he gave her a couple of strands of meat to swallow. She would have taken the whole pot, but he pulled it away despite her howls of protest. At the sound of Lili's cries, his wife opened her eyes. "More," she said weakly.

"Just a bit for now," Chang said, scooping more broth and meat into a bowl and carrying it to the bed. "Too much and you will be sick." He gestured toward the slabs of meat. "We have enough to last us many days if we are careful."

She raised her head for a better look. "It doesn't look like much meat from a whole deer," she said between slurps.

"I had to split it with Mr. Sun," Chang said. "And he and I ate in the forest, to build up enough strength to get back here to the village."

"Even so," she said, eyeing the slabs.

"It was a small deer," he said meekly.

She lay back and fell asleep. Chang gave the baby a few more spoonfuls to quiet her protests, and took some broth and meat for himself. He wrapped the remaining meat with care and hid it, along with the cooking pot and the knife, although it was doubtful anyone would be searching the hut now. Even the cadres and soldiers were starving.

When he awoke the next morning he cooked another pot of broth, using a bit more meat this time. Lili began demanding food as soon as the aromas reached her corner of the hut, and he fed her first, singing to her as he parceled the broth out slowly to avoid overextending her shrunken stomach. He could almost see the strength flowing into her tiny body with each mouthful. The sound of her slurps and gurgles awoke Mrs. Chang, and Chang fed her as well, giving her as much as he dared. He thought she seemed a bit stronger than the night before.

When she was finished, she closed her eyes and shook her head, as if to banish a thought. "It is very good," she whispered. "But...it does not taste like deer meat."

"How can you remember what deer meat tastes like?" he asked, trying to make light of her comment. "How can you remember the taste of any meat? It has been so long." At this, a sob caught in his throat, and he had to compose himself.

Her eyes opened wide. "What is wrong, husband?" she demanded. He waved the question away, but she persisted. "What did you do?"

He looked away, unable to meet her gaze. "I told you. We killed a deer."

Her jaw trembled and she had trouble speaking, but she grabbed his shirt in her frail hands and pulled him toward her. "Did you bury our son?" she demanded. "Did you keep your promise?"

Tears gushed from his eyes. "I promise you," he said, "this is not our son."

She ignored his words. "Did you bury him?" she demanded. "Did you bury him deep, so nobody could...?" She could not finish the sentence.

"This is not our son!" he insisted. The tears poured down his face.

"Tell me!" she cried. "What did you do?"

Chang Dongfeng looked heavenward while his wife's bony hands pumped like pistons against his sunken chest, and a sigh like the weeping of angels escaped his throat.

"This is not our son," he blubbered through his tears, while their daughter howled for food in the background. "We killed a deer."

Twenty

Yard upon yard of Asian and western delicacies stretched out on tables before Sturges's eyes. He was at a cocktail reception at the Peninsula Hotel in Kowloon. He'd been to a thousand of these things over the years if he'd been to one, and they were all the same: the same few locations at the city's top hotels and clubs, the same abundance of foods, the same mixture of Asian and Western faces that made up Hong Kong high society. He avoided the receptions whenever possible, but this was a charity event for underprivileged children and the newspaper was one of the sponsors, so his attendance was required. And oh yes: Olivia was going to be there. This was to be her first formal public appearance since the funeral.

She'd been out of town on business since Sturges's lunch with Ricco Tang. He hadn't had the chance to ask her why she told him one thing and Ricco another about Rupert's visit to China. He planned to clear up that part of the mystery tonight.

There was another reason why he wanted to see her, of course. The question she'd asked at her house that Sunday – *What if I let you take me to bed*? – kept replaying in his head. She'd said it was only a hypothetical question...but she hadn't said it was out of the question. He knew he might be fooling himself, but Sturges was an experienced and objective analyzer of the facts. It made him a good journalist. It made him certain, in this case, that Olivia Chen was offering herself to him. Now he had to decide: given all the peripheral considerations, did he really want that to happen?

He suspected the answers to his two questions were going to be mutually exclusive. If you accuse a woman of lying about the murder of her husband, is she then likely to climb into bed with you?

He walked through the hotel lobby and took the elevator to the top-floor restaurant. Twenty-eight floors separating two different worlds. The lobby, with its broad columns and potted palms and soaring, ornate ceiling, was Old Hong Kong frozen in time. The restaurant was all modern stainless steel and glass with a breathtaking view of the Hong Kong Island skyline, the opposite of the view Sturges and Brian Ross had observed from the American Club two weeks earlier. The typhoon had dumped oceans of rain on the city over the previous few days, and the lights across the harbor now sparkled in the cleansed air, spreading east and west along the waterfront like welcoming arms, climbing from the water's edge up the facades of office towers and apartment blocks, along the face of the mountains that made up Mid-Levels, and up to the beacon at the top of the Peak. For a moment, Sturges was again in the city of his childhood. Basking in the paternalistic embrace of British colonial governors. The air clean. The People's Republic a barely felt presence on the far side of a forbidden border.

The reverie lasted as long as it took him to glance across the room. Wu Zhemin, the mainland hatchet man, was standing against the far wall. He had buttonholed Sturges's boss, Ho Kai-ming, and was no doubt reminding Ho of his patriotic duty to support the motherland. Ho was a decent man, but like the other newspaper owners in town he knew it didn't pay to piss off Beijing. Local politicians, fellow businessmen and Hong Kong-based PRC officials regularly reminded publishers like Ho where their interests lay, and if gentle suasion didn't work, Beijing was happy to dispatch an oily thug like Wu to drive the point home.

Among the Chinese there were few publishers or journalists in town any longer who didn't soft-pedal news about the mainland. The *Star's* editor had given Rupert's vacated column to a local writer, and the man was already turning it into an empty vessel that didn't begin to approach Rupert's writing for erudition or vitriol. Sturges would probably receive a memo from Ho the following morning about the need to maintain "balance" and "sensitivity" in the paper's coverage of China.

He turned to get himself a drink in preparation for working the crowd, and found himself face to face with Ricco Tang. In Tang's case it was a bright scarlet face. "What ho, old boy," Tang said. He had a glass of champagne in each hand and held one out to Sturges. "I brought you a drink."

"Ricco," Sturges said, raising the glass in salute. "*Ganbei.* I see you're already well ahead of me. Careful: you know you don't hold your booze well."

"I've only had two or three," Tang said. "Or maybe five. Who's counting? I'm having fun, Bill. These are my people." He spread his arms to embrace the crowd. The points of light reflecting off diamond necklaces and jewel-encrusted wristwatches and platinum and gold almost matched the sparkling lights across the harbor. "Behold the disgustingly rich and locally famous of Hong Kong," Tang said expansively. "Do you have any idea how much money is represented in this room right now?"

"Tell me."

"I have no fucking idea," Tang said. But it's a shitload, I can tell you that old boy. Billions and billions of dollars. And I'm talking U.S. dollars – although I'm personally long on euros these days. Half the people here could pay for a duplex apartment in Monte Carlo with pocket cash. A few of them have their own private airplanes. They help keep Giorgio Armani and Bulgari and Gabbani & Dolci in business."

"Dolce & Gabbana."

"Them too. And look at the faces, Bill: hardly a round eye in the lot. Do we Chinese rock, or what?"

"Feeling all warm and ethnic this evening, are we Ricco?"

"I'm at home, Bill. I'm among my own." He blessed the crowd with a beatific smile. "I bet'cha I know everybody in the room. I grew up with half of 'em, for chrissake."

"Do you know the weasely little guy with glasses over there, talking to my boss?"

Tang stared in the direction of Ho Kai-min and Wu Zhemin and shook his head. "Never saw him. Who is he?"

"He's a spook from Beijing," Sturges said. "He followed you and me into the Sichuan restaurant the other day."

The smile on Tang's face weakened. "Are you serious?" he asked.

"Completely. Well, I'm assuming based on what he said that he's a spook."

"But you know for sure he was following us?"

"I am. He sort of kidnapped me after you left."

"He what? Why? What did he say?"

"He was interested in Rupert's murder."

"Rupert's...but if that's what he was interested in, why would he want to follow *us*?"

"Gosh, I don't know, Ricco. Maybe he was also chasing down the rumors about you and Rupert's wife."

"Come on Bill," Tang said, his face now deadly serious, "I told you there was nothing between us. And *sshh!* Claudia's here with me tonight." He glanced around, trying to spot his wife amid the jade and diamonds and couturier dresses. "If she even heard you joking about that..."

"Sorry, Ricco," Sturges said. "You know what *gwei-lo* humor is like. And I don't doubt that you're telling me the truth about Olivia. But you know, there's a way to end that talk once and for all."

"What's that?" Tang said, not sure he wanted to hear the answer.

"We could ask Olivia herself. She's right there." He pointed over Tang's shoulder and waved. "Here she comes," he said.

Tang swallowed hard. "You might be kidding about this spook chap being interested in me but you weren't kidding about people gossiping about me and Olivia, were you?"

"No, I was quite serious about that."

"And she really is walking up behind me right now?"

"Yep."

"Then I think," Tang said without turning around, "that I'm going the other way. Look!" he said, pushing past Sturges. "A billionaire is calling me. See you soon, old boy."

He melted into the crowd, just before Olivia walked up from the other direction. She was wearing an elegant but modestly cut black dress with a minimum of jewelry, as befit a recently widowed woman. Even so, Sturges thought she was easily the most stunning woman in the room. "Ah, the woman of my fantasies," he said, and they exchanged kisses on the cheeks. "I tried to call and your office said you were out of town. How was your trip?"

"Profitable," she said. "Wasn't that Ricco Tang you were just talking to?"

"Yeah. He had to go see someone about money."

"In keeping with the tone of the evening," she said. "I just handed over a shamelessly large check for the poor kiddies. Of course, I can afford it, can't I?" She slid her arm into his and looked up with a flutter of the eyelids, and Sturges could feel half the eyes in the room turn in their direction. "How about you, my late husband's great friend?" she said. "I got rich, and all you got out of this sad affair was a car. There must be something more I can give you."

"There you go Olivia, teasing me again."

"Who says I'm teasing? You certainly seemed interested when you came to my house the other Sunday."

"And you said it was too soon." He glanced around to make sure nobody was listening too closely to their conversation, and lowered his mouth to her ear. "Sex wouldn't be appropriate 'at this moment:' those were your words."

"You journalists are so literal," she said. "Anyway, that was a week ago."

"So what, it only took a week for the moment to pass?"

"I'm going to have to put you out of your misery sometime soon," she whispered. "Poor boy, your eyes are going to drop out of your head, staring at my boobs like that."

He was going to ignore the comment and ask what she really knew about Rupert's trip to China, but before he could get his mouth open a couple walked up and began dragging her away, chattering in Cantonese about introducing her to someone across the room. "Sorry," she said, giving him a good-bye pat on the cheek as she was pulled into the crowd. "But the idea we discussed is very interesting, Bill," she called out just before she disappeared. "Phone me at my office at the end of the week and we'll make a firm date to do something about it."

He was alone, with a flush on his cheeks and a bulge in his pants. The people who said Olivia was thoroughly Americanized had it right: Asian women were subtle and indirect; Olivia was as subtle as a knee to the groin. It sounded at any rate like she had decided that sex was in their future, so there was the answer to one of his questions. He wondered if it would be possible to finesse that and still get to the truth about Rupert's trip.

At the thought of Rupert, he felt a twinge of remorse for lusting after his widow so shortly after the murder – but only a twinge. Whatever Rupert's purpose in going to China, it was difficult to dismiss the photos Olivia had found on his computer. Whether he'd downloaded them to choose a young partner or just to relive old memories, he'd almost certainly done it out of lust. Why should Sturges feel guilty about having the same urges? Why should he feel guilty about satisfying the urge with any sexy woman who came on to him? How many come-ons had he turned down in the past out of a misguided determination to remain faithful, while his wife was spreading her legs for men all over town? He'd decided that if the opportunity presented itself again, he was ready. And what did Olivia's comments signal but opportunity?

But he'd deal with all that later. He switched into professional mode and started to make the rounds of the room, giving Wu a wide berth. After an hour of making small talk, nibbling on smoked salmon and *dim sum* and posing for photographs with people he barely knew, he said a few good nights and began working his way toward the exit. He was almost out the door when Elaine and Henry Sikorsky came walking in.

"At last, people I really want to see," he said. He had known the Sikorskys since he was a teenager. He was home from his first year at college, and they were fresh out of the United States and learning what summertime humidity in Hong Kong was all about. Over the years, the couple had watched Sturges grow into manhood, and he had watched Elaine become one of the premier cross-border traders in the city.

He gave them each a bear hug. "I haven't seen you guys in ages," he said.

"I just got back from one of my jaunts to the mainland," Elaine told him, "and I was planning to call you. How are you, anyway? Any new women in your life yet?"

Sturges considered the question and decided not to mention anything about Olivia. Elaine and Henry had also been friendly with Rupert, even though Rupe always looked askance at Elaine's insistence on trading with the enemy. Olivia no longer seemed reticent about starting a relationship with Sturges, but others, even those as close to him as the Sikorskys, might be put off by to the idea of Rupert's widow and his best friend hooking up less than a month after the murder. Anyway, there was very little to mention. Nothing had happened so far other than smiles and innuendo. "Nobody special," he said.

"Have you learned anything new about the murder?" Henry asked.

Sturges shrugged. "Bits and pieces. I'm still working on it, for old Rupe's sake as much as anything else, but the bits and pieces are fewer and farther between since the police here were ordered off the case."

"And you still don't know why he was in China?" Elaine asked.

"Well, I have some theories," he said. "If you promise you won't say anything to anyone until I print it..."

They nodded in unison.

"...there's evidence that he was there to buy antiques. But that's still unconfirmed. I'm hoping to pin that down one way or the other within the next few days."

"That's interesting," Elaine said. She and Henry gave each other a quizzical look.

"You say that like you don't believe it," Sturges said.

"I...well, no. It makes sense. We all know how important antiques were to him."

"And I know you, Mrs. Sikorsky. You've never been a good liar. There's something you're not telling me."

She flushed. "Actually," she said, "that's what I was going to call you about. I just happen to know where Rupert was on August 27th."

"The day before his body popped up? And where was that?"

"He was in Dongguan."

"Dongguan." This was nothing new. "We already know he arrived at the train station there that morning."

"But I know where he went after the train station," she said. "At least, I know one of the places he went."

"Which was?"

"One of the big restaurants in the city. I was at the same restaurant myself a couple of days ago, and my guest was a man who was sitting right next to Rupert there on the 27th."

"This guest: Chinese or Westerner?

"Chinese. An official from the Customs office. Why, is his race important?"

"Only, if you'll pardon the cliché, because we *gwei-los* all look the same to them. Are you sure he wasn't mistaking some other Westerner for Rupert?"

"He recognized him from a photo in your newspaper," she said. "I brought the paper with me from home that day. This guy looked at the front page and said, 'I saw that same man right here on August 27th.'"

"He still could have been mistaken."

"Look, Bill, this was a really local restaurant. The chance of any other *gwei-lo* being there, especially one who was as memorably fat as Rupert, is extremely small. The man I talked to was sure the man he saw and the man in the photo were the same. His colleague had also been there on the 27th and he backed my man up."

"Fair enough," Sturges said. "This helps fill in the timeline. We know Rupert cleared immigration at the Changping train station in Dongguan on the morning of the 27th. He had checked in for the 9:18 a.m. train from Hung Hom station in Kowloon that morning, which means he would have arrived at Changping around 10:25 a.m. Now, thanks to you, we know he was still alive and sitting in your restaurant a couple of hours later. Did your man say what time Rupert left the place?"

"He just said Rupe had lunch and left. Given how early the Chinese eat, that would have been around one o'clock, one-thirty."

"The medical examiner says Rupert died sometime in the late afternoon of the 27th," Sturges said. "Your man saw him in a Dongguan restaurant just a few hours before that. Rupe would have had time to leave the restaurant and return to Shenzhen before he was killed – it only takes about a half hour by high-speed train. But it's still possible that the murder took place in Dongguan. I don't suppose your informant was able to tell you what Rupert was doing in the city. Besides having lunch, I mean."

"Sort of," Elaine said. "That's why I sounded dubious when you said he'd gone to buy an antique. This fellow said he overheard Rupert in the restaurant talking to someone on his mobile phone."

"And this official speaks good enough English to understand what Rupert was saying?"

"He speaks no English at all. But he said Rupert was speaking Chinese – you know how good Rupe's Putonghua was. The official said Rupert kept asking whoever he was talking to about 'documents.' *'Ni you mei you zheige wenjian?'* 'Do you have the documents?' He said Rupert repeated the question two or three times into the phone. My man said Rupert also mentioned the Great Leap Forward a couple of times, which I found quite odd: nobody in China talks about that horror. Anyway, I have no idea how that reference might be connected to whichever documents he was asking about."

"*Wenjian*," Sturges repeated. "Did the fellow say whether Rupert indicated which documents he was interested in?"

"Unfortunately no," Elaine said.

"I mean, he could have to talking to whomever he was going to buy an antique from, and he could have been asking if the guy had documents certifying that the piece was genuine, something along those lines. I'll have to check with a linguist, but I think *wenjian* can also mean 'documentation.'"

"I guess that's possible," she said. "My Chinese is far from perfect."

"And you say he was talking about the Great Leap Forward? What the hell was that about?"

"That's all the man could tell me. He said Rupert used that official euphemism they use on the mainland to pretend the famine wasn't actually created by Mao: 'the three years of natural disasters.' That's all I know."

"Does that information help at all?" Henry asked.

"Every piece of information is potentially useful in a situation like this," Sturges said. "In a way though, it makes it worse."

"How so?"

"Up to now I've been working on several separate theories of the case. I thought I was narrowing it down. Instead, Elaine has just thrown another possibility into the mix. Every time I think I'm getting close to the truth of this damn thing, I find myself back where I started."

Twenty-one

"Documents?" Brian Ross said.

"That's what she told me," Sturges said.

He, Winston Wai and Ross were seated in a bar in Wanchai, just down the street from Police Headquarters. It was early evening. Flat-screen TVs showing the sport of the day flickered from inside the bars that stretched for blocks on either side of the street. Young professionals just finished with work streamed into the trendy bars, while middle-aged British men with pints of British beer in hand and Filipina girlfriends at their sides packed the less salubrious pubs. Chinese mamma-sans stood in front of the girlie bars, once the mainstay of the district, trying to lure passing men inside. "Beautiful girls, come see," they would call out, pulling at a man's sleeve. "Just one beer. Come." Rows of beautiful and semi-beautiful girls, all wearing tiny outfits, perched on stools behind the mamma-sans, chatting with each other or talking on their mobile phones, occasionally remembering why they were there and waving to a man who paused to look.

"And you don't have any idea what these documents might have been?" Ross asked.

"Everything I know was in today's story," Sturges said absently. The bar was open to the sidewalk and he was admiring a trio of young Filipina hookers who were trolling for early-evening customers. It was late September, still hot as blazes, and the girls were in identical summertime uniforms: platform heels, micro-miniskirts, bare midriffs, too-small tank tops with breasts spilling out the top. Long, silky black hair. Tight little asses. Like Olivia's ass.

"What was I saying?" Sturges asked.

"Documents," said Wai.

"Right, documents. Well, you know everything I know." Sturges's story that morning had detailed what Elaine Sikorsky told him about Rupert's presence in Dongguan. Sturges had also included the possibility – he was careful to portray it as only speculation – that Rupert was shopping for some antique in addition to documents.

Or in conjunction with documents. Or instead of documents. Or maybe Rupe had been on the trail of a story as they had originally suspected. Nothing was clear. Sturges's linguist friend had confirmed that *wenjian* could mean "documentation," and Wai now agreed with the man. "But why some perp would kill Rupert just for documents?" Wai asked.

"Some what?" Ross said.

"Perp. Means 'perpetrator.' Like they say all the time on '*Law and Order SVU*.' Didn't you see last night? Very good episode. Elliot is in trouble as usual..."

"It's not enough that my staff speaks bad English," Ross said. "These days they insist on speaking bad American English." He turned to Sturges. "So, despite this tantalizing piece of information, we're still no closer to knowing who our 'perp' was or why he killed Rupe, are we?"

Sturges could only shrug. His story had been a good example of enterprising journalism, it contained several new tidbits, but it had advanced the story only marginally.

Everything Sturges knew was *not* in the story, of course. He hadn't mentioned Rupert's apparent reference to the Great Leap

Forward. Printing what little Sikorsky knew of that would only have raised more questions than it would answer.

He also hadn't mentioned his fourth theory of the case, that Rupert had gone after young Chinese girls. That would still wait until such time as there was some corroboration. During their dinner at the Yacht Club a week earlier, Ross had said he was looking into Evelyn Chin's comments. "What about you?" Sturges now asked him. "Have you come up with anything on the buying-an-antique theory?"

Ross shook his head in frustration. "Nothing. We spoke to everybody we could think of who might have heard so much as a whisper about some major piece being smuggled into the city. None of them knew a thing."

"Well, we couldn't expect Rupe to be talking such a sensitive matter around," Sturges said. "I'm not surprised that none of your informants had heard about it."

"But it *would* be surprising," Ross said. "Think about it: he had to apply for a visa, which means Chinese security knew he was coming. They certainly would have been watching someone like him once he crossed the border, and Rupert was experienced enough to know they'd be watching, so there's no way he would have risked carrying a sensitive piece of art back across the border by himself. Assuming he did buy anything, he would have had to arrange for a professional to handle the actual transportation. That means at least one other person would have known about it.

"And judging by the comments Rupert made to Evelyn Chin, and given the fact that this quest was important enough to lure him across the border, this would have had to be the most important piece of art since the bloody Mona Lisa. No, laddie: it's very difficult to keep a thing like that quiet."

Wai chimed in. "We speak to art dealers, big-time smugglers, fellow cops who deal with smuggling: nobody has slightest idea that a major deal is in the works."

"So what are you saying? You don't think he was there to score an antique after all?"

Ross shrugged. "The story about an antique makes perfect sense and it would explain everything that we know took place, but in the end I don't think it holds up."

"I disagree," Sturges said. "Rupert simply might not have had time to discuss the deal with anyone before he was killed. The trip itself might only have been to confirm the existence and authenticity of the piece. The only other person who might have known about it at that point was the person who was going to sell it to Rupert – and that person wouldn't have been talking it around, because the simple fact of offering some super-important piece for sale could have landed him in trouble with the authorities.

"Rupe plans to examine the piece, authenticate it, cross back to Hong Kong, and only *then* make arrangements for the piece to be smuggled in. That way, even if the Chinese do discover what he's up to, he's already safely back home and out of their reach."

He took a big swallow of his beer. "Unfortunately for Rupert, someone put a bullet in his head before he could make the return journey, so those arrangements on this side were never made. That could be why nobody on this side had heard anything."

"Maybe, but we're still left with only the most circumstantial of evidence," Ross said. "We've found nobody who can quote

Rupert first-hand as saying, 'I'm going to China to buy an antique.' Somebody overheard Rupert saying the word 'documents' into his telephone, but that could mean anything. It's all a bunch of veiled references and informed guesses and hearsay."

"Actually, there's a point I haven't mentioned yet," Sturges said. "Ricco says Olivia told him that Rupert told her that he, Rupert, was going to China to pick up an antique."

"Bloody hell! That wee detail wasn't in your story today Sturges. Were you planning to tell me about this? Do we still have an agreement or not?"

"Easy," Sturges said. "I just heard this myself. And Olivia's been out of town, so I haven't had a chance to ask her about it yet. I want to see what she has to say before I use it in any way."

"You were both at that reception at the Peninsula last night," Ross said, not entirely mollified by the explanation. "I saw your photos in the newspaper this morning."

"But not in the same shot," Sturges reminded him. "We did speak very briefly, but I didn't have a private moment to ask her the question. I'm on it, though. I'm supposed to call her tomorrow to arrange a, uh..." He cleared his throat. "...a meeting." He hoped he wasn't blushing as the word came out of his mouth: Olivia's parting words suggested that it was going to be more than a simple meeting. "I plan to ask her about it when we get together." *Among other things.* "I promise I'll let you know what she says."

It wasn't clear if Ross believed the explanation, but waiting was his only option. "If *she* tells you that *Rupert* told *her* that he was after an antique, then that would pretty much tie it down," Ross said. "It would also mean she withheld information from us, and we'd have to have a word with her about that. But since we're officially off the case, I'll let you talk to her before I intervene."

"I'll tell you this," Sturges said, "whatever Rupe was up to, the powers-that-be over there are still concerned about the possibility of it being made public. Remember you were telling me about State Security's interest in the case? I think I met State Security face-to-face a couple of days ago, just as the typhoon was hitting us. They sent someone to personally lay some subtle pressure on me and my boss. I'm sure he was a mainland spook. Just thinking about him gives me the creeps." He shuddered, and told them about his meeting with Wu Zhemin, and about Wu showing up at the charity reception the previous evening.

"How you spell that name?" Wai asked. "Did he say who he works for?"

"He said he represented 'high-ranking people on the mainland.' That was enough to get my attention. Here, take his card. I made a copy of it."

Wai and Ross examined the almost-blank card. "This is it?" Ross said. "Nothing else gave you a clue who he was?"

"*Everything* gave me a clue. Including a dressing-down I got from my boss yesterday after Wu talked to him. Mr. Ho didn't threaten to fire me if I continued to pursue the story, but he came damn close."

"Interesting that they're now approaching you instead of me," Ross said. "But I guess they already know whatever I know." He looked around for a waitress to take an order for another round of beers. "Our people should be able to find out something about your Mr. Wu. And you say you're getting together with the lovely Ms. Chen?"

"For information," Sturges said, not too convincingly. "For information."

"Of course," Ross said, and he couldn't help keep a smile from curling his mouth. "Well, given our history, I'd best not try to tell you how to run your love life, laddie. I do hope, though..."

"Yes?"

"I do hope that when you see the poor widow, you keep your head long enough to remember to ask her what Rupert told her about his journey. You will do that this time, won't you?"

Twenty-two

Friday. Four weeks since Rupert's body was found. The conflicting theories of what lured him to his death swirled through Sturges's mind as he approached Olivia's front gate. She knew more than she had told him so far, of that he was sure. This time he would get a straight answer.

He pressed the doorbell. After a long moment her voice came wafting like music out of the intercom, inviting him in. There was a buzz and the snap of the lock unlatching itself. He pushed the gate open and took a deep breath. Be firm, he told himself. There are important matters to be resolved. Don't let her distract you.

The front door to the house opened as he shut the gate behind him. Olivia was standing in the entryway wearing a loose, floor-length caftan. The hall light behind her outlined her body beneath the feather-light fabric. He strained in spite of himself to see if she was wearing anything underneath, but she shifted position and extended a hand to draw him inside and the vision vanished.

She raised her face and planted a tender kiss on his lips, setting off electric sparks. He tried to remain in control of himself, but as he slid his arms around her back to give her a hug, she melted into him like butter, filling the hollows of his body with her curves, and his resolve evaporated.

"This is the nicest greeting I've had in a long time," he said.

"I haven't greeted anybody this nice in a long time," she replied, brushing his lips with hers again.

She had set the scene for seduction. Soft music. Lights dimmed. Her caftan plunged low in front and the deep shadows in the room exaggerated the contours of her body. She began reeling him in with her eyes and her voice, making no attempt at subtlety.

"The *amah*'s not here," she said.

How nice.

"I sent her out so we'd have the house to ourselves."

How very nice.

"I told her not to come back until Monday."

Fantastic.

Still, he made a final effort to turn the conversation toward matters he'd been so eager to resolve moments earlier. Chivalry dictated that before they fall into bed he make his doubts about her truthfulness known. No balling under bogus pretenses.

But she slid her hands up his chest and he couldn't get the words out. "Why so jumpy?" she said. "Are you not used to being with an older woman?"

"It's not...older?"

"I'll be forty-five in a few days," she said. "And a pretty spectacular forty-five, don't you think?" She held her arms out and did a pirouette, presenting herself for inspection. "I know young women are firm and enthusiastic, but I'm still pretty firm myself – and enthusiasm without expertise can wear thin pretty quickly. Don't you think?"

"Absolutely," he said, running his fingers over the bare skin of her neck. *Spineless coward.* "In fact, all of a sudden I'm considering giving up younger women for good." *Wimp.* "But before I commit myself I'd want to see some demonstration of this alleged expertise."

They circled each other like animals performing a mating dance. "Let me think," she said. "If I wanted to show a man what

I'm capable of...I guess I might start by giving him an inkling of what's in store for him."

She reached behind her back and pulled the zipper of the caftan downwards. Then she shrugged her shoulders, letting the garment fall forward along the slope of her breasts, catching it just before it revealed all. "Something like this," she says. "Would this be enough of a demonstration?"

He reached out and traced the tops of her breasts with the backs of his fingers. Ross's parting admonition came back to him, but Sturges was beyond voluntary action now. *I'll definitely ask about Rupert later.* "Not a bad start," he said with what little nonchalance he could muster. "But I'd need to see more than that."

She lowered her arms and let the caftan fall to the floor. Earlier question answered: she was wearing nothing underneath. Except now there was no underneath. She kicked off her shoes and she was wearing nothing at all.

The heat rushed to his face. He filled his hands with her flesh, massaging her nipples with his thumbs. "Enough talk," he said. "We should get rid of these silly clothes."

"In case you haven't noticed, dear, only one person in the room is still wearing clothes."

He managed to undress. She pushed him backward until he fell onto the sofa. She knelt between his legs and lowered her head. An image flashed through his mind: a vacuum cleaner hose skimming just above the surface of a piece of fabric...then suddenly sucking it in violently. A final thought flew past before he surrendered to sweet ecstasy.

They're true, he told himself.

Those stories about her: they're true.

~

An hour passed as if in a minute. And then another. They lay side by side, stunned. "That was beyond words," he said, gathering her into his arms. "And did I ever need it. It must be two months..."

"I needed it, too," she murmured, and he wondered how long it had been for her. Weeks? Months? Since before she and Rupert were married?

That reminded him of the reason he had come here. He could put it off no longer. "Actually there's something else I need," he said.

"I couldn't right now, Billy," she said into his shoulder. "You wore me out. We'll do it again in the morning, I promise. Let's sleep now." She slid her hand between his legs and gave him an appreciative squeeze. Despite his exhaustion, a jolt of pleasure shot through his mid-section at the thought of more to come.

But obligation called. *Courage.* "No," he said, "I mean I need to ask you about Rupert."

She rolled away from him and sat up with a sigh and a frown. "Gosh, lover boy," she said, "I wonder if you could have found a better way to destroy the mood."

"I'm sorry," he said, pulling her to him again. "I don't want anything to ruin this moment. But there's something I have to clear up."

She sighed again. "Let's hear it."

"It's about why Rupert went to China."

When she answered there was annoyance in her voice. "I told you what I know the last time you were here. I showed you those photographs on his computer. All I can do is guess what it all means."

"Those photos might indicate why he went, and they might not. I've thought about it a lot. Given his age and physical condition, it really doesn't seem likely that he was having sex with teenagers." *Or with anyone else.*

"That doesn't mean anything," she said. "I've thought about it, too. You know it's not unusual for some older men to get off just by looking, even if they can't do anything themselves. He could have been paying some young girl to perform while he watched and remembered the good old days, simple as that."

"What about the possibility that he was after some documents?" he said. "Do you know anything about that?"

"Only what I read in your story the other day."

"And the notion that he'd gone to China to buy some special piece of art?"

"That was in your story, too," she said. "Like I told you last time, I suppose that's also a possibility. I honestly don't know."

"Okay, but here's the thing: Ricco Tang says you told him that that's *precisely* why Rupert went."

She took a long time to answer, and when she did, annoyance had been replaced by wariness. "Are you saying I'm lying to you?" she asked. "Is that what you think?"

"I honestly don't know what to think. I asked you last time I was here why Rupert went to China, and you gave me speculation about some photos. I also asked you about antiques, and you

233

specifically told me Rupert hadn't said anything about that. You sounded like you were hearing the idea for the first time.

"Then I find out you'd told Ricco point-blank – before the murder ever happened – that Rupert was going across the border to collect an antique. You're telling me one thing, you're telling Ricco another. What am I supposed to think?"

She sat up and hugged her legs, resting her chin on her knees, and pondered an answer for what seems like an eternity. "The truth?" she said finally.

"I'd really appreciate that."

"The truth is, I did lie. To Ricco. Rupert never said anything to me about antiques, just like I told you. But he was acting very strangely those last days. Then I found the photos of the young girls, I knew about his past, now I had an idea of what had put him on edge. I'm ashamed to admit it but after that I searched through his desk, and I found a letter from the China Travel Service telling him his China visa had been approved. The fact that Rupert was planning a trip to the mainland for any reason at all was as big a shock as the photos.

"The girls in the photos looked like mainlanders, just as you said. I had to consider the possibility that the trip to China and the photos were connected. The whole idea made me nauseous. But more than that, I knew that both he and I could be hurt if my suspicions were right. I was desperate to find a way to keep him from going."

"I don't get it," Sturges said. "How could you be hurt by whatever he was up to?"

"I'm a tough girl, Bill," she said. "They don't call me the 'man-eater' for nothing. But if a story ever got out about Rupert dying in the saddle with some underage girl, I think I'd die of humiliation. Professionally, it could be devastating. What client would ever be able to look at me again with a straight face? So I told Ricco a white lie. To protect Rupert, but also to protect myself."

"But how did Ricco get involved in this in the first place? I'm still confused."

"Like I said, I needed to find some way to prevent Rupert from going to China, and I thought maybe Ricco could help. You know he and Rupert were close. I had an appointment with a client in Macau the next day, so I called Ricco and asked him to meet me there.

"Even then, face to face, I couldn't bring myself to tell Ricco what I really thought the trip was about. But as it turned out, I didn't have to: when I mentioned that Rupert was going to China, Ricco immediately told me what he'd heard from some antique dealer. The antique thing was a plausible reason for Rupert's actions. And frankly, I was happy to grab onto any theory that was different from what I suspected.

"Anyway, it fit my purposes. It would have been perfectly normal for Ricco to discuss some major antique deal with Rupert, and if he was planning some dangerous smuggling operation, it would have made sense for Ricco, as a friend, to try to talk him out of it. So I just nodded my head. I never specifically told Ricco what the trip was about, I just confirmed what he was already thinking. Whatever Rupert had in mind, I was hoping that a talk with Ricco would somehow bring him to his senses."

"Wow," Sturges said, more to himself than to her. Did any of this make sense? "You've got to realize how byzantine this all sounds, Olivia. Wheels within wheels within wheels. I'm having trouble getting my head around it all."

"I know," she said. She looked like a helpless little girl, and he had to fight to keep his mind on the job at hand.

"But why go to all that trouble?" he said. "Why didn't you just confront Rupert after you found the photos? Tell him you found it all despicable. Tell him he was endangering your position as well as his. Demand that he cancel his plans. Why all the subterfuge?"

She pursed her lips and shuddered. "I couldn't bring myself to do it," she said. "It was just so sordid. I looked at those pictures of those young girls and I felt sick. I couldn't bring myself to look him in the eye and ask him about it. If I was wrong, I'd have been accusing him falsely of a terrible thing. If I was right – well, I just didn't know how to deal with that. And anyway, you know how headstrong Rupert was. Once he made his mind up, that was it. I doubt I could have changed his mind no matter what his purpose was. So I hoped Ricco could somehow talk him out of going. I realize in retrospect how pathetic and implausible it sounds, but I didn't know what else to do."

"And that story about accidentally discovering what was on his computer?"

"That was all true. I found those photos of the young girls just like I told you."

"Rupert's dead, Olivia," he said. "Nobody else knows about the photos. If you were so intent on the whole thing going away, why show them to me at all? Why not just delete them and let the whole matter die a quiet death?"

"I considered that," she said. "But I can't really be sure that nobody else does know about the photos, can I? What if Rupert did manage to meet up with some teenage girl from that website while he was in China? He would have had to arrange that through someone, and what if that someone knew who he was? Since the murder took place I cringe every time the phone rings, wondering if it's going to be some blackmailer threatening to expose my late husband.

"You were Rupert's closest friend, Bill. I've been hoping you'd help me keep the thing buried for his sake, even though I know that might go against your journalistic principles. If God forbid word of the photos did get out, I'm hoping at least you could help me present it in the least harmful light. I know I should have been totally honest with you the first time you came over, but I really wasn't thinking straight then. It was only a couple of weeks after the murder. Just ten days after I'd put Rupert into the ground. There'd been the surprises with the will. I was still in shock from it all. I think I still am."

Each individual piece of the story fit with the next, but the total picture refused to come into focus. Could he bring himself to destroy this perfect moment, the first real joy he'd known since the break-up with Sarah, by rejecting her explanation? Could he afford not to? It's one thing to sleep with a woman knowing there might be unwanted consequences. It's another when you're not sure you can believe a word that comes out of her mouth.

He couldn't think straight. He felt used, like he'd felt when he learned what Sarah had been up to. He opened his mouth and his anger came tumbling out. "So," he said, "this whole elaborate ritual, the innuendos, the seductive clothing, the invitation to your conveniently empty house, the great sex – this was all meant to get a hook into me so you could call on a favor if you needed it?"

"No, please don't think that," she said. "I care about you: I've cared for years, and that's Gods' honest truth. I just couldn't do anything about it while Rupert was alive. I would have set my sights on you when he was gone even if I had never seen those photos. Please believe that, Bill."

Wishing your husband dead so you can be with another man: that was cold enough. But would she also do something to make it happen more quickly? He thought back to Ross's comment at the American Club: *Mrs. Rackley is the perfect suspect.*

Suddenly he couldn't breathe. He needed room to think. He stood and started to scoop up his clothing.

"What are you doing?" she asked.

"I'm going home."

"Don't leave. Stay with me."

"This..." He stopped, realizing nothing he could say would be appropriate. He began to dress. "You have to understand, Olivia," he said over his shoulder, "I haven't had a lot of luck with women lately. In fact, it's really been a miserable fucking couple of years. So you'll pardon me if I'm somewhat oversensitive."

"What: now you're equating me with Sarah? You think I'm like her?" All affection had disappeared from her voice. He couldn't tell if she was hurt, or furious.

Nor did he care at this moment. The heat rushed to his face again. "Oh, no," he said, wagging a finger in the air. "No no no no no. Don't you try to make me the villain here. I'm the one who's been lied to. I'm the one who's been seduced. Once I've had time to think it through, maybe I'll change my mind and everything you just told me will make perfect sense, and maybe we can continue whatever it is we have going. But for the moment I can't deal with another deception. I'm sorry, that's the way it is."

"I know I was wrong, lying to you," she pleaded. "But I've told you the truth now. That should count for something."

"Yeah. Well, under different circumstances it might." He turned and headed for the door, assaulted once again by the realization that for all their new intimacy, he still didn't know her at all.

Twenty-three

During the course of 1962, normalcy began to reappear in the Chinese countryside. One day the world was without hope; the next, military trucks pulled into Hong Xing Commune with emergency rations from the regional granaries. Without explanation and with no apologies, the communal kitchens were closed, permission was given by the Party for small private vegetable plots to be planted, and Chang Dongfeng and the other villagers were able to feed themselves once again.

The following year, Chang was absolved along with tens of thousands of others of the rightist crimes they hadn't committed, and he returned to Beijing with four-year-old Lili in tow. With government units depleted by death or political exile, many returnees like him were allowed to resume their previous jobs. Chang returned to the General Office, and his post as leader of the team cataloguing treasures for the People's Palace Museum.

Old colleagues – those who had not accused him falsely – welcomed him back with enthusiasm. Some who had denounced him also tried to ingratiate themselves, insisting they'd acted under duress. Chang could accept that that was true in some cases, but their lies had been responsible for the deaths of his wife and sons. He could not bring himself to look any of them in the eye.

His greatest bitterness was reserved for Wang Sheyu, his superior in the Bureau of Archives, who had reveled in Chang's downfall and personally delivered the news of his banishment. While others at least tried to make amends, Wang avoided him. When the two men finally found themselves face to face in a corridor one day, Wang grunted a brief greeting and tried to walk by. Chang grabbed him by the arm.

"Do you have nothing to say to me?" Chang asked.

"What should I say?" Wang replied.

"You heard what happened to my family during the famine?"

"I heard rumors," the man replied, trying to look away. "I sympathize if you suffered loss."

"I suffered more than 'loss'!" Chang said, holding his face close to Wang's and staring into his eyes. "My wife and my two sons are dead, and we all experienced horror beyond imagination."

"There were shortages here in Beijing," Wang said. "We also suffered."

"You and your family are all still alive. You do not know what suffering is."

"Your problems were not my doing."

Wang tried to pull away, but Chang held tight. "Is that so?" he said. "But we would not have been in that place if certain people had not spoken lies against me."

Wang refused to yield. "Many people said things at the time that were regrettable," he said. "It could not be avoided."

"Perhaps – in some cases." Chang moved his face closer to Wang's. "But I hold all those who falsely denounced me responsible for the death of my wife and my sons. And I warn you, comrade: do not let it happen again."

At this, Wang straightened and returned Chang's gaze. "You are warning *me*?" he said haughtily. "And what will you do? You are still being watched closely, my bourgeois friend. Everyone knows what you were then, and what you still are now. One false move and it is you who will suffer again."

"No," Chang said. "I allowed myself to be persecuted falsely once before. I will not allow it again. Heed my warning, comrade: anyone who causes me or my daughter pain in the future will regret it, and the suffering such a person experiences this time will be very real. I swear it on the graves of my wife and children."

He released his grip. Wang hesitated for just a moment, and then turned and strode away.

~

Chang stayed as far from politics as anyone in China could during that time, but through whispers at the office he learned that Mao was in danger of being shunted aside by a faction of the Party appalled at the havoc he had unleashed with his Great Leap Forward. None of Chang's colleagues dared speak candidly of the years of hunger just past, and certainly none would risk speaking ill of the Chairman himself, but in unguarded moments, some comrades allowed expressions of hope for better times to pass their lips.

Chang harbored no such fantasies. He knew the political struggle in the Party was not over, and Mao and his ideas could re-emerge triumphant at any moment. He knew that as long as Mao was alive, every Chinese citizen was in mortal peril. Delay in fleeing Nanjing had allowed his family to be massacred. Failure to heed his own caution in 1957 led to his wife and sons starving to death. Next time, there would be no hesitation: he would be ready for whatever came.

The moment he and his daughter had arrived back in Beijing, he'd begun to prepare for a quick exit should the need arise. He put money aside. He studied escape routes and means of transportation. He studied his potential enemies, alert for any hint of a new plot against him.

He did not have to wait for long. In 1965, two years after their return, word of new political maneuverings began to circulate in the capital. Soon after that, Mao announced the advent of the *Wuchan Jieji Wenhua Da Geming*, the Great Proletarian Cultural Revolution, a society-wide campaign of political cleansing and rectification. Cleansing was most urgently required, Mao declared, among the bourgeois revisionists at the head of the Party itself.

Again the entire nation took up Mao's call, this time with a level of violence unseen since the revolution itself. Political factions formed and splintered. Rival groups in schools, factories and government departments began attacking each other, each claiming to support Maoist doctrine, each accusing its opponents of betraying the revolution.

As before, Chang Dongfeng watched as some people were forced by circumstances into acts they would not normally commit, and he sympathized. He also watched with disgust as some used the turmoil to settle personal scores or advance themselves at the expense of others. He was sickened by the cruelty that was now displayed across the country.

Above all, this cultured and caring man, this champion of the nation's artistic heritage, could not forgive the wholesale destruction of priceless works of art and architecture that was now being carried out in the name of "Mao Tse-tung Thought." The destruction was the work of a particular element of Mao's latest campaign, the *hong weibing*, the Red Guards.

When Mao's initial attempts to dislodge the Party leadership went nowhere, he concluded that some extraordinary weapon was needed. He turned to the most credulous and uncritical segment of any society, its adolescents. The Maoists recruited, indoctrinated and equipped teenagers from all over the country to act as shock troops against the Party infrastructure. He whipped them into a frenzy, then sent them out to attack the "four olds:" old ideas, old culture, old customs, and "old habits of the exploiting classes."

How exhilarating! What *fun*! The youngsters, inexperienced in life and with no adults to establish boundaries, quite simply took leave of their humanity.

They attacked people in the streets. They invaded the homes of those named as targets while the police stood back and watched. They subjected their victims to days and weeks of public humiliation, parading them through the streets in dunce caps, making them kneel before thousands to confess imagined crimes. They tortured. They raped. They beat victims to death and buried others alive. They drove many to suicide.

And they plundered. By way of eliminating the "old" they defaced and smashed statues. They destroyed individual art collections. They demolished historic buildings. They desecrated Taoist and Buddhist temples: in Tibet, they ransacked temples and monasteries for religious books, paintings and statues, and then tore down the temples and monasteries themselves. By the time Mao realized they were beyond control and the Red Guards were disbanded, the damage they had caused to the national patrimony was incalculable.

Chang Dongfeng watched horror-struck as reports of the destruction came pouring into the General Office. Once again he concluded he had to do something to halt the damage. But what? And at what danger this time to himself and his daughter?

He gave no outward sign of his distress. At work he joined enthusiastically in the now-daily ritual of singing the Chairman's praise and reciting from the little red book of his quotations. Yet behind this façade of acquiescence, and despite his earlier caution, he was devising a plan to save what he could.

The plan he finally settled on was risky in the extreme. But then, just waking up in the morning was risky in the cauldron of hysteria that Mao Tse-tung had unleashed.

~

Chang's plan required the aid of two accomplices.

Many superb pieces looted from personal collections were being turned over to the government by the Red Guards, or sold to the government directly by the owners before the vandals could get their hands on them. In the midst of the chaos, those foreigners willing to brave the journey to China could continue to purchase antiques at government-run Friendship Stores and take them away, all perfectly legally. Chang's challenge was to bring these two elements, the art and the art-lovers, together.

He first needed someone with legitimate access to those antiques; someone who without raising suspicion could take control of pieces that he, Chang, would personally select. Then he needed a foreigner to buy these designated pieces from the first accomplice and take them out of the country for safekeeping.

For the first he chose a long-time friend, a fellow veteran of Yanan, now an official in the Shanghai office of the bureau that oversaw the sale and export of antiquities. This man had also been denounced during the anti-rightist campaign. He too was disillusioned with communist rule, and appalled at what was now taking place.

Chang's position as museum curator already took him from city to city to inspect the new pieces flooding into government warehouses, and to select the cream of the items for the museum. Now he purposely undervalued some of the very best pieces, and sent them instead to the personal attention of his accomplice.

That was not all he sent. Working alone at night in his museum office, he selected dozens of as-yet-uncatalogued masterpieces from Chiang Kai-shek's crates. He slipped these into a false bottom in his briefcase and smuggled them past guards who were too preoccupied with political concerns to do their jobs, if they bothered to show up for work at all. He gave these items false labels and sent them off to his Shanghai confederate. As each item left his hands he felt a pang of guilt, but the feeling lasted only as long as it took to picture Mao's teenage monsters swarming into the museum and destroying whatever Chiang Kai-shek been unable to spirit to Taiwan.

Recruiting a foreign buyer for the plan was infinitely trickier, but Chang thought he knew just the man. He was an Englishman from Hong Kong named Rupert Rackley, who despite his youth had demonstrated extraordinary knowledge and empathy for all things Chinese.

~

In 1964, a year after his arrival in the Orient, Rackley had traveled to Beijing and managed to interview Chang about the organization of the new museum. The story Rackley wrote showed a profound affection for his subject. Chang had to be careful about being seen with a foreigner, but the subject of their mutual interest was benign, and when Rackley made a return visit the following year, the two men found a way to spend time together. They sipped tea and discussed the intricacies of Song glazes. They debated the relative merits of Tang versus Western Han pottery horses. After swearing Rackley to secrecy, Chang unwrapped several items of indescribable delicacy that his team had just catalogued, and Rackley was moved to tears by their beauty.

Once the chaos began in 1966, word of the destructive rampages of the Red Guards began to leak out. Chang could have told Rackley the true extent of the damage. But visas for any foreigners, even journalists posing as tourists, had now become scarce, and at any rate for a Chinese to meet with a foreigner at that point was plain and simply out of the question.

In early 1967, though, a window of opportunity presented itself. The chaos had reached a crescendo. Railroads, docks, factories and schools had all but ceased to function. The terror and destruction of the Red Guards continued. The country was close to civil war. Mao had no choice but to call on the army – whose leaders he had initially earmarked for attack – to restore order. The Cultural Revolution was "postponed for the time being."

Slowly, the army brought the chaos under control. Red Guard units were reorganized or disbanded, and some of the most incorrigible members were exiled to rural villages. Rackley managed to obtain a tourist visa during the lull and traveled to Beijing that February, and Chang took the gamble of meeting him to explain his plan.

Rackley was appalled when he learned the real extent of the damage being done. "The bloody animals!" he exclaimed. "If only I could do something to help stop them."

"In fact, there is something," said Chang.

"Anything. Just tell me."

"I have to warn you: it could be very dangerous."

Rackley brushed the warning aside. A bit of danger was a part of the foreign correspondent's game, was it not? And the idea of saving at least part of China's art outweighed any hesitation. "Tell me what you have in mind," he said.

"It's quite simple," Chang told him. All Rackley had to do was stop in Shanghai en route back to Hong Kong and meet Chang's accomplice there through the local Friendship Store. Then he would start buying according to a list the accomplice would provide, and have his purchases shipped to Hong Kong. Just like any other customer. Except that Rackley would be receiving items of quality and value that no other regular customer could dream of obtaining. The accomplice would certify the purchases as legitimate and arrange shipping through regular channels. Rackley had to come up with real cash, but Chang saw to it that the pieces were priced for him at a tiny fraction of their real value.

After that, Rackley would not even have to appear in person. When a new shipment arrived from Chang, the accomplice would smuggle a note to Rackley in Hong Kong using a code they had devised to describe the new arrivals. Rackley would then cable the accomplice using generic terms to describe what he wanted. "I have a buyer seeking a nice pottery horse from the Northern Wei period," he might write, having been advised in advance that a masterpiece of the genre was sitting in the Shanghai accomplice's safe. Or, "I wonder if you have any good quality porcelains from the Yuan in stock." A request for a set of blue-and-white Qing Dynasty *lingzhi* bowls could result in a pair stamped with the seal of the Qianlong Emperor, one of the greatest patrons of the arts in Chinese history.

"You will be doing the nation a favor," Chang told him when he laid out the plan. "You should expect something in return for your service and the danger you are facing."

Chang's proffer was this: The pieces from the original imperial collection were official national treasures and were to be guarded with care. Among the rest, from every twenty-five items that Rupert was able to get to Hong Kong, he would be allowed to choose one for his personal collection.

Once the madness on the mainland had run its course, Chang explained, he and Rupert would see that the rest of the pieces were restored to the museum, or some other appropriate official body. If something were to happen to Chang, Rupert pledged to see on his own that the pieces were eventually returned to Chinese ownership.

"It's an extremely generous proposition," Rackley said. "But I would do this for the sake of art alone. These pieces should be preserved for all of mankind to enjoy."

"Nevertheless, you will be doing China a service," Chang said. "Your generosity and the risk you are taking on behalf of the country should not go unrewarded."

And so the operation began. There was nothing unusual about someone in Rackley's position opening a small business on the side – Hong Kong was a city of entrepreneurs. He established a shell company with an address in the Hollywood Road antiques district, and printed cards identifying himself as an antiques trader. He had company checks and invoices printed to make his purchases look as unremarkable as possible. He gathered what cash he could, borrowing from friends and relatives with the promise that they would receive an attractive return, and began making contact with Chang's man in Shanghai.

He bought modestly at first so as not to arouse suspicion: a half dozen items one time, a dozen the next. Even so, his stash grew quickly: Chang was eager to get as much as possible out of the country as fast as prudence allowed. When Rackley's cash began to run low he placed a couple of pieces with a well-known art dealer in Hong Kong and was staggered by the huge prices they fetched. Armed with ample cash and mounting anxiety over the fate of China's artistic heritage, he increased the pace of his purchases.

By late July every inch of storage space in his small bachelor apartment was filled, and cartons and scrolls were spilling onto the floors. Buddhas and Earth Spirits, Guanyins and tomb guardians, horses and riders, intricate jade and soapstone carvings of gods and mortals, stared from every surface. The cupboard in his dining room opened to reveal not everyday dishware but priceless blue-and-white and *famille-rose* porcelains. His medicine cabinet was stuffed to the hinges with Qing Dynasty snuff bottles. The night he staggered into his bathroom at one a.m. after a wedding banquet at which far too much Cognac was served, and almost relieved himself on a box of rare Song jades, he realized a new arrangement was in order.

He rented an office on the fringes of Central district. He furnished it with a desk, a chair, powerful lamps, and rows of floor-to-ceiling shelves. He installed dehumidifiers and air-conditioners, and a metal door with industrial locks, and started to transfer his treasures – he allowed himself to think of them as *his* treasures, even though he knew his ownership of most would be fleeting – to their new temporary home.

Many a night after telexing his copy to the newspaper in London he would rush to the office like a smitten lover stealing away for a rendezvous with the object of his desire. He would triple-lock the front door, ensconce himself behind the desk, and examine the treasures under the lamps.

True to his word, he put the original museum items aside, each carefully wrapped and labeled. But there was little difference between those and the rest. Chang was a man of superb taste and surpassing expertise, and every item Rackley obtained was of museum quality. There was another box that Chang had asked Rackley to keep separate, and after debating with himself, Rackley opened it one night and found documents inside. He pulled one out and skimmed it: his written Chinese was still only marginal, but he could make out that it was an official document dealing with the museum project. Paper held no interest for him: he returned the box to the shelf and went back to the art.

He would examine one or two pieces per evening, making sketches and taking extensive notes in large notebooks he kept in the desk. He selected his one twenty-fifth of the stash with great care. At times he would abandon an early choice when a more desirable item came along in the latest batch.

The size of the secret horde was building rapidly, but as it turned out there was no rush to get it catalogued. After a short interlude, the Maoists regrouped in April of 1967 and resumed their attack on the Party leadership. There was no letup to the turmoil in sight.

Rupert's relationship with Chang Dongfeng had a long time yet to run.

Twenty-four

Olivia telephoned. She sent text messages. She left voice-mail. "Call me," her voice pleaded. "We have to talk. I want to see you." Sturges ignored her.

Staying away wasn't easy. The memory of those hours in bed – and on the floor, and a couple of other places he could recollect only vaguely – was intense. The mere appearance of her phone number on his phone led to stirrings in his groin. This was passion of a type he had never experienced with Sarah. He couldn't be sure, the initial feelings of lust and love are difficult to distinguish, but he was beginning to suspect that what he was feeling went beyond mere physical attraction. Avoiding Olivia meant he didn't have to put his feelings to the test.

One of the reporters stuck his head into Sturges's office. "Some guy named Ross called," the reporter said. "He gave me a message for you."

"Ross called *you*?" Sturges said. The man was a middle-aged reporter who covered education and other mundane topics. He rarely got out of the newsroom. He had never done a story remotely connected to Rupert's murder. Why would Ross call him, of all people? "What's the message?"

"Here," the reporter said, and handed him a hand-scrawled note. "*Must meet most urgent,*" it said. "*Home & office not safe. Discreet location? Reply soonest text only.*" The note contained a phone number that Sturges was not familiar with.

What the hell was going on? And where might they meet that was discreet? He supposed he could rent a hotel room – with cash, in case whomever Ross was worried about was somehow monitoring Sturges's credit card transactions. They did that, didn't they, monitor credit cards? Winston Wai's TV cops all did that.

How's this for paranoia, he asked himself. He didn't even know who or what he was supposed to be paranoid about but already he was looking over his shoulder. He had allowed the approach by Wu Zhemin to rattle him after all. But Ross's note left no doubt that there was something to be wary of. *Home & office not safe*. He couldn't call to ask what was going on. *Reply soonest text only*. At least it took his mind off Olivia.

So where could they...wait: Ricco Tang. Ricco owed Sturges for lying to him. Providing the premises for a private meeting would be a way of making amends. Ricco's office, perhaps – or even better, his home. He lived in a monster complex, a beehive of dozens of apartments with numerous entrances. It was nestled in a cleft in Mid-Levels, just past the point where the road climbed straight up from the flats of Central and then branched east and west across the face of the mountain. A person could drive into one of the ground-level entrances to the complex and nobody watching from outside would have any idea which of the apartments he was headed for.

He pulled out his cell phone to call Tang, then stopped. If it was unsafe to call Ross, it stood to reason that it was unsafe to call Ricco. They – or he, or she, or whoever the hell it was – might hear him asking to use Ricco's apartment.

He was passing a small stationery store; he walked inside and asked if he could use the phone behind the counter. It used to be common practice in Hong Kong, walk off the street into someone's shop and ask to use the landline. Local calls were free; people rarely refused. Now almost everyone had a mobile phone and the practice had all but disappeared, but Sturges laid on his most effusive Cantonese, pretending his phone battery had just died, and the woman in the shop was happy to let him use her phone.

Tang was equally happy to let Sturges use his apartment. "As long as you're not planning to bring Olivia," he said. "You're not planning to bring Olivia, are you?"

Sturges assured him he was not. Tang asked how long and Sturges said he didn't know, an hour or so. Tang asked what it was all about and Sturges told him to mind his own business. "Claudia and I were going out tonight anyway," Tang said, sounding disappointed at being excluded from the intrigue. "I'll call the *amah* and tell her to let you in. I'll also have to let the Gurkha at the gate know you're coming. Uh...what names should I give him?"

"Just tell the guard that two *gwei-los* and a Chinese will be arriving separately and will be giving your name and address."

Tang realized he wasn't going to learn anything more. "Well, make yourselves at home," he said. "Please don't drink all my good wines."

Sturges next walked into a 7-Eleven, satisfied himself that nobody was watching, and bought a SIM card with pre-paid minutes. He walked behind the racks of potato chips and packaged pastries at the rear of the shop and slipped the new card into his phone. He texted Ross the time and place of the meeting, received an immediate reply, then removed the SIM and dropped it into the shop's trash can on his way out.

"James Bond, eat your goddamn heart out," he said aloud, but again with more bravado than he felt. He stepped into the street, fighting back a new feeling of dread, and hailed a taxi for lunch at the China Club.

~

Ricco and Claudia Tang's apartment was decorated with understated good taste. Most Chinese, if they could afford it and were not too tight-fisted to shell out the cash, opted for glitz and flash, lots of stainless steel and glass. The Tangs' living and dining rooms were all leather and wood, with carved Chinese and Tibetan furniture and very expensive Asian carpets on the floors. Tang's collection of paintings, porcelains, statues and carvings was smaller than Rupert's, but considerably more selective and far better displayed.

The Filipina housekeeper brought them drinks and snacks, and then Winston Wai escorted her to the servants' quarters behind the kitchen and told her to stay there. When Wai returned, Ross leaned forward and spoke with urgency in his voice.

"I'm afraid you might be in a wee bit of danger, laddie," he said. "We don't have anything on your Mr. Wu yet. But Special Branch have meanwhile picked up indications that another mainland security operative might also be in town, one we are familiar with this time, a vicious little bugger named Ng. I'm told that whenever he shows up, something unpleasant happens. Do you remember the attack on the editor of *View* Magazine a few years back?"

"How could I forget?" Sturges said. "They chopped the poor bastard's hand off. Luckily, the doctors were able to sew it back on. The word was that the attack was the work of local triads who were angry at an exposé of their operations that *View* had run."

"That was accurate as far as it went," Ross said. "We later developed information that those triads were acting at the behest of mainland State Security. If you recall, *View* was also running some sensitive stories about the mainland's post-handover operations in Hong Kong, things the mainland authorities considered their private affair. Of course, they consider everything a secret, don't they? The attack was their subtle way of telling the *View* editor and anyone with like ideas to back off."

"And this guy Ng was in town at that time? Did your people definitely tie him to the *View* attack?"

"There was nothing we could take to court," Ross said. "But we knew for sure he was in contact with heads of the triad gang that carried out the attack both before and after it happened. And remember when that radio commentator was beaten up last year? The one who was arguing loudly for full democracy here?"

"Don't tell me: Mr. Ng just happened to be paying a visit that time, too."

"So our people tell me," Ross said. "And that time he was accompanied by some of his own wee muscle boys from the mainland. Special Branch are pretty sure they're the ones who did the beating in that case."

"What are you saying? You think Ng might be here to rough *me* up now?"

"We have to assume it's possible," Ross said. "This Wu fellow went to the trouble of coming down here to warn you off the story. Then for good measure he talked to your boss about getting you to back off. And what happened? Within days, you published a new story about Rupert being on the trail of some documents, along with a few other new tidbits. In essence, you told them to piss off. So now they've sent Ng in — perhaps to take up where Wu left off."

"You think they've decided verbal warnings aren't going to work."

"It's a logical assumption, don't you think? You know as well as I do that the folks in Beijing are used to getting their way. Since polite persuasion failed to convince you, it would be no surprise if they turned to their black ops people to deliver their message more forcefully. If Special Branch's tip about this Ng fellow is correct and he really is in town, you'd best be very careful, my friend."

"*If* Special Branch's tip is correct,'" Sturges repeated. "You scare the shit out of me, and you don't even know for sure that Ng is here?"

"We're pretty sure it's him. And it's smart to be safe, laddie. Wu took the trouble to search you out, and now we have this information about Ng's apparent arrival. It would strain credulity to think that the two men's appearances are not connected."

"Do we know what this Ng looks like or where we can find him?"

"No," Ross said. "That's what makes this especially difficult. We know he exists, we've tracked his comings and goings, but none of our people has ever actually seen him."

But Sturges needed no further convincing. "We know the mainland authorities are at their worst when they believe their prerogatives are being threatened, as they obviously believed about the *View* exposés and those radio commentaries," he said. "If Ng has been sent to Hong Kong to take care of me, that means they consider whatever I've been writing to be in the same category as those things. Whatever Rupert was up to and however he was killed, it's making them extremely nervous to think the story might get out. My God, what the hell did Rupe have on them?"

"I don't suppose you'd consider backing away from the story," Ross said.

"You know I can't do that."

"I thought you had too much integrity, but I had to ask."

"Thanks. But it looks like I'm going to need more than compliments on my integrity. Your text message implied that I'm being watched, and maybe my phone is tapped. Is that the case?"

"Everything we saying is off record, right?" Wai said. "This one you don't write nothing about. Okay?"

Sturges nodded, and Wai spoke: "Yes, we think you are being monitored. So you have to be careful what you say on phone. Get second phone or new SIM card, like you do today. Look around you all the time. Check locks on doors and windows.

"These very serious people," Wai said, accentuating the obvious. "I deal with this type a lot when I was in Triad Bureau. They don't mind to beat people up or kill them. You got to be careful, Sturges."

"Since you know what they're up to," Sturges asked, "isn't there something you can do to make them back off before they do...whatever they plan to do?"

"If we could find them, sure," Ross said. "I could have a couple of our lads stop them for an ID check on the street. If there's anything suspicious about their documents we could even send them back across the border."

"But that would let them know we were on to them."

"That's the point. If they know we're watching they might hesitate to do anything rash." Ross glanced at Wai, who nodded in confirmation. "With some proactive strategy on our part and a wee bit of luck," he told Sturges, "you might not get the shit beat out of you."

Twenty-five

Olivia's call came through the newspaper switchboard this time. Sturges couldn't keep putting her off forever. Even if the elusive Mr. Ng was tapping his personal phone, it was unlikely he'd be tapping the paper's main telephone line, so it was probably safe to talk. "Hi," he said as casually as his tangled emotions allowed.

"You've been avoiding me," she said.

"Really? Whatever gave you that idea?"

"Bill, this is silly. I swear I was not using you. Not the way you were thinking – although I wouldn't mind using you again the way we used each other the other night. That was pretty spectacular. And I'm not easy to impress in the bedroom."

"We didn't spend all that much time in the bedroom per se, as I recall."

She giggled, and a picture of the two them flailing away flashed through his mind. He could feel the contours and crevices of her body. It was lucky he was sitting behind his desk at the moment. If his staff had gotten a full frontal look at him, he would have been mortally embarrassed.

His resolve evaporated. Enough high-minded abstinence. "Okay, I apologize for avoiding you. There's an awful lot going through my mind at the moment: Rupert's death for starters, the mystery surrounding that, falling in—" He stopped himself before he blurted out something he might regret later. Was he really falling in love with her? "...falling *into* bed with you. All that stuff." He didn't mention the possibility that men had come to town to chop his hand off. "Let's get together tonight and talk."

"Just talk?" she said.

"We'll see what comes up."

~

He meant to be businesslike this time, he really did. They had to discuss their relationship in an adult manner. He'd gone over in his mind what he was going to say to her. He'd practiced it in front of the mirror before he left his apartment.

A waste of time. The moment he was inside her door they were at each other like rutting animals. None of this he-fumbles-with-her-blouse-buttons, she-maneuvers-his-shirt-over-his-head stuff you see in the movies. They both went straight for the genitals. She opened his pants so fast that sparks almost flew from the zipper. He threw her on her back and tore off her panties. Then he was inside her, and that was the last thing either of them remembered clearly for the next hour.

"I can't believe we just did that again," she gasped.

"You were amazing," he said.

"*You* were amazing."

"We were both amazing. I'm amazed at how amazing we were.'"

"Maybe you should always ignore me for several days before we get together."

"You make it sound like we're going to do this on a regular basis," he said. "I'm not sure I can take it."

"You sound surprised."

"Surprised at...?"

"My enthusiasm in bed. I thought after the other night..."

"Well, you know, you hear things," he said. "But people exaggerate. You don't always know what to believe."

"You mean some of my previous male friends...?"

He shrugged. "Guys. You know how it is."

"Anyway, you shouldn't be."

"Surprised?"

"I told you what people call me: 'The Man-eater.'"

"So you did. Now I know where the nickname came from."

She giggled. "Actually, you don't. You don't know, and nobody else knows. It's literally true."

"What's literally true?"

"The nickname."

~

"I don't get it," Sturges said.

"You're really going to find me amazing after you hear this," she said. She rolled over to face him. "Apparently my father and I almost starved to death during the famine that followed the Great Leap Forward."

He nodded. "I know about the famine," he said.

"I'm sure you know the general story," she said. "What I'm going to tell you next is not so widely known. A lot of people turned to cannibalism during the famine. And those people included us. The thing that saved my father and me at a critical moment was human flesh."

He let that sink in for a moment. He swallowed and said: "I'm learning not to dismiss anything out of hand these days. Go on."

"I only recently learned this myself. My father told me about it just before he died. I've read up on the whole era since then, and it wasn't terribly uncommon during the famine. People were literally insane with hunger. Some ate their dead neighbors, some ate their relatives, some ate each other's children – sometimes they even ate their own children. According to my father, when it happened to us, my two brothers had already starved to death, and he and my mother and I were all on the brink."

"When are we talking about?"

"It was 1961, near the end of the famine. We were living in a village near Macau, where my family had been sent in 1957 because of my father's alleged rightist crimes."

"The Anti-Rightist Campaign," Sturges said. "I didn't realize he'd been caught up in that. But Rupert once told me that your father came from an aristocratic background, so I guess it's no surprise that he was targeted. And I suppose you were in some rural village 'learning from the masses' during that period?"

"I was born in the village seven or eight months after the rest of them had arrived from Beijing, and I was only a toddler when the famine came, so I don't remember any of it. But according to my father..."

And she recounted the family's story, detail by gory detail. "My father said that as terrible as it was, that little boy's flesh got him and me through the worst of it. We built up our strength enough to make it until the famine ended. Unfortunately, it was too late to save my mother."

"I'm speechless," Sturges said.

"I'll bet," she said. "Imagine how I felt when I first learned about it. But my father lived through all that craziness, the Nanjing massacre, the war against the Japanese, the civil war, the retribution after the Communist victory, the Anti-Rightist

264

Campaign, the Great Leap, the Great Famine, the Cultural Revolution. He personally got to know Mao and Chou En-lai and all the other big guns during his time in Yanan. He had some pretty amazing stories to tell. And one of the most amazing is that yours truly is a man-eater in the most literal sense of the term."

He rolled onto his back and stared at the ceiling.

"Hey," Olivia said after several minutes of silence, and she poked him in the ribs.

"What?"

"Now's the moment when you're supposed to say, 'Honey, I understand, there's nothing to be ashamed of, this doesn't affect our relationship.'"

"Honey, I understand, there's nothing to be ashamed of, this doesn't affect our relationship," he said. Still staring at the ceiling.

"I wouldn't mind a bit more enthusiasm when you say it," she said. "What's up?"

"Nothing."

"Something."

He hesitated. "There is something," he finally said. "It's nothing you said or did. I could be in a bit of danger because of working on the murder story, and I can deal with that, but I'm wondering if you could be in danger if we began being seen together in public." He recounted what Ross and Wai had told him about the mainland thug Ng.

"My God," she said when he had finished. "But this isn't...this shouldn't be happening."

"Of course it shouldn't be happening. But you know what the Party is capable of when its interests are threatened. I have to believe that what the cops told me is true."

"I believe them," she said. "What I mean is, it's bad enough that they killed Rupert. I never expected them to threaten you, too."

"'They'?" he said, turning toward her. "Who are 'they'? Do you know something you haven't told me?"

"No, no," she said. "By 'they' I just mean the Chinese. The Communist Party. Someone on that side killed Rupert. Now some mainlanders are apparently threatening you, too." She snuggled in closer and wrapped an arm around him. "Lying here with you like this, I've been feeling safe for the first time since the murder," she said. "I like the feeling, Bill. I don't want it to end."

Twenty-six

Their personal relationship was settled, to the extent that he and Olivia would continue seeing each other. He'd run her comments and explanations past his journalistic antennae, he'd searched his soul, and he was satisfied that she was telling him the truth. As convoluted as the truth was.

They'd have to take care not to move too quickly or too openly. They didn't want their relationship to become fodder for newspaper columnists and Internet gossip. With finesse and luck, the future would work itself out. And if not...he would savor the moment.

Sarah's sleeping around had wounded him more than he liked to admit. He'd felt wronged, he'd felt betrayed, but most of all, if he was honest with himself, he'd felt stupid. Here was old Bill playing the faithful husband, while his wife was slinking around town and fucking heaven knew how many other men. "I did nothing wrong," he told himself. "I'm the wounded party. I deserve the company of a fantastic woman."

And if after all there was criticism of Rupert's best friend and Rupert's widow taking up with each other after Rupert's murder? He'd given that extensive thought, too, and he had his answer ready. In the words of the writer, anyone who didn't like it could take a flying fuck at a rolling doughnut.

He left Olivia's house and steered the Morgan through the deserted roads of Stanley, heading for his house on the Peak. Like Rupert, he could never have afforded to buy the house on a journalist's salary – square foot per square foot, the Peak was some of the most expensive real estate in the world. But Sturges's

267

mother had been the granddaughter of a former governor. She was a member of Hong Kong's elite. She had inherited two pieces of prime real estate on the Peak.

Bill, the only surviving family member since his mother's death five years earlier, had moved back into one of the two houses after Sarah left town. It was the house he'd grown up in on Severn Road, a narrow loop of road that fronted one face of the mountainside. He rented the other out at a hundred thousand Hong Kong dollars a month – almost thirteen thousand U.S. Even in the still-depressed real estate market, the houses were worth seven or eight million U.S. dollars each. If he and Olivia did end up together, what would their combined net worth be? He started to calculate, then stopped: he was getting way ahead of himself.

He braked for the sharp left turn that would take him out of Stanley Village and along the southern end of the island. The way home was mostly tight and twisty two-lane roads carved out of the island's mountainsides by the British decades earlier. The kind of roads the Morgan was made for. It was four in the morning: there would be little or no traffic about. It was a glorious night, the moon was bright, the top was down, and a touch of coolness in the night air caressed his face, signaling that the long summer was finally coming to an end. Sturges was feeling his manhood after his joust with Olivia.

Okay, he told himself. Let's see what this baby can do on a real driver's road.

He shifted down to first, jerked the wheel hard to the left and pushed the gas pedal to the floor. The Morgan slid around the tight turn with its tail hanging out and then straightened for the uphill run to the Chung Hom Kok peninsula. Halfway there he came upon a Ferrari on a short straight; he caught the driver napping and flashed past with a slight wave of the hand. The way Stirling Moss used to wave, Sturges thought with a smile, whenever Moss passed one of his hapless opponents.

The Ferrari driver rose to the challenge, but there was no safe place to pass for the next mile or so and Sturges knew the way intimately: he'd been driving these roads for twenty-five years. With skill and care he could stay ahead at least until the flat stretch along Repulse Bay, despite the Ferrari's superior handling and power.

He barely lifted off the accelerator as he took a left-hand bend on a tight, inside line; in his rear-view mirror, he saw the other driver run wide and have to correct. The wobble put the Ferrari back by several seconds. Hah! Like Fangio humbling the Ferraris during the 1957 German Grand Prix.

He was still several seconds ahead when he crested the hill at Chung Hom Kok. The Ferrari closed the gap on the downhill run toward Repulse Bay, but the road was twisting and barely wide enough for two cars: there was still no safe place to pass at the speed they were going and the other driver clearly didn't have what it took to try. Sturges left his braking a bit late at the bottom of the hill where the road curved hard left onto the bay front. He slid into the oncoming lane, missing a minibus coming in the opposite direction by inches. The Ferrari, paying more attention to the Morgan than to the road, got all out of shape once more...and the driver abandoned the chase.

The red car slowed to a crawl, shrinking rapidly in Sturges's rear-view mirror; Sturges covered the straight along Repulse Bay in less than thirty seconds and put the car into a drift around the uphill left-hand bend at the end. Rupert would have been proud, he told himself, patting the car's dashboard and enjoying his small victory.

He was on the Peak ten minutes later. He crested another hill and began to navigate the narrow maze of lanes that led to his house, admiring the sight of the city lights spread out like a blanket far below, when his phone rang. It was Ross.

"It's the middle of the night," Sturges said. "Don't you cops ever sleep?"

"Where are you right now?" Ross asked. There was urgency in his voice.

"I'll be pulling up to my house in another minute. Why?"

"You're out in the car? That's not good. That's definitely not good." He heard a muffled conversation, and then Ross was back. "You'd better turn around and meet me at Police Headquarters, laddie. I want to arrange some protection for you. Quickly."

"What's up?" Sturges asked. The policeman's tone frightened him.

"I just got a call from my men. We've now confirmed that Ng, the mainland enforcer, is in town, for one thing," Ross said.

"And for another?"

"We intercepted a phone conversation. They're definitely after you. If you were inside your house, I'd say lock the doors and windows and grab a cricket bat and hunker down until we could got there, but since you're out and about..."

"We Americans tend to have baseball bats," Sturges said. "But is this for real this time? You're sure this Ng fellow knows who I am and cares about what I write?"

"Oh, he most definitely knows you, and he most definitely cares. There's no longer any question about that. My *local* staff, you see, are the ones who told me about Ng's history and the fact that he's here in Hong Kong right now." Ross had put unusual emphasis on the word "local."

"And...?"

"They told me in Cantonese."

"Which you'd expect, given that they're all Hong Kong Chinese," Sturges said. Annoyance was creeping into his voice. What the hell was Ross babbling on about at this hour of the morning? "I don't see what--"

"They used the Cantonese pronunciation of the man's name." He paused. 'Ng Chi-ming.'"

"I still don't – oh, shit!" Chinese characters and transliterations flashed in Sturges's mind. "Of course!" he shouted. Wu Zhemin, Ng Chi-ming: different dialects, different pronunciations, same scumbag. "Damn, I should have made that connection. And the son of a bitch was sitting right across from me in my own office! I told you he was a weasel."

"I'm far less interested in his personality right now than in what he and his men are apparently aiming to do to you."

As they spoke, Sturges approached the end of Plantation Road. A silver SUV was parked in the driveway of a row of houses. As the Morgan passed by, the SUV's engine rumbled into life and its headlights switched on.

Sturges eyed the car in his rear-view mirror. He couldn't be sure it was the same SUV that had accompanied him and Wu from the Sichuan restaurant the previous week, but everything in him said it was. "Ross, I think I'm in trouble," he said.

"What's wrong?"

"I think I'm being followed...by one of Wu's cars. He's right behind me."

"Can you get into your house safely?"

"I don't think so. I have to get out of my car to unlock the front gate by hand. They could jump out and grab me."

"Do you think you can outrun them? Get to Police Headquarters?"

"I can try. It depends on how good the driver of the SUV is," Sturges said. "He sure as hell can't get in front of me on Severn Road." It was an old, one-way road, barely wide enough for one car in some places. "If I can gain enough of a lead on him by the time we get back to Peak Road, I might be able to stay ahead all the way down the hill. It would help if you had a couple of cars waiting for me at the bottom. Preferably with lights flashing. That might scare them off." He hoped.

Ross pictured the route from the Peak to Central. "It should take you no more than seven or eight minutes at this time of night — five or six if you're any good. I'll scramble some cars to wait for you at the bottom of Garden Road. Put your foot into it, laddie. Show Rupert he was justified in leaving you that lovely car of his."

Sturges slid the phone into his shirt pocket. The SUV's high beams were on and the lights were reflecting directly into his eyes, almost blinding him. There was still a chance this was just a bad driver: the Chinese could be as oblivious when they drove as when they walked down the street. But his gut told him this driver knew exactly what he was doing.

He signaled for a right turn as if to continue along Plantation Road, and the SUV veered right to follow. Then he jammed the gear lever into first, jerked the wheel to the left and floored the gas pedal to plunge downhill onto Severn Road. The driver of the SUV stood on his brakes, did as quick a turn as a large car can do in a very narrow space, and shot after him. Once again a powerful car was chasing him, but this time the racing was for keeps.

There was no way to go fast on Severn Road. At some points, fifteen miles an hour was almost reckless. Speed bumps spaced along the track could tear a car's underside out if taken too fast. At least it was impossible for another car to get by, and again, Sturges could almost drive the road blindfolded. He used his knowledge of the twists and turns to gain a half second here, a second there. The SUV's modern suspension navigated the speed bumps better than the Morgan's – the persistent rattle in the wood frame behind Sturges's head was even louder than normal, and at times he thought the car was going to shake itself to pieces – but the SUV was also too wide for what was originally built as a track for sedan chairs carrying rich and powerful colonials to their mountainside retreats. More than once he saw sparks fly from the doors of the SUV as it scraped against the concrete foundations of apartment buildings or the stone balustrades along the cliff side. Despite the danger looming in his mirror he had to laugh: if they were in a movie, this would be the slowest car chase in film history.

He was thirty yards ahead by the time he'd finished the loop and was back at the intersection with Plantation Road. He put his foot to the floor again, navigated the bend above a schoolyard and dived downhill. He stood on the brakes and put the car into a power slide around the hairpin at the bottom; another two tight switchbacks and he was hurtling downhill at high speed toward Central. Behind him, the SUV got tangled momentarily on the tiny bridge that leads to Peak Road. Another few seconds' advantage; another bit of space between him and men intent on doing him harm.

The curves along Peak Road were tight and he was using almost all the road, even on blind curves, and praying that no car was coming up the hill. Despite his advantage, by the time he neared the bottom of the hill the SUV had closed most of the gap; on the short straight stretch at the bottom, the driver pulled out to his right in an attempt to pass and block him.

Too late: by the time the SUV's front bumper was even with the Morgan's rear wheel they were at the end of the straight, and both were standing on the brakes for the left-hand switchback that led onto Magazine Gap Road.

Sturges had the inside line. He negotiated the turn with inches to spare between his right-hand door and the stone retaining wall on the cliff side. The SUV, caught on the outside of the curve, slid wide and into the wall. "Keep making mistakes, motherfucker," Sturges thought. "Please."

Accelerating, braking, running at full revs in second gear, sliding wide to block any attempt by the SUV to get in front. Like Senna using all the narrow road at Monaco in 1992 while Mansell, in a faster car, tried every which way to get past.

As he stood on the brakes again for the right-hand hairpin at May Road, the SUV made another lunge. The car's nose rammed the Morgan's rear bumper. The Morgan's rear end swung violently outward, but Sturges held the car on the road, then sawed at the wheel wildly for the left-hand switchback onto the final stretch.

He barely navigated the tight, looping overpass that led onto Garden Road. The SUV driver overcooked again it and skidded into the guardrail on the overpass before managing to straighten out and roar after his prey.

This run down the mountainside was wider than the stretch they'd just navigated, but so steep and bumpy that driving it at even normal speeds was precarious. At the speed Sturges was traveling it felt almost like skiing on black ice down the face of a vertical cliff.

Only a couple of hundred yards more, he told himself as his speedometer needle leapt past a hundred kilometers per hour. Only a few more seconds. Please God that Ross has kept his word and his men are waiting for me at the bottom. Please God that I can keep the car on the road that long.

He swept out to the right as he passed the old colonial governors' mansion with his tires barely gripping the asphalt. As he approached the U.S. Consulate building on the left, with the SUV closing in rapidly, the road widened to four lanes – and down the hill, from around the final curve, he saw blinking lights reflecting off the buildings ahead. Ross had come through!

Now if only Sturges could stop the car before he killed himself.

There were two exits from the bottom of Garden Road, separated by high guardrails. The two right-hand lanes led up and across an overpass toward Admiralty. Those on the left led sharply down and into a right-angle turn toward Central. Both routes were blocked by police cars.

The only option was to stop, and there was only one way at this speed. He'd seen racing drivers and movie stunt drivers do it. He'd tried it once himself on a wide, flat surface at half the speed he was going now.

First he had to claw off what speed he could. The car clipped the apex of the final left-hand curve by the U.S. Consulate and drifted out to the far right-hand lane. He stood on the brakes again, so hard that smoke poured out of the front wheels. He shifted down at the same time, sending the overworked engine up to maximum revs, then shifted down yet again.

The engine screamed in protest. The car slowed, although not as much as he'd hoped. With only fifty yards left to the bottom of the hill, he yanked the wheel hard to the left with one hand, and pulled the handbrake up with the other.

The rear end of the Morgan swung around a hundred and eighty degrees. The front end was now pointing uphill, and the car was sliding backwards toward the police cars at the bottom. The cops standing by the cars broke and ran. The Morgan continued sliding for several seconds, while Sturges stood on the brakes with all the strength in his body.

And then the car stopped.

The other driver, unfamiliar with the road and caught unawares by Sturges's sudden maneuver, shot past the sliding Morgan. He tried to brake and turn, but he was going too fast and he'd left it too late. The SUV's rear end slid out until the car was perpendicular to the roadway. It slewed sideways, balancing for a split second on its downhill wheels, then it flipped, bouncing like a beach ball until it came to a violent halt against the guardrail. It teetered there for a moment, dissipating its final bit of stored energy while the laws of physics decided which way to send it.

The car toppled back the way it had come, hitting the roadway with a crash of metal and glass.

~

The cops had watched the scene unfold from the sides of the road. Now they swarmed over the SUV, attempting to extricate the two men inside.

Sturges sat in the middle of the road, the Morgan pointing uphill, hands grasping the steering wheel so hard his knuckles were white. He heard a shout nearby and realized it was Ross's voice. "Are you all right Billy boy?" Ross was calling.

Sturges couldn't reply. His heart was pounding furiously and his whole body was trembling from adrenaline and naked terror. In his mind's eye the road was still rushing uphill at him. He did a mental MRI for internal injuries or broken bones. Sensing none, he gave a barely perceptible nod of the head. He knew that trying any more ambitious a move than that would be a mistake: he'd have no control over his body.

There was shouting all around, and through the fog he heard a voice crackling over a police radio. The cops at the crumpled SUV were calling for an ambulance. One man unconscious and just barely breathing, the voice said. The other: no pulse.

After a long pause to allow his heart rate to return to somewhere near normal, Sturges tried to climb out of the car, but his legs were like jelly and he collapsed back into the seat. He composed himself, then willed himself upright again. Ross grabbed one arm. Winston Wai grabbed the other.

"This is crazy, guys," Sturges rasped as the two men led him to a police car. "This kind of shit doesn't happen in real life."

Twenty-seven

Ross called two days after the chase. "Our wee friend Wu has left town," he said.

"You let him go just like that?" Sturges asked. "What if he comes after me again?"

"We had nothing to hold him on. We can't prove that he was involved in what happened to you. Even if we had something, trying to detain him would have put us into a competition with the mainland authorities that we had no way of winning. They bundled him across the border at two o'clock this morning – I sent Winston to make sure he really left town. We did make it clear to the mainlanders that we knew why Wu and his friends had come to town, and told them that if he ever showed up again we would bring him in for questioning. They're denying it all, of course, in public and in private. But we have the bodies of those two mainland thugs to back up our side of the story."

"It would have been nice before you let Wu go if you'd found out what his bosses are so eager to keep hidden," Sturges said. But he knew Ross was right. The Hong Kong government wouldn't have supported Ross if he'd tried to take the questioning any further. And Wu wouldn't have told them anything if they tried.

"My reporters were told the two bodies have already been claimed by the mainland authorities and will be following Wu across the border by this afternoon," Sturges said.

"In fact," Ross said, "they're being put onto a train bound for Guangzhou as we speak. There's nothing we could have done to keep them here, and it wouldn't have done us any good. There's no mystery how the two died. There's nothing more the bodies could have told us. The Hong Kong government was officially informed that the grieving families in the Northeast, where the two men ostensibly come from, are desperate to have the men's bodies back home for proper funeral rites, and of course our leaders fell all over themselves to do the humanitarian thing for the poor relatives."

"And to sweep the whole thing under the rug," Sturges said. "Yeah, we got a photo of those so-called 'relatives' crying and burning ritual paper money at the crash site yesterday morning. If you believe the official story, the Chinese authorities identified the two dead men, located their families up near the Russian border in Heilongjiang and transported them down here to be with their late loved ones, all within hours of the crash. The only way they could have done all that so quickly would be to fly them down here on military jets."

"Speaking of flying, how's that Morgan of yours? That was a masterful job of driving the other night, but I can't imagine things like that are easy on a twenty-year-old car."

"It's in the shop," Sturges said. "I really put the poor thing through the wringer. I'm sure I over-revved the engine. There's a humongous dent in the rear where that sonofabitch in the SUV rammed me from behind. I flat-spotted all four tires when I spun her to a stop. And the damn thing's rattling so loud from banging over those speed bumps on Severn Road that it's driving me nuts. I'm having her torn down and reassembled from scratch. The mechanic says it's going to take at least three weeks."

"You should take good care of the old girl," Ross said. "She saved your Anglo-Yankee arse."

"So it seems," Sturges said. "Although we really don't know what the specific danger was, do we? I mean, there was the chase, but we never had a chance to question the two thugs to ask what they had in mind for me if they'd caught me. Any evidence that might exist of a plan to injure me has departed the SAR along with Mr. Wu and the two bodies."

"Actually, we do have something. Now, you've earned this story, I'm not going to try to talk you out of printing it, but none of this came from me ..."

Sturges waited.

"We found some items in the SUV. There was a map of the Peak, with your house circled and your name and address hand-written at the top." Ross paused.

Sturges digested that. "You said 'some items,' plural."

"Yes. Well, there were also a couple of brand new meat cleavers on the back seat."

Sturges felt his heart miss a beat. "Jesus," he said under his breath.

"Indeed. We're confident they didn't come all the way to Hong Kong to cook you a meal, laddie. We assume they were planning to use those choppers on some part of your body, like they did with that other editor."

"Animals!" Sturges snorted, trying to clear his mind of visions of the two men coming at him with choppers raised. "So now what?"

"Given the known links between the car chase and Rupert's death, we'll have a legitimate reason to reopen the murder case."

"But surely they'll close you down again as quickly as they can."

"They'll let us thrash around for a decent period and then quietly call it off again. But as long as the local media are crawling all over the story, I suspect our mainland friends will keep their hands off you. I personally told them that if anything happens to you going forward we will hold them responsible, and we will say so very publicly."

"Do you think that's going to scare them off?" Sturges asked.

"It should do, for now. The foreign press corps up in Beijing pays attention to what happens in Hong Kong. If we down here were to accuse the Chinese authorities of being behind an attempt to murder you, a respected newspaper editor, in order to cover up another murder, those reporters in Beijing would pick the story up in a flash and send it around the world.

"Beijing is used to accusations of human rights abuses against its own citizens, but being accused of violent attack on a prominent foreigner is not the kind of publicity they'd welcome. So yes, I think they'll back off for the time being."

"My goodness, Mr. Ross, it almost sounds like you think reporters play a useful role in society."

"From time to time," Ross said. "From time to time."

Sturges laughed in spite of himself. "Well, I hope 'the time being' lasts for a good long while. Remember, you promised you were going to make sure I didn't get the shit beat out of me."

"Let's not set our sights too high," Ross said. "Keeping you from being beaten has now become a secondary consideration. Given all that's happened, I'll settle for just getting you out of this alive."

Twenty-eight

Sturges re-read the follow-up stories on the car chase, only to shut down his computer in frustration. His reporters had located plenty of people willing to comment on what was happening – there was never any shortage these days of "analysts" and "experts" willing to venture an opinion about any subject that came down the journalistic pike. But it was all filler: speculation and personal opinion substituting for hard fact. The mystery was as impregnable as ever.

He walked to the elevator lobby, where Winston Wai was waiting. Ross had assigned Wai to watch over Sturges following the car chase. "I don't normally have my detectives do guard duty," Ross had said, "but I want one of my best people keeping an eye on you until this thing cools down. Wai is tough as nails. And he knows as much about the case as either of us. Maybe the two of you can toss it around while you're spending time together and come up with some answers."

Ross was probably right, a second attack on Sturges in so short a period would be too blatant for the Chinese to explain away. But Wu Zhemin's parting words kept coming back to haunt him: *I am always prepared for any eventuality.* The menace was still real, and the choice of Wai as a bodyguard seemed apt. The man exuded menace of his own, a result, Sturges figured, of the kind of people Wai had dealt with for most of his career. He'd spent the past six years in the Homicide Bureau. Before that, he'd been a member of the police Organized Crime and Triad Bureau.

People in Hong Kong threw the word "triad" around carelessly to describe almost any Chinese thug, the way "mafia" is used to refer to any powerful group of questionable character. But like the real Mafia or the Japanese Yakuza, triad societies were serious and violent organized criminal networks with roots in China going back two and a half centuries. The modern-day gangs preyed on the ethnic Chinese communities of Asia and large western cities. They had names like the *Sun Yee On* and the *14K*. They engaged in the same activities as their Italian and Japanese counterparts: drug trafficking, money laundering, extortion, prostitution, gambling, Internet crime.

And murder. Triads – the term described individual members as well as the organizations – had no compunction about doing violence to others. Just like the men who had attempted to attack Sturges. He supposed he should feel some remorse for having helped those two to their deaths, but the thought of what they had planned to do to him negated any sympathy he might feel. Only particularly brave or foolhardy cops volunteered to do go toe-to-toe with people like that by joining the Triad Bureau.

"Ready to go, detective?" he said to Wai.

"The boss says stay close to you," Wai said. "Where we going?"

"I thought I'd buy you and me a drink. I can use one."

"*Aiyeeah*, cannot. I'm on duty. But you have a drink, I come along and have cup of coffee." Wai gestured toward the elevators and smiled a crooked smile. It was his attempt to be friendly, but he was almost more frightening when he smiled than when he didn't. He was short, with more angular features than the typical Cantonese. His body was that of a flyweight boxer, spare and compact, like a compressed spring that might uncoil at any moment. Somebody or something had broken his nose in the past, and now it traced a lopsided "S" from his eyebrows to his upper lip. A scar meandered from the corner of his left eye and over his cheek. The two ragged lines gave the face the look of a teapot that had been dropped and glued back together imperfectly, and a smile only magnified the mismatches.

Wai's English and his love of American detective shows were engaging, but Sturges was under no illusion: if there was to be more violence in his immediate future, it was as likely to originate with Winston Wai as with the people Wai was guarding against.

~

Sturges took them to the Captain's Bar at the Mandarin Oriental Hotel. The place was packed with young Chinese and Western professionals from the offices of the big banks and financial corporations, who traditionally came here to drink and laugh at the end of the working day.

Few people in Hong Kong had been laughing recently. There had been five years of debilitating recession, and then, just as it looked like the recession was finally ending, along came SARS, the disease that killed several hundred people outright and scared the rest of the population half to death. The break-up with Sarah had come in the midst of all that, and then Rupert's murder, and Bill Sturges had yet to find much to laugh about. But SARS had been defeated, an economic recovery was now in full swing, and for most people, the laughter had returned.

"Ever been here before?" Sturges asked. He had ordered a martini. Wai, sticking to protocol, had ordered coffee.

"Sure," Wai said. "Three years I do undercover work for Triad Bureau. Got close to the *Sun Yee On* — they even consider me for membership. Those triad *dai lobans* like to take their people to expensive places like this. Give them lots of face, you know?"

"Three years undercover with the *Sun Yee On*? That must have been pretty precarious stuff."

"For me not so big deal," Wai said. "My family is from Chiu Chow."

"Aha," Sturges said. Chiu Chow: the corner of the Chinese coast where Guangdong and Fujian provinces meet. Famous for its distinctive cuisine. Famous – like Sicily to the Cosa Nostra or Naples to the Camorra – for supplying members to gangs like the *Sun Yee On*. That helped explain the aura of danger surrounding Wai. "So you're used to dealing with people like those thugs State Security sent to attack me."

Wai shrugged.

"So much for the 'high degree of autonomy' Beijing promised us before the handover, though," Sturges said. "The reality is that Beijing gives us all the autonomy we want, except when it decides it wants to take matters into its own hands, and then it does something like this."

"You sound surprised," Wai said. "Hong Kong part of China now. Beijing can do what they want, nothing you and me can do about it."

"You're right, of course," Sturges said. "It's no more than what many of us have expected all along. I remember how so many Chinese here were bursting with patriotic pride when the handover came. The last of the foreign invaders being kicked off Chinese soil, China made whole again. I wonder how many of those people still feel that way now that we've all had a taste of what Chinese rule is really like."

"Hard to say," Wai said. "Lots of older Chinese people still feeling patriotic."

"What about you? If you had your choice for Hong Kong, given everything we've seen in the past six years, what would it be: part of China, or still a British colony?"

Wai laughed. "I not gonna answer a question like that from a reporter. But I can tell you," he said, gesturing around the room, "young people like these not so happy British are gone. It's not just they don't like that Beijing mess in Hong Kong affairs now and then. They worried Hong Kong gonna be swallowed up whole by China. They don't want Hong Kong becomes just like every other Chinese city.

"Maybe economy is getting better here, but why? Because Beijing open the gates, allow millions of Mainland China people to come across border to shop, and everyone welcoming mainlanders with open arms right now. But almost every Hong Kong Chinese people speak Cantonese. What these same people gonna say when more people here speaking Putonghua than Cantonese? What people gonna say when mainlanders buy up all the goods and all the apartments and use up all the services? Already freedom of the press no longer as free as it was when British were here: what's it gonna be like a few years from now?

"Some people still happy that *gwei-los* no longer in charge," he continued, "but they want Hong Kong stays special. China told us we gonna have 'one country, two systems.' People here like the 'two systems' part." He looked around the bar again. "A lot of these young people just as unhappy Hong Kong has become part of China as Rackley was. Already I hear some of them saying, 'I'm not Chinese; I'm *Hongkonger.*'"

"Rupert would be delighted to hear that if he were still with us. Anyway, Ross suggested you and I discuss his case to see if we can come up with any new ideas."

"I got nothing new," Wai said. "We already talk to everybody we can think of. No luck. What about you?"

"The same. It always comes back to the same question: what was Rupert doing in China? And nobody I can find can give me a definitive answer. I'd love to know what reason for the trip he gave to the press office at the Chinese Foreign Ministry when he applied for his visa. I'm still amazed they gave him the visa at all."

"To press office?" Wai said.

"Yeah. Any journalist who makes an application for a China visa has to tell the press office where he plans to go in China, what he plans to do and who he plans to see. "

"Journalists don't just go to visa office in China Resources Building like everybody else?"

"We have to go through a different procedure," Sturges said.

"Did you ask Foreign Ministry what reason Rackley give them?"

"We did, and Ross said he did too, but we all got the usual answer, which was no answer at all."

Wai pulled out his notebook and scribbled a note to himself. "Maybe I find person who handle Rackley's application and ask him," he said.

"There are only a few people in the press office that we journalists normally deal with, so you won't have a lot of names to consider," Sturges said. "But good luck if you think any of them is going to tell you anything."

"Maybe you got to ask the right question," Wai said.

"I think I know how to ask questions," Sturges replied.

Wai smiled his syncopated smile. "Maybe," he said without looking up from his notebook, "you got to ask in Chinese."

~

The phone rang. Sturges groped for the receiver. It was Wai.

"You sleeping?" Wai asked.

"Not any longer," Sturges said. "What time is it?" It felt like he'd been asleep for only ten minutes.

"Almost midnight,"

He was right: he had been asleep for only ten minutes.

"You get dressed again real quick, okay? I come pick you up," Wai said.

"You just brought me home a half hour ago. What's up?"

"Somebody we got to meet."

"Now?" Sturges fumbled for the lamp switch. "Who is it?"

"You wait for me downstairs," Wai said. "*Faai di-laa!* Hurry up!"

~

"Do you want to tell me where we're going, or is it a secret?" Sturges said once he was in Wai's car.

"Going to Kennedytown," Wai said. "I can't talk on telephone, maybe somebody listening to your conversation like before, you know?"

"I'm getting used to the idea," Sturges said. "Who are we going to see?"

"Guy from Foreign Ministry press office."

"In Kennedytown at one in the morning?"

"What'chu think: somebody from Chinese Foreign Ministry going to invite us to his office to give us secret Communist Party information?"

They rode along the waterfront on the northwestern tip of the island. Kennedytown was one of the last parts of the island to be gentrified, with new apartment buildings and fancy restaurants starting to appear, but for the most part it was still a warren of half-century-old public housing estates and decrepit low-rise buildings lining narrow streets and alleys.

Wai parked and led the way on foot. At the entrance to one alley a half dozen young Chinese sat on tiny plastic stools around a small table, lifting noodles from bowls of soup with their chopsticks and sucking them into their mouths with loud slurps. Twenty yards farther on, Wai stopped at an entryway set between overflowing garbage cans. A back-lit plastic sign in Chinese characters was on the wall.

"The name of your friend?" Sturges asked, pointing to the sign.

"Name of restaurant," Wai said, and he cocked a thumb in the air. "Best Chiu Chow food on Hong Kong side."

They climbed two flights of narrow stairs, dodging trash and broken furniture, and entered what looked like a private apartment. It was furnished with the same round-top tables and plastic stools they had seen in the alley. Only one of the tables was occupied at this late hour. The people there turned briefly to inspect the newcomers, then turned back to finish their meal.

A man greeted Wai, and they exchanged a few words in what Sturges assumed to be Chiu Chow dialect. The man disappeared through a door and returned moments later with a small tray of thimble-sized teacups filled with a deep orange-yellow liquid. To English speakers this was "Iron Buddha," a particularly high-octane preparation of oolong tea. The traditional beginning and end to a Chiu Chow meal.

Wai picked one up and poured the bitter liquid down his throat, and began to order. Sturges threw back a cup and felt a jolt of caffeinated energy flow through his body as the tea ran down his gullet. He drank another. "Okay, I'm awake now," he said.

Ten minutes later the food arrived. Whole steamed crab, served cold. Dumplings stuffed with chives. Braised goose. Broad rice noodles swimming in a dark broth along with pig offal, duck meat, preserved vegetables, bean curd and braised hard-boiled eggs. A pot of tea. Two large bottles of San Miguel beer.

"I thought you don't drink on duty," Sturges said.

"I'm off duty," Wai said. He reached for the teapot and poured boiling water over his plastic chopsticks to sterilize them. "Dig in," he said, digging in.

"It's a bit late for so much food," Sturges said. They had finished dinner less than four hours earlier. But the aromas were delectable. They raised their beer glasses to each other and took a sip. Sturges dipped a dumpling into sauce and popped it into his mouth. They ate silently for five minutes while the party at the other table paid their bill and left. Then Wai picked up his phone and punched in a number. Fifteen minutes later a Chinese man in his mid-thirties walked into the room.

Wai and the man chatted for a couple of minutes in the same dialect Wai had used when they entered the restaurant. The man looked agitated, and Sturges could tell that Wai was trying to reassure him.

Finally they turned to Sturges. "This my friend from Foreign Ministry," Wai said in a low voice. "He don't want you write his name." The man whispered something in Chiu Chow. "Sorry. He don't *tell* you his name. We just call him Mr. Wong, okay?"

"Whatever you like. Good evening, Mr. Wong," Sturges said. "Thank you for meeting us." He reached into his pocket and offered a name card to the man, but "Wong" waved it away.

"Please understand, Mr. Sturges, this is very dangerous for me," the man said. "I speak only off the record, okay?"

"I won't identify you or your agency in any way," Sturges assured him.

"No, no. You cannot write anything in your newspaper. I only speak to help you understand the situation. Do you agree?"

It wasn't what he'd hoped for, but he had no choice. "Agreed," Sturges said.

"Then please, ask your questions," Wong said.

"Well, we know Rupert Rackley, the newspaper columnist who was found dead in China last—"

"I know who Mr. Rackley was," Wong said.

"Of course. He obtained a visa for China, and being a journalist, he would have had to apply through your office. So my first question is, were you involved in processing his visa application?"

"I was," Wong said.

"Did you interview him personally?"

"No – why you are taking notes, Mr. Sturges?" He jumped like someone who had suddenly discovered that his chair was on fire. "I thought we agreed."

"We did agree," Sturges said. "I'm only taking notes for my own benefit."

There was another heated discussion in Chiu Chow, and Wai again turned to Sturges: "Maybe you do this without notes? Just casual conversation. Okay?"

"No problem," Sturges said. He capped his pen and slipped his notebook into his pocket. Wai smiled. Wong may or may not have relaxed slightly; it was difficult to tell.

"Now, again: did you interview Mr. Rackley personally?"

"No," Wong said. "But I reviewed his application.'

"I assume that the application listed his reason for wanting to travel to China?"

"It did."

"Can you tell me what that reason was? Was he going to gather information for his newspaper column?"

"No. He assured my colleagues he was not planning to write any story. He said he wanted to go to Dongguan to see the art museum there. The Dongguan museum is rather famous, and Mr. Rackley said he knew the curator from before the Cultural Revolution. He said he just wanted to visit the man and look at the museum's latest acquisitions."

"That's all? He gave no other reason for wanting to go?"

"None. Not on his written application, not in the interview with my colleagues."

"You gave him the visa, so I assume you and your colleagues were satisfied with his reason for the trip," Sturges said.

"Not really."

Sturges was unsure what to say next. "I'm sorry," he said. "I don't quite understand that last answer. You did not approve of his reason for the trip? Or you didn't believe he had told you the real reason?"

"We knew Mr. Rackley was no friend of China. We knew he was not in the habit of hopping across the border just to visit museums. We doubted he was telling the truth about what he planned to do in China."

"But you gave him the visa anyway."

"We did."

"What *did* you think he was planning to do once he got into the mainland?"

"We had no idea what he was planning to do."

Sturges glanced at Wai, whose face gave away nothing. He turned back to Wong. "I'm still confused," he said. "Here was someone, as you say, who was no friend of China, you thought he was lying on his application, you had no idea what he really planned to do, yet you approved his application? The People's Republic is not normally so magnanimous with people it doesn't trust. May I ask why?"

Wong wrestled with himself for a minute before answering. "Whether or not we believed him..." he began. He cleared his throat and started again. "Whether or not we believed him was beside the point."

"I'm afraid I still don't understand."

"I mean, we were told to give him a visa. The reason he gave for wanting to go was not important."

"Give him the visa...no matter what?"

Wong nodded.

"And who told you to give him the visa?"

"You absolutely guarantee that none of this is going to appear in the newspaper?"

"Again, you have my word."

The man hesitated for another moment, and then said, "We were told by our superiors in the Foreign Ministry."

"Yes, but who...?"

"Please, Mr. Sturges. I cannot be more specific than that. We receive our orders. We don't ask questions. We gave Mr. Rackley his visa."

"And Mr. Rackley said nothing about any plans aside from visiting this museum curator and looking at antiques?"

"Nothing. We discussed the matter among ourselves at some length, just to make sure we had all the facts straight before we issued the visa."

"Do you remember this curator's name? The one Rupert said he was planning to visit?"

"I am sorry, I do not," Wong said. "It just wasn't important. But the museum has a website. I'm sure the name can be found there."

"Do you know if he actually went to the museum? Do you have any idea what happened to him after he arrived in Dongguan?"

"Watching over visiting journalists is the job of the security services," Wong said. "My office just issues them visas." He looked from man to man. "Is there anything else you wish to ask?"

Sturges looked at Wai, who shook his head.

"I guess not," Sturges replied.

Wong stood abruptly. "Then I must go. I know Mr. Wai personally, Mr. Sturges, and he has vouched for you, so I will trust your word. Please do not betray me. It would cause me much trouble." He started to walk out of the restaurant, but turned back for a moment and said: "I am sorry – that Mr. Rackley died. I enjoyed reading his column."

~

"What'chu think?" Wai asked.

"I'm not sure," Sturges said. "At least we now know that Rupert told the Chinese that the reason for his trip was antiques. Looking at antiques, that is. He didn't say anything about buying them. But at least that's something more than we had before. It's partial confirmation of one of our theories of the case. I suppose. In an extremely tentative sort of way. *If* Rupert was telling the truth on his application, that is. But Wong didn't think he was telling the truth. Shit! I have no idea what it means."

"He said it don't matter if it was truth or not," Wai said.

"That's the fascinating part." It was clear from Wong's remarks that somebody on the Chinese side wanted Rupert to come to China. As if they were luring him across the border in order to murder him. Murder was not the kind of thing foreign ministries did, so the ministry would almost certainly have issued the visa on orders from the security services. "It confirms our suspicion that somebody in a powerful position had a hand in the matter. But we still don't know what Rupert's real motive for making the trip was."

"Maybe Rupert tell them the truth."

"That he had suddenly decided to go to China after thirty-five years just to visit a museum? I seriously doubt that," Sturges said.

"I mean, Rupert could visit and then buy, no?" Wai said. "Maybe this curator got some special pieces he want to sell personally. Like a side business? Nobody on mainland in a better position to get his hands on valuable antiques than guy who runs art museum. Grave robbers come to sell stuff to museum, head of museum buys five piece for museum, buys two more to sell in private. Maybe your sources right: maybe Rupert went to buy antiques after all."

"Maybe. Another 'maybe' to add to our extensive collection of 'maybes.'"

"Remember," Wai said, "you promise not to write anything about this meeting."

"You do know who 'Mr. Wong' is, though, don't you?" Sturges said.

Wai shrugged. "Strictly between us? His name Zhang Guanghua. He served three years at Chinese embassy in Washington, why his English is so good."

"What else do you know about him?"

"Not much to say," Wai said. "His names, *Guang Hua*, mean 'Great China.' Kind of names parents give their kids during Cultural Revolution to show they are patriotic."

"His parents might have been patriotic, but it looks like Guanghua turned into a closet democrat. Anyone who likes the stuff Rupert used to write about China is not exactly toeing the Party line. That's probably why he agreed to speak to us."

"Not really," said Wai.

"What, then?"

"He speak to us because he's my cousin. My mother and his mother are sisters."

"One cousin a mainland government official and the other a Hong Kong cop who almost joined the Triads?" Sturges said. "That's priceless."

Wai dismissed the comment. "Cops, Communist Party, that stuff not so important," he said. "You should know: to Chinese, family is still most important thing of all."

Sturges surveyed the man with enhanced respect. "I've got to hand it to you," he said. "You've just confirmed one of the major elements in the mystery: that somebody high up wanted Rupert dead, even if we don't know who it was. I never could have gotten that information on my own."

"Who loves ya baby?" Wai said, prying open a pink-and-white crab shell.

"I beg your pardon?" Sturges said.

"*Who loves ya baby*? You don't recognize?" Wai looked up with his lopsided grin. "Favorite saying of *Kojak* – best TV detective of all." He waved his chopsticks in the direction of the dishes on the table. "Food getting cold," he said. "You should eat."

~

Well, Sturges thought as he walked into his house, that was worth getting up in the middle of the night for. One more indecipherable bit of information to add to the puzzle. If he could find just one person who could tell him unequivocally what Rupert was doing in China...

His answering machine was flashing. A call had come in just after he left for the meeting with Wai. He punched the replay button and a voice with a Germanic accent came drifting out:

"Hallo, Mr. Sturges. My name is Fritz Giesler. I'm sorry for calling you so late, but I just returned from an extended trip out of town and I see that you have left me many messages, so I'm thinking maybe it is something important. You can call me tomorrow morning at my office, maybe, and we can talk, *ja?*"

Twenty-nine

Fritz Giesler looked the part of a grave robber. His head was shaved as smooth and shiny as the lid of a Ming Dynasty ginger jar. He wore a small diamond stud in his left ear. He had an elaborate handlebar mustache, and a faintly Oriental cast to his eye. His body was lean and agile – well suited, Sturges thought as he studied the man, to sliding down a narrow shaft into a dark, dank burial chamber.

He showed Sturges to a chair in his small but elegant office, located not far from Evelyn Chin's showroom. "Please, sit," Giesler said. "Can I get you a drink? I have a beautiful and very old highland single malt."

"I'd like that," Sturges said, and, remembering Brian Ross's admonition: "Just a splash of water, please. You're a connoisseur of beautiful and very old things, then, Mr. Giesler?"

"It's my specialty, Mr. Sturges." He handed Sturges a drink and sat facing him. "So, how can I help?"

"I'm trying to figure out why Rupert was in China," Sturges said. "He had vowed never to go back."

"So he told me, on more than one occasion," Giesler said. "Considering my specialty, I assume you called me because you suspect his visit there had something to do with antiques."

"It's one of the very few things I can think of that might have led him there. Only something that excited his imagination in some unusual way would have done that, and the thing that excited him above all was Chinese art. So, yes: you're a highly regarded expert on the subject, you knew him personally. Do you think antiques were somehow involved?"

"I do not just think, I am convinced of it," Giesler said. He rose and walked to a row of filing cabinets. "Do you know anything about Chinese art?" he said over his shoulder.

"Mainly bits and pieces that I picked up from Rupert."

"Then I tell you a story," Giesler said, returning with a folder full of documents. "Ancient civilizations all over the world have long been complaining about Western imperialists stealing their treasures, *ja*? The most famous example is the friezes that a British diplomat named Lord Elgin stole from the Parthenon in the early 1800s. Those have been in the British Museum since 1816, and the Greeks desperately want them returned."

"I do know about those," Sturges said. "What do they have to do with Rupert?"

"Patience, please," Giesler said. "Chinese civilization, as you also know, has been around in one form or another for five thousand years. And the tradition for much of that time has been for the Chinese to be buried in tombs, along with artifacts from this world for the deceased to use in the next life. Not everyone, of course, but Chinese of any stature have traditionally been buried like this.

"So we are talking two hundred fifty or so generations; hundreds of thousands of tombs scattered across the Chinese countryside, containing what are often priceless antiquities. Enormous amounts of artifacts have already been dug up, but there's still a huge amount sitting in the ground waiting to be found."

"And waiting to be smuggled out of the country – by local officials in many cases," Sturges said.

"Precisely. On the one hand the Chinese are fiercely protective of their cultural heritage. On the other hand they've been selling it out the back door as fast as they can. Now they want it back - or at least the best of it. The central government is helpless to stop the kind of local-level corruption that accounts for most pieces leaving the country in the current period. But it does want to recover the very best pieces from abroad, many of which left the country long ago. A lot of these show up periodically at auctions, and I'm sure you know that the prices are quite spectacular: millions of U.S. dollars for a single piece in many cases."

"So the Chinese have to buy back for millions of dollars what they've allowed to be stolen from under their noses," Sturges snorted.

A condescending smile crossed Giesler's face. "Correct in principle," he said, "but like the Parthenon friezes, not all of this art has been 'allowed' to be stolen. And until recently it has not been the government that does the buying back. It persuades 'patriotic' citizens on the mainland and here in Hong Kong to buy the expensive pieces and 'donate' them to the motherland."

Sturges drummed his fingers on his leg. "I assume this story is leading somewhere," he said.

Giesler drew out one of the documents he had taken from the file cabinet. "It is," he said. "You have heard of the *Yuanmingyuan*?"

"The Old Summer Palace in Beijing," Sturges said. "The building was sacked in the mid-1800s by British soldiers."

"Partly right," Giesler said. "It was far more than a building, first of all. The Chinese name, *yuan-ming-yuan*, means Gardens of Perfect Clarity. The site took in a huge area with several gardens, plus lakes, Chinese pavilions and temples, and European-style palaces. Here," he said, raising the document, "is what the French writer Victor Hugo wrote about the place:

"'There was, in a corner of the world, a wonder of the world; this wonder was called the Summer Palace. Art has two principles, the Idea, which produces European art, and the Chimera, which produces oriental art. The Summer Palace was to chimerical art what the Parthenon was to ideal art.'

"Both British and French soldiers were involved in the sack of the gardens in 1860," Giesler said. "The French got there first and looted much of the treasures. Then our friend Lord Elgin, who by now was the British high commissioner to China, decided to teach the Chinese a lesson for torturing and killing a group of western hostages not long before. He ordered the gardens destroyed – over the objections of the French, by the way. This has to be one of the few cases in recorded history in which the Frogs have demonstrated a sense of principle.

"For three days, British troops burned whatever they could. The Chinese buildings were mostly wood and the fire destroyed them completely. The European-style buildings were made of stone, so some rather extensive ruins were left when the Brits were finished the job."

"I never knew the details," Sturges said.

"It was no secret, even back then," Giesler said. He read again from the Victor Hugo document:

'The devastation of the Summer Palace was accomplished by the two victors acting jointly,' Hugo wrote. 'Mixed up in all this is the name of Elgin, which inevitably calls to mind the Parthenon. What was done to the Parthenon was done to the Summer Palace, more thoroughly and better, so that nothing of it should be left. All the treasures of all our cathedrals put together could not equal this formidable and splendid museum of the Orient.'

Giesler looked up again. "To the Chinese mind, the sacking of the Summer Palace was one of the major outrages the country suffered at foreign hands during the 19th and 20th centuries. It's all of a piece with the taking of Hong Kong by the British, the loss of Taiwan to the Japanese, and so forth. You can understand how retrieving what they can of those looted artifacts ranks high on their nationalistic agenda. They look on those Summer Palace treasures in much the same way as the Greeks look on the Parthenon friezes – which, ironically, are now known to the world as 'the Elgin Marbles.'"

"This is all fascinating," Sturges said, "but I still don't understand what it has to do with Rupert's death."

"Now we come to it," Giesler said, sliding several photographs out of the folder. "The most widely known of the looted pieces – because several have been sold at auction in recent years for very high prices – are bronze castings of the heads of the twelve animals of the Chinese zodiac." He tapped the photographs with his finger. "They were taken from a bronze water clock that was cast for the Yuanmingyuan in 1744.

"Three of those heads, of the ox, monkey and tiger, were sold at auctions in Hong Kong in 2000 to a state-owned mainland company. Early this year, a Hong Kong businessman bought the pig head from a New York collector. And just last month, the same businessman bought the horse head from a Taiwanese – you had that story in your newspaper. All those heads have now been donated to mainland museums."

The sale of the horse head had indeed been big news in Hong Kong. "That's five of the twelve," Sturges said. "Do we know where the other seven are?"

"The rat and the rabbit are in a private collection in Europe. About the remaining five, nobody knows. At least nobody who's telling."

"You'd think the prices these things are bringing would tempt whoever has them to put them on the market," Sturges said.

"*Ja*, you would," Giesler said. "The horse head brought almost nine million U.S. dollars. But the dragon's head would probably bring the highest price. The dragon in Chinese lore symbolizes fire, energy, truth and light, power – all kinds of auspicious things. That would make it especially attractive to a Chinese buyer."

"You still haven't said – wait!" Sturges paused, assembling the pieces in his mind. A smile spread over his face. "Don't tell me Rupert was on the trail of one of the missing heads."

Giesler raised his palms in the air. "As you said: the possibility of acquiring a piece of art like this is one of the few things that might have dragged him over there."

"And I know exactly what would have gone through his mind," Sturges said. "Not only would this have been an incredible addition to his collection, but he would have loved owning a symbol of China's humiliation. He probably would have called a press conference about it just to pour salt into the wound. But you haven't given me a concrete answer. Do you know for a fact that this is why Rupert went to China?"

Giesler toyed with the photos, composing an answer carefully. "I cannot say with one hundred percent certainty," he said finally. "I mean to say, Rupert never looked me in the eye and said, 'Well, Fritz, I'm off to China to buy one of the Summer Palace heads.'"

The elation Sturges had felt moments earlier started to drain away. "But you said you're sure he was after antiques," he said. "He must have said *something* to you."

"It was a combination of things," Giesler replied. "First, he came by here half a dozen times in the weeks before he was killed, pestering me for details on how antiquities are smuggled across the border."

"It's possible he was going to write about smuggling in one of his columns," Sturges said, "maybe as a way of focusing on Chinese corruption. That was one of his favorite topics."

"No. I asked him. He swore it was not for publication, only for his own knowledge. That's what made me suspect he was thinking of doing some smuggling himself."

This was somewhat encouraging. "Go on," Sturges said.

"He made other remarks during this period, but the most interesting came in early August, the day after the sale of the horse head. He came by my office that day, and of course the story of the sale was all over the front pages. I made some remark about how China was relying on foreigners to retrieve the dignity it had lost to them in the first place. Rupert replied: 'There is still a lot more of China's precious property out there, my dear Giesler – property as significant as this." He pointed at the photo of the horse head when he said it. 'And not all of it will help China regain its dignity.'"

"That was pretty standard Rupert," Sturges said. "It still doesn't prove that he was after one of the heads – or that he'd personally go to China to get it."

"Ah, but I have not finished. He was here again in mid-August, just a week or so before the murder, pressing me again for details about smuggling. I could not resist: I said, 'Rupert, if I were a betting man I would bet that *you* have plans to smuggle in some major piece from the mainland.' And – I am not sure what made me say it, I guess it was all the fanfare about the sale of the horse head the month before – I said to him, 'I would not be surprised even if you had a line on one of those missing animal heads from the Yuanmingyuan.'

"I expected him to brush it off," Giesler continued. "Instead, a conspiratorial look came over his face and he said: 'You're very clever, my dear Giesler. I cannot reveal the details at the moment, but I do have something big in the works. Extremely big. People are going to be writing about me soon, just like they wrote about that man who bought the horse head last month. And when the Chinese see what I have, the buggers are going to eat their livers in anguish.'"

Sturges spread his hands, waiting for the final answer.

"That is all he would say," Giesler told him. Sturges sank back in his chair, deflated. "I wish I had more definite information," the German said, "but he would not tell me what the extremely big thing of his was. He said I would have to wait. Then a week later, the newspapers say he has been found dead in China. I have to believe that there was a connection between the murder and the extremely big thing. And this being Rupert, I have to believe this extremely big thing was a special piece of art. I cannot guarantee it was one of the Summer Palace heads," Giesler said, "but I am convinced it was."

"But wait," Sturges said. "The British and French took their booty home with them. The seven heads whose whereabouts are known were all either returned to China from abroad or are still abroad, according to you. If Rupert was after one of the remaining five heads – what makes you think it might still have been *inside* China?"

"Historians have proof that Chinese citizens also took part in the plunder of the Yuanmingyuan," Giesler said. "Some of the water clock heads could have been left behind by the Europeans, and later stolen by locals. For all we know, the remaining five heads have never have left Chinese soil."

"I guess it's plausible," Sturges said, but without much conviction. "What doesn't fit is the murder. Was whatever he was after so important that the only way to stop him was to kill him?"

"Remember," Giesler said, "these artifacts have a very special significance to the Chinese. I am sure they would go to extreme lengths to hold onto them."

"Perhaps," Sturges said, "but all they had to do was arrest Rupert once he had his hands on the head, or whatever he was after, and throw him in jail for dealing in stolen goods. Or even better from their point of view – although this would have been alien to their way of thinking – they could have confiscated the goods and expelled him, with a lot of noise about how he snuck into China under false pretenses and was caught making an illegal purchase."

"How would letting him go have been better?" Giesler asked.

"Think about it," Sturges said. "After nurturing his hatred for thirty-five years, and with all the careful planning a caper like this would have required, to have himself held up to public ridicule as a liar and a thief – to be defeated so publicly by the people he hated – would have been almost impossible for Rupert to swallow. I don't think he ever would have gotten over it. My point is, they didn't have to shoot him: they could have just embarrassed him to death."

"Nevertheless," Giesler said, "I am convinced he went there to buy one of the heads. Getting his hands on it and sneaking it out of the country just as the government is spending a fortune to bring the other heads back – you know as well as I do: Rupert would have done anything, even go to China, to get even for what they did to him in 1968."

Thirty

Nineteen sixty-eight: assassinations and riots in the U.S.; demonstrations and strikes in France; wars and chaos in Asia. A miserable year for almost everyone.

For the Sturges family, 1968 was intensely personal. George was killed in January, cornered by the Viet Cong in Saigon during the Tet Offensive and shot at point-blank range. Rupert's torment in Shanghai followed less than two months later.

The Maoists were still struggling to bring the Red Guards under control early that year. Rupert had wangled another visa and had gone to report on the political situation, but also to rescue what further pieces of art he and Chang Dongfeng could save from the rampaging mobs. Bill was already inconsolable at his father's death, and when he didn't hear from Rupert for ten days, the boy smelled danger. "He's in trouble, I'm sure of it," he cried.

They had to endure another week of uncertainty before word was finally relayed from the British Consulate in Shanghai: Rupert been rescued from the clutches of a band of Red Guards and was now recovering in a hospital. His injuries were not life-threatening, a consular official told them, but the torture he'd suffered had been severe. He would be sent back to Hong Kong as soon as he was able to travel, but they were warned that it would take him some time to heal.

The Hong Kong he returned to was not immune from the violence and disruption enveloping the world. There had been anti-British riots and bombings in the streets the previous year and dozens were killed. Refugees from the mainland were now pouring across the border by the thousands to escape the chaos of the Cultural Revolution. China's streets, the refugees reported, had become battlefields, as opposing political factions went at each other with a vengeance. Bodies floating down the Pearl River into Hong Kong waters daily were vivid confirmation of what was taking place just a short distance away.

Rupert was admitted to Matilda Hospital on the Peak, far above the violence. His physical injuries began to heal, but it soon became clear that the psychological scars would be more resilient. He would sit for hours at his window, staring at ships plying the South China Sea below, rarely speaking to anyone. When he did speak it was to curse the Chinese – not just the leaders, but all of them. He'd always treated the Hong Kong Chinese with respect and friendship, insisting on speaking Cantonese or Mandarin with them, but now if he spoke to the nurses and orderlies at all it was to snap orders at them in English.

One afternoon, Bill walked into the hospital room to find Rupert in the throes of a nightmare. His face was red and contorted. His arms and legs thrashed beneath the covers. *"Kill the bloody bastards!"* he was screaming. *"Kill them all!"*

When the boy tried to shake him awake, Rupert shot upright with a wild look in his eye. He grabbed Bill's wrist in a death grip and stared straight through him. "At least we saved some of it, didn't we?" he cried out to nobody in particular. "By God, we did save some of it." Then his eyes rolled up in his head. He released his grip and fell back on the pillow, to resume his troubled journey back to normalcy.

~

Nineteen sixty-eight also brought change to Chang Dongfeng, as life-transforming as the Japanese assault on Nanjing thirty-one years earlier.

For almost two years, while the Cultural Revolution ebbed and flowed, Chang kept his head down. Mao had initially trained his sights on the top level of the Party, those who posed the most serious threat to his continued leadership, but there was no guarantee of safety at any level. Once again people hurled accusations in order to settle personal scores, or to pre-empt a denunciation of themselves by denouncing another first, or to fill a quota when there was no one legitimate to accuse.

Several of Chang's colleagues had already been labeled "capitalist-roaders" and "poisonous weeds." Some had been paraded in front of mobs to be struggled against and some had been beaten viciously. Some had simply vanished. The archive team's expert on Ming Dynasty landscape painters, one of the country's most prominent art historians, left home for work one morning and never arrived at his office. Twelve days later his body was dumped on his doorstep, battered almost beyond recognition.

Chang had put out feelers to detect the slightest sign that he personally was in danger. He learned what he could about his enemies and their habits: any piece of knowledge might be useful if he found himself threatened. In mid-March, his preparations paid off.

He was awakened after midnight by a frantic knocking on his door, and he opened it to find a colleague from the archives office. The man pushed his way into the apartment, looking behind him to make sure nobody was watching. "They are coming for you," he said in an urgent whisper as soon as the door was shut.

"Who is doing this?" Chang asked.

"Wang, the head of the section. He has gathered evidence of your bourgeois activities – so he says."

"Wang," Chang said. The man Chang held most directly responsible for the deaths of his wife and children. "It is no surprise," he said as black thoughts flooded his mind. " The man is evil. When is he planning to do this, do you know?"

"Any day. Perhaps even today. After the group recitation from Chairman Mao's writings he plans to step forward and denounce you. He will cite your dedication to preserving old artworks, which he will say is a violation of the Chairman's order to destroy the four olds."

"Are others involved?"

"Wang's usual group of toadies will support him, but he is the ringleader. You realize–" The man paused, searching for the right words. "The rest of us will do nothing to support Wang, but we cannot speak openly in your defense. Given your background..."

Chang signaled that he understood. "What will you do now?" the man asked.

"I will protect myself and my daughter," Chang said, and then: "Wait." He opened a drawer and took out an envelope. "I will trouble you for one more thing," he said. "Wait a couple of days, and then see that this envelope gets to the head of the General Office. But be careful that no one knows it came from you."

The man took the envelope and scurried away without asking any questions, and Chang began to activate his escape plan. He had already prepared the route: first to Shanghai and then Guangzhou, ostensibly to inspect new art treasures that had fallen into government hands. He had made the same trip several times in the past eighteen months as part of his official duties, so his preparations for another trip had raised no eyebrows. Nor was his intention to bring Lili along in any way suspicious: the schools had all been closed for more than a year by the chaos, and children had nothing to do.

He pulled out bags that were packed and ready and checked the contents a final time: clothes, money, identification documents. A few other items, small and easy to hide, that he had snuck out of his office in anticipation of this moment. He now added food to last them for several days, and slipped a sharp knife into his pocket. Then he sat and reviewed his plans step by step to make sure there were no loose ends.

An hour before dawn he shook Lili awake and told her to dress quickly. "Where are we going, Papa?" she asked, rubbing her eyes.

"We are going on the trip I told you about," he said. "Hurry."

~

They moved through the frigid darkness at a rapid pace, giving anyone they encountered a wide berth. "Papa," the girl said at one point, tugging at his tunic. "I thought we were going to the train station. This is not the right way." The station was located southeast of the Forbidden City, but Chang was taking them northward.

"We will go to the station soon," he said. "We have to make a short stop first."

As dawn was breaking they reached Desheng Gate, which ran through the old city wall directly north of the Forbidden City. Chang wrapped his daughter in a blanket and sat her down inside the gate. He told her to wait for him no matter what, and then, with a sigh of determination, he continued alone into a park that lay just outside the wall.

He had always assumed that if he were targeted again, the man behind the plot would be Wang Sheyu, who had denounced him in 1957. *Know your enemy if you can't avoid battle,* Sun Tzu had written. On his return from Taishan, Chan had set out to know everything he could about Wang. He learned that Wang came here to Taiping Park every morning before work to do *tai chi chuan,* the stylized, centuries-old Chinese exercises. It was a tranquil spot, popular with intellectuals who liked to sit by its pond and contemplate the world. Chang himself had visited the park several times over the last year to watch Wang from afar.

Chang now took a position behind a tree with an unobstructed view of the pond, and waited, shivering in the late-winter cold. Ten minutes later, true to form, Wang appeared. He laid a bag on the grass, removed his coat, and faced the pond. As the sun burned through the morning mist he began the slow, methodical rhythms of *tai chi.*

Wang was fully engrossed in the ritual, concentrating on his movements and blocking out all else, when Chang walked up to him from behind. "Engaging in a bit of old culture, comrade Sheyu?" Chang said when he was only three yards away. "My, my. What would Chairman Mao have to say about this?"

Wang almost jumped out of his skin at the unexpected intrusion. "Chang!" he cried, turning in the direction of the voice. "Why are you here? What do you want?"

"I have a problem," Chang said. "I thought you might help me solve it."

Wang knew he was the last person Chang would come to for help. "What is this ridiculousness?" he said warily. He took several small steps backward as he spoke. "Your problems are no concern of mine."

"You are wrong," Chang said, closing the gap between them. "For the problem, you see, is you."

"I do not know what you mean."

"But you know full well. You accused me falsely in 1957. I am told that you plan to accuse me again – perhaps this very day." Chang took another step forward. "It would be a very big problem for me if you did that."

Wang backed away again. "Someone is telling you lies," he said in a voice tinged with fear. "I plan no such thing."

"Oh, I expect that my information is correct," Chang said.

"And what will you do to stop me?" Wang asked, now defiant. "Will you cry like a woman? Will you fall to your knees and plead with me to spare you? You know there is nothing you can do to escape your past. Your fate is sealed, yours and that of your daughter. She would have been better off to have died in the famine with the rest of your family."

Chang fought to keep his voice even. "You asked once before what I would do if my daughter and I were threatened again," he said. "I think the time has come to show you." While he spoke, he slid his knife out of his pocket.

"What is that in your hand?" Wang asked.

Chang showed him the knife. Wang raised his hands in front of his body. "You would not be so stupid as to attack me," he said.

"You seem very certain about what I will and will not do," Chang said. "But you do not know me at all." He raised the knife suddenly high above his head, and rushed toward Wang with a cry.

Wang screamed in fright and lurched backward, forgetting that he was at the lip of the pond. He flailed his arms, trying to keep his balance, but in vain. He toppled like a tree into the water.

For a moment he disappeared. Then he burst through the surface, churning the water frantically, eyes wide with fright. "Help me!" he screeched. "I cannot swim!" Chang watched with satisfaction as the man thrashed. The first part of his plan had worked: he had forced Wang into the water without having to lay a hand on him.

Now for the second part. With an exaggerated sigh, he put the knife in his pocket and knelt by the edge of the pond. "I only want to scare you into leaving us alone," he said. "I trust you have learned the lesson. Here," – he held out his left hand – "grab hold and I will pull you out."

Wang snatched at the proffered hand and held on for dear life while Chang pulled him toward the bank. As soon as he reached the edge of the pond, Wang grabbed for the shoreline with his other hand to pull himself up. But Chang placed his right hand on top of Wang's head, and shoved downward with all his might.

Wang's head disappeared underwater again. Chang shook his left hand loose from Wang's grasp, placed it on Wang's submerged shoulder and pushed down on that as well.

Wang's hands broke the surface and grasped in desperation at Chang's arms, but Chang had the man's head and shoulder in a death grip. He counted slowly to ten, watching the frigid water churn into a white froth beneath his eyes. "This is for my wife," he said calmly. He counted to ten again. "This is for my son, Mingfu." The twitching under his hands slackened, and again he counted. "This is for my Xilian."

One of Wang's hands disappeared under the water. "And this is for my daughter, Lili, who is lucky to be alive — no thanks to you, you worthless piece of shit."

The other hand went limp and slid from sight. Chang continued to hold the body down, feeling for any remaining signs of life. He loosened his grip, and the body sank completely. "And that is for me," he whispered.

He stood and dried his hands on Wang's coat. Then he pulled a piece of paper from his own bag. It was a suicide note, ostensibly written by Wang, printed by Chang on machinery from the archives office. Chang had spent weeks copying Wang's signature, and when he was satisfied he had it right he placed the forged signature at the bottom of the note. Now he slid the note into Wang's coat.

The envelope Chang had given to the friend who warned him contained an anonymous accusation: that Wang had given information about the Cultural Revolution to the British Embassy; that he had revealed state secrets in return for passage to Hong Kong for himself and his family. The forged suicide note was an ostensible confession by Wang that confirmed the false accusation. His treason had been found out, the note said, and Wang was taking his own life to avoid persecution.

It was all a fabrication, but there would be no visible marks on the body once it resurfaced to indicate that the death had been anything other than suicide, and Chang knew that nobody would bother to investigate the death very carefully anyway. Wang had been despised by most of the archives staff. His death would rid them of a vile presence. It would also help them fill their quota of denunciations.

Chang had briefly considered murdering Wang's wife and children, to make Wang suffer the way he, Chang, had suffered. But he could not bring himself to take the life of innocents. No matter, he thought: Wang's family was now doomed anyway. Suicide by a Party member was considered a betrayal of the Party, and like the family of a landlord, the family of a traitor was automatically judged guilty. Once Wang's body and the note were discovered, his widow and children would be ruined. Never again allowed to hold meaningful jobs. Exiled to the countryside where, if they survived, they would endure misery for the rest of their lives.

Chang hoped that in his final moments, Wang realized how complete Chang's revenge had been. *"What will you do?"* the supervisor had asked with contempt. Chang had known from the time he returned to Beijing what he would do. The knowledge that he had carried it off brought him a small measure of peace. "Now, comrade," he said, staring at the spot where Wang had gone under, "your suffering is truly the equal of mine."

He turned to fetch his daughter, and take her from this hell forever.

Thirty-one

Sturges was mulling over his conversation with Fritz Giesler when Olivia called.

"What are you up to, lover?" she said. "Thinking of me?"

"Actually, I was," he said. "What do you know about the animal heads from the water clock at the Yuanmingyuan?"

It took a moment for her to reply. "The whats from the what? Is this a trick question I have to answer before I get any more sex?"

"I take that to mean you've never heard of them before."

"I don't have the slightest idea what you're talking about. I mean, of course I know what animal heads are. And the Yuanmingyuan is the Summer Palace in Beijing if I'm not mistaken. But what's a water clock?"

"It just might be the answer to what your husband was up to when he was killed," he said. "Among many other things on the grounds of the Summer Palace when it was razed by the British and the French, there was an ornate clock, which was driven by water, and which had the heads of the twelve animals of the Chinese zodiac on it..."

"Okay."

"...and those heads, or at least some of them, were among items that were looted by the European soldiers when the gardens were destroyed. The heads, those whose whereabouts are known, are now extremely valuable artifacts. When I say 'extremely,' I'm talking several million U.S. apiece."

"I think I can guess what comes next: these heads are what Rupert was after in China?"

"It's distinctly possible he was after one or more of them," Sturges said. "Thinking back now, did he ever say anything to you that suggests those heads might have been involved in his plans in any way?"

"Nothing that I can recall," she said. Another pause. "But wait a minute: what do these heads look like?"

"They're bronze," he said. "Smooth and shiny for the most part. Roughly, I don't know, twelve inches, eighteen inches high? A couple of them have been auctioned off or purchased here recently, and the last one, the horse head, went for a fortune."

"Sure, I remember reading about that," she said. "It was just a month or so back. There were photographs in all the papers if I'm thinking of the right one."

"That's the one. Did Rupert ever mention anything about those heads, or the Summer Palace, or anything that might be connected to them?

"I'm sure he would have commented on the auction at the time it took place: he always had a comment about anything in the news that had to do with antiques. But I don't have a specific recollection of any reference to the horse head or any of the others. I'm not much help, am I?"

"You and everyone else," he said. "Could you give it some thought, though? If you can remember anything he said shortly before his death that was even remotely related to the heads, it might help solve the mystery."

"I'll try, but don't hold your breath," she said. Then, in the little-girl voice she could do so convincingly: "Am I going to see you tonight? It's been several days. Maybe if I had a little sensory stimulation it might jog my memory..."

How many guys have a beautiful woman begging them for sex? What guy, in a situation like this, could keep his mind on anything else? "I can definitely help you there," he said. "Why don't you come to my place for a change? I'll arrange a sexy meal, like oysters and Champagne, and then I'll stimulate the hell out of your senses."

"I can't wait," she said, and her tinkling laugh came pouring out of the telephone like flecks of fairy dust. "What's the dress code?"

"As little as possible. You won't be wearing it for long, anyway."

"That's what I like to hear. Eight-thirty okay? If I could I'd come and rip your clothes off this very moment, but I have to see an important client early in the evening. I'll get rid of him as quickly as I can, baby. I don't want to be away from you for one minute longer than is absolutely necessary."

"Eight-thirty's a long way away."

"I won't be a minute late. I promise."

He hung up, shifting in his seat as he did so. Her effect on him was remarkable. He was like a teenager, walking around with an erection half the day. No matter what he was doing or whom he was talking to, he found his mind wandering to her.

He tried to tell himself that she wasn't going to chew him up and spit him out like she'd done with her previous boyfriends, but he knew her reputation – she had told him herself: "The Man-eater." Was it too much to hope that this boyfriend was going to survive?

The Art of War by Scarlett O'Hara: *I'll think about that tomorrow.*

Today, life was good.

Today, he was going to enjoy every minute.

Tomorrow? Who the hell ever knows about tomorrow?

~

Eight thirty passed. Nine p.m. Thirty of his precious minutes with Olivia gone.

Nine twenty-five. She'd promised she wouldn't be late.

The phone rang. "Bill? I'm sorry baby. Something came up at the last minute."

"Are you all right?" he asked. He feared she was going to cancel the evening.

"I'm fine," she said. "I had to run home to pick something up, that's all. I'm walking out the door now. I'll be there in a half an hour at most. Do you miss me?"

"Very much," he said. "I don't like things like this cutting into our time together."

"I don't either, my darling. But I think you're going to like this thing very much," she said.

"What do you mean? What thing?"

"Wait until I get there. You'll see."

~

The housekeeper opened the door and Olivia walked in to the popping of a champagne cork. "I was afraid you'd have drunk it all by yourself," she said, giving Sturges a kiss so tender his knees buckled.

He poured two glasses and they walked to the living room window to take in the view. It was a clear night, and the lights of the harbor spread out below almost as far as the eye could see in either direction.

"My God, this is magic," she said.

"I grew up looking at this view every day," he replied. "I used to stand here as a small child and pretend I was the emperor, and everything down below was my domain. All these years later and I still get a thrill every time I see it. But it's not often that it's this clear any more. You brought the clean air with you."

"That's not all I brought." She reached into her bag and pulled out a manila envelope. "You asked me to try to remember anything Rupert said or did that might be relevant to those heads from the Summer Palace. After we spoke, I thought I recalled some things I'd seen on his desk just before his death. That's why I went back to the house, to see if my memory was correct. And it was." She handed the envelope to him, beaming like a schoolgirl who's just pleased the teacher.

He opened it and pulled out the contents. "My, my," he said softly. "I'll have to forgive you for being late after all."

The envelope contained newspaper stories, academic articles and photographs of the Yuanmingyuan heads, all apparently downloaded from the Internet. There was an artist's impression of what the water clock might have looked like before it was dismembered, along with photos of the seven heads whose whereabouts were known and the artist's guess of what the missing five would look like.

"You say Rupert was looking at these things just before he was killed?"

"I caught a glimpse of this drawing of the clock as I walked by his desk only a day or two before he left for China," she said. "I didn't think much of it at the time. He was always looking at photos and drawings of antiques – he must have had a thousand of them. I figured this was just the usual stuff. But then what you said earlier today got me to thinking.

"After the funeral, I stuffed Rupert's things into boxes and threw them all into the spare bedroom along with the antiques that I moved. Tonight was the first time I've gone through any of the boxes carefully. And sure enough, there was this envelope with all these photos and articles."

She watched as he studied the items one by one. "Does this help in any way?" she asked. "You didn't really tell me much about the clock or the heads when we spoke earlier."

"It's still only circumstantial," he said. "I'm not going to get too excited yet. But I would say that this, along with what I've been told, is the most compelling evidence we've found so far of why he was there." And he recounted his conversation with Giesler.

"These all prove that Rupert was interested in the heads," he said. "And the fact that he was studying them just before his trip to China means Giesler could be right: one of the heads might have been what Rupe was after."

"And those pictures of the young girls? Do you have any further thoughts about those? I'm almost afraid to ask."

He shrugged. "I still don't know what to make of those, Liv. Rupert downloaded some photographs, that's all we know. We know of his past interest in young girls, but the pictures don't tell us anything except that he was apparently still interested. We have no evidence that he'd actually done anything about his interest for many years. In fact, we have absolutely nothing except the timing to suggest that those photos are related to his trip to China in any way whatsoever. My advice is to let it be. With what you just brought me, the antiques scenario is looking far more likely."

She seemed comforted by the idea. It wasn't conclusive – nothing in the case was conclusive – but it made sense. "So what's the next step?" she asked.

"First thing tomorrow I'm going to take these clippings and photos to some of the people I've already talked to. Deputy Commissioner Ross, for one."

"This is exciting," she said, more animated than he'd seen her since the murder.

"How's that?"

"The possibility that Rupert was about to get one of these heads, I mean. It reminds me of my father. Whenever he was on the trail of a major piece it was like the whole house was filled with electricity. It was all he could talk about for days."

"I'm still amazed at the passion people like your father and Rupert work up for this stuff," Sturges said. "I appreciate the beauty, of course. But for them, it's as if art were the only important thing on earth."

"In my father's case that was almost true," she said. "His life was devoted to two things: China's art, and keeping me safe."

Thirty-two

Tall red characters reading *Beijing Zhan* – Beijing Station – stood atop the roof of the massive building, set between pagoda-like clock towers. Chang Dongfeng and Lili had arrived at the first stop on their flight to safety.

The breakdown of order and the closing of factories and schools had freed people to do as they pleased, and many had chosen to travel, some for political reasons, some just to escape the chaos in their hometowns. Train stations were alive day and night with people arriving, departing, waiting for trains that were frequently hours or even days behind schedule. As far as Chang could tell there had been no witnesses to the scene at Taiping Pond, although he could not be certain. But once inside the station he and his daughter could melt into the boiling mass of humanity and disappear, like drops of rain falling into the ocean.

He plunged into the station with Lili in tow. They forced their way onto a platform to await the train for Shanghai. When it pulled into the station almost twenty-four hours later, they were indistinguishable from the hundreds fighting with fists and elbows to get through the doors and windows and onto hard wooden seats. Once in place it was almost impossible to move until the journey was over. But they were leaving Beijing, and that was the only thing that mattered. As dawn broke, the train chugged slowly out of the station, carrying a thousand souls with a thousand different stories of a world gone crazy; carrying Chang and his daughter away from doubt and danger, and rolling toward salvation.

In Shanghai they fought their way aboard a second train, this one bound for Guangzhou, and they repeated the maneuver in Guangzhou, boarding the first train heading south along the western bank of the Pearl River. With every passing mile, Beijing and its peril receded into the distance.

Chang said little to the people around him. Once in Guangdong province, if forced to speak, he would say – in the *Toisan* dialect he had mastered during their earlier exile – that he and the girl were returning to his native village to share revolutionary experiences and spread the word of Mao Tse-tung Thought. It was a standard answer these days, and one people accepted without question.

They reached Zhongshan, north of Macau, and bought tickets on a local train that would take them to the southwest. The overburdened stationmaster told him this train ran only every few days in the best of circumstances. Given the disruption, no one could say when it might actually arrive. "If you're not on the platform," the man growled, "you'll miss it for sure. Find a spot along with everyone else and wait."

So they waited, jammed cheek by jowl with hundreds of others. Some in the crowd were old. Some had injuries, and some were ill. There was little to eat. There was no sanitation. Calls of nature required stepping gingerly over the bodies sprawled out on the platform, leaving the station, finding a reasonably clean spot to squat in the nearby trees where hundreds of others had already been for the same purpose, and then finding one's way back. One time Lili became confused among the crowds, and Chang feared he had lost her.

During the wait Chang conversed with the woman next to them. She was the wife of a university professor named Chen. She told Chang her husband, who was lying beside her, had been accused of "bourgeois tendencies" by his students. He was held for a week and submitted to daily struggle sessions. He finally dragged himself home with broken bones and bruises all over his body, and during his recuperation he'd developed pneumonia. Now they were heading for his home village, where she hoped he could recover in safety.

Chen lay under his blanket during the entire time they were on the platform, groaning in pain, coughing incessantly. His wife fed him what little food they had, carried his waste away in a chamber pot, and wiped the sweat that poured from him in Southern China's springtime humidity.

It was the middle of the third night when the train finally arrived. Everybody grabbed their possessions and jumped up, preparing for the battle to climb aboard. The injured professor's wife shook him, but there was no movement beneath the blanket. She shook him again. As Chang watched, she slumped forward and began to cry silently.

"Can I help?" Chang asked.

"Too late," she said between sobs. "He is dead,"

The man's face was cold. Chang could find no pulse. "You are right," he told the woman. "There is nothing you can do. Hurry, or you will miss the train."

There was no time to make arrangements for a burial, no time for the simplest of traditional observances. The woman hesitated for a moment, then nodded her head and pushed her way into the crowd without another look. Chang stayed with the body for a moment out of respect. At least, he told himself, this man's misery is over.

He had more than respect for the dead in mind, however. Once the woman was out of sight he felt under the blanket and felt in Chen's pocket for the man's identity card. He slid it out and replaced it with his own. Then he grabbed Lili and joined the jostling mob.

They took the train as far as the town of Jiangmen and then climbed off and headed south again, now on foot, now hitching rides on the occasional passing horse cart. Twelve days after they'd begun their flight in Beijing, they reached Hong Xing Village.

Chang was shocked to find the villagers who had survived the famine almost as emaciated as he'd left them six years earlier. "We eat enough to stay alive," Cheung Je-luk, their old friend, explained, "but there is never enough to fill our stomachs. We are always hungry."

It was early April and *Ching Ming*, the traditional grave sweeping holiday, was approaching. For the first time, Lili would have the chance perform her filial duty by visiting the graves of her mother and brothers. The Cultural Revolution had come to Hong Xing as it had come to every town and village in the country, but the residents were too jaded from previous experience and too hungry to do anything more than mouth the current slogans and wave their little red books in the air a couple of times a day. There had been one or two ritual denunciations and struggle sessions in the village, but they were only for show, and nobody had been harmed. There was no danger that the Changs would be bothered by anyone for observing the old rituals of ancestor worship.

Tradition was only one reason for the visit to Hong Xing, however. Chang had selected it as one more stop on their journey. For they were now within walking distance of Macau – and from there it was only a boat ride on to Hong Kong, and safety.

Two days after their arrival, he trudged to the site in the hills where he had buried his first son, Mingfu. He uncovered the remains and transferred them to a clean sack. He had also brought some animal bones with him in a second sack. He returned to the village and dug two new graves next to that of his wife. The remains of Mingfu went into one, the animal bones into the second.

Together, father and daughter cleared the burial area of weeds and rubbish. They burned a large circle around the gravesites to complete the ritual cleansing. They lit incense. They placed dishes by the graves holding a chicken and several eggs, which Chang had bought as they passed through Jiangmen and Je-luk had cooked the day before. Only Chang, watching his daughter burn fake money for her mother's and brothers' use in the afterlife, knew that the grave of Xilian was empty of human remains.

As he stood at the site of his family's destruction, the horrors of the famine came rushing back. He could feel the old hunger tearing at his insides. The moment the ritual acts were completed he tore the chicken to pieces, and he and Je-luk devoured their portions like animals. Then Chang and Lili stood and bowed. One more step towards safety.

Over the previous year and a half, Chang had smuggled out a large number of extremely valuable antiques with Rupert Rackley's help. Now he carried a roll of official documents, ones he had judged too precious to let out of his sight. He would take custody of the entire hoard from Rackley once he and his daughter arrived in Hong Kong and keep the items safe until sanity returned to his homeland and they could be sent back to where they belonged.

Chang would not be returning with them. After all he'd seen and endured, he could never love China again. He'd allowed Rackley to keep a small portion of the smuggled pieces for his trouble, and at Rackley's urging, Chang had also earmarked some pieces for himself. Pieces valuable enough that when sold on the international market, they would provide the funds to start a new life in Hong Kong.

~

Cheung Je-luk made the arrangements for their escape. A man she knew would guide them to the border with Macau. She gave them peasant's clothing to wear, even more ragged than what they had brought with them from Beijing. She had identity cards made for them using the name of the dead professor, Chen. In the event that they ran into a military patrol, the cards would not explain why they were wandering in the countryside, but they would at least identify them as residents of a local village instead of political refugees from the capital.

Chang tried to convince Je-luk to come with them. She was poor and alone – her husband had died of starvation along with so many others. But as miserable as her existence was, the thought of change was too much for her to contemplate. "My place is here near the graves of my husband and my ancestors," she told Chang. As he turned to leave, she pressed another document into his hand. "This is your daughter's birth certificate," she said. "I found it among the village records. For now, you will want to hide her identity. But someday she will want this. People should know who they really are. And if you are stopped, this will help prove that you are from here."

Once again, Chang Dongfeng was on the run, slinking through the night, hiding by day to avoid capture. This time he headed east instead of northwest, with his daughter at his side. This time the enemies he was evading were his own countrymen. They could not avoid others entirely along the way, but their disguises were good and they aroused no suspicion. At any rate, most of the people they encountered were just like them, refugees who wanted only to disappear into the darkness and continue on to a better life.

They approached the western edge of Macau on the third night. Only a ridge of hills now separated them from the border. The lights of the Portuguese-run enclave blazed like a welcoming beacon on the far side, far brighter than anything Chang had ever known in Shanghai or Beijing. They were about to move out when they heard voices.

A half dozen men came around a bend in the road seventy-five yards ahead, and in the moonlight Chang could see that at least one of them was carrying a rifle. The three dived into the underbrush, but too late: the approaching group had spotted them.

Chang told the guide and Lili to remain where they were, while he scrambled farther into the bush. He found a clearing next to a tree and began digging frantically in the soft earth. When the hole was big enough he dropped the documents he was carrying, all but Lili's birth records, into it. He covered the hole with dirt, and covered the dirt with twigs and leaves. Behind him, he heard the sound of a rifle bolt being slid into place, and voices shouting in the local dialect for Lili and the guide to show themselves.

Chang took a moment to pick out landmarks in the blaze of lights from beyond the hills, triangulating the position of the buried items as best he could. Then he walked casually back to the edge of the road, hitching up his pants as if he'd been relieving himself in the bushes and feigning surprise at the sight of the strangers.

At least they were not soldiers, only a group of villagers drafted into nighttime duty to intercept would-be escapees. In fact, they were less interested in preventing people from fleeing than in extorting whatever of value the escapees might be carrying.

The man with the rifle pointed it at Chang, who was clearly the leader of the trio, and ordered all three to empty their pockets. The guide, having been accosted on previous runs, was carrying nothing of value. Lili also had nothing. Chang had been warned that this might happen, and had placed two silver coins in his pocket. One of the cadres snatched them away – missing the dozen additional coins Cheung Je-luk had sewn into the buttons and lining of Chang's jacket.

There was nothing in their looks or voices to suggest their capture might be worth anything more. The man with the gun barked a few questions, more for show than anything else. Then he gave an order and the patrol marched off into the night.

Chang started to return for the buried documents, but the guide grabbed his jacket. "There are also soldiers on this road," he hissed. "They will not be so lenient if they find us. And look: it is already getting light. It will be too late to make the crossing. We must hurry."

The thought of leaving the documents behind was devastating, but there was no choice. Chang looked around, again trying to preserve the shape of the surrounding hills, the bend in the road, the placement of trees, in his mind. "Where are we?" he asked the guide. The guide pointed northeast and west and grunted the names of nearby villages, and Chang also committed those to memory. He prayed the landmarks would one day allow him to recover the documents.

They resumed their journey eastward toward the lights, and freedom.

~

They were able to make the crossing just before sunrise, first across narrow inlets to Taipa, one of Macau's two major islands, and then by sampan to the mainland portion of the tiny enclave. Once there they had no trouble blending in with the local residents and fellow refugees who thronged the narrow streets.

The guide had given Chang the name of a Macau snakehead, a smuggler of people who could be trusted to take them by junk to Hong Kong. It took two days of questioning people along the seafront to find the man, a grizzled old Macanese with a mouthful of gold teeth who was loading cargo onto his boat when Chang and Lili approached.

The deal was done quickly. The man relieved Chang of half his remaining silver coins, then stuffed father and daughter into the hold of the boat. He gave them food and water for two days, packed the rest of the hold with bits of rigging and household implements in order to hide them from view, and set sail with the tide. Junks like this were a common sight on this stretch of water, and the forty-five-mile journey from one European enclave to another passed without incident.

They were dropped past midnight in the New Territories and made their way to downtown Kowloon. Once there, they were home free: the Hong Kong government was turning back nobody who made it safely across the border. A harried refugee coordinator tried to direct them to a settlement in northern Kowloon, but Chang insisted they had relatives on Hong Kong Island and wanted to search for them there.

During one of his trips to China, Rackley had assured Chang that if he ever made his way to Hong Kong, Rackley would take care of him and his daughter for however long was necessary. He had given Chang an address and a phone number, and as part of his escape preparations Chang used to chant them to himself at night, committing them to memory. The Englishman had also whispered the amount of money that pieces like the ones they were smuggling out could bring on the open market. It seemed an astronomical sum to the mainland archivist and he was skeptical about the claim, but it spoke of salvation. If Rackley was right, the sale of just a few pieces would be enough to support him and his daughter comfortably while he built a new life.

He and Lili crossed the harbor and made their way to an enormous squatter settlement that was spreading across the hills above North Point. Refugees were setting up temporary homes, buying or scrounging materials to build crude shelters on the slopes. Chang found them a spot on a hillside: it was small and surrounded by filth, and just level enough to stand or lie on, but for now it would be home. Unlike the thousands of other refugees around them, Chang knew this home would only be temporary.

Now to locate Rackley and be reunited with the hundreds of priceless antiques that would become both his sacred responsibility, and the key to his and Lili's future.

Thirty-three

They hadn't yet solved the crime, but in the meantime, Sturges had the makings of a great story. Murder in the midst of the quest for a long-lost treasure. Colorful characters. Political intrigue. Cannibalism – no, he'd probably leave that out. But he also had that key factor, plausibility: Sturges had read about the sack of the Summer Palace and confirmed everything Fritz Giesler had told him. Knowing Rupert as he did, he had no doubt that one of the water clock heads would have been prize enough to persuade Rupert to break his long-held vow and visit the country he hated.

"Rupert's infatuation with Chinese art, combined with his contempt for China and its leaders: that's got to be what killed him," Sturges told Ross and Wai. "I'm convinced of it now."

He looked from one cop to the other, seeking agreement. "Come on guys," he said when they hesitated. "Everything we have points in that direction." He went down the list:

Ricco Tang, who knew Rupert well, suspected he was on the trail of some antique. Evelyn Chin, who knew him equally well, thought the same thing. Giesler was convinced of it – and he had evidence that pointed toward the precise antique Rupert was after. Rupert had pressed Giesler for information on smuggling artifacts. He'd told the Foreign Ministry he was going to Dongguan to look at antiques at the local museum, and Elaine Sikorsky's contact placed him in downtown Dongguan, not far from the museum, just hours before the murder. Sikorsky's information about documents fit easily into the antiques scenario.

Olivia, whatever she knew or did not know in advance of Rupert's trip to China, had now provided the most compelling evidence of all: Rupert had shown unusual interest in the water clock heads only days before he was killed; immediately after he had commented to Giesler about those same water clock heads with great excitement.

"Maybe it wasn't art for art's sake," Sturges said. "Maybe his ultimate goal was to stick it to the Chinese. But one way or another it looks like art is what finally drew him across the border for the first time in thirty-five years."

"The way you tell it, it all sounds perfectly plausible," Ross said. "But let's be honest, laddie: it's still only supposition. And I'm not even talking about whether we have the kind of evidence that would hold up in court. There are difficulties with the story from an everyday, common-sense point of view."

Sturges sighed in frustration. Ross was right of course: just about every fact they had was open to different interpretations. Each new revelation was like a golf putt that rims the cup and circles a few times, but refuses to drop.

There was one overriding problem with the scenario as well, and that was Beijing's reaction to the murder. The untoward interest in the case at the highest levels of the Party, the shutting down of the police investigation, the dispatching of Wu Zhemin in an attempt to squelch the story, the attempted attack on Sturges: it all suggested that Rupert had been on the trail of something so sensitive that some mainland official would kill Rupe in order to keep it out of his hands, and kill or maim anyone else who looked too closely into the murder. That didn't square with the notion that all Rupert was after was a piece of art.

"Maybe some high-ranking Party official was involved in the illegal sale of one of the heads, and Rupert learned about that," Sturges suggested. "That would provide a connection between the two." The heads had become a symbol of Chinese unity. The Party was relying on the themes of unity and patriotism to keep itself in power. In the midst of that, it would be a terrible indictment of the Party if some high-level member were found trying to sell off a major piece of the country's history. "Rupert would have loved to be able to write about that," he said. "And the bastards would be desperate to keep such a thing quiet."

"I don't like it," Ross said. "It would be embarrassing for the Party, sure, but I doubt it would be embarrassing enough to drive the leadership to murder, especially the murder of a foreigner. They've caught Party officials red-handed doing far worse than that and only thrown them in prison."

"Rupert wasn't some party official they could easily shut up," Sturges said. "He was out of their reach – until he crossed the border at any rate. And his column gave him a platform for broadcasting any Chinese embarrassment far and wide. If he had come across a scandal like that he wouldn't have hesitated to write about it, and his column had a broad readership. He'd have had the motive, the means and the opportunity to turn it into a public relations nightmare for the Chinese leadership. Finding him suddenly within their grasp in a situation like that..." He raised his hands in surrender. "I don't they'd have hesitated for a moment to take extreme action."

Wai was shaking his head. "Got to be realistic," he said. "You right about Chinese leadership willing to do anything to stay in power, but you think some senior official in China gonna risk lose face and go to jail for only few million dollars' worth of art? *Aiyeeah:* low-level officials and bank clerks, they steal more than that every day."

Nobody had an answer to that. All they could agree on in the end was that whatever the *Guojia Anquan Bu* was so desperate to hush up, it almost certainly had to be more than the simple fact that Rupert Rackley knew the location of a missing artifact. They were still only part way to the truth.

"Have you talked to Ricco Tang since all this new information has come our way?" Ross asked.

"I haven't seen him since my run-in with Wu, except for a very brief encounter at that charity reception the other night," Sturges said. "Why?"

"He's a ranking expert on Chinese antiquities," Ross said. "We have all this new information about Rupert and antiques. And Ricco withheld information from you before. Maybe he knows something more that can tie it all together. I'd love to find out that your theory of the case is right, laddie."

Thirty-four

As soon as Chang Dongfeng had settled himself and Lili in the refugee encampment in North Point, he located a telephone and dialed the number Rackley had given him.

"Master is asleep," the *amah* informed him in Cantonese, and she slammed down the receiver before he could give his name or leave a message.

He called four more times over the next two days, but *Lok-lei Sinsaang*, as "Mr. Rackley" was approximated in Cantonese, was always asleep. In frustration, Chang put on his most officious voice and demanded in formal Cantonese to know why Rackley would not take his calls. That had the desired effect: the Chinese will treat equals and subordinates like dirt, but they bow quickly before the voice of authority. Rupert had only recently been released from the hospital, the *amah* informed Chang with deference, and was still recovering from serious injuries. He spent much of the day in bed.

That explained the situation, but Chang needed more than explanations at this point. He was almost out of cash. Lili was complaining of hunger. Decisive action was needed.

He grabbed Lili by the hand and they trekked along the harbor front to the Central district, and then up the steep hill to Mid-Levels, asking the way as they went. Chang was struck by the quiet neatness of the neighborhood, such a contrast with the chaos of China and the teeming and squalid squatter settlement where they'd spent the last couple of days. But this was no time to admire the scenery. They found the street number Rackley had given and walked to the fourth floor. He rapped on the door.

Even as the door started to swing open, it occurred to him what he and his daughter must look like. They were still dressed in peasants' rags. They hadn't washed in days. They stank. The *amah* took one look at what appeared to be two beggars at the door and started to slam it shut.

Chang shot an arm out and stopped her. He squared his shoulders, fixed her with a gaze and announced in his most commanding tone: "We are not beggars, despite our appearance. I am an official of the Chinese People's Government, from Beijing. My daughter and I have made our way to Hong Kong experiencing great danger to see my good friend Rupert Rackley. Open the door, woman, and go fetch him. *Now!* We will wait here." He pushed his way inside, dragging Lili after him, while the maid scampered off to the bedroom with Chang's command ringing in her ears.

The smell of cooking wafted out of the kitchen, reminding him how hungry they were. But Chang was mollified by the notion that their journey was over at last. Soon enough they would be eating good food in their own comfortable apartment – nothing as grand as this one, he thought, eyeing the spacious and richly furnished rooms, but something new and nice. His friend and co-conspirator would appear in a minute to transform their lives.

In the end, it took more than twenty minutes, while father and daughter stood fidgeting in the entryway. When a door at the rear of the living room finally opened, a very different Rupert Rackley from the man Chang had come to know in Beijing hobbled through.

~

Rupert looked like an old man, gaunt, unkempt, shuffling slowly toward them with the help of a cane. His hair was uncombed and stuck out in all directions. As he came near, Chang could see the blotches from cuts and bruises still discoloring his face and neck.

Even more jarring was his manner. The man Chang had known as warm and engaging was now distant and cold. Chang didn't yet know what had happened in Shanghai. He couldn't know that at that moment, Rupert despised the Chinese. All Chinese.

"Mr. Rackley," Chang said, speaking Putonghua in the formal Chinese manner and bowing slightly. "I understand you suffered an accident. I hope you are recovering well."

"I am recovering slowly," Rupert replied in English. He could not bring himself to revert to Chinese no matter who his visitor was. His voice was brittle with contempt, and he glared at Lili as he spoke in a way that made her father uneasy.

Chang reverted to English, but it was a struggle. He'd hardly used the language since the family was exiled from Beijing in 1957. He hadn't spoken it at all during their years in Taishan. On their return to Beijing in 1963 he'd destroyed all his English-language books and periodicals, along with any other evidence of "bourgeois" inclinations, and spoke the language only on the rarest of occasions.

"I am...pleased...to see...that you, ah, improve," he said. Lili started at the strange sounds coming from her father's mouth.

"I am sorry, ah, to arrive at your door...without...inviting," Chang continued. "I tried to ring telephone many times." When Rupert offered no words of encouragement, Chang went on: "This is my daughter, Lili. We are running for two weeks. We walked across the border to Macau, and we came here on boat. We have spent the last nights in *Beijiao* – in, ah, North Point. I apologize to impose, but I ask if we can wash a bit. And perhaps...something to eat? The child has no decent food in so many days."

Rupert ordered the *amah* to show them to a bathroom. When they emerged twenty minutes later, somewhat more presentable, bowls of food and rice were sitting on the dining room table. After a moment's hesitation the two visitors sat. Chang reached tentatively for the chopsticks; when Rupert said nothing Chang signaled to Lili, and they began wolfing the food down.

They finished in minutes, and Chang laid his chopsticks across the top of his rice bowl. "I apologize for our manners," he said to Rupert, bowing his head. "The food is delicious." He glanced with unease at the *amah*, who was hovering behind them, and said in a lowered voice, "I have something else to ask."

"Go ahead," Rupert said. "She speaks no English."

"I am wondering," Chang said: "The items you purchased in China: they all arrived safely?"

At this, Rupert told the woman to clear the dishes and leave the room. When she was gone, he said: "Everything is here. Everything is safe."

Chang sighed with relief. "Thank goodness," he said. "I knew you would take great care with such treasures, but even so, the mind creates many worries." He paused again. "I can see the items soon, yes?"

"See them? Of course," Rupert replied.

"Thank you – thank you for everything you have done. And as soon as I am settled I wish to take possession. Of course, you may keep certain items, as we agreed."

"The items are quite safe right where they are, Mr. Chang. I doubt you would be able to find a better or safer place to store them. And I'm sure you'll agree that we should continue to keep their presence here a secret for the time being."

"Yes, yes, I am sure they are safe," Chang said. His English was coming back as he spoke. "But protecting them is heavy responsibility. I am grateful to you, and Chinese people will be grateful to you, for taking this burden. But now that I am here I can no longer ask you to carry such burden. It is my duty to take responsibility for the items. Until it is safe to return them to Mainland China."

"Indeed," Rupert said. "Well, since you raise the subject, there is something I've been planning to discuss with you – assuming I ever saw you again." He shifted in his chair and continued: "I did take on a heavy responsibility, as you say. I did so at considerable risk to myself. I always knew, of course, that there were dangers from the Chinese authorities. But this" – he pointed to the bruises on his face – "has been my reward from the 'grateful Chinese people.'"

"I am – please, I do not know what happened to you, Mr. Rackley. You say your injuries were made by the Chinese people?"

"Of course, how thoughtless of me. You would have no way of knowing. Let me bring you up to date." And he proceeded to tell Chang of his ordeal in Shanghai.

Chang lowered his head when Rupert finished speaking. "I am truly ashamed and sorry for your pain," he said. "Many of my countrymen have also suffered because of the madness that has overtaken China. Thousands of them I am sure, perhaps many thousands. I myself have suffered, as you know. Still, this is no excuse for such behavior to a guest. It is all because of..." He stopped himself. Even in the safety of Hong Kong he could not bring himself to speak aloud what was in his mind: *It is all because of this maniac, Mao Tse-tung, who is destroying China for his own political purposes.*

"Thousands may well have suffered," Rupert agreed, showing how little the world yet realized the true extent of the mayhem. "But it appears that many, *many* thousands are eagerly taking part in what you rightly call this madness. I'm afraid it will be a long time before I can forgive the Chinese people, no matter how grateful they might be.

Chang started to reply, but Rupert cut him short. "There is nothing for you to say, Mr. Chang. So please, just listen. We both agree I took on a heavy responsibility on behalf of the Chinese people. Given the outcome, I believe I am entitled to greater compensation than we originally agreed to."

Again, he put up a hand to stop Chang from replying. "Please: this is not a discussion, nor a negotiation. I have decided that one in twenty-five of the pieces is not sufficient to pay me for what I have gone through. Not nearly sufficient. Instead, I have decided that I will keep half of the items. The rest I will return to you as soon as you have secured a safe place to store them. Or if you choose, I will continue to safeguard them for you."

Chang flushed, running Rupert's words through his mind to make sure he had understood. When he could speak, he said: "But this is..."

Rupert waited, arms crossed, chin raised.

Chang summoned his courage: "These items are the property of the Chinese people. They include some of the greatest treasures collected by our leaders over the past one thousand years."

"I beg to differ, Mr. Chang," Rupert said. "Legally speaking, they are all now my property, although I realize that legality might be an alien concept to a citizen of the People's Republic of China. I purchased the items from an official branch of the Chinese government, following all proper procedures and paying the full asking price. I have the receipts of purchase. I obtained official permission to export the items, all chopped and signed by the relevant Chinese authorities, and I have the shipping papers from the state-owned shipping company to show that they were exported according to your country's rules and regulations. I have documents from Hong Kong Customs showing that they were brought into the colony legally. I would be within my legal rights to keep the whole lot.

"However, I am not a greedy man, nor am I unfair. As I said, I will keep half. I will relinquish any claim to the rest, and those are yours to take – on behalf of the grateful Chinese people. Of course, I expect that you will want to keep some of the pieces for yourself. You will need money to get yourself and your daughter established. And to rent a place to store the rest of the items."

Lili could see that her father was becoming agitated as Rupert spoke. She started to ask what was happening, but her father squeezed her arm as a signal for her to be quiet. "Surely, Mr. Rackley, there must be some way—"

Once again, Rupert cut him off. "As I said, Mr. Chang, this is not a negotiation. I have made up my mind. The law is on my side.

And if you cause any trouble..." He paused, to make sure Chang was paying attention: "...if you did that I would be forced to reveal how some of the treasures of the Palace Museum made their way to Hong Kong. I don't think the Communists would look kindly on their property being stolen, do you? If I did say anything, you and your lovely daughter would be in danger of retaliation by Beijing's agents."

"Lili and I are safe here in Hong Kong," Chang said.

"Do you think so?" Rupert asked. "But this place is crawling with underground Communist Party cadres, Mr. Chang. Just look at the riots and bombings they instigated here last year. They could easily get at the two of you. Especially if someone told them where to find you."

"We are not important enough to occupy their attention," Chang said.

"A servant of the Communist government who smuggled priceless works of art out of the country and then escaped himself...with who knows what government secrets in his head from his years in the General Office? Oh, I think they would consider you extremely important, Mr. Chang," Rupert said. "I think Mao Tse-tung himself would consider you important under the circumstances, and I think he would want you captured and returned to Beijing, or killed here in Hong Kong if returning you is not possible. And we both know that the Chinese people will do anything, no matter how vicious, no matter how violent, no matter how insane, that Chairman Mao wants. Don't we?"

A shudder ran through Chang's body. Rupert would have no way of knowing what secrets Chang was carrying in his head, but he might have looked at some of the documents Chang had sent along with the antiques. They contained information the Party would most definitely be unhappy to see made public. The Communist Party might forgive the smuggling of a few antiques, but Party secrets were absolutely sacrosanct. It would never forgive anyone who revealed them. Rupert was right: Chang and Lili were vulnerable, and being in Hong Kong was no guarantee of protection.

There might eventually be some way, legal or otherwise, to get the treasures back from Rupert, but at the moment Rupert had him at a disadvantage. Chang had no money, he had no income, and he knew nothing about British law or what his rights might be. Common sense dictated that he agree to Rupert's terms. He would get himself and the child settled, and then see what options might present themselves.

"Then I have no choice but to agree, Mr. Rackley," he said as evenly as he could. "Half the pieces are yours. I will take the other half as soon as I am able."

"I thought you would see reason," Rupert said.

Chang pushed himself from the table and stood, and Lili jumped up next to him. "You once told me you would take care of us if we reached Hong Kong," he said. "I hope that part of our agreement is still intact. I would like to ask you for a small amount of money. Just enough to buy us some decent clothes, and food for my child, and a clean place to stay. An advance against my half of the items, so to say."

"Of course," Rupert said, staring at the young girl with an intensity that frightened her. He reached for his wallet and pulled out three red hundred-dollar notes, a considerable amount of money at the time. "This should take care of your immediate needs."

Chang took the money. He would find them a safe place to live. More important, he would create new identities for them. He would use the forged mainland identity card with the dead college professor's name to obtain official new Hong Kong identity cards. From now on, Chang Dongfeng would be known as Chen Weihan. Little Chang Lili would become Chen Lizhu. In their own conversation the two would use the Mandarin pronunciation of their new name, *Chen*, but the local Chinese, seeing the name written in characters, would automatically call him by the Cantonese pronunciation, *Chan*, which would disguise them even further.

The two Changs, soon to be Chens (or Chans), bowed to Rackley and backed toward the door. "I will return as soon as I have better dress," Chang said.

"There's no rush," Rackley said. "The items are not going anywhere."

"Soon," Chang repeated.

"As you wish," said Rackley. He looked again at the little girl, and what might have been a smile creased his face for the first time that day. "Your daughter really is most lovely, Mr. Chang," he said. "How old did you say she was?"

Thirty-five

Dinner with Ricco Tang at a Yunnanese restaurant. Different food this time – cold shredded chicken with peanuts and fresh chili, wild mushrooms, dishes featuring the province's famous salty ham – but the topics of conversation were once again antiques, and Rupert Rackley.

"You know about the sacking of the Summer Palace in 1860," Sturges said between bites.

"Of course," Tang replied. "*An outrage against the Chinese nation,*' '*a festering wound on the Chinese soul*' – waving his chopsticks in time with his words – "*blah-blah-blah*." He lifted a small slice of ham sandwiched between opaque white rectangles of steamed milk and placed it on Sturges's plate. "Try this, old boy," he said. "Yunnan ham is luscious."

"I'm glad to see you accepting the outrage with such equanimity," Sturges said. "As for Yunnan ham, I've been eating it since I was a boy. So you naturally know about the heads from the water clock at the Summer Palace?"

"I've been hearing about those bloody heads since *I* was a boy. My grandfather was a rabid nationalist. He was born several years before the revolution – the 1911 revolution, I mean, not the one in 1949 – and China had recently suffered two more humiliations: the defeat by Japan in 1895, and western military intervention during the Boxer Rebellion in 1900. Grandpa was perpetually outraged at the whole world for the injustices that foreign powers had inflicted on China.

"Luckily for us, he wasn't outraged enough to stick around Shanghai for the Communist takeover. But even after he found a safe refuge for the family in colonial Hong Kong, he always resented the British. From the time my siblings and I were old enough to understand, he taught us about the terrible things they had done to us Chinese. And the sacking of the Summer Palace was high on his list."

"And yet here you are, perfectly at home with the Brits, and the Japanese, and just about everybody else for that matter."

"I'm a pragmatist, Bill. I've gotten what I need out of the Brits, and the Japanese, and the Americans, and the Chinese Communist Party, too. I have my pet peeves but I don't let them rule my life the way they ruled my grandfather's. But I'm rambling: what about the water clock?"

"I think one of the water clock heads might be a part of what got Rupert killed," Sturges said.

"You think somebody killed Rupert, what, to steal one of his antiques from him? But why would Rupe have carried a valuable piece like that into China? That doesn't make any sense."

"Steal?" Sturges said. "No, you don't understand. I think Rupert might have planned to *buy* one of the heads while he was in China." There was skepticism on Tang's face. "This isn't just guesswork, Ricco. You told me yourself you thought Rupert was about to score a major piece of art." He recounted what Giesler had said, and about the photos and news articles Olivia had seen Rupert looking at just before his death. "From a contemporary collector's point of view, Chinese art doesn't get much more major than those heads. And we now have strong evidence to indicate that he was after one of them."

Tang looked at him through narrowed eyes. "You're not putting me on, are you old boy?" he said.

"What kind of a question is that? You know I've been working non-stop on Rupert's murder. I don't have time for games. I still don't have all the pieces to the puzzle, but I'm pretty sure this was one of them."

"Hmm," Tang said. What looked like a smile played at the corners of his mouth.

"You don't seem impressed."

"Oh, I'm quite impressed with all the work you've put into this."

"But not with my conclusions?"

"I don't think one of the water clock heads is what Rupert was after, no."

"Why not? You have to admit, getting his hands on one of those heads would have been a major coup for him. The heads are not only famous, they're pieces the Chinese would have been hugely unhappy to see in the hands of an avowed antagonist like Rupe. I don't think he could have resisted the chance to get his hands on one if it came along."

"Well, there's the thing," Tang said with a shrug of the shoulders. "You obviously don't know: it just so happens that the chance did come along — but a long, long time before he was killed."

Sturges waited for him to continue, but Tang pulled another morsel from the dishes in front of them and chewed quietly. "Please go on," Sturges said.

"I mean," Tang said, "Rupert didn't have to go to China to buy one of the heads, because he already owned one."

Sturges wasn't sure he'd heard correctly. "He *what*?"

"You heard me. He already owned one – the best one of all, in fact: he had the dragon's head."

"How do you know this?" Sturges managed to ask.

"I saw the bloody thing with my own eyes. Rupert showed it to me once."

"When? Where? You never mentioned this earlier."

"Why would I mention it?" Tang threw up his hands. "I didn't know until a moment ago that it might have anything to do with the murder. Besides, I promised Rupert that I'd never tell anyone about it." Although," he muttered, more to himself than to Sturges, "since he went and got himself killed, I suppose I'm released from that promise."

To Sturges, the importance of the revelation was obvious. If Rupert already owned the dragon's head, it was unlikely that a second head would have been tempting enough to lure him across the border. All he'd have had to do to rankle the Chinese was bring the one he owned out of hiding and show it to the world. "Tell me," he said, "where exactly did you see this head?"

"It's been right here under China's nose for years," Tang said. "Rupert rented a storage locker in Chai Wan. He kept his really special pieces there, things too valuable to keep on display or whatever. But Olivia got his entire estate, didn't she? She must know about the locker."

"I don't think so." There had been no mention of the locker or the items in it that day at the lawyer's office, and Olivia had seemed genuinely surprised just a couple of days ago at Rupert's interest in the heads. Which meant, Sturges realized, that the dragon's head might still be in the locker, waiting to be discovered. "And you say Rupert took you to this locker?"

Tang nodded. "It was his big secret. Well, given everything we've learned in the last six weeks, I guess I should say it was one of his big secrets."

"If it was such a secret why did he let you in on it?"

"Hah! Because he was Rupert, that's why," Tang said. "One night after dinner he and I got to arguing about whose collection was better. I don't think he would have showed me the head even then, but we'd had an exceptional amount to drink, even for the two of us. The argument was getting quite heated, and he finally pounded the table and said, 'Right! I'm going to show you something that will settle the argument once and for all.'

"We rode out to Chai Wan and we stopped outside a building, but before he would let me out of the car he swore me to secrecy about the locker and anything that was inside it. Then he took me in and showed me what he had."

"When exactly was this?"

"Well....mid-1997, I guess," Tang said. "Yeah, just a short while after the handover. If you recall, Rupert was sick at the notion that the country he despised had taken ownership of the city he loved. A lot of old Hong Kong Brits felt like that, of course. Couldn't accept that the Chinese had taken back Britain's last great colony. I used to tell them, 'Get over it, chaps,' but you know, some of them—"

"The dragon's head, Ricco?"

"Sorry. Well, all Rupert really wanted to do that night was drown his sorrows. I think part of the reason he let me in on the secret was to show that the Chinese hadn't beaten him completely. They'd taken something precious from him, but he still had something of theirs that they wanted very much."

"Did you realize at the time how valuable the head was?" Sturges asked.

"I knew its historic value, so I knew it would be worth a lot of money. And Rupe was right about it settling the argument: that piece trumps anything in my collection. I was envious, and given what the Brits did to the Yuanmingyuan, I must admit even I felt a twinge of nationalistic displeasure at seeing the head in the hands of a bloody Englishman."

"Why didn't you tell Brian Ross about the locker?"

"For the same reason I never told you. Ross never asked me anything about Rupert's collection. And Rupe had hundreds of pieces. How was I to know that the ones in the locker might have any more relevance to the murder than the ones on display in his house? I mean, this is all stuff he's had for years. And the bloody locker isn't something I think about on a regular basis. I just saw it that once, in an alcohol haze. Rupert never mentioned it again after that night. Sometimes, to be honest, I wonder if I really saw what I think I saw."

"Ross didn't ask you about the Summer Palace heads because he didn't know about them himself when he talked to you. But that locker could be very important. Could you find it again?"

"Rupert didn't give me an address," Tang said. "We were sitting in the back seat of his car on the ride over and I wasn't paying any attention to the route we took. And like I said..."

"You'd had a lot to drink. I get it."

"...so, yes, it's all rather hazy. I might be able to find the place again, but I shan't make any promises. Chai Wan is a big area. And even if I could find the building, that doesn't mean we could get inside the locker."

"Why's that?"

"How are we supposed to open the door?" Tang said. "I don't have a key. From what Rupert told me that night, Olivia didn't know about the place while he was alive, so I'm guessing she didn't have a key back then either. And you just said you don't think he left her one in the will. So even if I could lead you to the locker," he said, "I couldn't tell you how to open it."

"I'm sure Ross could break into it if need be."

"I don't know about that," Tang said. "Rupert was really serious about security. There's a massive steel door. It would be like breaking into Fort Knox."

"But wait," Sturges said. "On second thought, breaking in might not be necessary."

"What do you mean?"

Sturges smiled. "We might already have the key."

Thirty-six

They cruised for an hour through the streets of Chai Wan, a sprawling district on the northeastern corner of Hong Kong Island. Much of the construction in the district was recent, but there were still large expanses of old apartment blocks and commercial buildings, and Tang was sure the locker was in an older building.

"It looked sort of like that one," he said, pointing out the car's window. Winston Wai rolled the car to a stop, but after a moment Tang shook his head. "Nope, that's not it. Sorry it's taking so long, chaps," he said. "It was late at night when Rupert and I got here, just like now, and the lights in the building were out. I couldn't see very clearly."

"And you'd had a lot to drink," Sturges said with resignation in his voice.

Tang had been right about Olivia: she knew nothing about a secret locker or its contents. "I think Rupert mentioned something about a safe deposit box once," she told Ross when he called to ask. "Is that any help?"

"Stop!" Tang cried suddenly. He stuck his head out the window and peered at the façade of a building rising in the gloom.

Sturges followed Tang's gaze. "That doesn't look like the kind of place you'd store valuable goods," he said.

"It isn't," said Tang. "I mean to say, Rupert said he purposely chose a nondescript building like this so nobody would think there might be valuable artifacts inside. I'm going for a closer look." He walked to the building entrance. He leaned forward to examine a rusting metal plate by the front door. He straightened with a smile on his face and waved at the men in the car. "This is the one!" he shouted.

The other three hurried to join him, and Sturges took a look at the nameplate. "*Glorious Prosperity House*," he read out loud.

"You're sure this is it?" Ross asked.

"Now that I see the name, it all comes back," Tang said. "I remember thinking it was an awfully grandiose name for an old derelict like this. But you know us Chinese: anything to bring good luck. And a prestigious name is supposed to bring good luck."

They followed him through the entrance. Wai flashed his badge at an old caretaker who was dozing in the lobby, and after a brief exchange in Cantonese the man pointed to a door that led down a flight of stairs. The corridor at the bottom was lit by a single bulb. The place smelled of mildew and rot. Piles of junk were strewn haphazardly on the floor, almost blocking the passage. As they picked their way around the debris with the help of Wai's flashlight, a rat scurried between their legs before disappearing into a hole in the wall.

Most of the rooms off the corridor were covered by nothing more than unlocked wooden doors. A couple had no doors at all. The room at the far end of the corridor, though, was protected by a heavy steel door set inside a reinforced metal frame. A pinpoint of red light in a glass panel on the wall next to the door indicated that a security alarm had been activated.

"This is it," Tang said. "I remember this door. It's like something you'd find in a bank vault."

The beam from the flashlight showed that the keyhole was square in shape. Ross and Sturges exchanged a glance, and Ross produced the keys Sturges had given him. He picked out the one with the square blade and fumbled with it until the four edges lined up with their counterparts in the keyhole, and then it slid in easily. Ross gave it a sharp twist. The muffled sound of tumblers falling into place could be heard, and the light in the alarm panel changed from red to green. "Two keys down, one to go," Ross said.

Wai gave a push and the mass of metal slid open on soundless hinges. Cool, clean air wafted out, shunting aside the foul smell in the corridor. "Full-time climate control," Ross said. "You were right, Ricco. Rupert wasn't mucking about."

The wall surrounding the door had been reinforced: it was three or four times as thick as those of the other rooms in the corridor. The door itself was two inches thick and made of seamless stainless steel. Not a spot of rust, not a scratch marred its burnished surface. Sturges ran his fingers over the smooth exterior. "This looks like it could stop a bazooka blast," he said. "It must have cost as much as one of his antiques."

Ross reached for a panel of light switches just inside the door. The lights came up slowly, and the men could see that they were in a single large room with rows of built-in stainless steel cabinets and shelves. Like the door, everything in the room was of top-quality construction. The walls were spotless, and the floor was laid with glistening white tiles. Dozens of large and ornate cloth bags and boxes, the type traditionally used to hold Chinese artwork, sat on the shelves. The cabinets presumably held similar items.

Sturges and Tang moved forward toward the objects, but Ross pulled them up short. "Don't touch anything," he said. "This is all evidence." He and Wai pulled on latex gloves and the two policemen began unwrapping the items. The two cops and Sturges were hoping the locker would finally provide the answer to some of their questions about the murder. Tang's hands were trembling at the thought of the treasures about to be revealed.

"*Wah*," Wai said softly as piece after piece was uncovered. There was a white jade carving of staggering intricacy. There was a prancing bronze horse, probably from the Western Han period, whose grace matched that of the famous flying horse of Gansu. There were indescribably beautiful porcelains from the Song and Qing, each one so pristine it might have been fired only a day earlier. There was a two-foot-high seated Buddha of gilded bronze with a crown of precious jewels. "Ming Dynasty; no, probably Yuan," Tang pronounced after a quick look. There were more bronzes, ceramics, scroll paintings, each more exquisite than the last.

"Like we find King Solomon mine," said Wai.

"More like being taken to a private room and shown the finest items in the National Palace Museum," said Tang.

"You sound like you're seeing it all for the first time," said Sturges.

"I am," Tang said. "When Rupert brought me here he showed me the dragon's head, and that was all. He wouldn't let me unwrap any of these other pieces. I had a picture in my mind of what the rest might be like, but actually seeing them all like this...I don't know what to say."

"It really is breathtaking," Sturges said. He was snapping photos of the items with a small camera.

"It's more than breathtaking," Tang said. "Can you pick some of those porcelains up and show me the bottoms?" Wai did as he was asked and Tang leaned close, examining the surfaces for telltale imperial markings. He finished his inspection and said: "This is just off the top of my head, and I haven't seen everything yet, but there are dozens of pieces here. If you take what pieces of this quality have sold for recently as a starting point, and extrapolate from there: my God." He looked from man to man with eyes wide. "There has to be a hundred million U.S. worth of art here at a bare minimum. That is...assuming the head is still here."

"It is." It was Ross's voice. He'd wandered to the far corner of the room and opened a cabinet door about thirty-six inches square. The door swung down on sturdy hinges and clicked into place to form a horizontal viewing platform for whatever was inside. He'd pulled the item from the cabinet and rested it on the door, and now he removed the bag that was covering it. "Gentlemen," he said, "unless I'm mistaken, I give you the dragon's head from the Summer Palace water clock."

The statue flashed like gold as the light caught the bronze surface. It was about a foot and a half high. A relatively unexceptional casting compared with the intricacy of many Chinese dragon carvings, but its significance escaped nobody in the room. Here was an artifact that hadn't been seen in public for more than a hundred and forty years. An artifact that the Chinese government would want returned almost as fervently as it wanted the island of Taiwan.

"I think I have an idea how Howard Carter must have felt when he opened Tutankhamen's tomb in 1922," Sturges said, snapping photos of the head from every conceivable angle.

"I think I have an idea how the lovely Mrs. Rackley is going to feel tomorrow," said Ross, "when she finds out that she's the owner of another hundred million dollars' worth of art. *U.S. dollars*, did you not say, Ricco?"

"That's what I said," Tang replied, staring in wonderment at the treasures around him. "This baby alone is worth at least ten million."

"It's exciting stuff, but unfortunately it pretty much destroys our theory that Rupert was after one of the Summer Palace heads," Ross said. "And that being the case, I don't see how any of this is relevant to the murder. It looks like it's just more of Rupert's art collection."

"So what do we do with it?" Sturges asked.

"You were at the reading of the will. Aside from your car, Rupert left everything to Olivia, right?"

"That's right. Which means everything in this room, including the head, is hers – in addition to the houses and the cash and everything else she already knows about."

"Then we'll leave it here for now, until she arranges to pick it up," Ross said. "I'll hold onto the key for safekeeping in the meantime, just in case this does turn out to be evidence." He turned to admire the dragon's head. "Is there anything at all to indicate how Rupert got hold of this beauty?"

"Only this," Wai said. He had pulled out several large books containing Rupert's drawings and notes. There was a drawing of the head at the back of one of the books, with notes indicating that Rupert had obtained the piece in 1985, but there was nothing about where it had been over the previous hundred and twenty-five years or how Rupert had gained possession of it. There were also boxes of photographs, all in color and professionally printed, of each of the items in the locker.

"Nothing else," Wai said. "One more mystery for your mystery collection, hey boss?"

"If only we could ask Rupert himself," Ross said.

"Nothing about this on any of his e-mails," said Wai.

"Oh?" Sturges said. "When did you see his e-mails?"

"When we looked through his home computer," Ross said. "We examined the hard drive right after the murder. I told you at our first meeting that we'd looked through his private effects."

"That's right, you did," Sturges said. And Olivia had told him the other night that the cops had looked through everything. "You didn't mention the computer – but of course you'd have looked at that along with everything else." He contemplated the information for a moment. "And you found nothing on the hard drive that might help explain his trip across the border? Nothing unusual or suspicious? No references to a major piece of art? Nothing at all relating to the looted art of the Summer Palace?"

"Nothing," Ross said. "There was nothing on that computer that helped us in any way – in fact, there wasn't much of anything there at all. It doesn't appear that old Rupe used the thing for much except to write his columns. We did find a bit of routine e-mail traffic and occasional browsing of antiquities websites, but that was it. Nothing that we could even remotely connect to the murder. And believe me, our people went over that hard drive with a fine tooth comb."

"I'm sure they did," Sturges said, suddenly not sure of anything.

He pulled out his phone and started punching in a number. "Who are you calling?" Ross asked.

"The Widow Rackley."

"To tell her she's even richer than she thought?"

"That, yes, but I'm more interested in what she might have to tell me."

The prospect of another meeting with Olivia sent a jumble of emotions racing through his mind.

What an incredible woman, he thought. That face. That fantastic body. That voracious sexual appetite.

And I, he thought; I William Sturges; *I'm* fucking her.

Amazing.

But all that was suddenly of secondary importance. A more urgent question now dominated his thoughts.

He wondered: who was actually fucking with whom?

Thirty-seven

Olivia begged him to come by immediately, despite the late hour. "I was afraid you weren't going to call tonight," she told him. "The more we're together, the more I hate it when we're apart. Please be quick."

He walked through her door twenty minutes later and she rushed forward to embrace him, but he put his hands out and held her at arm's length. "That's not what I came for tonight," he said.

Her face registered confusion. "What's going on?" she asked.

"What's going on is you've been lying to me again."

She opened her mouth to protest. She closed it and turned away. "I thought we already went over that," she said. "I didn't tell you the whole truth right away because I was trying to protect Rupert's reputation...and my own privacy."

"You're referring to what you did or did not tell Ricco about why Rupert was going to China?

"Yes. I explained all that to you."

"You did explain it. You said when Ricco came to meet you in Macau, he was under the impression Rupert was about to buy some major antique somewhere."

"That's right."

"You informed him that Rupert was planning a trip to China, and you told him, or you implied, that that's where the antique would be coming from. You misled Ricco because you didn't want him to know the real purpose of Rupert's trip, which was to hook up with some underage girl. At least that's what you feared Rupert's real purpose was."

"Exactly." Tears were welling in her eyes.

"And all this after you found those photographs of young Chinese girls on Rupert's computer."

"Yes, yes."

"All this *before* Rupert actually made the trip. Before he was killed for his troubles."

"I told you..."

"Well, you see, that's the first problem, Liv. Are you aware that the police looked through Rupert's computer? Immediately *after* he was killed?"

"I – well, I don't know exactly what they did," she said. "I said they could look at anything they wanted. I was too distracted to pay much attention. But I suppose they would have looked at the computer, too, although I have no idea what they might have found there. I told you, I don't know much about computers, except how to send emails and surf the Web."

"That's probably a good thing for all of us. Because I can tell you this: those photos of the young girls that you were so worried about were nowhere on the computer, and never had been on the computer, at the time the cops inspected it."

"But they were!" she insisted. "I showed them to you. The police must have missed them. And how is my lack of knowledge a good thing?"

He closed his eyes. "Because it helped me catch you in a lie," he said. "If you did know anything about computers, you'd know it's easy for an expert to determine when something was downloaded. In other words, if those photos had been on Rupert's computer when the cops examined it, Ross's technicians would have found them.

"But they found no such thing," he said. "There was no sign of those photos, period – which means Rupert didn't download them before he left for China. That can only mean *you* must have downloaded them onto the computer – after the cops were finished looking through it, and before I came to your house that first day. And if Rupert never downloaded those photos, that means there was no reason for you to mislead Ricco in Macau – before Rupert was killed. So that was a lie. And then you showed the photos to me – after Rupert was killed – and fed me the whole story about giving Ricco a phony reason for Rupert's trip. Another lie.

"Which means...I'm not sure what it means. Were the photos a red herring, Liv? Did you download them and show them to me to send me off in the wrong direction in case I was closing in on the real reason for the murder?"

"If that's what you think—"

"I don't know what else to think."

"Your mind is made up, then," she said. "It's useless for me to argue. But what does it matter, anyway?" she said, turning to face him. "We finally know the real reason for the trip: that's the important thing, isn't it? He was after one of the Summer Palace heads. He was after a major antique after all. You said so yourself"

"It does matter, because that was yet another lie. Yes, I did speculate that Rupert was after one of the heads, but I based that largely on the articles and photos you brought to my house that night. But Ross says there was no trace of those articles and photos of the heads on Rupert's hard drive, either. There's no evidence in other words that Rupert ever downloaded that material."

"He clipped them out of a magazine, then," she said. "Who cares where he got them? The point is, I saw him looking at them just before he died."

"I care," Sturges said, "because it turns out that there was no particular reason for Rupert to be reading up on the dragon's head or collecting photos of it just before he died...because he already owned it. He'd owned that head for almost twenty years!"

For the first time since they'd been together, she seemed flustered. Her face flushed. She clasped her hands together as if to keep them from trembling. "What are you talking about?" she demanded, almost shouting. "Since the murder I've looked through every piece of art he owned, and I haven't come across that head or anything remotely like it. There was nothing in the will about the head – you were at the reading; you know exactly what he left me."

"What I now know is that he left you a great deal more than either of us thought. I know because I just saw the dragon's head for myself a half hour ago. It's in a storage locker that Rupert kept here."

"A storage locker? Where?"

"In Chai Wan."

"So that's what Ross was calling about earlier tonight," she said.

"That's it all right. Rupert took Ricco there once several years ago, and Ricco led us to it tonight. There were also a lot of other magnificent antiques in that locker."

"Oh, God, more antiques," she said, wringing her hands. "I don't know where I'm going to put them all. I can't deal with this."

"These are quite safe where they are," Sturges said. "And you should probably leave them there for the time being. Ricco reckons the items are worth a hundred million U.S. dollars or more. You don't want to leave stuff like that sitting around your house."

He searched her face for a clue to her thoughts. Would she keep up the pretense? Would she come up with some new story? "You're worth three times as much as you thought, Liv," he said, hoping to keep her talking. "You're a very rich chickie indeed."

Her face darkened. "And what do you think," she snapped, "that this was all about money?"

"Like I said, I don't know what to think."

"Right, right," she mumbled, but her mind was clearly elsewhere. Then a sigh of resignation. A decision made. "I'm not a very good liar, am I?" she said.

"Good enough to keep me off balance for a time. But the story you made up was much too convoluted. It was inevitable that you'd trip over your own lies at some point."

"I did lie, of course," she said. "Not about Rupert's wealth. I really knew nothing about that. But about the photos of the young girls, about the photos of the animal heads, about what I told Ricco. It *was* all meant to throw you off the track so you wouldn't find out what had really happened. But it has nothing to do with money. There's more to this story than you could begin to imagine. I wanted to tell you the truth all along, but I had to protect myself. And my father. And even Rupert, may the son of a bitch rot in hell. That's why I misled you."

"Your father and Rupert are past protecting."

"I still have their reputations to worry about," she said.

"You have yourself to worry about, Liv. There are criminal penalties for obstructing a murder investigation. It's called perverting the course of justice, and Brian Ross isn't going to look very kindly on it when he finds out that's what you've been doing from the start. I might still be able to help you – if you come up with a very convincing story. But it had better be the truth this time."

"If I talk to you will you promise not to write about it?" she said. "You could do that much, couldn't you?"

"How much eventually appears in the newspapers is beyond my control, and hardly the most important thing at this point. What's important right now is the murder of your husband. Who was like a father to me, in case you've forgotten. If you know something more about that, you're going to have to tell what you know. You really don't have much choice."

"I can't tell you the story if you won't protect me," she said.

"Up to you. But whether you talk to me or not, I'm going straight to Ross to tell him everything I do know, about your faking the photos of the girls, about the articles, about our conversations, about all the things you've been keeping from him and lying to the both of us about. He'll get the truth out of you. Then I'm washing my hands of the whole thing. And that includes you."

She stared out the window for a long time, arms folded across her chest, deep in thought. "I didn't kill Rupert," she finally said. "Whatever else you think about me, I didn't do that."

"I'd like to believe that," he said. "But you know who did kill him, don't you?"

"Sit down," she said. "This is going to take a while."

371

He sat. "I'm listening."

"That Sunday at my house, you asked me about my marriage to Rupert. The time has come to tell you that story."

"I'd say that's long overdue."

"Maybe," she said. "I'm not sure you'll still feel that way after I've finished. It's not a pretty story."

Thirty-eight

Chen Weihan, as Chang Dongfeng was now known, used the several hundred dollars that Rupert had given him to buy new clothes for himself and his daughter, and he paid a week's rent for a simple but clean room in North Point. Bathed, shaved and looking more like the ranking authority on Chinese art he was than a ragged peasant, he made his way to one of the prominent antique dealers on Hollywood Road. He opened a bag containing two pieces he'd selected from his half of the items in Rupert's storeroom, two exquisite blue-and-white plates with a period mark on the bottom indicating when they were fired. He unwrapped the plates with care. He placed them on the counter. The dealer almost lost his composure.

"Are these genuine?" the man gasped.

"I assure you they are," Chen replied.

"They are magnificent!" the dealer exclaimed. Then, realizing he'd allowed more enthusiasm to show than good business practice dictated, he straightened up and affected a stern look. "Where did you get them?" he said.

"They have been in my family for generations," Chen said. That was a lie of course: they had been in some other family's personal collection for some unknown period, until that family was forced by contemporary politics to part with them. But the only people who knew the truth were Chen and the unfortunate family members. If they had not already been beaten to death by Red Guards. "My great-grandfather was a prolific collector in" – he picked the name of a city at random in order to further the lie – "Ningbo."

"They were made for the Xuande Emperor in the early Ming," Chen continued, and that was the truth. The imperial mark on the bottom proved their provenance. "They were authenticated many years ago by some of the leading experts in China, when men in China still cared for such things. I am heartbroken to have to part with them, but my daughter and I escaped with nothing much but the clothes on our backs and these two precious items. I need money for us to live on. Do you think you can sell them for me?"

It was all the dealer could do to keep from drooling at the prospect. "I expect that I can," he said, caressing the cool, smooth surfaces of the porcelain. "I will charge a small commission, of course."

"Of course," Chen said, trying to appear knowledgeable. For all his expertise in art, he knew nothing about the art market. "I wonder, do you think they are worth much?"

"I will have to examine them more closely, and I would like to invite some colleagues in for consultation, but I think I can safely say, yes, they are worth a very handsome amount." The dealer pulled an approximate dollar figure from his store of knowledge; now it was Chen who had to hold onto the counter to keep from collapsing in shock. His mind whirled. It took him a moment to realize that the dealer was still speaking. "I said, will you leave them with me for a day?" the dealer asked.

"How much did you say they are worth?" Chen said.

The dealer repeated the figure.

"That is what I thought you said," Chen replied, wiping a speck of perspiration from his brow. He had no idea who in this city could be trusted. Given his experience with Rupert, his instinct was to trust no one. "Please begin your examination," he said. "I will stay here with the plates until you are finished. I have nowhere else to go."

~

He took the pieces home with him that night, gripping them tightly all the way, imagining potential thieves on all sides. The following morning, returning for an appointment with one of the dealer's best customers, he splurged on a rickshaw to reduce the chance of being robbed en route. When the customer saw the pieces his eyes grew wide and he became short of breath. "You described them accurately," he told the dealer between gasps. "They are truly beautiful."

Haggling followed, but less than might have been expected. The collector was determined to have the plates at any cost and he made little attempt to hide it. Two hours after he arrived at the shop, Chen walked back out with forty thousand Hong Kong dollars in the bag where the plates had been.

It was more money than he ever dreamed he'd see. Enough by itself to keep him and Lili housed and fed decently, if not extravagantly, for several years if they were frugal with their spending. His mind was busy recalibrating the relationship among himself, Rupert and the secret stash of art. It was now clear that by selling only a small portion of the pieces they had spirited out of China, both he and Rupert could be rich beyond – well, beyond Chen's wildest imagination, at least.

But Rupert's claim to half the treasure was not motivated by money, Chen realized that. It was revenge the man was after. The pity was, they could have talked it out. Had not Chen also suffered grievously at the hands of his countrymen? He could understand Rupert's fury. He could empathize.

But Rupert would not listen to reason. Chen sighed. He was not sure which emotion was stronger, sympathy for his erstwhile friend, or anger at his betrayal.

His first stop was one of the city's British banks, which the art dealer had assured him were safe and reliable. After an assistant manager spent an hour explaining the details of modern savings and checking accounts, Chen opened one of each, and with no small amount of trepidation, he handed the bulk of his newly acquired fortune to this stranger.

Just days earlier he had been a dirt-poor refugee, a supplicant barely surviving with the aid of handouts. Now, as he wandered absently among the low-rise, arched façades of Queen's Road Central, the small bankbooks in his hands informed him that he was an established citizen with money in the bank. More money in fact than most of Hong Kong's four million residents could boast of. Certainly far more than any of his fellow refugees had. They'd been flocking in by the scores of thousands since the Cultural Revolution began, in search of safety and a better life. Chen Weihan had found that better life almost with a snap of his fingers.

Safety was still a primary concern. His next stop after the bank was to rent a proper apartment for himself and little Lili in one of the newer buildings in North Point. He could have afforded something even better in one of the colony's best Chinese neighborhoods, but his tastes were simple after thirty years of living with communism. And he knew he and his daughter must remain as anonymous as possible.

He assumed Rupert was correct when he said the colony was crawling with communist agents. It was possible, however unlikely, that one of them might be on the lookout for Chang Dongfeng, former PRC official. A low-ranking official, to be sure, but if the communists learned what was in the documents he had smuggled out of China, nothing would stop them from trying to get them back, and very likely from shutting Chang's mouth for good.

Maybe the ploy of leaving his ID card on the body of a dead university professor in the Zhongshan train station had worked. Maybe some railway clerk in that remote town had bothered to check the body before disposing of it. Maybe that person had found the ID card with Chang's name and Beijing registration on it, and had not merely thrown it away, as a lowly clerk in those turbulent times would normally be expected to do. Maybe the apparent death of one Chang Dongfeng had been reported to the Beijing authorities. Maybe someone in Beijing who might know of Chang and care about his whereabouts now believed him dead. Maybe he had made a successful escape.

Maybe maybe maybe. Too many maybe's. As remote as the threat appeared to be, the potential cost of carelessness was very great indeed. So he and his daughter would keep their heads down and begin to build their new lives quietly.

Their living arrangements were taken care of. Money was no longer a worry. To disguise himself further, Chen adopted western-style dress, like many westernized Hong Kong Chinese. That and the cultivated and American-accented English of his youth, which was coming back to him rapidly, would set him apart from the hordes arriving from the mainland with only peasant rags on their backs and one or another Chinese dialect in their heads. It would all allow him to pass for someone who had been in the colony for some time.

He began to introduce himself around town as William Chen, taking a western name for the first time since he had shed the name Peter as he fled the horrors of Nanjing. He enrolled his daughter in a government school as Olivia Chen Lizhu, and he hired a woman to tutor her in English in the evenings. Their disguises were as complete as he could make them. Now he could return his attention to Rupert Rackley and the smuggled treasure trove.

~

Rupert's distaste at having to deal with anyone Chinese notwithstanding, and setting aside the new ground rules he had so arbitrarily established, he was good to his word.

He took Chen to the office where he was storing the art. He allowed Chen to inspect the goods to make sure nothing was missing. He showed Chen the pieces he, Rupert, had put aside for himself. They included some of the best, but the division was equitable in both quantity and quality. "The rest is yours," he told Chen. "You are welcome to leave everything here, where it will be quite safe, or you can find another storage spot – or ship it all back to Beijing if you wish. It's entirely up to you."

Now that he had examined all the items, however, Chen had another concern. "What of the documents I sent?" Chen said. "They are not here. Did you keep them? Did you read them?"

"I did indeed," Rupert replied. "I have had a considerable amount of spare time these last couple of months, waiting for the injuries inflicted by your countrymen to heal. Reading has helped to pass the time. Some of the documents were most interesting, I must say. Fascinating, in fact. I imagine the mainland authorities would be extremely unhappy if they were ever made public."

"I see," Chen said, tight-lipped. "And?"

"And what?"

"And what do you plan to do with this information?"

"For now, nothing," Rupert said. "The documents will be my insurance. They are proof of your actions: stealing the country's treasures, and more important from the Communists' point of view, stealing their secrets. I have put the documents in a safe place. Should anything untoward happen to me, there are instructions for them to be made public, along with detailed information about you and your daughter and how you smuggled the lot into Hong Kong. If nothing does happen to me the documents will remain secret, along with the pieces of art."

"You should know that those documents are only copies I made, re-creations of the originals," Chen said.

"Perhaps," said Rupert. "But I'm sure the information they contain is genuine, or you wouldn't have gone to the trouble of smuggling them out. This is information the Communist Party would definitely not like the world to know about, and it would not look kindly on any citizen who revealed it."

"You can't think I would reveal the information at this point," Chen said. "As you say, that could place us in great danger."

"True," Rupert said. "But I will keep the documents just the same, thank you."

Chen breathed deeply. Rupert had figured all the angles. The only option at this point was to take possession of his half of the treasures as quickly as possible before Rupert changed his mind about those as well. "I will not risk my daughter's safety," he said. "You can be assured of that."

"Ah," Rupert said, "that is something else I want to discuss."

"You want to discuss what? I don't understand."

"I too am concerned about your daughter's safety. She is such an innocent young thing, and these are dangerous times. You are new here, and unschooled in the ways of a free society like Hong Kong. Despite all your precautions, I really don't think you can give her the kind of protection she needs."

"She will be safe with me," Chen said.

"I *really* don't think so," Rupert insisted. "I said that I am keeping those documents as insurance against your making any trouble, and that is the truth. But I also have another reason."

"And what is that?" Chen asked.

"I would like to suggest an alternative arrangement for your daughter's safety." Rupert's face flushed, making his scars stand out in sharp relief.

"In fact," he said, "I believe I shall insist on it."

Thirty-nine

"I don't believe it," Sturges said when Olivia had finished the tale.

"It's true," Olivia told him.

"Rupert wanted to *buy* you?"

"He wanted me, any way he could get me. He was ready to make it a cash transaction if that's what it took. Remember, he was still young at this time, and still seriously into young girls, and since he was used to paying for their services, paying for me wouldn't have been much different from his point of view.

"The main thing, though, was that he was bent on revenge. Against the Chinese in general, but against my father in particular. He had gone to China earlier that year to follow up on the scheme my father had drawn him into, and he'd been abducted and tortured for his troubles. In Rupert's damaged mind, my father had come to personify all the wrong that was done to him by the Chinese people. The only way he could get even was to hurt my father in return – and he realized that more than anything, hurting me was the likeliest way for him to succeed. Taking me as his own would have satisfied all his lusts."

"Don't tell me your father went along with this."

"My father tried to talk him out of it. But Rupert wouldn't listen. He threatened my father with the same thing as before: to let the mainland authorities know my father's real identity, to tell them what he'd done and where he and I could be found. My father knew that could be a death sentence for the both of us."

"My God," Sturges said. He paced the room, trying to digest this information about the man he had revered. "But how would he have explained your presence in his home if your father had agreed to his demand?"

"He wouldn't have had to explain at all," she said. "You've heard of *mui tsai*?"

"The 'little sister' system, sure." Young Chinese girls sent to live with wealthier families to work as household servants. The girls' parents received a cash payment. "For some young girls, it was the ticket to a better life."

"It was also common for the girls to be sexually abused in their new homes," Olivia said.

"I know the colonial government routinely turned a blind eye to certain traditional Chinese practices here," he said. "Plenty of local Chinese men still had concubines when I was growing up, for example. But the blatant buying and selling of little girls, that can't still have been legal here as late as 1968."

"It wasn't," Olivia said. "The Hong Kong government had outlawed the practice years earlier. But people kept it up, and nobody really cared, or even noticed. A young girl living in a wealthy person's house, ostensibly as a family member of the household staff, was perfectly normal. Nobody would have thought about it twice."

"But legal or not, you were only ten years old at this point. What kind of monster...?"

"My age was what saved me. Even for the noted child-fucker Rupert Rackley, I was too young."

"I'm starting to feel sick."

"I warned you this wasn't going to be pretty."

"You didn't prepare me for this. So: what finally happened?" He glanced at the wedding ring she was still wearing. "I guess your father finally gave in after all?"

"My father couldn't change Rupert's mind," Olivia said, "but he was able to strike a deal: Rupert agreed to wait until I turned fifteen. At least the perverted bastard was willing to let me become a young woman before making me his sex slave."

"Fifteen. His favorite age back then. It's like you were a steer being fattened by a breeder before being sold for your meat."

"Exactly," she said. "Except that my father never intended to go along with the deal. Rupert kept reminding him about the agreement as I was growing up, and my father always assured him it was still on, but all the time, he was making other arrangements."

"And those were?"

"He built up a considerable amount of cash, at first by selling a few more of the smuggled antiques. He had sincerely planned to send all the pieces from the original imperial collection back to China some day, but Rupert's blackmail forced him to change his plans. He went into the antiques business, using some of those pieces as his original stock, and those combined with his superior knowledge of the subject meant he did very well.

"Next, he began sending money to a U.S. bank account, and during business trips to the States in the early '70s he used that cash to buy some prime real estate in the San Francisco area.

"And then, shortly before my fifteenth birthday, he quietly shipped me off as well," she said. "Not to California, where Rupert might have thought to look for me, but to a small boarding school buried in the heart of Michigan. He enrolled me under my original name – he had brought my birth certificate along when we made our way to Hong Kong and he used that to register me. He arranged for me to live on the income from the San Francisco real estate, and then he cut off all contact with me. He smuggled me into Middle America and hid me there just as Rupert was about to get his hands on me."

"This is an awful lot to take in," Sturges said. "I always knew Rupe was bent. But my god: I never realized just how much."

"I didn't want to destroy your image of your good friend," she said. "But mainly, I never told you or anyone else about any of this because it's all just so damn embarrassing. I did end up marrying the son of a bitch, after all."

"I'm still waiting to hear about that," he said. "I know he continued to have dealings with your father, although I now realize those were very different from what I'd imagined. But how in the world did it end in you two getting married?"

"Would you like a drink before I go on?" she said. "The story gets a lot worse from here."

~

When he learned that Chen Weihan had tricked him, Rupert was furious. "Bring her back and keep your side of the bargain or I will expose you to the Communists!" he thundered. "I will destroy you!"

"Do whatever you like," Chen told him. "Olivia is the most precious thing in the world to me. Thanks to the Japanese butchers and the Chinese Communists she is the only family I have left. Now that she is safe where you can never find her, I do not care what happens to me. Publish your story if you wish."

"You can still make this right," Rupert said. "You might have changed your appearance and your name – Mr. 'William Chan' – you might dress like an Englishman and talk like an American, but you and your daughter are still Chinese through and through. You have schooled her in Chinese tradition and I am sure she will do whatever her father tells her. Order her to come back and she will obey, whether she wants to be with me or not."

"As long as she is a minor I will not give her to you or anyone else," Chen replied. "And when she becomes an adult she will choose a partner by herself. I made a bargain with the devil early in my life, and then I brought my daughter into a terrible world. I will not bring pain into her life again."

~

"Now wait," Sturges said to Olivia. "Don't tell me that after all this you came back to Hong Kong and married Rupert *voluntarily*."

"I did come back, and in the end it was my decision to marry him, yes," Olivia said. "But there was nothing voluntary about it."

She explained: "As I said, I wasn't allowed to contact my father for years, until I was a grown woman, and even then he kept my location secret. But by 1993, when my bank asked me to return to Hong Kong, I'd been gone for twenty years. I was now a mature woman, an established professional. Married and divorced."

"I never knew—"

"There's a lot you don't know. The point is, it appeared after all that time that it was safe for me to come home. My father told me Rupert was by now acting perfectly normally, collecting his art, drinking at his clubs, mingling with *gwei-los* and the local

Chinese. He said Rupert was even civil to him when they ran into each other at antique auctions. He'd stopped asking about me and stopped threatening my father. The only place his anger at the Chinese still showed was in his writing, and that was directed mainly at the Communist leadership. The chance to return home came along and I was delighted at the idea of starting over and seeing my father again on a regular basis. I figured I'd have no problems once I got here. As it turned out, I was wrong."

"Rupert hadn't let it go?"

"Not at all. Oh, he made it look that way at first. As soon as he heard I was back in town he came to me and apologized for his actions. I couldn't forgive him, but he convinced me that the trauma of his experience had made him act as he did and that he had long since moved past that. I really thought my father and I were home free at last.

"But he was just biding his time. A couple of years later he showed up at my father's office with the draft of a story he'd prepared for the newspaper. It contained details of my father's life and extensive excerpts from the documents my father had smuggled out. He again threatened to publish the story unless I married him. He told my father, 'It might be late in the game, old chap, but you made an agreement, and you will honor it or else.'"

"And you really thought after all that time that your father was still in some kind of danger if Rupert did publish the information?"

"Think of the timing," she said. "This was early 1995. Just six years after the 1989 bloodbath in Tiananmen Square; only two years before Hong Kong, and its citizens, would again come under Chinese rule. The Communists had shown in 1989 what they were still capable of. In another two years they would no longer have to sneak around in Hong Kong; they were going to own the place. They'd promised to leave Hong Kong to its own devices for fifty years, but you remember what it was like as 1997 approached. Nobody was really sure of anything. Yes, to answer your question: even all those years later, if the Communists learned the things my father had done, we were afraid of what they might do to him."

"And Rupert was still lusting after you."

"Not in the usual sense of the word," she said. "I don't think Rupert ever had sex with a grown woman in his entire life, so I was no longer his type. It was revenge against my father that he still lusted after. Twenty-five years after the fact, the worm was still eating at his brain.

"I did what I could to discourage him. I told him I despised him. I insulted his manhood. I allowed myself to acquire a very public reputation as a party girl and a sexual predator, hoping he'd be too embarrassed to marry me. But nothing I did could change his mind, and in the meantime the stress was affecting my father's health. I had to take the pressure off, and in the end there was only one way to do that: I agreed to marry Rupert."

"Even though your father didn't ask you to do it?"

"He didn't have to. I'm a Chinese daughter, Bill. I was raised to honor and protect my parents. You of all people should know: it's more than learned behavior with us Chinese. After five thousand years, it's programmed into our DNA."

She had sacrificed her own happiness to save her father. A typically Chinese thing for a child to do. He could not bring himself to ask her to marry Rupert, so she did it on her own. If she had sliced off a piece of her flesh to save him, her sacrifice would not have been more in keeping with tradition.

"I can't imagine what it must have been like, sharing your bed with a man you hated," Sturges said.

"That at least I never did," she said. "I told him I'd be civil whenever we were forced to appear together in public, but if he ever tried to touch me I'd cut his goddam hand off. I also told him, if any harm comes to my father because of your actions, I swear to God I will see you dead."

"Apparently he got that message at least," Sturges said. Chen Weihan had died in bed, of cancer, aged eighty-two, less than a month before Rupert was killed. Untouched by Rupert. Secrets still intact.

Forty

Sturges paced the room, trying to take it all in.

"You still haven't fully explained the threat Rupert was holding over your father's head," he said. "What's in those documents that would get the Communists so worked up?"

"According to my father, the information would seriously damage the Party's image if it were ever made public," she said.

Sturges flashed a look of skepticism. "There wasn't much of an image to damage by 1995," he said. What could the documents possibly contain that the world didn't already know by then? The truth about the Great Famine and the Cultural Revolution was already in the public domain. The world had watched the Tiananmen massacre unfold on live television. The world was well aware of Beijing's continuing suppression of human rights.

Yet businessmen continued to pour billions of dollars into the country. Tourists continued to arrive by the planeload. "Foreigners occasionally make noise about dissidents being arrested or Tibetans being abused," Sturges said, "but in the end the world doesn't really care what the Chinese Communist Party does."

"That's true," she said, "but according to my father, it wasn't a question of what the rest of the world knew. It was what the Chinese people themselves might learn. He said the documents contained proof that for the previous sixty or seventy years, the Party had systematically lied to the Chinese people.

"Remember, by the time of Tiananmen, the Party's ideological underpinnings were rapidly disappearing due to Deng Xiaoping's reforms, and its legitimacy was being undermined by corruption.

389

My father said the information in his documents could have led to a final collapse of public support. He said it could have destroyed the Party."

"If you say so," Sturges said. "And with both your father and Rupert now gone, you're the only one left who knows what's in those documents. If they're as incriminating as you say, who knows, you could still be in danger."

She shook her head. "I never read the documents myself," she said.

"Never?" he said. "But that would mean...*nobody* knows what was in those documents. Neither Rupert nor your father ever showed them to you or anyone else?"

"No one else as far as I know. My father had no copies: he had sent them all off to Rupert with the antiques they smuggled out. Rupert did make copies, and he waved them in my face in a drunken rage one night, telling me how he could still use them to ruin my father any time he chose, but I didn't get a chance to read them."

"And you never saw them again after that?"

"Once. Following that drunken scene I watched him lock the documents back in his safe – he was too drunk to realize I was watching. Later, I called in an expert to find out how to get the safe open. Then one day not long before Rupert left for China, I waited until he went off to one of his clubs. I opened the safe and took the documents out."

"Then the documents are safely in your possession!" Sturges said with relief. "You had me worried for a minute. But I'm still flabbergasted that you've never looked at them. I mean, they played such a major role in your life."

"I never read them and no, they are not in my possession. As soon as I took them out of the safe, I burned them."

"Oh God," Sturges said, covering his eyes. "Tell me I didn't hear that correctly."

"You did. I didn't know what they contained and I didn't want to know. I just wanted them out of our lives once and for all."

Sturges flopped into a chair, dumbfounded. "You destroyed them without so much as peek?" he said. "You have absolutely no idea what was in them?"

"I know the general subject matter because my father told me that. One item was his personal account of the Great Famine, based on our family's experience in Taishan."

A written account of the famine, of course. That would explain why, when Rupert was in Dongguan asking about documents, Elaine Sikorsky had specifically heard him refer to "the three years of natural disasters" – code for The Great Famine.

"There was also a pack of sensitive documents that passed through my father's hands while he was assigned to the Party archives office in Beijing in the early '50s," she said. "And there were minutes of meetings of the Party leadership in Yanan in the late 1930s. My father was one of the few educated people who made it to Yanan in those early days. He was assigned to sit in on meetings and take notes."

It took a moment before Sturges could speak again. "You burned first-hand notes of what the leaders of the Chinese Communist Party were saying to each other in private in the late 1930s – just after the Long March was completed?" He shook his head in disbelief. "Do you realize what you destroyed? This was a period when Mao Tse-tung was maneuvering furiously for control of the Party. The debates you're talking about shaped the Party's future, and there are still a lot of unanswered questions about what happened during that period. You had the answers in your hands – and you destroyed them. The loss to the historical record is beyond calculation."

He ran a hand across his forehead. "But forget about history. This was personal. This was information sensitive enough pose a mortal threat to you and your father. This was information important enough to make you marry a man that you hated. This was information, according to your father, that could have brought the Party to its knees. And thanks to your lack of curiosity, it's all gone."

"I didn't care about any of that," she said. "It might be history to you, it might have been the means to an end for Rupert, but whatever was in them, those documents had been a sword hanging over my father's and my heads for decades. To me, they were nothing more or less than an evil that had to be eliminated. So I did just that."

"Now I really am going to be sick," he said. He closed his eyes and massaged his temples, trying to come to terms with what he had just been told.

"Okay," he said finally, "tell me how Rupert was killed. I think I'm beyond shock at this point."

Forty-one

The doctors had done all they could. Chen Weihan was dying. When Olivia asked how long, they could only shake their heads and say, very soon. A few weeks at most.

She brought him home from the hospital so he could die in his own bed. As soon as she had him tucked in, he signaled for her to come near. "Sleep, Papa," she told him. "You need the rest."

He shook his head. "I will soon have all the time in the world to rest," he said. "Before then, there are things I must tell you – things you never heard before. Come." She pulled a chair close to the bed and took his limp hand in hers, and he began to tell her the story of their family.

He told her about the massacres in Nanjing, and his escape from the Japanese. He told her about his life in Yanan. He told her about the early days of the communist government in Beijing, and how Mao's collectives almost destroyed agriculture. He told about the big character poster he had written during the Hundred Flowers campaign in 1957 and the part it played in the family being sent to its fate in the countryside.

"With your family background you probably would have been sent away anyway, Papa," she said. "You have nothing to apologize for."

"But you never knew your mother or your brothers," he said. "For that, I feel great remorse."

He told her about the Great Famine, how her mother had cared for her and the two boys at the cost of her own health; how he had turned away the man who suggested swapping the body of the older boy, Mingfu, for the body of the man's daughter, and how he had buried Mingfu in the forest instead. He paused, shutting his eyes in an effort to dull the pain, and then he told her how he had given in to the offer to swap Xilian's body so that the rest of them could live. He told her how he, Chang Dongfeng, and she, Chang Lili, had survived by eating the flesh of their neighbor's child.

She was horrified. But what could she say? He had done what he had to do. He had acted out of love. In the end, he had saved their lives. She patted his hand to show she understood, and allowed him to continue.

"Do you remember when we were making our escape?" he asked. "Just before we reached Macau. It was nighttime, and some men came along the trail and began to question us."

"It's all just a blur, Papa," she said. "Mostly I remember being terrified during that whole journey from Beijing. It took a long time after we arrived here for the fear to go away completely."

"I know," he said. "There was much to be frightened of. But you must know this: I had brought some official documents with me when we left Beijing. Those were originals, not copies like the ones Rupert took. When those men approached us outside Macau, I ran into the trees. I buried the documents so the men would not find them.

"After they left, I wanted to go back and dig up what I had buried, but our guide told us we had to hurry if we were to reach Macau before daylight. I hadn't gotten you safely to that point, a few steps from freedom, only to fail you at the last minute because of some scraps of paper. You were the most important thing in the world to me. So I left the documents behind."

"And you were never able to retrieve them?" she asked.

"You know that I have never returned to the mainland," he said. "Many refugees from that time have gone back to visit since the opening up, but I could never bring myself to return to that cursed country."

A spasm of pain rippled through his body, and she pushed a plunger to send a shot of morphine into his veins. It took a minute for him to catch his breath and she tried to quiet him, but he insisted on resuming. "I'm coming to the most important part," he said.

"I mentioned those buried documents to Rupert once, many years ago, while you were in the United States. It came out during one of the arguments he and I used to have. I wanted to taunt him, so I told him that there was a stash of even more valuable documents than the ones he had, and I said he would never get his hands on those. I told him more than I planned to and I regretted it at the time, but now I'm glad I did it – because now I want you to do something for me."

He paused again, this time to consider his words carefully. "I want you to tell Rupert something after I'm gone. The fact that I told him about those buried items will make what I want you to tell him believable. But I only want you to do this if you can be sure you will not suffer any harm. Promise me that."

"Whatever you say, Papa," she said. "Tell me."

He said nothing for a long time, and she thought maybe the morphine had knocked him out. Then his eyes popped open, and his voice was suddenly strong. "When I am gone, I want you to destroy Rupert!" he cried, squeezing her hand so hard it hurt. "For the pain and anguish he caused us. For forcing you into marriage and making you waste years of your life with a man you detest. I want you...I want you to destroy the monster."

"But how can I do that?" she asked. She suspected this was the pain and the morphine talking, but the next words out of his mouth told her she was wrong.

"I have a plan," he said. "I have been working on this plan for many years."

~

Chen Weihan let another spasm of pain pass before continuing. "I want you to tell Rupert that before I died, I told a friend of mine where I buried those documents, and my friend succeeded in digging them up," he finally said.

"Is this true?" she asked.

"Only partly," he said. "I did once send a friend to look for them. But all I had was a vague recollection of the place I buried them, and there's been so much development since we were there. I am told that much of what was then countryside has been swallowed up by the cities. My friend found nothing. I doubt I could have found the items at that late date if I had gone myself.

"But Rupert will have no way of knowing that," Chen said. "Tell him my friend did find the documents, and I had him take the documents to the city of Dongguan, and give them for safekeeping to an old colleague of mine who runs the museum there. And here is the main point: I want you to tell Rupert that if he is willing to retrieve the documents personally, you will instruct my contact in Dongguan to turn them over to him. Tell him this was my dying wish."

"But Papa," she said, "he won't believe that. He won't believe you would do him such a favor after he's been so horrible to us."

"He will be suspicious, of course," Chen said. "But you must tell him that more than anything, I wanted the truth about the Communists to be told, and the truth is in those documents. That is why I took them in the first place, to get my revenge against the Communists for what they did to your mother and brothers. Play to his vanity; tell him I said his newspaper column is the perfect vehicle for exposing the Party's actions. Tell him that as much as I hated him for what he did to us, I recognized in the end that he was the best one to tell this story to the world. Tell him I said that if he would do this thing, it would go part way toward atoning for the harm he had done us."

"But," he said, grasping her arm even tighter, "you must emphasize that he has to go to Dongguan personally. Tell him these are the arrangements I insisted on. You will not authorize the release of the documents to anyone but him. Tell him that."

"But even if he believes this story," she protested, "you know Rupert won't go to China."

"You are wrong," the old man said. "For these documents, he will go. Rupert has read the copies. He knows that if the information were made available to the Chinese people it could destroy the Party's credibility. He admitted to me that because he only has copies, the Party might be able to limit the damage by claiming the copies are forgeries. But if he had original documents, with all the official chops, to show the world, it would make his story more believable.

"If you tell him my contact at the Dongguan museum has the originals, he will go to China. If it meant he could bring harm to the Communists," Chen Weihan said, "I'm sure Rupert would travel to hell and back."

~

"So nothing is left," Sturges said. "You burned Rupert's copies. The contact in Dongguan, if he even exists, had no copies. Your father had no copies: he left the originals in some anonymous hole in the ground in the Chinese countryside. Could you find your way back to where the two of you were stopped that night?"

"Impossible," she said. "I was just a kid, it was the middle of the night, we'd been on the road for days. And my father ran into the trees alone to bury the items. We'd have to dig up an entire forest, and I couldn't even be sure at this point if we were digging in the right forest. And anyway the hole is probably covered by a housing estate or a shopping mall by now."

"And you're sure you burned all of Rupert's copies?"

"I burned all the ones I took from his safe."

He detected a hesitation in her voice. "You sounded a bit uncertain there," he said. "Are there any other copies out there?"

"I'm not entirely sure," she said.

"What does that mean?"

"Not long before my father died, Rupert and I were having one of our periodic arguments. I told him I'd seen him put the documents in the safe and I would destroy them if I ever got the chance. He laughed and said: 'You'd be wasting your time. I made more photocopies of everything I took from your father. And I've hidden *those* copies where you'll never find them.'"

"Then more copies do exist. Copies of copies. Christ, it's hard to keep up with this story."

"Maybe they exist and maybe they don't," she said. "I've searched every corner of the house since he died and I've found nothing. They kept a desk for him at the newspaper, but the editor told me there was nothing in it but some rubber bands and paper clips. Nothing was mentioned in the will about any documents, as you know. And I guess there weren't any documents in that storage locker you found or you would have told me about them by now."

"Nothing there except your hundred million dollars worth of art, and Rupert's notes and photos of the pieces," he said. "We checked every square inch of the room."

"Then maybe he was lying about making additional copies," she said. "If he was telling the truth, I have no idea where they might be."

"Damn!" Sturges suddenly cried.

"What?"

"The safe deposit box! The one in Tsuen Wan that was accidentally destroyed just after the murder. There must have been something valuable in that box or he wouldn't have bothered to leave me the key. I'll bet anything that's where he was keeping a set of the documents."

She sighed. "I told you there was a lot you didn't know about this story."

"You also said it would get worse, and you weren't kidding. But you still haven't finished. Your father devised this elaborate plan to entice Rupert into China in order to destroy him, and your telling Rupe the original documents were in Dongguan was the first part of the plan. What was the second part, Liv? How did Rupert die?"

"I've been hoping we might still be friends once this was over," she said. "I'm afraid there's not going to be much chance of that once you've heard the rest."

"You told me you were innocent."

"I said I didn't kill Rupert. I didn't say I had nothing to do with his death."

He rolled his eyes. "Just finish," he said. "Please."

But now she was crying. "I never wanted any of this," she said.

He could believe that. Who could conceive of such a tangled web of deceit and revenge, let alone wish for it? But if she was looking for sympathy, Sturges had none left to give. "Tell me or tell Brian Ross," he sighed. "One way or another, this story is finally going to be told."

Forty-two

Chen Weihan had guessed right. Hatred of the Communists overrode all other considerations in Rupert's mind. The prospect of returning to the mainland to retrieve the documents made him almost physically ill, but Rupert knew the Communist Party's hold on power was shaky despite its economic successes. He knew the public was increasingly questioning the Party's claim to legitimacy. He knew that China as it was could not last, part capitalist, part communist; partly open to the rest of the world, partly still closed off by censorship and authoritarian rule. To take possession of documents that might destroy that the Party's hold on power, no matter how tenuous the possibility? For that, yes, Rupert would go to China.

Sturges had also guessed right. Most of his suppositions and discoveries along the way had been accurate. Rupert had gone to China in search of information for an article. The information in the documents was going to be the "big news" he had hinted at to Evelyn Chin and Fritz Giesler in the weeks leading up to the murder. The original documents were the tool he was planning to use to "knock their socks off." These were the documents Elaine Sikorsky's contact in Dongguan had overheard Rupert asking about. Rupert really did think he was going to meet the curator of the Dongguan museum: he had told the Chinese Foreign Ministry the truth as far as he knew it, even though he was actually repeating a lie meant to entrap him.

"Okay," Sturges told Olivia, "we're in late August. Your father is presumably dead by now."

"He died July thirty-first," she said.

"And you have now given Rupert the impression that he's going to be given the original documents if and when he gets to Dongguan. But wait: then you sent Ricco to try to talk him out of going. That doesn't make any sense."

"It does if you knew Rupert," she said. "Several weeks before I met Ricco in Macau, I ran into him at a public reception, and a photographer took shots of us together. The pictures were nothing, me giving Ricco an innocent kiss on the cheek, but Rupert was insanely possessive of me even though he never loved me. Before I went to Macau, I left the photos on Rupert's desk, just to infuriate him.

"And you know what he was like: nobody could ever talk him out of anything once he'd made up his mind. I was sure that sending Ricco to talk to him out of going, especially after Rupert had seen those photos, would only make him more determined to go."

"Wow," Sturges said. "You are really a piece of work. Thank God *I* never did anything to get on your bad side. So, finish the story: how did it finally happen?"

"I told Rupert the story as my father had instructed, and Rupert bought it," she said. "He agreed in principle to go to Dongguan – but there was the problem of his getting a China visa. Given the way he'd attacked the Chinese over the years, it was highly unlikely they'd give him one under normal circumstances. But my father had thought of everything. So when Rupert went off to submit his visa application, I carried out the next step of my father's plan."

She made an appointment at the central government's Liaison Office in Hong Kong. She was directed to a low-level clerk, as was normal, but the message she delivered was anything but normal: she had information about mortal danger to the Communist Party. She told the clerk she would only give the information to an official from the office. She gave the clerk her telephone number, and left. "Sure enough, the next morning, I received a call from a man asking me to meet him in Victoria Park."

"And this was the official you had asked for?"

"I can't say for certain who or what he was. He didn't give me a name or a title. But he did refer obliquely to my visit to the Liaison Office the previous day, so I knew this was the call I was waiting for."

"What about when you met face to face? Did he at least say he was contacting you on behalf of the Chinese government?"

"He said nothing. He didn't show me any credentials. He just began asking questions. All I can tell you is that he was one of the scariest people I've ever met."

"Probably State Security," Sturges said. "What did you tell him?"

"Pretty much the truth. I told him about the documents and what I little I knew about what the contained. I told him that copies had been smuggled out of Beijing during the Cultural Revolution. I didn't say who had smuggled them, just that Rupert had the copies. I said he planned to publish what he knew of the documents' secrets in any case, but he hoped to get his hands on the originals from Dongguan before he published anything, and he was about to apply for the visa in hopes of traveling to Dongguan."

"Did the man ask why you were being so helpful to China? You and your father hadn't exactly been active in the pro-Beijing camp."

"He did. I told him that even though my father had fled during the Maoist era, he still had great love for the motherland. I told him my father's dying wish was to stop Rupert from doing anything that could harm the country."

"And he believed you?"

"I have no idea, but the story was perfectly credible. Plenty of Chinese who suffered under Mao still remain loyal to the country, if not the Party. All I know for sure is that a couple of days after I spoke to the man, Rupert got his visa. I assume they issued it because of what I told them. I can't imagine why else they would have given him one."

Sturges shook his head in wonderment. "Your father really did plan this out to the last detail," he said. "And then?"

"The man in the park gave me a phone number to call, somewhere across the border in Guangdong. He said to call it with a pre-paid phone card. I did as he said, and a second man answered, and he'd clearly been briefed. He told me to give Rupert the same phone number I had just called, and tell him it was the number of the man he was to contact in Dongguan, the curator of the museum. He told me to follow Rupert to the train station the morning he was planning to leave. Once Rupert was through Hong Kong Immigration, I was to send a text to the same number to report that he was on his way."

"And you followed those instructions?"

"I did exactly what the man on the phone told me to do. I drove Rupert to the train station myself. I watched him go through Immigration. I sent the text on the same phone card and then tossed the card into a trashcan as I left the station. And that was that."

She paused and lowered her head. "Three days later, the police called to say that Rupert's body had been found."

"That was that?" he repeated. But that was plenty. She'd dangled irresistible bait in front of Rupert. She'd told the Chinese he had information that could threaten the Party, and plotted with them to lure him to a place where they could get their hands on him. Once Rupert stepped off the train in Dongguan, he was at their mercy. What more was there to do? "And now you're sitting here telling me you didn't kill him?" he said.

"I was just the messenger."

"And your message lured him to his death." Scenarios ran through his mind like a movie: Rupert arriving at the museum thinking he's about to be handed the scoop of his life; being grabbed instead by security thugs and manhandled into a waiting car; being driven into the countryside and then pulled out of the car in some isolated spot by a riverbank; a gun being pressed to the back of his head...

"What did you think was going to happen?" Sturges said. "Did you think Chinese State Security was going to give him a stern lecture about the importance of loving the motherland and then send him on his way?"

"I had no way of knowing what would happen," Olivia said. "And anyway, I had no choice. My father had made the request on his deathbed. It was my duty to honor his wish."

"I see. Tradition was to blame for all this, is that it?"

"I know you can't understand."

"Don't patronize me, Liv. I grew up here. I speak the language. I know the Chinese and how they think almost as well as you do. I also know that filial loyalty is not a recognized defense for conspiracy to commit murder."

She stared at the floor and said nothing.

"Did your father ever say what *he* thought would happen next in this little scenario of his?"

"We never discussed that specifically."

"But you knew what he was thinking. The two of you could guess what would happen to Rupert once he got to Dongguan."

"I guessed they would stop him," she muttered.

"Stop him from what? From getting hold of documents that didn't exist? From meeting someone at the museum who wasn't there? When he got to the museum, what, they were going to jump out and waggle their fingers and shout, 'Nanny-nanny boo-boo, we fooled you'? Is that what you guessed?"

"Of course not..."

"They were going to 'stop him,' all right: they were going to stop him permanently."

"I suppose."

"You suppose? Jesus Christ! You *knew*, Olivia. You said it yourself: you knew what the Party was capable of. You knew the Party would stop at nothing, *will* stop at nothing, when its interests are threatened. And what could threaten its interests more than documents that might prove it's been lying to the Chinese people from the start? You knew they would stop Rupert from revealing what he already knew was in those documents. And how could they be absolutely sure he would never reveal anything...except by killing him?

"It's bad enough that you've lied to me all this time," he said. "Please don't insult my intelligence any further. You and your father knew full well that in sending Rupert to China you were sending him to his death, as surely as if you'd put the gun to his head and pulled the trigger yourself."

Forty-three

Questions answered. Facts tied down.

Now what could Sturges do with it? What would Ross be able to do with it?

"I don't apologize for what I did," Olivia told him before he left her house. "Rupert was a monster. He almost destroyed our lives. He deserved what he got. I owed it to you to tell you what happened because you and he were close friends, and also because you and I are...you and I *have been*...close. But I won't repeat the story to the police. I'll deny I ever said any of it."

"Ross trusts me," he said. "If I tell him you said it, he'll believe me."

"Maybe so," she said, "but the last I heard, the authorities here still need proof to convict a person of a crime."

And without her confession, what proof was there? The documents in question were irretrievably lost. There was no proof that Rupert had done any of the appalling things Olivia said he'd done. There was no record of what Chen Weihan had asked his daughter to do as a result of Rupert's actions, and there was no evidence to prove she had done any of the things her father asked. Any attempt to obtain even the most peripheral confirmation from the Chinese liaison office would be futile. There was nothing except her words to back up the whole incredible story.

Even if all the rest could be proved, there was one final, glaring hole in the narrative: there was no evidence to link Olivia's actions directly to the murder itself. She'd been given no names, no job titles by the scary man in Victoria Park, or by the voice on the phone "somewhere in Guangdong.'" There was nothing concrete to tie the two men to the Chinese government, and even if there had been, there was no information as to who had actually pulled the trigger to end Rupert's life, or where it had happened, or whether the killing had any connection at all to the preceding events. For all anyone knew, Rupert could have been the victim of a completely random act of violence, whose timing shortly after Olivia's encounters with the two mystery men was sheer coincidence. Anything else was improvable conjecture.

A butterfly stirring the air in Beijing today can theoretically cause storms in New York next month, but there was nothing to prove that an approach by Olivia to the liaison office in Hong Kong had set a murder in motion in Guangdong.

In the end there was only Sturges's account of what Olivia had told him – which she was prepared to deny – plus the same extremely circumstantial evidence they had gathered before the conversation with Olivia ever took place. Sturges was no lawyer, but he could see that what they did have did not add up to a solid prosecution.

It might not even be enough for a news story. Writing a story based entirely on what one person has told you, when that same person is going to call you a liar and deny she ever said any of it the moment the story appears, does not make for convincing journalism.

Before he left her house, Olivia had urged him to keep their conversation secret. She had dangled the image of an enticing future. "We could have a beautiful life together, Bill," she said. "We obviously have feelings for each other. We have all the money we could ever want – far more than we could ever spend. We could do anything we want, go anywhere we please." All they had to do was wait for a decent interval, let the case fade away before making their relationship public. The victim's best friend taking the victim's widow as his wife: it would be almost biblical in its symmetry.

And why not? Rupert had been traumatized in 1968, true, but his suffering was nothing compared to that of Chen Weihan and millions of other Chinese citizens, and Rupert had had thirty-five extremely comfortable years to get over the pain. There was no excusing his actions. The man Sturges had admired all those years had been a beast.

Olivia's father had suffered beyond imagination, and just when he thought he and his daughter had finally reached safety, Rupert had prolonged the suffering, taking the daughter by force, blackmailing Chen right up to the day he died. In the end, Chen had merely evened the score. Illegally and violently to be sure, but under the circumstances, who could call his actions anything but justice? Sturges could not bring himself to criticize the father.

So, the ultimate question: did Rupert's actions, even seen through the prism of ancient Confucian tradition, justify what Olivia had done? Loyalty to ones parents was admirable; arranging the murder of another human being might be taking it a bit far.

Even if Olivia could be forgiven, Sturges wasn't sure he could he devote the rest of his life to a woman who could lie and kill so easily. "I'll have to think about it," was the most he'd been able to tell her.

He went home and thought about it half the night, and just before he finally nodded off, he reached a decision: he could not keep the information secret. He had valuable evidence in a criminal investigation that he was bound to turn over. He had a duty to his readers to write the story. And, yes, as Ross had said earlier...he had a duty to Rupert.

Rupert was a Hongkonger who had stood up for Hong Kong while its rich and powerful were happily selling out Hong Kong's freedoms to Beijing. Ross and Sturges had owed it to Rupe to find out who had killed him. Now that they had found out, they owed it to him to let the world know.

Rupe might have been a twisted and vengeful extortionist, but there were remedies for that kind of thing, and in civilized society they didn't include a bullet to the back of the head in some remote part of the Chinese countryside. The old boy deserved a bit of justice, too.

Forty-four

Sturges sat bolt upright and looked at the clock. Already past 10 a.m. He hadn't meant to sleep so late. He leapt out of bed and was about to reach for the phone to call Ross and tell him what he'd learned from Olivia...when the phone began to ring.

"Is that Mr. Sturges?" The voice this time had a strong East London accent. Sturges recognized it as that of Ian Williams, the mechanic who was rebuilding the Morgan.

"Make it quick, Ian," Sturges said. "I have work to do."

"Right. Well, I found something in the car, Mr. Sturges," Williams said. "It's real strange. I think you'd better come take a look."

Williams paused. "Was that quick enough?"

~

The car was stripped of its metal bodywork. Williams pointed to a space in the metal-and-wood skeleton just behind the driver's seat. Normally, what he was pointing to would be empty air between wooden struts. This space was taken up by a metal box, secured to the wooden upper frame with bolts and glue. "It was sitting there when I got the body panels off," the mechanic said.

The box was locked. "But something's definitely in there," Williams said. He bounced the car on its springs and something rattled against the insides of the box.

"That's the same rattle that's been driving me crazy," Sturges said. "I thought a piece of the frame had been knocked loose during the car chase."

"Do you want me to break the box open?" the mechanic asked.

"No, wait," Sturges said. "I have a feeling the police will want to look at this. Let me make a call."

Ross and Wai were at the garage in no time. Ross produced the last of the keys Rupert had left behind, the one with the cardboard slogans attached. "What do you think, laddie?" he said. "Three out of three?"

The key slid easily into the lock, and the top of the box popped up.

"*Mo-gun*," Sturges said, grabbing the piece of cardboard on the key ring and holding it in the air. "This wasn't a coded message after all. Rupert was literally telling me, 'Look in the Morgan.' But why not come right out and say it? The crazy old bastard could have told us the whole story and saved us a hell of a lot of trouble."

Ross reached inside the box and pulled out a fat envelope. Inside the envelope was a stack of documents, hand-written in Chinese. On top of the stack, attached with a clamp, an affidavit typed in English:

> "*The enclosed are photocopies of documents that Mr. Chang Dongfeng, alias Chen Weihan, a civil servant of the People's Republic of China at the time, smuggled out of China during 1967 and 1968 with the help of Mr. Rupert Rackley of Hong Kong. The copies have been made in a notary's presence and have been read by Mr. Rackley and certified as true copies of said smuggled documents.*"

A detailed list of the documents followed. The affidavit and each of the documents were signed by Rupert, and next to the signature he had imprinted his personal chop in red ink. The affidavit was attested to by a notary, a solicitor at a prominent Hong Kong law firm, and dated May 1993. The same month Rupert had rented the safe deposit box in Tsuen Wan. Shortly after Olivia had returned to Hong Kong from the United States. Chen Weihan was not the only one who had planned ahead.

"That's definitely his signature and his chop," Sturges said. "As for the documents, my Chinese is good, but I don't know if it's good enough to read all of this."

"It's also not your problem," Ross said. "This is evidence in a criminal investigation. My people will translate the documents. Don't worry: you'll get a look at the translations as soon as they're done." And then, to the mechanic: "Don't touch that box until we can dust it for fingerprints. In fact, don't touch the car at all any more until I tell you it's okay." He weighed the documents in his hands. "Maybe these will be the break we've been looking for," he said to Sturges.

"If they're what I think they are," Sturges said, "they're the key to the whole mystery."

"Oh?" Ross studied Sturges's face. "Don't tell me you've finally turned up some information that's actually going to be useful."

"For chrissake, Ross!" Sturges bellowed, "I've turned up three-quarters of the information we've had in this goddam case so far."

"And we still don't know anything for sure," Ross reminded him.

"Don't we now?" Sturges smiled and draped an arm over Ross's shoulder. "Brian my man," he said, "how about you buy me a drink and some lunch, and I'll tell you a long and fascinating story? Then you can tell me if my information is useful or not."

He chuckled to himself. "This is going to be so fucking useful, in fact, that I think nothing less than a twenty-five-year-old Macallan will be appropriate to the occasion."

Forty-five

Ross called: the translations were finally en route from police headquarters. Sturges had held off writing anything until he could see what the documents said, praying nothing about them or Rupert's secret treasures would leak out in the meantime. Olivia was certainly saying nothing to anyone, including Ross. Ross had brought her in for questioning after hearing Sturges's story, and true to her word, she had denied everything.

"He's invented it, every bit of it," she'd told Ross. "You know what journalists are like. If they can't nail down the facts, they'll make them up. I do feel sorry for him: he so wanted to be able to solve the murder of his old friend and mentor. I guess this is his rather pitiable attempt to do so." She batted her eyelashes and lowered her head. "I'm afraid poor Bill also had sexual designs on me, and when I rebuffed his advances, well..."

Ross knew she was lying. But without evidence to back up what Sturges had told him, there was nothing further he could do. "This is not over, Ms. Chen," he'd said as he showed her to the door. "Keep yourself available for further questioning."

How to deal with Olivia was now Ross's problem. Sturges was struggling with his own. Even once he had the translations in hand, he wasn't sure how much of a story he'd be able to put together. If what Olivia had been told about the documents was accurate, quoting them would provide an interesting enough tale, but a full explanation of their history, how they got to Hong Kong — how they were connected to Rupert's murder — required details that only Olivia could provide. Without her corroboration, he wasn't sure he'd be able to write anything about how the murder took place and what was behind it.

There was a knock on the door and a courier dropped off the translations. The only thing to do was get to work and see what came of it. He locked the door, closed the blinds, turned off his mobile phone, and began reading.

~

It was all as Olivia had described. Chang Dongfeng/Chen Weihan's notes from Party meetings in Yanan. Documents relating to agricultural production and collectivization in the 1950s. Chang's first-hand account of village life during the Great Famine.

The Politburo minutes were dated between 1938, when Chang arrived in Yanan, and 1942, when Mao began one of his periodic "rectification" campaigns to terrorize his followers into unquestioning obedience, and Chang's access to the leadership was cut off. But he had already recorded several years of debate over policy and ideology, and details of the struggle for Party leadership then raging between Mao and his rivals.

Plenty of grist for the historians' mills here, Sturges concluded when he'd finished reading, and it didn't all paint Mao in a good light. But Communist infighting had never been a pretty sight, and Mao's maneuvering en route to securing the leadership was generally known by now. There was no particular threat to the Party's survival here that Sturges could see.

The only things of mild interest were a couple of early references to Taiwan. If the island had become a major rallying point for Chinese unity today, Chang's notes revealed that both

Mao and Chou En-lai had dismissed it back then as a separate and not overly important nation.

"In order to defeat Japan's war of aggression," Mao had written in 1938, *"the soldiers and people of the two great nations of China and Japan, and also the oppressed nations of Korea, Taiwan, etc., should join in efforts...to establish a mutual united front of anti-aggression."*

"The oppressed nations of Korea, Taiwan, etc." Mao saw Taiwan as a separate country. The documents quoted Chou En-lai in a similar vein. So much for Taiwan being an inseparable part of the mainland, as the Party now claimed. In fact, the island's status had always been open to debate. It was annexed by the Qing emperor only in 1683 and ruled by Beijing until the Japanese took it in 1895; occupied by the Nationalists in 1949 and officially returned by Japan – to the Nationalist government, not the Communist government – in 1952; self-governed ever since.

Formally part of China, then, for a mere two hundred and twelve years — a blink of the eye by Chinese reckoning – ruled independently of Beijing for one hundred and eight years since then, and not even considered "Chinese" by the leaders of the Communist Party for much of that time. Mao's and Chou's early references to the island might cause the Party leadership some embarrassment if they were widely circulated, but they were hardly a regime-changer at this late date.

Perhaps something in the other documents...?

Once ensconced in the General Office, Chang Dongfeng again became privy to the highest classification of official documents.

Between 1949 and 1957, he documented the falsification of production figures. He detailed the poor performance of the agricultural sector under the Communists. He recorded the peasants' resistance, futile as it was, to collectivization and communization. Most damning of all, the documents illustrated the central role Mao's utopian ideas and his pseudo-science played in the creation of the Great Famine. The material Chang had gathered before being shipped off to the countryside, and which he later smuggled to Rupert when he returned to Beijing, left no doubt about the Great Helmsman's direct role in creating what was arguably the greatest holocaust in human history.

That much had already been made public, however. Detailed accounts of the famine itself were also starting to emerge by the time Sturges read Chang's notes, but the authors were mostly scholars and journalists who had gathered second- and third-hand accounts, or residents of the cities where the famine had been less serious. Chang's memoir was a rare first-person account by an educated and literate witness to the genocide – how else to describe the purposeful death of five percent of the population? – that had taken place in the Chinese countryside.

What stood out most in his account was the attitude of Party cadres who visited Hong Xing to enforce the rules that perpetuated the famine. Chang wrote that only one cadre in all that time was distraught or brave enough to speak his mind about the human extinction occurring all around them. He confided to the heads of Hong Xing that "a new class struggle" had been declared by the Party; that China's peasants had been designated "the enemy."

"The Party leaders have told us the peasants must be struggled against even more earnestly than we struggled against the landlords and rich peasants," Chang quoted the man as saying. He'd been told this directive came "from Chairman Mao himself."

Here was truth the Party would never openly admit. Here was contemporaneous evidence of Mao's contempt for his fellow citizens and his responsibility for the slaughter. But it was already well documented that Mao had been receiving reports of the starvation as it happened. It was already well documented that he blocked all attempts to alleviate the suffering. Whether or not Mao had personally branded China's peasants as the enemy, he had done nothing to reverse the decision. Whatever else the Chairman might have said, it was clear he never told his comrades: "Do whatever it takes to stop our people from starving to death, and do it now."

The disdain for human life beggared belief, but Mao's lack of empathy was hardly unique. Concern for humanity at large has never factored greatly into Chinese thinking. Twenty-five hundred years after Confucius, the guiding philosophy of the average Chinese is much the same as it was in his time: defend the family, and the powers on high can worry about the rest. The factory owner in modern-day China rarely considers the consequences of stuffing toxic chemicals into processed food, or manufacturing counterfeit medicines that lack any healing ingredient: those outside the family circle who might suffer from these poisons are someone else's concern.

With the one-child policy and the coming of modern urban living, Chinese households are shrinking; elderly parents are now often cut off from their children; Confucian notions of family are being altered by circumstance. With modern communications, glimmerings of a broader social consciousness are starting to filter in from the outside world.

But slowly. The casual disregard for human life among much of the population still staggers even those who profess to know China well. Mao had only taken this attitude to its logical conclusion. "We are prepared to sacrifice three hundred million Chinese for the victory of the world revolution," he once boasted. From 1959 to 1961, he went a significant way toward making that boast a reality. During the ten years of the Cultural Revolution, millions more died.

And yet he is still venerated by the Chinese people, especially the young ones who never suffered under his rule and have been taught very little about it. Those Chinese know only the miraculous improvement in the general standard of living that the Party has wrought since Mao's disappearance from the scene.

The cost of that progress is only starting to become appreciated. The flood of new vehicles has outstripped the capacity of the new roads. The refurbished towns are disappearing beneath blankets of oily smog. The water, the soil and the people are being poisoned by industrial, agricultural and human waste. And the effects of China's development are not only being felt inside the country. As prosperity spreads and consumer demand increases, the country sucks in everything around it, like a terrestrial black hole. A scenario previously given scant attention is now posited seriously by academics and sociologists: If the multitudes in China (and India) begin consuming food, and oil, and steel, and wood, like Americans and Europeans have done for so many decades...how long before there's no longer enough to go around?

But the Chinese will not be denied. Since the institution of the one-child policy, an entire generation of only-children has grown up in China. These "little emperors" are used to getting anything they want. They throng the new, modern shopping malls, snatching up designer watches and haute couture and fine wines, eating in exotic new restaurants, toying with their mobile phones and other electronic devices, and thinking, like their counterparts in the developed world, that this plentitude is their due. Having tasted all this, would these self-entitled millions accept anything less?

Unlikely. Certainly not without a very noisy fight.

At the same time, those who know the Chinese know that for all the outward trappings of normalcy, the potential for the mass hysteria that characterized the Maoist era still lies not far below the surface. Unrest, wherever it is directed, could tear the country apart again. The Party has no choice but to continue feeding the beast it has created, while it scrambles to conceal any information that could tarnish its image and fuel further unrest. So the public is fed a highly selective account of the Cultural Revolution and Mao's role in it. If the Great Leap Forward and the famine are mentioned at all, it is with a euphemism – "the three years of natural disasters" – as if bad weather and not Mao's self-aggrandizement and contempt for human life were to blame for the disaster.

To many of the uninformed young, content with their lives and ignorant of the truth, the man who killed tens of millions and destroyed the lives of many millions more just a generation earlier is a hero today. "I love that man," they say of Mao, and there is no irony in their voices when they say it.

At the time Chang Dongfeng smuggled these documents out, the public release of such information would have been political dynamite. It might well have led to the overthrow of the Party. But by the time of Chang's and Rupert's deaths, most of the information now in Sturges's hands had already been published, in memoirs and academic papers that had flooded out of China since Deng Xiaoping's Reform and Opening.

The fact that production figures had been falsified? Common knowledge for decades. It continued to the present day. No great revelation there.

Taiwan? However questionable Beijing's claim to the island, it was now officially recognized as a part of "one China" by almost every nation and international body. Chang's revelations were thirty years too late to make any practical difference in that debate.

The Great Famine? Books had already been written about that, and more were on the way.

The revelations in Rupert's documents, interesting as they were, were no longer damaging enough by themselves to bring the Party to its knees, no matter how fervently Chen Weihan and Rupert Rackley might have wished it so.

~

Enough musings for one day. It was almost three a.m. Sturges's mind was fogged from an overload of information. He sent a memo for the Saturday duty editors to read when they arrived in the morning: major story coming for the Sunday edition. How major it was going to be, and exactly what it would say, would have to wait until he could think straight.

He did know that whatever he ended up writing would drive the final nail into the coffin of his relationship with Olivia. Another love affair gone to hell.

I'm a good-looking guy, he told himself as he drifted off to sleep. I'm intelligent, I'm sophisticated, I'm considerate, I'm well off financially.

Why can't I catch a break with women?

Forty-six

Saturday afternoon. Sturges had worked at home all day to avoid distractions. He'd decided he would run with the contents of the documents. They had the ring of authenticity, and he had Rupert's affidavit to back them up. If Beijing decided to challenge their authenticity, its denial would be met with skepticism: everyone knew the Chinese never hesitated to twist the truth when information that embarrassed the Party was involved.

But the rest of the pieces, the story of the murder itself, had still not fallen into place. A story of this magnitude had to be rock solid if the public was to have confidence in it. The public was going to have serious difficulties with that if the Chinese government was questioning the underlying facts, and a central player in the drama, Olivia, was calling the rest of the story a lie.

He had followed Rupert's dictum. He'd learned not just what had happened, but also why. It would hurt if he'd come this far, only to be unable to publish the full story.

The phone rang. "Sorry to bother you at home, chief." It was Janson Cheung, the Saturday duty editor. "It's getting a bit late. How's the story coming?"

"Slowly," Sturges said. "What's up?"

"You said to let you know if anything new came in."

"And?"

"You're going to want to see a press release that just arrived," Cheung said. "I emailed it to you a minute ago. It should be in your inbox."

Sturges found the email and opened the attachment. It was a press release, as Cheung had said:

Hong Kong, 20 October, 2003 – A trove of priceless Chinese antiques, many of them smuggled out of the country for safekeeping during the height of China's Great Proletarian Cultural Revolution and stored in a secret location in Hong Kong ever since, is to be returned to the Chinese government, Ms. Olivia Chen Lizhu announced today.

Ms. Chen, a prominent banker based in Hong Kong, says dozens of the pieces, estimated to be worth hundreds of millions of Hong Kong dollars in all, were smuggled out of China in 1967 and 1968 by her father, Chen Weihan, and her future husband, Rupert Rackley. The two men, who both died within the last three months under differing circumstances, were renowned experts on ancient Chinese art.

Ms. Chen says the scheme to safeguard the artworks was instituted by the two men as Mao Tse-tung's Red Guards were rampaging through the country, destroying innumerable examples of priceless art and architecture. Some of the pieces removed for safekeeping were from the pre-revolutionary imperial collection in Beijing's Forbidden City, according to Ms. Chen. That collection now makes up much of the exhibits in the Palace Museum in the Chinese capital, and the National Palace Museum in Taipei.

"My father and Rupert were appalled at the destruction taking place in the name of Maoist ideology in the late 1960s," Ms. Chen said in a statement. "Their common love of art had brought them together several years earlier, and they jointly devised this scheme, at enormous risk to their own safety, to save important elements of China's patrimony from possible destruction.

"My father and my husband were heroes and should be applauded for their selfless actions. But China is now a modern and peaceful nation, and it is time for the treasures the two men rescued to be returned to their rightful owners, the Chinese people."

Further details of this remarkable story will be provided by Ms. Chen at a news conference to be held this afternoon, Monday, 20 October, at 2 p.m., in the law offices of MacGyver and Wong, 20th floor, Prince's Building, Central.

Smart, Sturges thought when he'd finished reading. Olivia and her lawyers knew the story was bound to come out soon, and they wanted to get her version out before the sordid details leaked. Paint her father and Rupert as good guys who only had China's interests in mind, instead of two bitter old men bent on revenge against each other. Paint herself as a friend of China and a protector of its property in case the eventual release of the information in the documents might yet make her a target of Beijing's anger.

The stipulations in the embargo meant that the information in the press release would dominate the Monday morning newspapers, plus radio and television. Olivia was probably planning to show off some of the antiques from the locker at her Monday afternoon press conference, especially the dragon's head, which would add another sensational twist to the story and keep her in front of the story for a second day. Or so the lawyers had probably figured.

What they didn't realize was that they'd also solved much of Sturges's problem.

He now had Olivia's own word that her father and Rupert had smuggled out antiques, to pair with Rupert's sworn statement that they had smuggled out documents. He could use the press release as a stepping-off point for everything she had told him about the smuggling operation.

The embargo Olivia's lawyers had placed on the press release also presented a new problem, however. Journalistic practice meant neither Sturges nor anyone else could publish the information in the press release until Monday morning. It was already several days since Ricco had revealed the secrets of the locker and Olivia had revealed the secrets of the murder. Sturges had held his story back to wait for the translations, hoping no other journalist would get wind of the details in the meantime. Having to wait yet another day now that part of the story was out in the open made him extremely uneasy. But he had no choice.

He called Cheung on the city desk. "The press release is what I needed to make the story work," he said. "Unfortunately, we'll have to hold the entire package until Monday's paper, which makes me nervous as hell: I'm not sure we can count on our local colleagues to adhere to the embargo. But it gives me more time to write, and nobody is going to have as complete a story as I have."

"Any idea how long the story's going to be?" Cheung asked. "We'll still hold the front page as you ordered, but I could use a better idea of how much space we're going to need inside."

"A lot," Sturges said. "I'm going to want a box with excerpts from some documents that play a central role in the story. I have photographs of a lot of those pieces of art Rackley's widow is going to be talking about on Monday, including one really spectacular piece that's never been seen in public before. We'll beat her on her own story by running the photos in the Monday morning paper before her press conference ever takes place."

But a major obstacle remained: how to wrap Olivia, the smuggling of the documents and the artifacts, and Rupert's murder all into one neat package. He tried one formulation after another, but midnight arrived and the answer did not arrive with it. He still had nothing to corroborate what Olivia had told him about the motive for the murder, or the murder itself. It would be he said-she said at best, and what she was going to say if he went ahead with the story was that he was lying. He still didn't have enough support for a story of this magnitude.

He gave up again and fell into bed. Maybe a miracle would come along in the next twenty-four hours and solve his problem.

Forty-seven

Grissom Lam swore in his most florid Cantonese.

The instructions left by Rupert Rackley along with his will had been specific, and Lam had carried them out to the letter — all but the dispatching of a particular envelope, which was to go out precisely forty-nine days after Rackley's death, whenever that date might occur. The day had now arrived: October 18, a Saturday.

Lam had placed the envelope on his desk before he left the office the previous evening, intending to send it first thing in the morning. But he'd been called out early on an emergency matter, and it had taken all day to get that resolved. A package like Rackley's had to be sent by registered mail – it couldn't just be dropped into a mailbox – but it was now late Saturday evening and the post office was closed for the weekend. There was no way to mail it before Monday.

The only one who knew about the envelope was Lam himself. The precise date it was to be sent couldn't have been all that important: Rackley had no way of knowing in advance when he would expire. *Mou mantai*, Lam tried to tell himself. No big deal. If the envelope went out a day late, or even two, who would know the difference?

Lam would know. And he prided himself on his reliability. If given a task by a client, he performed it. Not only that, this envelope was addressed to Bill Sturges. Judging by recent events – a high-speed car chase involving a mainland hit team, in *Hong Kong*! – it seemed quite possible that Sturges could soon end up like Rackley. Lam was determined to send the envelope while Sturges was still around to receive it. Following his clients' instructions to the letter was the least he could do for the five thousand Hong Kong dollars he charged them per hour.

"Celia!" he shouted. No answer. His secretary, like the post office, had finished working for the weekend.

He walked to her office and rummaged around in her desk. Where did she keep the phone number of that courier service the firm used? What was the *name* of the bloody courier service? Senior partners shouldn't have to concern themselves with such trivia.

He swore again, and punched the speed dial to call Celia's mobile phone.

Forty-eight

Sunday. The doorbell rang at eight a.m. Sturges stumbled out of bed, still half asleep. He buzzed in the caller. He opened the front door. He was suddenly very much awake.

A man in a black leather jacket was standing on the front steps, his head and face obscured by a black crash helmet and visor. An enormous black motorcycle was parked just outside the gate, poised for a quick getaway. Panic wrapped its fingers around Sturges's throat: another hit man sent by Wu Zhemin to finish him off! Ross had predicted that Beijing would back off for a time. But Ross hadn't considered that the Chinese might want to get at Sturges before he was able to publish whatever else he might learn, and international public opinion be damned.

The visitor's black-gloved hand began to rise. Sturges raised his arms in a reflex of self-protection as the hand reached towards him...and handed him a large envelope. The hand retreated briefly, and returned with a receipt for Sturges to sign. He scribbled a shaky signature, and the courier roared off without a word. Sturges listened as the sound of the bike's engine faded into the distance, while his heartbeat returned to something close to normal.

The envelope bore the letterhead of Lee, Li, Lai, Lo, Lam, Leung & Gillespie, Rupert's lawyers. Sturges tore it open with trembling hands, half expecting a threat of legal action if he published anything Olivia had told him. But wait: the press release had said Olivia was using a different law firm. What could Rupert's lawyers be sending him at this late date?

There was a second envelope inside, also addressed to him, and the handwriting on this envelope was Rupert's. The envelope contained a letter, notarized like the copies of the documents, and dated 2001:

"My Dear Bill,

"If you are reading this letter, it should be 49 days since my death," the letter began. *"According to traditional Chinese belief, I will by now have been judged by the gods. I fear the judgment will not have been favorable.*

"I have no way of knowing at this writing how I will have died, or what information you may have in hand by the time this letter arrives. I'm sure, however, that there will have been many details to attend to – funeral arrangements, execution of the will and so on. Even though those will not have been your responsibility, you will have been involved to one extent or another, and I wanted to allow time for all the fuss to be dispensed with before you read this. I want your full attention for what I am about to tell you."

The letter included information that Sturges and Ross would have killed for weeks earlier: information about the operation to smuggle artifacts and documents out of China; an explanation of the three keys and the locations of the safe deposit box in Tsuen Wan, the box hidden in the frame of the Morgan, and the storage locker in Chai Wan.

"I can assure you that the documents are authentic. Chen and I discussed them in detail after he arrived in Hong Kong. Given their sensitivity, I made two copies of the set I already had in hand, and hid each of the sets individually. The political and historical value of the documents will be obvious to so astute a journalist as yourself."

A full description of the facts behind Rupert and Olivia's marriage followed. Some differences in interpretation aside, Rupert's story matched what Olivia had told Sturges:

"You already know that I am a flawed human being. On top of that, I have allowed anger and humiliation to control me and distort my judgment for more than three decades. I have done things that I regret, and I have hurt people, particularly Olivia and her father.

My only explanation (there is no excuse for my actions) is that I have never been able to overcome the pain and fury that grew inside me likely a cancer following the events of 1968. I offered China my unequivocal love, and instead of returning that love she turned on me with violence. Try as I might, I have been unable to rid myself of the humiliation of that rejection.

"I plead guilty to weakness and vindictiveness, and throw myself on your mercy, my dear Bill. There was much good that you and I shared in life. I hope you will not let the bad that I have done overshadow the good completely."

The letter also contained Rupert's rationale for keeping half of the antiques the two men had smuggled out:

"I never intended to sell those pieces for profit," he wrote. *"When Chen first reached Hong Kong in 1968 with Olivia – they were then known by their real names, Chang Dongfeng and Chang Lili – the trauma from the torture I'd undergone was still fresh. I trusted no Chinese, him or any other. It's true that I decided unilaterally to keep one half of the pieces instead of the 1/25th that Chen and I had agreed on. But I did so to continue to keep them safe from the Chinese themselves.*

"I did sell some of my portion over the years and converted the proceeds into real estate holdings and other investments, and also purchased other extremely fine pieces along the way. The dragon's head from the Summer Palace water clock, which you may or may not have yet seen, is the most spectacular of the latter. How I obtained it and from whom must remain a secret, for these were the conditions under which I was allowed to buy it. It and the remainder of my half of the smuggled pieces, along with some other superlative pieces I bought on the regular market, are safe in the Chai Wan locker.

~

Sturges no longer needed Olivia's confirmation for most of the facts. If she wanted to call Rupert a liar, let her try: dying declarations like his letter tended to resonate with the public. Sturges would get in touch with the lawyer who had notarized the letter to confirm its authenticity, but he was confident the old boy had written the truth, and he'd be able quote the letter without hesitation.

He still couldn't publish one key point; namely, that Olivia and her late father had arranged Rupert's murder. Hong Kong's British-inspired libel laws would not allow that, even if he quoted her directly. But he could connect Rupert's fateful trip to the smuggled documents, and the documents to Rupert's blackmail of Chen Weihan. He could detail how Olivia was forced as a result of the blackmail into an unwanted marriage. He could quote Ross as saying she was being questioned about her possible role in the murder. *"Ms. Chen is currently helping the police with their enquiries, according to Deputy Chief Commissioner Ross:"* that was the formulation the libel laws allowed. The public would fill in the blanks.

The meaning of the second notation on Rupert's cardboard tag – *rongren*, "patience" – was now clear. Be patient, Rupert had been telling him; wait forty-nine days, and all will be explained.

"You alcohol-befuddled old pervert," Sturges said aloud. "If you'd have given me all this information along with your will, like a normal, clear-headed human being, we would have been able to retrieve the documents before your safe deposit box was destroyed. We could have gotten it all out into the open before some thugs attempted to murder me to keep it quiet. What the hell were you thinking?

~

Monday morning. Sturges's anger at Rupert had dissipated. He had the morning's newspaper spread out in front of him on the kitchen table and he was reading his story for the third time. Feeling very pleased with himself.

Ross called. "Did you see the story?" Sturges said. "I don't want to be immodest, but I think it turned out great. And you have to hand it to old Rupe: that final settling of the score—"

Ross cut him off. "Can you come to my office?" he asked.

"Sure," Sturges said. "I just have a couple of things to—"

"It's urgent," Ross said. "Get your arse over here now."

"Right away," Sturges said, wondering: *Now what? I thought this was over and done with.*

Forty-nine

"She's gone," Ross said as Sturges appeared in the doorway. "Scarpered. Did a runner."

Sturges turned to Wai. "She take it on lam," he said, confirming the news.

Sturges had no idea what they were talking about. "Who's gone?" he asked.

"The Widow Rackley. She's disappeared."

"She's due to give a press conference this afternoon," Sturges said. "How can she be gone?"

"She might surprise us and show up at that press conference, laddie," said Ross, "but I seriously doubt it."

"This is a joke, right?" Sturges said, looking to Wai and back to Ross for confirmation. The look on the men's faces told him they were serious. "Okay, it's not a joke. But I mean, where could she be? Hong Kong is too small a place for anyone to hide for long."

"That would be accurate, assuming she were still in Hong Kong," Ross said. "Her office staff received a message from her early this morning. If anyone asks after her, the staff were told to say that Ms. Chen has left Hong Kong and will be traveling for an indefinite period."

"I go to her office to see message myself," said Wai. "Time stamp says e-mail from her arrived 2:30 a.m. – means 2:30 this morning our time. I go to her apartment, most of her clothes and personal items are gone. Housekeeper says she left early yesterday morning with two large suitcase."

"Two-thirty a.m. our time today would have been yesterday evening London Time," Ross said. "Yesterday afternoon New York time. Yesterday morning California time. She could have sent the message from anywhere."

Sturges plopped himself into a seat to think the situation through. "How could you let her get out of Hong Kong in the first place?" he asked. "Didn't you realize she might leave rather than face more questioning? Don't you cops take a person's passport in a case like this?"

"We need a court order for that, but I would have needed solid evidence of her involvement first. We did inform Immigration to contact us if there was any indication she was trying to leave the territory, but neither Immigration nor the airlines have any record of her flying out. "

"What about the ferries, to the mainland, to Macao? Did you check those?"

"That's what we doing when you get here," Wai said, and he pointed to his computer. "We look for Chen Lizhu, Lizhu Chen, Olivia Chen, Olivia Chen Lizhu, ..."

"Every permutation of her name you can think of," Ross said, taking up the narration. "There's no record of her passport being used at either ferry terminal, on Hong Kong or Kowloon side. We checked with the cruise ship companies too. Nothing."

Sturges walked around behind Wai and looked over his shoulder at the computer. "She's a permanent Hong Kong resident like the rest of us, so as you know, she doesn't need a passport to leave Hong Kong," he said. "We can enter and leave using only our Hong Kong ID cards, and we can enter Macao with them, too. Chinese like her can enter the mainland on their ID cards as well."

"Of course we know that," Ross said. "But the name on her ID card is the same as the name on her passport. We checked with Immigration at the ferry terminals for her ID card: nothing."

"Wait," Sturges said, and he turned to the window to think. Something Rupert had written in that final letter. Something about names.

"It was Chang. Chang something. Yes!" he said with a snap of the fingers. "Chang Lili. That was the name she was given when she was born. Her father got them new identities when they arrived here in '68. But Rupert mentioned their original names in the letter I got yesterday."

"So he did," Ross said. He returned to the computer and began tapping in information, while Sturges and Wai leaned over his shoulder in anticipation.

The screen refreshed itself. Information from the Immigration Department database appeared. "Bingo!" Ross said. "One Chang Lili passed through immigration at the Hong Kong-side ferry terminal yesterday morning at 8:48 a.m. Given the facts of this case, I seriously doubt Olivia would risk traveling to the mainland, even if it was only to transit to the States or somewhere else, so she most likely headed for Macau.

"She would have had to fly *out* of Macau on her U.S. passport, meaning she'd have had to use that on her arrival there as well. I suspect that when we check with Macau immigration, we'll find that a Ms. Olivia Chen Lizhu, U.S. passport holder, entered around 9:40 a.m. yesterday. But how could she get hold of that second ID card?"

"I can guess," Sturges said. "Olivia told me that when she and her father left the commune where she was born for the final leg of their trek to Hong Kong, the commune leader gave him her original birth certificate. She could have shown up with that at some point to apply for a second ID card here, and the system would have had no way of knowing that Chang Lili and Olivia Chen were the same person."

Olivia had been two people all along: the decisive, assertive, modern western woman on the surface, the obedient Chinese daughter beneath it all. And now she was two people in legal fact.

The things you grow up with never leave you completely. He'd been struck by her repeated use of the phrase. Now he understood.

"I go call Macau airport," Wai said, heading for the door. "See which flight she get on and where she go to. This one *werry* smart lady," he muttered as he disappeared down the hall.

Ross and Sturges were left staring at each other. Neither spoke for a long time. "You can probably extradite her, can't you – once you find out where she went?" Sturges finally said. "Hong Kong has extradition treaties with most of the major western countries, assuming she's gone to one of those."

"Extradite her on what basis?" Ross said. "And to what end? We do have extradition treaties, yes, but countries require solid evidence of a crime before they'll transport a person. Especially if that person is one of their own citizens. All we have is your word about what she told you about the murder, and that's just hearsay. I was hoping to break her during a second interrogation session with the help of Rupert's letter, but even with that I wasn't holding my breath. She's one smart lady, as Wai said. If she's back in the States, where she would most likely go, there's precious little hope of our getting her back here by force with what we have right now. Not," he added after a moment's thought, "that I very much care."

"How can you not care after everything we've been through?" Sturges said.

In response, Ross reached into his desk and pulled out a sheet of paper. He placed it on the desk in front of him and stared at it. "This is my letter of resignation," he said after a moment. "I drafted it several days ago, before I interrogated Olivia. I was planning to hand it in even before this latest twist in the case. "

"You're not going to see this through to the end?"

"This *is* the end," Ross said. "We've done all we could, and unfortunately it wasn't enough. You did tell the story as completely as it could be told – my compliments on that, by the way: I have new respect for the journalist's profession. But we agree that we don't have enough hard evidence to mount a prosecution. Perhaps some new evidence will come to light in the future that gives the prosecutor grounds to proceed against her, but I hold out no great hope of that. And if such evidence does come along, my successors will handle it. I'm through."

"But why now?" Sturges asked. "Like you said, it's only a year until you reach retirement age. Why not just wait it out and collect your full pension?"

"Because I can't stomach it any longer," Ross said. "A few of the lads and I remained on the force after the handover in hopes of reinforcing the professionalism that had been built into it by 1997; keeping the troops on the straight-and-narrow while the new administration took hold, as it were. And I think we succeeded.

"But there was nothing I or any other individual could do to influence the actions of the new Hong Kong government – or the decision-makers up in Beijing who pull their strings. The Communists promised to keep their hands off our legal system for fifty years, but you saw how they manipulated this case from the start. It's what so many of us warned about at the time of the handover: not so much blatant interference by Beijing in Hong Kong's affairs, as a slow and steady chipping away of our freedoms from behind the scenes. And I'm sorry to say that's what it's come to. I for one will no longer be a party to it."

"So now what?" Sturges asked. "Back to Scotland after all these years?"

"Scotland!" Ross exclaimed. "To freeze my arse off? Christ no. I've been in the sunny climes for too long to go back to that. No, I'm going to do what a lot of my former colleagues have done: go into the private security business here. What with all the cross-border traffic these days, and all the crime and corruption on the other side, the private agencies here are desperate for experienced investigators who know the language and the people. I've already had several offers, and the work pays exceedingly well – far more than I'm earning now. Who knows: I might open my own agency someday. I'm a competent enough manager, don't you think?"

"None better," Sturges said.

"You might even join me," Ross said. "You've proved yourself to be a hell of an investigator. What do you think? Could I persuade you to give up this silly profession of yours and do some honest work for a change?"

"I don't think so," Sturges said. "It was great working with you on this, Brian, but I'll stick with journalism. It gives me all the excitement and gratification I need. I'll continue to consult you as a news source, of course," he added.

"And I'll treat you like I treat any bloody journo: with suspicion and contempt," Ross said. There was a smile on his face when he said it, and affection in his voice.

Fifty

Late October. Seventy-eight degrees cool. Seventy-one percent humid. Sturges strolls the path that circles the Peak, reveling in the autumn sunshine. The summer heat has finally broken, the worst of the humidity is gone and the air will be dry, by Hong Kong standards, for a few short months. The saga of Rupert's death is fading from public consciousness.

Was Rupert justified in risking danger to get his hands on documents whose impact might have been less than monumental? Of course he was. It could have been a big story. That's what journalists did.

Was the story big enough to justify murdering him to prevent its publication? To the Party's way of thinking, without a doubt. The Party has never allowed intrusions on its private deliberations or threats to its survival to go unpunished. At the time it killed Rupert the Party didn't know for sure what was in the documents or whether they truly posed a challenge to its power, but it couldn't take a chance that they did. So it removed the threat in the way it knew best.

But Rupert did not go quietly. He gave a final twist to the knife before he departed the scene. A final settling of the score. In his letter to Sturges, Rupert revealed that there was one more exception to the provision in the will leaving everything to Olivia:

"The items in the Chai Wan locker," he wrote, *"are the equal for artistic merit and historic importance of those that exist anywhere in the world: the Palace Museum in Beijing, the National Palace Museum in Taipei, museums and private*

collections in New York, Washington, London, Paris, Tokyo. They constitute an international treasure, and as such they should be accessible to the world. I have therefore arranged for them to be displayed properly, and for the public's access to them to be guaranteed.

"*A copy of a codicil to my will is enclosed here,*" the letter said. "*In it, I bequeath the entire contents of the locker to the British Museum in London.*"

Sturges had just finished reading the letter that Sunday morning when Grissom Lam called.

"Mr. Lam!" Sturges almost shouted. "The material you couriered over this morning, especially this bit about the antiques going to the British Museum: it's incredible!"

"I called to make sure you got the letter," Lam said. "Mr. Rackley's instructions were very clear about dispatching the envelope to you: '*Precisely forty-nine days after my death.*' All very Confucian, eh?" He chuckled. "The old boy might have had his falling out with China, but in many ways he was more Chinese than us Chinese."

"That he was," Sturges said. "And I'm planning to run a major story tomorrow on his life and his murder. Now that the antiques in the locker are a more prominent part of the story, I'm going to send a photographer today to shoot pictures of them all. I took a few shots myself, but given the information in the letter, I want a professional to do them over."

"Oh, you won't be able to do that," Lam said.

"I don't see why not. The pieces don't belong to Mrs. Rackley. Rupert left me a key to the locker," Sturges said, putting emphasis on the word "*me*." "Deputy Commissioner Ross of the police is holding the key for procedural reasons, but I have no doubt he'll let my photographer in. We won't disturb anything, of course."

"And I don't doubt that your photographer would be most careful," Lam said. "What I mean to say is, there isn't anything in the locker for him to shoot."

"But there is. I saw it all myself just a few days ago."

"A few days ago, yes. Today, no. The pieces are no longer in Hong Kong, in fact. I had everything packed up and shipped to London two days ago."

"Two days ago!" Sturges said. "Why would you do that when you knew the collection was about to become public knowledge?"

"That was also part of Mr. Rackley's instructions," Lam said. "All the pieces were to leave for the U.K. on the forty-*eighth* day after his death. As I said, his instructions were quite specific."

"But how did you get into the locker?"

"He left me a key, too," Lam said. He chuckled again. "Rupert thought of everything."

Sturges hung up and immediately called Ross. Ross was back on the line in an hour, laughing so hard he could hardly speak. "It's been cleaned out!" he managed to say. "Not a single bloody thing's left in the locker except the shelves. Didn't you say Rupert never had sex with a mature woman?" Ross asked. "Well I'm telling you, Billy boy: he screwed Olivia royally this time."

"Does she know what happened?"

"I called her and told her just a few minutes ago," Ross said.

"What was her reaction?"

"She just hung up. Didn't say a word."

~

And now she was gone, without a goodbye, without giving her press conference. No wonder: instead of spinning the story her way, she would have had to answer questions about how everyone, including her dead husband, had outwitted her instead.

Olivia might challenge the bequest to the museum from wherever she had fled to, but she'd said before she disappeared that she was going to give the pieces to the Chinese government; Rupert's ploy was no great loss to her. At any rate, the items were never hers to give away. Lam had assured Sturges that the codicil to the will was a legal and binding document.

Beijing would almost certainly try to claim the pieces, but the Chinese would be forced to fight the custody battle in the British courts. They wouldn't get the pieces back without a lengthy fight, if they got them back at all. Rupert had bolstered his claim to the antiques, and his right to give them to whomever he pleased, by sending the museum the original Chinese sales receipts and shipping documents, with their official stamps attesting to his ownership.

Greece had been trying to get its possessions back from the Brits for a hundred years, with no luck so far – and Lord Elgin had never obtained a receipt from the Greeks when he looted the Parthenon.

~

So it's over. Sturges has told Rupert's story in a way he's proud of, even if this small victory has come at large cost. The image of the man he looked up to for forty years has been destroyed. His relationship with Olivia, which seemed so promising only a short time earlier, is already a memory.

Brian Ross's wish has been fulfilled: he's learned how Rupert's murder happened, even if he has no way to bring any of the perpetrators to justice before he leaves the force.

Olivia has left China and Hong Kong behind, no doubt for good, having fulfilled her father's dying wishes and having gained her own revenge on the man who persecuted them both. As Ross said, it's up to the prosecutors to decide whether to try to bring her back, but prosecutors are famously hesitant to bring cases they don't think they can win.

So Olivia, wherever she is, might get away with murder after all. She might even escape public censure. Once Hong Kong has fully digested Sturges's story, it's entirely possible that instead of being condemned, she'll be pitied for the torture she and her father endured. It's even possible that she'll be admired, for being so faithful a Chinese daughter: nothing is looked upon with greater approbation by the Chinese than the honoring of tradition.

In murdering Rupert, the Communist Party has stamped out one more perceived threat to its existence, gained itself a bit more time in its struggle to survive China's transition to the modern era. But the Party's future is no more certain than that of Olivia. The dynasty could fall apart suddenly, as dynasties have done periodically throughout the country's history. This one will certainly disappear sooner or later: no dictatorship lasts forever and the Chinese, with their long view of history, are surely aware of that. The Party might be tossed aside by a population that finally can no longer stomach its corruption and arrogance. Or it might modernize itself out of power, as the despots in South Korea and Taiwan did. Whatever the method, China can't endure forever as it is now, half Leninist dictatorship, half modern state guided by the rules of international civilization.

It's like they used to say about dishes like chop suey: half an hour after you eat them, you're hungry again. They don't last.

And Rupert? Rupert has obtained a measure of the justice that Sturges and Ross said was his due. The story of his death has been told after all. The artifacts he loved so dearly are well out of Beijing's reach. The dragon's head will finally reside in public view, for the first time in a century and a half, along with other items from the imperial collection – right alongside the infamous Elgin Marbles.

China broke Rupert's heart and poisoned his mind. It snatched away his Hong Kong while the whole world watched. Ultimately, it took his life.

But he landed a final blow, a final slap to the Chinese face, before he slipped from sight. He did it to get even for the loss of Hong Kong. He did it to get even for his own humiliation.

As always, his actions changed nobody's thinking. But one final time – this time from beyond the grave – Rupert Rackley has had the last word.

The End

Acknowledgements

This book would not have been completed if it hadn't been for the repeated encouragement of my brother, Steve, who kept on urging me forward each time the search for an agent or a publisher came tantalizingly close to success, and then failed to materialize. I also received encouragement and help along the way from a number of friends and associates. They include Jennifer Janin, the head of the Voice of America bureau in Hong Kong while I worked there as an editor, who was the first to read several early chapters, and to cheer me on. Aviva Layton, a professional literary editor, provided many helpful suggestions for changes. The late James Berggren, a prodigious collector of Chinese antiquities, walked me through the intricacies and subtleties of Chinese art, which plays a central role in the novel. Jimmy Ross, a Scottish friend, initiated me into the pleasures and protocols of single-malt whisky.

The quote at the start of Chapter 26 is a paraphrase from Kurt Vonnegut, in his novels *Slaughterhouse-Five* and *Slapstick or Lonesome No More!*

"Why don't you take a flying fuck at a rolling doughnut?
Why don't you take a flying fuck at the moooooooooooooon?"

Mao Tse-tung's and Zhou En-lai's descriptions in the 1920s of Taiwan as a separate and distinct "nation," as opposed to an inseparable part of China, are reported in *The Chinese Communist Party and the Status of Taiwan, 1928-1943* (Pacific Affairs, the University of British Columbia), a 1979 study by Frank S.T. Hsiao and Lawrence R. Sullivan.

The characters in the book are pure literary invention, but the various events depicted, including those in the life of Chang Dongfeng – the Nanjing Massacre, the Anti-Rightest campaign, the Great Leap Forward and the great famine that followed, the Cultural Revolution, Deng Xiaoping putting China on the road back to sanity after the death of Mao – are all historical fact.

I am indebted for information about China to the first-rate scholarship of many authors. There are too many to list here, but there are several books that are particularly relevant to the writing of this novel:

*Two books by Harrison E. Salisbury, *The Long March* (MacMillan London Ltd., 1994), which recounts his personal retracing of the route of the epic journey that the young Communist Party of China undertook in 1934-35; and *The New Emperors, Mao and Deng* (HarperCollins Publishers, 1992), which provides valuable insights into the lives and personalities of these two towering figures.

The Long March by Sun Shuyun (HarperPress, 2006), a China-born writer and film producer who also retraced the route of the Long March, and along the way debunked some of the myths that surround it.

The Private Life of Chairman Mao (Chatto & Windus, 1994), by his personal physician, Li Zhisui, who according to his own recollections and to photos included in his book, was at Mao's side almost constantly – including during defining moments in the history of the People's Republic of China – between 1955 and Mao's death in 1976. The book reveals many details of Mao's personality and of the inner workings of the Communist Party's early years as ruler of China.

The Rape of Nanking by Iris Chang (Basic Books, 1997), a detailed account of that atrocity and an analysis of the militaristic culture of wartime Japan that helped lead to the massacre.

*Two books on the Great Leap Forward and the devastating man-made famine that followed: *Hungry Ghosts* (John Murray [Publishers] Ltd., 1996), by Jasper Becker, one of the earliest works to detail the full extent of the horrors that Mao unleashed during the years 1959-1961; and *Mao's Great Famine* (Bloomsbury Publishing Plc, 2010) by Frank Dikötter, which makes telling use of detailed information that the author was able to unearth since Becker's book was published.

Mao's Last Revolution by Roderick MacFarquhar and Michael Schoenhals (The President and Fellows of Harvard College, 2006), one of the more extensive and authoritative studies (in English at least) in what is now a very long list of books about the Great Proletarian Cultural Revolution.

THE AUTHOR

Barry Kalb spent 25 years as a reporter on three continents, for the Washington Evening Star, CBS News and TIME Magazine, and as an editor for the Voice of America. For 10 years, he taught journalism at the Journalism and Media Studies Centre of Hong Kong University. He has lived in Hong Kong for more than 35 years, writing about China as a journalist for part of that time, and observing the Hong Kong and Mainland Chinese at close range. He and his wife now divide their time between Hong Kong and Thailand.

Also by Barry Kalb

Cleaning House
A whimsical look at good and evil,
mass death and divine displeasure

You Can Write Better English
A handbook aimed at native speakers of
Chinese and other Asian languages